Bo

Threesomes

EDITED BY
BRIT M

Contents

1 3 5 7 9 10 8 6 4 2

First published in the US by Ravenous Romance as *The Virgin Threesome*
(2010) and *Three in Love* (2009)
First published in the UK in 2013 by Black Lace,
an imprint of Ebury Publishing
A Random House Group Company

The Random House Group Limited Reg. No. 954009

Addresses for companies within the Random House Group can be found at:
www.randomhouse.co.uk

A CIP catalogue record for this book is available from the British Library

The Random House Group Limited supports The Forest Stewardship
Council (FSC®), the leading international forest certification organisation.
Our books carrying the FSC label are printed on FSC® certified paper.
FSC is the only forest certification scheme endorsed by the leading
environmental organisations, including Greenpeace.
Our paper procurement policy can be found at:
www.randomhouse.co.uk/environment

Printed and bound by CPI Group (UK) Ltd, Croydon, CR0 4YY

ISBN: 9780352346735

To buy books by your favourite authors and register for offers, visit:
www.blacklace.co.uk

The Virgin
Threesome

Chapter One

Marissa ran her thumb around the condensation on the whiskey tumbler that Lita had filled with cherry vodka and ice chips. It was still mostly full. The chipped Manchester United logo on the outside brought a tiny grin to her lips—Lita and her footballers. That was one of the things Marissa's best friend had brought back from her internship overseas: a passion for soccer that Marissa tried to indulge. The other thing, her freshly discovered interest in erotica, was the subject of their girls' night in. Sometimes she wondered how intertwined those two interests were for her friend, especially when Lita was purring over her life-sized posters of players.

"I'm serious," Lita said as she strode back into the living room and flopped onto the couch, her pint glass full again. She hit play on the remote and the sighing, wriggling, moaning couple on the screen slid back into motion. "There's so much porn out there that doesn't suck."

Marissa rolled her eyes, taking a sip of her drink. The tingling cherry burn numbed her tongue for a brief second. "I don't see what you see in this."

The man and the woman on the screen were half-lit in their bedroom. It was almost soft-core, obviously amateur, and neither person was particularly attractive to her. The stack of movies Lita had brought over with her leaned next to the DVD player.

"Maybe you like the heavier stuff," Lita said.

"Give me a break." Marissa sighed. "Have you ever known me to be into any of . . . that stuff?"

Lita gave her a look, eyebrows raised.

"What?" Marissa said.

"Honey, I don't think you even know if you're into any of 'that stuff,'" she said with her fingers making quote marks in the air. "You haven't had a date since you broke it off with Jeff, have you?"

Marissa sipped again. "No."

"I'm serious," Lita said. "I respect your pickiness, but the only two guys you've been with have been so vanilla they made me want to cry for you."

"Just because I don't sleep around—"

"Not what I meant," Lita said. "It's official: tonight isn't just girls' night in. We're going to go through these movies until something gives you a real kick. You've got to have a kink buried somewhere under your good-girl persona."

She climbed off the couch and hit the eject button on the DVD player. She popped the disc out, put it in its case, and selected something else. Marissa couldn't quite make out what the cover of the new one was and Lita turned it facedown before coming back to the couch and pushing play once again.

Marissa almost protested, but honestly, she was curious. Jeff had been very—nice. She always dated nice boys, and the two she'd stayed with long enough to feel comfortable getting intimate with were no exception. It wasn't that they hadn't made her come, or been generous, because they had. It was just that she got the feeling that Lita might be right. Her friend enjoyed sex with a passion she proudly shared, all the time, and Marissa, well, she had never gotten the kind of rush out of it that Lita did. So maybe something *was* missing.

And no matter that Lita kept calling her a good-girl, she regretted having made it to her twenty-sixth birthday with only two men on her scorecard. There were so many missed opportunities that kept her up at night, imagining what it might have been like. Frankly, she wanted to be done with that side of herself and explore a little more.

"All right," she said after a long pause while the credits of the new movie scrolled past. "That sounds like fun."

Lita didn't quite do a double take, but it was a near thing. "Good," was all she said.

Marissa held back a grin. It was nice to surprise know-it-all, experienced, wicked, well-traveled Lisa a little bit. On the screen, the movie began without much fanfare directed towards a plot. A blond woman with gravity-defying breasts and a brunette girl who looked much younger were cuddled up next to one of the typical porno-hunks. Marissa made a face.

"I know where this is going," she said.

"Not into the mainstream boy's porn?" Lita chuckled.

"Yeah, me neither. Give it a shot, though. You might like the camera angles or something."

The vodka still burned her tongue as she took another swallow. The melting ice chips had watered it down a bit, and it was high enough quality to actually *be* sippable, but it was still strong. The girls on the screen were ooh- and ahh-ing over the man's cock as they both stroked and squeezed him. Marissa had to admit it was big—as thick as the smaller, younger actress's hand where her fingers were wrapped around him, long enough for them both to have room to touch. A brief tickle of warmth shot down her spine. She had never been a . . . a size queen, but it was interesting to look at in their hands, made to seem larger by their worship.

Lita pulled her legs up and rested her chin on her knees, drawing Marissa's attention briefly away from the screen. It was weird but not too weird to be watching this together. They'd talked about sex together since they were teenagers; shared every detail and compared stories. She was sure Lita didn't mean anything by it, either. She'd never seen her friend with a girl, not once, and Lita wasn't shy.

"What?" she said, looking over at Marissa.

"Nothing," she said. "How many movies did you bring, anyway?"

"A lot," she said with a smirk.

Marissa checked out the television again, watching the blonde bob her mouth up and down the actor's cock while the brunette played with his balls. This time it didn't give her any reaction—it had just been the scene with their hands on him. "Then let's switch," she said. "Pick something, I don't know, something you think will shock me."

"I can do that," Lita said.

She wobbled a bit when she stood, putting her empty pint glass on the table. Marissa tucked her feet under her and buried her toes in the crease of the couch cushions while Lita fiddled with the DVD player and changed the disc again. She picked something from the middle of the stack.

"Close your eyes," she said. Marissa obediently put her hands over her face. "I'm going to just skip to a scene and see if you have to put a cushion over your head until I turn it off."

"I hope it's not gross," Marissa muttered. "I'm not trying to figure out what might make me throw up."

"It's not gross, it's just . . . well, you'll see."

The couch dipped as she sat down again, and sound blared out of the TV: wet groans, slaps, grunts. Marissa lowered her hands even though Lita hadn't said to yet and her breath caught. She fumbled for the remote and hit pause. The still screenshot showed a toned, lanky blond man with his mouth open in a silenced cry, his eyes squeezed shut. His arms were pinned beneath his back, legs in the air with cuffs around his ankles and cords binding him spread to the bedposts. A man's broad hand spanned the back of his thigh with fingers gripping the flesh tight enough to mottle it white. His partner was a large man, broad in the shoulders and hips with muscles corded in his legs as he crouched to fuck into his bound companion. The camera was angled to catch the slightest view of the bigger man's dick disappearing into him, the sheen of lube and sweat glistening under the performance lights. This was the opposite of the soft-core amateur video with which Lita had started the night.

With a suddenly shaking finger, Marissa hit play again. The couple swung into motion, the man on the bottom letting out a hearty moan as he thrashed and struggled aimlessly. His cock bounced on his stomach with his movements. Pre-come left a shining trail on his taut abs. Marissa had to swallow. Heat flared in her belly and up her spine in a wave. The bigger man's hand slipped up the blond man's thigh to his calf, bending him further backwards. The cord holding his ankles up were suddenly slack. He moaned and whimpered, eyelids fluttering.

"Not going to change the disc?" Lita whispered, as if afraid to break Marissa's trance.

She swallowed, hard, and took a gulp of her drink to cool the heat building in her. "No, I don't think so."

The top unclipped the cords and eased the blond man's legs down, massaging them with his large palms. After a moment he was all the way up to his hips, stroking them and teasing the hard, flushed cock with his fingertips. The blond man stretched on his lap. His hips rolled suggestively, as if begging for the other man to start moving again, keep fucking him. Instead, the larger man edged back and slipped out of him. He let out a groan.

"Turn over," the top murmured.

His voice was low and husky. Marissa shivered. She wanted to spread her legs and ease the pressure of her thighs pressing together, but it seemed too embarrassing with Lita right there. Instead, she leaned forward slightly, her pulse pounding. The blond man rolled onto his stomach. The leather binding his wrists together didn't appear so tight that it cut into him, but it looked sturdy. Marissa rubbed a thumb over her wrist bone and imagined what that must have felt like.

She almost gasped along with him as his partner grabbed him by the hips and pulled him up onto his knees with his face buried in the bed. The top braced his own cock with his thumb and guided himself back inside the other man in one slow, slick glide. After that it was a flurry of pounding and fucking, the bigger man hammering into him hard enough that his hips made slapping sounds impacting the blond man's ass.

Marissa's clit throbbed. She wanted to put a hand down her panties and finish herself off—it would be quick. They were so hot, two masculine, sweat-dripping bodies colliding and sliding together. The top was so strong, so powerful. The sight of all those muscular planes instead of curves and soft plush bodies seemed to light a fire in her. If she'd ever suspected she might like women, this experiment proved her preferences. Men, and more men. The blond man was shaking under his partner, whining, and finally the other man wrapped a loose hand around his cock. It took two strokes and he was coming, the thick liquid dripping over the bigger man's fingers and between their legs. A moment later, he groaned out his release as well, and wrapped both arms around the blond man's chest. Marissa wondered if he was going to pick him up, but they just rested together, the blond man caged in the other's embrace.

"Wow," Lita said as the screen faded out. "You *liked* that."

Marissa put down her glass and cast a glance at her. "I—yes. I did."

"Okay, well," she said. "I've got more. Lemme grab one . . ."

She almost laughed. "I don't think I can handle another!"

"Just let me show you this," Lita said. "Test a theory."

"What, do you wonder if it's the boys I like, or the tying-up part?"

"I kind of suspect you like both, honey," Lita said, flashing a grin over her shoulder as she sifted through DVDs. "Shit, I can't believe you thought you were vanilla all these years. You never read a kinky book, or thought about it, or anything?"

Marissa sighed. "I've been busy. You know that."

"So," Lita said quietly. "This is going to be kind of personal, but you never thought about anything but boring ol' Jeff or guys like him when you get off?"

"Maybe I did, maybe I didn't," she said.

"Uh-huh," Lita murmured, returning to the couch. "You're keeping secrets."

"Well," Marissa gave in. "I really didn't know I liked—that."

"Guy-on-guy action," Lita clarified in a singsong voice.

"Yes. Guy-on-guy action."

They burst into giggles as the next movie started. The surreal quality of being turned on watching porn with her best friend was starting to wear off, and Marissa uncurled her legs to get comfortable, bracing her feet on the coffee table. She fought a blush as her panties stuck damply to her skin. She'd liked the boys, all right. It wasn't—that big of a surprise, really. She liked watching men kiss; it made her smile. It hadn't ever lit such passion in her, but she'd never seen men fucking before, either.

Lita scene-skipped through the introduction and hit play as soon as the two men on screen started stripping their shirts off. There was a woman sitting on the couch in the room with them, her skirt pulled up around her hips and her hand caressing herself through her panties. The men, both shaggy-haired and cutely unkempt, threw glances at her as they moved closer together. One put his hands on the other's belt and jerked it open, prompting a sigh from the woman watching. Marissa thought her jaw might drop. The ardor she'd been feeling before, which had cooled during her conversation with Lita, came rushing back. Things low in her body tightened with desire as she watched the woman direct her partners into touching each other, broad fingers petting hard muscle and tugging at hair. The men kissed with obvious passion, their mouths sliding together as they groaned and clutched at each other. Hands wandered.

"Come over here," said the woman on the screen.

They broke apart to look at her, their gazes sultry.

She shimmied out of her top and skirt. Only her thin silky underwear stood between them and her. Marissa bit her lower lip. The sting did nothing to quell her need. She almost gasped as the men collapsed artfully onto the couch with the woman, one on either side, and their hands found her body. The woman grasped at them, hands on their arms as they fondled and stroked her. In tandem they palmed her breasts, squeezing and massaging; as one they slipped fingers into her panties and teased her. The silk came off a moment later, baring her wet pussy to the camera and their exploring hands as one pushed his fingers inside and the other rubbed his thumb in tiny circles over her clit.

"This is—" Marissa said, hoarse. She cleared her throat. "Hot."

"Yeah," Lita said. "I've done it. Been the filling in a sandwich, I mean."

Marissa turned to her, eyebrows raised. "When?"

"While I was in Europe," Lita said, blushing. "I went to this spa, and I didn't realize it was—you know, really really full service—until I asked for two masseurs and ended up getting the happiest ending I've ever heard of."

Marissa almost laughed. "You had a threesome with two male prostitutes?"

"They aren't prostitutes," Lita grumbled. "And I don't know if I paid for it or not—the bill didn't change between when I got there and when I left. So I think they just wanted to and did it."

"Oh, wow." Marissa giggled. "Now I know why you didn't tell me."

"Anyway," Lita said, redirecting the conversation. "I'm telling you, it's worth it. You can feel them on both sides of you, and they can hold you twice as tight and touch you twice as much. It's . . . overwhelming."

"Oh," Marissa sighed.

"You don't have to sound like that," Lita said. "You could find someone. Or two someones."

"Give me a break," Marissa groaned. "I can't go into a bar and say, hey, are any of you comfortable with a bisexual threesome?"

"Honey, that's what the Internet is for."

Marissa made a face. "That's not safe."

"It is if you exercise caution and practice safe sex," Lita said. "And you don't have to go through with it. Just . . . you should really check some sites out. See if anybody's looking for what you're looking for."

"Maybe," Marissa said.

She turned her eyes back to the television to see one man licking the woman's nipples while the other knelt up and offered her his cock. She sucked him with gratuitous moans. Lita stood and went to the kitchen again, but Marissa was entranced by the writhing trio on the screen. The men kissed briefly over the woman's head. Marissa bit down on her knuckle to hold in a sigh of desire.

Lita didn't come back until the scene was nearly over, and Marissa hit "stop" on the remote. They sat on the couch for a comfortable, quiet moment, sipping drinks and enjoying each other's company.

"At least now that you've got the degree and the job, we can hang out more," Lita said.

"And you're back from your spa adventures," Marissa replied with a grin.

"I guess I should call a cab," Lita said, glancing at the clock. "I have to work in the morning, and I don't want to walk home."

"Okay," Marissa said.

"Let me know if you want me to send you some links," she said.

"I will," she murmured.

Marissa put the glasses in the sink, including Lita's, which she had left along with the half-empty bottle of cherry vodka. She'd be back to get them soon enough. The apartment was quiet and still. Marissa rubbed her eyes with the heels of her hands, leaning one hip against the counter. It was late. She had to work the next day, too, but she couldn't get the thought out of her mind— should she e-mail Lita and ask for those websites? It wasn't something old Marissa would have ever dreamed of. In fact, it seemed impossible. But the image of those men petting and kissing the woman in the porn movie wouldn't get out of her head, either. To be pressed between them, watching them kiss; the thought sent a bolt of desire through her body. She shivered.

Her resolution had been to explore more, do new things, stop being such a goody-two-shoes. Fuck men she liked, and enjoy it, when she wanted to. There was a part of her that whispered incessantly that no self-respecting woman wanted to sleep with two men at once—but it was the same part that kept easing her into relationships with plain vanilla boys like Jeff, who'd left her out of what seemed like sheer boredom. There was no *spark*. But, Marissa was sure, if she was caught between a pair of gorgeous men, there would definitely be something happening. At least a spark, if not a wildfire.

So on the way to take a shower before bed, she opened her laptop and fired off a quick e-mail to Lita: "Send me the list."

Her breath stuck in her chest for a moment after she clicked send. Just because she'd asked didn't mean she was going to go through with it. She repeated that to herself as she shut down the computer and made her way to the shower. She would just—look. See what other people were posting, what their fantasies were, and how they compared to these desires she found herself with.

Marissa turned on the shower, tested it for warmth, and stripped out of her clothes. The damp lace of her panties dragged teasingly against her skin as she stepped out of them. She cupped a hand over herself, feeling heat and wetness. Her fingers slid on her pussy. She held in a gasp and rolled the pad of her middle finger over the stiff button of her clit, back and forth, pleasure like lightning racing from the simple touch. After a moment she made herself stop, breath heavy, and climbed in the shower. The wall of hot water forced a sound of relaxation from her. It massaged the tightness in her back, and tickled down her legs.

She turned to let it wash over her face and down her chest, a hot wave pressing against her breasts, which were heavy with need to be touched. The men in the movie had taken turns feeling up their partner. She wondered how it felt to have two hands on her breasts, belonging to two different men. Would one squeeze harder than the other, use his fingernails more to pinch her nipples? She lifted her hands, one cupping each of her breasts, and tried to imitate the differences. With one hand she lifted and massaged; with the other she played with her nipple, but her hands weren't quite big enough and her fingers were slender, girlish.

The water continued to spray down on her, teasing the firm nubs of her nipples, peaked with want. Marissa slid her hand down her belly and let her fingers find her clit again, one on each side, stroking deftly up and down. The pleasure built slow, like a spring coiling tighter and tighter in her as she worked her hips against her hand, never speeding the pace, simply letting the orgasm build. It hit like a blow, sudden, a burst of ecstasy that made her cry out once in the privacy of her shower, water sluicing down her legs and between her fingers. She trembled, gasping.

She hadn't managed to have much of a fantasy, she admitted to herself, but the need to come had been too urgent. Next time, she would make a game of it—imagine the naughtiest, newest things she had never done with anyone. Make herself come thinking about having a man's dick in her hand and another fucking her at the same time, their bodies above her.

Marissa finished her shower and crawled into bed half sated, a thousand thoughts of erotic encounters haunting her into sleep.

*

The alarm went off too early. Marissa smacked her lips, the ugly morning-after taste of old liquor in her mouth, and slapped the snooze button. As an assistant professor only in her second week of work, she could hardly afford to be late, but her head was swimming as she sat up, sheets tangling around her legs. She hadn't had that much to drink the night before, but the one glass of vodka had caught up with her. A stumbling trip to the bathroom to comb her hair and brush her teeth left her squinting into the bright lights above her mirror. There were shadows under her eyes. Her dreams had been normal, weird, and totally not sexual, which surprised her. Maybe the movies hadn't made as much of an impression as she thought they had.

All the same, as soon as she finished throwing her clothes on and putting her tea in hot water to steep, she turned on her laptop. Her heart sped a bit as she refreshed her e-mail but nothing was waiting—Lita must not have seen the e-mail, or had time to respond yet. Marissa closed the lid with a click and sighed. Not even she knew if it was a sound of disappointment or relief.

With the new job, Marissa wondered if she would even have the time to pursue this new thing, or if it would be best to keep the desires to herself and use them to aid her own hands in getting her off at night. Would she be able to face her young, handsome students—to be honest, not much younger than she was—with the knowledge that she liked to watch men fuck? Would she think about the boys who she sat close to in ways she never had before? She cursed, retrieved her tea, and sipped it standing over the stove.

The only way to find out was to go, and her first class started in an hour. The past two weeks had been interesting and terrifying, but the students were good, and so was the material. The auditor who slipped in and out to rate her progress, on the other hand, nearly gave her heart attacks. She had trouble not looking at him, speaking straight to him, or asking for approval. He always ghosted out without a word a moment before class ended. It was nerve-wracking; she didn't know how people put up with it. But of course she would, because she *wanted* to succeed with this job. It was what the past eight years of her life had been leading up to.

Marissa gathered up her bag, gulped the rest of her tea so fast it burned her tongue, and walked out the door of her apartment. The second-floor patio all the apartments shared was shielded from the bright September sun, but it was still too hot, and she fanned herself with a paper snagged out of her bag as she clattered down the wooden steps to the parking lot. A note was stuck under her windshield wiper: "Hey hon, hope work's great today. I'll talk at you later!" She smiled and tucked it away. Her neighbors probably thought she had a girlfriend if they saw the note and who left it, but that was just Lita's way of showing her affection.

On the drive to the university she thought about the movies again and decided she should find some of her own if she could. It would be worth a trip to the adult store down the street, so long as none of her students ran into her there. That would be mortifying.

She parked in the administrative lot with a rush of

pleasure. The joy of being able to call herself a professor and say "Doctor Ford" still had its new-car shine. She was proud of herself. She was sure it would wear off around halfway through the semester and become *work*, but for the moment, it was like every day was some kind of special reward. The classroom was empty when she breezed in and started setting up her notes, the book the class was reading, and a few pieces of emergency chalk in case she lost the one on the blackboard tray. She didn't have a room with a dry-erase board or a projection screen—the trials and tribulations of being an associate professor and not tenured.

One day, she thought. *One day I will be.*

She just needed to work hard, be on time, teach well—and make sure the auditor noticed. As if the devil called by thought, the man himself strode in. Marissa froze, hands above her notepad and ass halfway to her chair.

He raised an eyebrow.

She feigned a smile, which she was sure came off too nervous, and sat. He wedged himself into one of the desks. He was an older man, dark hair graying at the temples but still thick and rather lustrous.

Marissa cleared her throat once and managed a timid, "Hello."

"Good morning," he replied casually. She smiled wider.

"I'm just going to go grab a coffee before the class starts. Do you need anything?" she asked. "Or is that not allowed?"

He returned her smile. "I'm fine, thank you."

She eased out of the classroom, trying for suave and

unconcerned, but nearly fainted as soon as she stepped out. He held her potential career in his hands and he was so unreadable. It was the first time he'd ever said a word to her, and she still had no idea if he thought she was a total idiot or not.

A trip to the bagel place in the lobby of her building for a coffee took twenty minutes, and when she returned, a few early students had arrived. One, Evan, was always early and he always had a cream-cheese-laden bagel with him. She wondered how she'd missed him in the lobby shop's line—his dreadlocks were distinctive in a crowd, tipped with red beads that clacked together when he shook his head. She smiled at him and he returned it.

The auditor seemed to note her interaction, and that made her hide a grimace behind her coffee cup. What if she came off as too involved with her students? With the narrow age difference, that was a professional danger. But at the same time, wasn't she expected to take on favorites and potential research assistants?

Thankfully, the hour struck on the bell tower clock outside, its song ringing in through the cracked window in the corner. She stood and picked up her battered copy of *Paradise Lost*, ready to lead the class—even the last-minute stragglers—on a tale of wonder and woe.

The auditor slipped out halfway through, and Marissa let out a tiny sigh of relief that prompted titters from her students. She blushed, stammered, but continued with barely a moment's delay. She was only human. The rest of the hour went on without a hitch.

As soon as the class ended and the last of her students trickled out, she collapsed in the uncomfortable instructor's chair. No one needed the room for another two hours, so she tilted her head back and rubbed a hand over her eyes. The sound of a clearing throat made her jump so hard she nearly knocked the chair over.

"Are you all right?" her auditor asked, frowning.

"Oh, Jesus," she said with a shocked laugh. "I'm so sorry, I was just—I have a bit of a headache."

"I wanted to let you know you've been doing exceptionally well for a beginner," he said. He flipped open his folder of notes. "You engage your students without allowing them to lead you off track, and you manage to keep them awake during Milton."

She made an affronted face.

He smirked. "Not everyone likes Milton," he said.

"Surely you jest," she said. A weight had flown off of her shoulders. He was grading her well!

"Never," he replied affably. He snapped the folder closer. "So, keep up the good work. And try not to get so nervous. I'm not your boss. I'm just here to tell them where you might need more practice, if you do. And so far, so good."

She ducked her head, cheeks burning. Was it that obvious? "Thank you," she said.

"All in a day's work."

She looked up in time to see his well-shined boot disappear out the door.

Chapter Two

Marissa let her messenger bag drop off of her shoulder with a heavy thud just inside her front door. Her back was aching—she should never have worn heels to teach, not even small ones. Her feet felt pinched and they throbbed with every step. She kicked off the shoes, sighing, and padded in her stockings into her small kitchen. A burning curiosity nagged at her to check her personal e-mail now that she was home, and see if Lita had responded. She denied it, mixing herself up a cup of tea and arranging a few frozen, ready-to-bake stuffed pasta shells in a pan.

It was hardly gourmet food, but she was hungry and too broke to justify dinner out. She poured sauce over the frozen shells and turned the oven on, not bothering to wait for it to preheat before she slid the pan inside.

There was nothing else to be done now. The sink was empty of dishes; her floor was neat and didn't need to be mopped. She sipped her tea and wondered nervously what Lita would have sent her, if she even had the courage to look at singles sites and find someone to make her desire

a reality, if she could go through with it. She just wasn't
sure if she wanted to go so far. But truly, it couldn't hurt
to look, so Marissa carried her mug of tea with her into
the living room and powered up her laptop.

The first three new e-mails of the day were advertise-
ments, but the fourth was a reply from Lita. She hesitated
for a moment, reminded herself that all she was doing
was taking a look, and opened the e-mail. Lita's only text
was a smirking, winking animated icon. Below were five
links: three to places with names like "Kink and Coffee"
and two for more generic-sounding singles sites. Had
Lita used all of them? Had she found partners this way?
Marissa couldn't imagine her outgoing, gorgeous friend
needing to use a website to find a date, not even just for
one night. But maybe she had specific things she was
looking for, too, just like Marissa.

She took a deep breath and closed the e-mail. How
did she even know yet that she really wanted to try sex
with two men? Maybe she just enjoyed watching men
together, and she could do that from the privacy and
safety of her own home. The thought of having to find
someone on a listing who wanted what she wanted—and
she hardly knew what that was—then arrange to meet
them, and possibly turn them down, or worse, go to a
hotel with them—It was too much. That was something
other women did.

As soon as she thought it, Marissa scolded herself.
Meeting strangers for sex was something other women
did, and she wanted to try being somebody different for
a while. Maybe her new self was the kind of woman who

would go out and take things into her own hands that way. She just—didn't know. And it was frightening, new, fraught with complications.

Instead of reopening the e-mail and following the links, Marissa pulled up her search page. First, she needed to do research. She typed in "porn stores" and her ZIP code, then blinked at the huge list that came up. There were so many. She'd bought her vibrator and her other personal toys online; she'd never set foot in an adult store. That was a much easier first step to exploration than hooking up with a stranger or two.

The oven timer dinged and she retrieved her dinner, sitting down with it on the couch in front of her laptop. She ate as she surfed through the site listings and reviews of them, ruling out the ones customers had said were sleazy or creepy.

When she finished with her meal, she wrote down the addresses of the two nearest her, closed the laptop, and went to change into a more comfortable outfit. She slipped off her silk button-up and professional slacks and stood in her underwear in front of her closet for a moment, considering. It was just a quick trip out, so she grabbed a pair of jeans and a tank-top.

Not to mention, people were less likely to recognize her from the university if she wasn't dressed up. Just in case. Though honestly, if she encountered anyone she knew in an adult store, they would have as much embarrassment on their hands. She smoothed her hands over the jeans, flattening out the creases left from the wire hangers she'd never replaced, and slipped into a pair of tennis shoes.

Marissa climbed into her car and eased it out of the apartment's lot. Her mind drifted to the class auditor as she drove. He was so enigmatic. The fact that they'd finally spoken did nothing to erase that image. He was playful, she could tell, but seemed to enjoy having her on edge. That must have been part of his everyday job, though, to keep new and old professors alike on their toes.

She hoped against hope that he really thought she was doing okay and hadn't just told her that to soothe her. Six years of post-grad work was half the time it took most people for their doctorates, she knew, and she wanted to make the most of hers. An early suspension or firing if she wasn't any good would definitely offset her plans, not to mention make it difficult to pay back the mountain of student loans she'd accumulated.

Before she could dwell more on her job, she approached the first store on her right. She pulled into the parking lot as the sun was starting to dip to the horizon. It was still hot in September and the sun still set late. Four other cars were in the lot. She straightened her spine, looked up at the purple cursive "Priscilla's" on the sign, and went inside.

The clerk, a young-looking woman, smiled at her. "Do you need any help today?"

"Oh." Marissa sputtered, then cleared her throat. "No, that's all right."

The girl smiled and went back to reading the paperback in her hand. Marissa blew a breath out hard enough to ruffle her bangs and wandered farther inside. The store was built in an old house, with some of the "rooms" still intact: the main room with the register where she was standing held clothes and costumes. She ran her fingers over a shiny vinyl corset and glanced at matching boots. A flush of heat ran down her spine. She moved further inside, glancing at clothes and accessories.

There were two doorways on the side wall. She glanced in one and saw racks of toys. Her cheeks warmed. There were two men perusing the walls. The next room was full of movies. She stepped into it and inspected the labels on the shelves. They were surprisingly detailed. Skipping past the racks of DVDs labeled things like "teen girls" and "MILFs," she found the corner rack: "gay."

Marissa glanced around the empty room and ran her fingers along the cases, selecting one at random and pulling it out. There were two burly men dressed as construction workers on the front. She made a face and put it back. Big hairy guys weren't her thing. The next DVD featured boys so young-looking they made her feel a little guilty. She put it back as well, feeling a bit discouraged. Where had Lita found a movie that was so gorgeous, so sexy, but still dirty? She didn't want some boring, badly produced crap.

She skipped down a shelf and picked out another. This one made her raise her eyebrows. The men were cute, and it was about "office workers" in their suits and ties. They looked clean-cut and handsome, indeterminate age but definitely not teenagers. She turned it over and looked at the screenshots on the back, shifting on her feet. A slow pulse of arousal rippled through her as she checked out the frames of men kissing, stripping each other, one leading another along by his tie with no shirt on—yes, this was the one. She tucked it under her arm and was almost all the way out of the room when one more rack caught her eye: "bisexual." She hesitated.

It was probably the girl-girl-boy stuff. She swallowed, thinking of the video with the woman and her two lovers, and flipped through a few of the movies. They were all two or more men and one woman. Some made her frown—they looked violent, kind of icky—but finally she found a movie with two long-haired rocker types and a normal-looking blond woman between them, wearing a corset and heels. They were kneeling at her feet.

That one, Marissa snagged. She held her head high and marched into the main room again. Her DVDs felt hot in her hands. The clerk smiled at her again, as if she were buying groceries, and rang her up. Marissa's face felt like it was a thousand degrees. Her hands trembled a bit as she took her wallet from her pocket. It was so public, but nobody was going to say anything. She hated how silly and embarrassed she was. This was the kind of thing exploring her sexuality and growing up was supposed to prevent: humiliation about what she wanted, a fear of admitting her desires.

Once outside, her purchases in a nondescript black bag, she took a deep breath and sighed. Maybe it just wasn't in her to be unashamed and open like Lita. But she wanted to. She wanted to be able to buy porn and toys and find men without having to feel wrong or ridiculous.

It was getting late. She climbed in her car and headed back home.

The air was cool and the sky dark when she parked her car and climbed the stairs to her apartment, bag in hand. The slow burn of her desire built as she closed her door behind her and took out her movies, fanning them in her hands like a pair of cards. Now, in the privacy of her home, she felt—naughty, in a good way, not just embarrassed. She unwrapped them, walked to her DVD player, and stuck in the one with the office-worker men.

After making sure her door was locked and her blinds closed, she retrieved her vibrator from her bedroom and shimmied out of her clothes. Walking into the living room nude made her shiver and glance at the balcony doors, which were completely covered by the thick blinds. All the same, it gave her a thrill. The movie was on its menu screen. She selected play, snuggled down on her couch, and tucked her legs under her.

Maybe she wouldn't like it a second time. She watched with bated breath as the two men who came on screen—in suits and ties, looking like characters from *Mad Men*—and flirted with each other, making heavy eye contact and brushing hands together over the desk between them. Her tension wound as the scene unfolded. Finally, after a groan-inducing pickup line, the man with the gelled brown hair grabbed the other by his tie and yanked him into a wet, open-mouthed kiss. Their tongues were visible briefly, twining slickly together, as they shifted, leaning together over the desk.

Marissa gasped a bit when the man being kissed swept all the papers off the desk and crawled up onto it, the brown-haired actor using his tie as a leash. The sight of the red silk wrapped around his fist as he maneuvered his partner's head, guiding him, made her pulse race. It was almost as good as the bondage in Lita's movie. *Yes*, she thought to herself, *I definitely like the kinky parts.*

She pressed her fingers to her pussy, feeling her own heat and dampness, and pressed her thighs tighter together, digging her toes into the couch. The men onscreen were stripping each other; clothes came off with yanks and grunts, both of them seemingly unwilling to break their kiss. The man on the desk jerked the other's belt open and unzipped his pants. Marissa held her breath. That slim but still masculine hand slid inside the gap in his pants and drew out his half-hard dick. The brown-haired man gasped, hips canting forward into the touch. She watched him harden further while the hand stroked and squeezed, until his cock was pointing up at his belly.

The man on the desk smirked at the camera and bent forward, mouthing at the other's cock. It was hard to tell who was in control now—the brown-haired actor was moaning, hands petting the other's back and shoulders while he sucked him. The camera caught each wet, spit-slick glide up and down, the way his lips plumped with the pressure and how every few moments his tongue licked out past the suction of his mouth to tease at the flesh he couldn't reach.

Marissa picked up her vibrator and turned it on low, laying it in the crook of her lap. With her thighs pressed together and her legs tucked under her, the firm pulses of the toy seemed to echo through her whole lower body, not just her clit. It was erotic, charged, but not enough to make her come. She wanted to wait until the movie got further along, maybe orgasm at the same time as the actors. They were so, so hot. She'd never been so turned on so quickly in her life. How had she missed this? How had she never noticed how much this aroused her?

Simple: she'd never tried to find out.

With a moan of her own, she watched the men part, saliva stretching in a glistening line between one's mouth and the other's erection. His eyes were half-lidded with desire. They were actually into it, not just faking, she thought. At least they could pretend chemistry.

"Fuck me," the brown-haired man said, stroking himself.

The man on the desk grinned. "Okay, boss."

He slipped down off the desk and shucked his pants, revealing his own hard-on. Marissa lifted her hands to her breasts, tweaking her nipples between her fingertips. Small bursts of pleasure followed each pinch. The brown-haired man caught him in another quick kiss, then bent over his own desk, pants around his thighs while the other man was totally nude. The camera followed him as he walked around behind his partner, grinning, and plucked a condom from somewhere on the desk. He rolled it over his cock and stepped closer, rubbing himself along the crack of the other's ass.

Marissa thumbed the power up a notch on the vibrator and shifted to spread her legs a bit and ease it between them, putting pressure on her clit and sending sharp sparks up her spine. Her back bowed and she moaned. She closed her eyes for a brief second to revel in the sensation.

"You're already slick," the man on the film said.

"I got myself ready for you," the brown-haired man purred. "Stretched myself with my fingers and fucked myself 'til I came. I want your dick."

The dialogue might have been corny, but it made her whole body flush with need as she imagined the actor before the filming with his fingers in himself, pleasuring himself, his mouth open and lips damp. She shuddered. The man in the movie did the same, shifting his hips and pushing his cock against the other man. The actors and Marissa both gasped as the man on top thrust into him in one smooth stroke, until his hips met the smooth curves of the other man's ass.

"Oh, fuck," the brown-haired man groaned, his voice almost cracking. "Yeah, yeah!"

The top groaned, clutching at his sides with white-knuckled hands and pounding into him. The sound of flesh hitting flesh and their moans came from the television. She saw his hand slip down his body, grasping his own cock where it bounced between his thighs. He whimpered, head bowed to the desk, and he rocked back into the fucking. Marissa couldn't catch her breath. She panted, pressing her vibrator harder against her clit as the pleasure built and built.

She climaxed almost at the moment the actor did, his come splattering over his hand and the desk. Her breath stuck in her throat as she shivered through the waves of ecstasy. The other man on the video bent low over his partner's back, grasping at his shoulders, and cried out as he finished. They collapsed onto the desk together, breathing heavily. The screen faded out and another scene started.

Marissa pressed the stop button on the remote and turned off her toy, taking a moment to catch her breath.

There was no doubt about it—this turned her on, so much. It made her come. She dropped her head back against the couch and sighed. Watching men have sex really, really did it for her in a way nothing else quite could.

Except possibly a woman sandwiched in between them. She pried herself off the couch and shut down the TV, going to clean up. As she collapsed into bed later, freshly scrubbed from a quick shower, the sheets slid over her bare skin. It was more erotic than it had ever been before. She stared up at her darkened ceiling, wondering if any of those links would have a way for her to see men together in real life, not just on video . . . To be in the same room, smell the sweat and hear their luscious noises.

Or to join in.

Suddenly, it seemed more viable.

After a long, arduous day teaching the merits of Milton to one class and basic composition to several others, Marissa was unbelievably grateful to walk into her quiet apartment. She'd spilled her coffee that morning, though thankfully not on herself; lost her only pen halfway through the day; and gotten so unnerved at the presence of the auditor that she managed to forget the ends of a few sentences.

There was nothing quite like standing in front of a room of cynical college students with your mouth hanging open, going "um, uh, er—" while you tried to remember what you'd said before and where you were going with it.

The auditor had finally lessened her tension by rolling his eyes at her and quirking a grin. While a part of her was horrified that he was laughing at her, most of her brain just relaxed. If he was trying to make her calm down by showing her that she amused him, then he understood he was making her nervous by sitting there stone-faced and imperious. She knew she needed to find a way to be less intimidated by his presence. He seemed like a good guy with no intent of being cruel to her or grading her down. Like he'd said, he wasn't there to get her fired, just to tell her bosses where she might need training. That wasn't so bad.

As she made herself a fresh cup of tea, she tried to think through why she was so nervous in front of him. She'd never been a bad test taker, and this was another kind of exam. She needed to pick up the pace, teach better, and learn to be more at ease in the classroom. But how?

Marissa cupped the hot mug in her hands and went to sit on her couch. It sank under her, comfortable and soft. Her eyes fluttered closed. The mug between her fingers was warm and soothing. She'd managed not to think about the e-mail from Lita all day, but now that she was home alone again, it crept to the forefront of her mind. Should she check some of the links?

The night before in the darkness of her bedroom, freshly sated, it seemed like the perfect idea. She could find a male couple who would find it erotic to have a woman watch them, or join in. In the evening light after a long day at work, it seemed more like a pipe dream.

"It can't hurt to look," she repeated to herself under her breath.

That much was true. If she found nothing, then she found nothing, but did she want to be the kind of woman who let opportunities slip by without grabbing for them? Did she want to be the kind of woman who let the voice in the back of her head—which was pretty insistent about hooking up with strange men being something good girls never did—dictate what she allowed herself to enjoy? Lita always said that being raised by her grandmother had done some damage to Marissa's self esteem, but she'd never believed her friend.

Her grandma had been sweet, supportive, and helpful. It was just that she had so many old-fashioned ideas about womanhood and femininity. Marissa was a bit chagrined to realize how much of that she'd really internalized when it came down to it. She couldn't enjoy her sexuality the way Lita did because she was ashamed. She didn't want to be that way. It wasn't *her*. She wanted freedom and erotic development.

So, with a fortifying gulp of hot tea, she opened her laptop.

The only way out of this morass of old-fashioned

silliness holding her back was to do the things she'd only ever dreamed of, do the things that embarrassed her, take what she knew she wanted, deep down. She had walls to knock down.

Marissa opened the e-mail again and clicked on the "Kink and Coffee" link because it seemed the most cute and simple. The entry page warned her that the site was for viewers eighteen and older. She stifled a smile and clicked through. The main site was understated in browns and golds, with a message board and a few links to other websites. It seemed to be locally oriented, too, not national. She entered the message board, found the room entitled "Looking For" and was immediately surprised at how many listings there were just for her state. There were that many people looking for "kink and coffee" together, who had fantasies they wanted filled?

It made her feel—better. Lita was such a force of nature that it was hard to judge sometimes if her way was the best way. But here were all these normal people, all looking to hook up and find their desires. Marissa bookmarked it and began to sift through the listings.

The first thing she noticed was that there were women posting, not just men. Some wanted things she found odd, like foot massages, but others made more sense to her: role-playing, dress-up, games. One caught her eye, halfway down the first page. "Two bisexual men looking to celebrate an anniversary with a like-minded woman." She took a quick sip of her tea to wet her suddenly dry mouth. That sounded like what she thought she might want.

Should she click? The mouse hovered over the link for

a moment as she thought about it. *It couldn't hurt to look*, she thought one more time. She clicked. The posting had a longer paragraph inside. "We're about to have our anniversary, and neither of us has been with a woman in that time. We want an adventurous, kinky, self-confident woman who would like to spend the weekend exploring all the combinations we could make with three people. If you're interested, please e-mail us with a photo. We can talk about it."

Marissa sat her laptop on the couch and stood, leaving the page open as she went to the kitchen. Her thoughts were consumed with images of her between them, watching them kiss and touch while they rubbed their bodies against hers. She shuddered. It was hard to put together any kind of dinner when all she could think about was sex—dirty, kinky sex.

Though it took longer than usual, she eventually succeeded in putting a chicken and pasta dish in the oven to bake. She pulled her cell phone from her pocket and dialed Lita's number. The other end rang and rang, then went to voice mail.

"Hi, hon," Marissa said. She licked her lips, nervous. "I think I might—I might—oh hell. I think I want to answer one of those ads on the sites you sent me. What do I do? Should I do it? I don't know. Call me."

She hung up and heaved a sigh.

"I'm such a grown-up," Marissa muttered to herself. "I have to call my best friend to decide if I should even think about hooking up with a guy."

Well, that was what best friends were for. She flopped

back onto the couch to wait for her dinner to bake and turned on the television, this time to watch the news. She didn't quite feel up to another night of adult film entertainment. Her fingers lazily tapped at the keyboard of the laptop at her side. The ad was still there. It was phrased nicely. If she e-mailed them with her picture, would they send one back? How did she politely decline if she didn't think they were hot?

What if it was a couple she knew? How would you get past that? How embarrassing would it be to answer a friend's sex ad and not even know until it was too late and they realized it was you? She made a face at the news-anchor blathering along on the TV. Lita would be able to help her. She'd done stuff like this before.

Her phone buzzed. She flipped it open and saw only a text message, from Lita: "On a date. Call you tonight. I think you should do it."

Marissa read it twice and closed her phone again.

She picked up the laptop with trembling hands, her breath speeding with nerves. It was just an e-mail. She clicked their e-mail link and composed a succinct message, then attached a photo of herself Lita had taken a few months back.

"I might be interested in spending a weekend with you. I am very new to this, though, and very shy. Please go easy on me. I've attached a photo. Thanks!"

Hitting the send button felt like cutting loose strings that were holding her whole body up. She collapsed back into the soft cushions of the couch and closed her eyes. It was done. She might end up with a date to screw two men, who were a couple. She rubbed her eyes with one hand. That wasn't so hard. It was the rest of the deal that she might not be able to go through with.

A moment later, her e-mail dinged. She nearly jumped, then scrambled to open the reply. He must have been at his computer to respond so quickly. With her pulse in her throat, and a familiar tingling creeping up her spine, she read his answer: "A new shy girl, huh? You're lovely. What made you want to answer our ad? Here's a picture of us, too."

Marissa opened the attachment. The picture was of two men, arm in arm. One was taller than the other by a bare inch or two. The taller man had olive skin and a wide smile, curly black hair cut short. The other was pale as Marissa herself, the kind of porcelain skin that seemed to reflect sunlight, and appeared to be a natural blond. His eyes were bright blue. Together they made a beautiful contrast. The tingling firmed into the tightness of arousal in her belly as she imagined them together: kissing, hands tangled in hair, their bodies pressed together.

She responded, "You're both handsome. I decided to answer your ad because I want to explore myself." She paused, considering how to frame her words. "I like watching men together. I think I'd like being with two men at once. I've never tried, and I don't want to let my whole life go by without giving it a shot."

She sent it before she had time to worry that it was too honest, too personal. If she was even considering sleeping with these guys, or they with her, there had to be some level of honesty, right? And she knew she would never be able to fake Lita's suave sexual pull.

At best she seemed like what she was: a delicate, easily embarrassed bookworm who spent most of her time alone, reading. They needed to understand that going in to the whole mess. She wasn't as demonstrative or as outwardly sexual, but she wanted to try. They might be willing to help. Or, maybe they wanted an experienced woman, and they'd turn her down.

The reply pinged back quickly again. "I'm curious—how old are you? What else have you never tried that you might like to, if we do this?"

Marissa tapped her keys without typing anything. "I'm twenty-six. How old are you guys? I honestly . . ." She paused again. "I honestly don't know what I like. I haven't had much experience. Is that a problem? Like I said, I want to explore. I want to discover things about myself. I'm adventurous."

The reply back came almost instantly, and had more picture attachments. "Adrian says he's into helping you figure out some things. You sound sweet and nice. And you're attractive. We're both into adventurousness, too. Before we make a date to meet, if you wanted, what do you think of these pictures? It might give you a hint about what you want to try."

She opened the attachments without taking a breath. Her heart was pounding. The first photo was a much more amateur shot than their original picture. It showed them kissing, eyes closed. The darker-skinned man had his hand on the other's jaw, holding him in the embrace.

She cycled through to the next picture and her breath caught. This one showed no faces, but the skin contrast let her know who she was seeing: a man on all fours, though the photo cut off at his shoulders, and another fucking him. The camera was angled down at the point where they were joined, and she knew it was them, pictured their faces in her mind's eye to go along with the erotic photo. Another showed the blond man, the other man's hand fisted in his hair, with a cock in his mouth. He was eyeing the camera with a sultry look, lips wet and plump around the dick stretching them. His expression was absolutely *wicked*.

Marissa slid a hand between her legs as if drawn by powers beyond her control. The photos showed them again, this time fully clothed and embracing in a kiss. The last was a picture of the blond man with the other man on his back, his skinnier frame pinning his partner to the bed as they writhed together. Marissa stroked herself with gentle fingers, teasing the pleasure in her groin tighter and tighter as she scrolled back through again. The picture of the blond man sucking cock was the hottest, she thought, because he was looking right at the camera, and by extension, his partner.

She drew her hand away from herself long enough to type: "So hot, I can't even stop looking. I want you, both of you."

It was the dirtiest thing she'd ever sent in an e-mail, though that wasn't saying much. She clicked the button all the same and went back to the pictures, rubbing her fingertips in small circles around her stiffened clit. It was a slow, heady pleasure.

The reply: "Let me guess—you're touching yourself?"

She gasped a little, using her free hand to respond, "Yes."

"Show me?"

She paused, breath heaving, and weighed the options. Should she? If they were honestly thinking about having a "date" with her, they'd see her this way. She would just make sure not to have her face in the photo. She scrambled for her phone and shucked her business-casual slacks. Thankfully the blinds were still closed from the night before. She angled the phone to have a full view of her fingers and her pussy, spreading her legs wide. She snapped two shots as she stroked herself and checked them on her phone: the shot showed only her taut lower stomach and her slick cunt. She e-mailed them to herself with a quick press of her phone's camera functions button.

The minute it took to reattach the photo to the e-mail from the couple was almost torture. She was so close to coming, so aroused by how new and strange this experience was. She was having cybersex with a stranger. She shuddered, sending the files with the note: "I think I'm about to come."

The reply was so fast she knew they must have been taking their return photo as she took hers. It was a shot taken with a webcam, she thought, that showed the blond man sitting on the other man's lap. His back was to the camera, his legs over the arms of a desk chair. Strong, dark hands were holding him up by his ass. The picture captured a single moment of their fucking, but the darker man was grinning over his partner's shoulder at the camera. His eyes were half-lidded with arousal but his face was open and amused, pleased. He seemed so—interesting.

"Us, too," was the reply.

Marissa cried out as she came, arching her back and pushing a finger inside herself at the last moment, imagining it was one of them.

The oven dinged in the other room. She panted for breath, shivering with aftershocks, and typed another response as heat flushed through her. "Thank you for giving me a try."

She sent it and closed the laptop, staggering to her feet to turn the oven off.

Lita would be amazed. Marissa had sent two strangers a picture of her most private parts and masturbated while they sent her photos of themselves in the act. And it had been so, so scorching hot.

She knew without having to ask her friend for the advice that she was going to make a date to meet them. The e-mail interlude had only cemented her desire to fulfill herself, her needs, her wants. They wanted the same things she did, it seemed, and they were all consenting adults.

Marissa smiled to herself, because she refused to feel any shame. This was what she wanted, and she was going to do it, old-fashioned morals be damned. She'd earned it.

Chapter Three

The next morning found Marissa sitting in her empty classroom with a fresh cup of tea, staring at the wall. She'd checked her e-mail with quivering fingers that morning and found a response from the men. Their names were Paul and Adrian—the blond man was Adrian—and they were respectively thirty and twenty-eight. They both had clean bills of health. They liked to go to movies and read, which was nice, she thought.

And they wanted to set up a meeting date with her over dinner on the coming Saturday.

Lita had never called her back the night before, which must have meant that her date went well, whoever it was with. She didn't begrudge her friend the fun, and honestly, it was probably better to handle this on her own and not let someone else's expectations guide her. She would do what felt right and avoid what made her genuinely uncomfortable. That shouldn't have been so hard to figure out, but it was, and so she was still staring at the wall letting her tea cool when the auditor walked in.

"You look preoccupied today," he said. "I keep telling you to relax."

She blinked, feeling her face heat and hating it. He raised an eyebrow. "It's nothing. I'm sure I'll do better today. I don't know why I get so nervous."

If only he knew. Today it wasn't the class that had her nerves on edge. It was the fact that she was trying to decide whether or not she should meet a couple from the Internet and decide if they wanted to all have sex. She glanced at him one more time as he took his customary seat closest to the door. He was a handsome guy—that might have been where all the stupid nerves came from. It was always harder to be suave and interesting in front of attractive, classy older men who happened to be grading her.

Now that she thought about it, she'd had that problem once or twice in her own college career. It made sense. She wasn't afraid of being graded badly—he just got under her skin. Strong jaw, thick, glossy hair with a touch of gray that curled just so over his ears like he didn't care enough to cut it, the faintest, roguish hint of stubble on his cheeks: he was her type, when it came to older guys.

Marissa took a sip of her tea as her students began to filter in, pondering her realization. Maybe that would make the class easier; knowing she had a little crush might make it go away, or at least keep it from pestering her and making her act like an idiot. Honestly it made her feel a little dumb that she hadn't put two and two together about her own reaction to him. He wasn't "smoking hot" as Lita would say, so he hadn't dinged her radar immediately, just slipped under it to be a cute nuisance. But, she knew nothing about him, and he was her auditor, so it really didn't matter if she thought he was nice looking.

Still, when she stood to start the class, she felt his eyes on her. It almost brought her to a stumbling halt again, but she powered through the tingle of awareness and kept talking. Students rustled in their bags for the paper they were supposed to turn in. She marked in her head which ones were sitting still with abashed looks. They'd be staying after to beg her for forgiveness and an extension. She hadn't decided yet if she'd give it—was that fair to the others? What would the auditor say?

She shook herself and collected the neatly stapled stacks of paper from each row of desks, tapped them on hers to straighten them out, and tucked them in her bag. Now, it was time to get on with the lecture.

It was, as she'd suspected, easier now. But she also added a few flourishes and made a point to catch the auditor's eye once or twice. He was smiling. He might not have known how she conquered her nervousness, and she was glad about that, but he seemed pleased that she'd managed it. She held onto the hope that he'd grade her well after all.

Marissa managed to delay opening her laptop by picking up take-out, eating her dinner, and watching a few episodes of a crime drama on television. By the time she'd finished all that, her fingers were practically itching to open their e-mail again. She still wasn't completely sure of her response, but, really, why not say yes to a normal date? There were no guarantees on the table. She could go, meet them, and see if she was still comfortable with taking things a step further.

That in and of itself was a huge step.

It was easy enough to power up the laptop and re-open the e-mail. She sat staring at it for a long while, considering what she would say, what she wanted to do. A part of her said no, that she'd be better off just finding another guy like Jeff who was nice and normal, and seeing if it worked out this time. The rest of her knew that wasn't the way to go. It hadn't worked before, her whole life. It wasn't going to work now.

So she clicked "reply" and typed out a short answer. "Yes, I'd like to meet with you to talk about this further. I can't make any promises yet, but we can see over dinner, right? I want to try. What do you say? Saturday at six?"

Sending it was easier than making the decision to agree. It almost felt like a weight had lifted from her shoulders. She was really going to do it, this new, crazy thing. She was going to meet a staggeringly beautiful male couple and talk about fucking with them. The first thing she thought was that Lita would be proud—and then Marissa realized that she herself was rather proud.

This really was the kind of freedom she wanted, the kind of woman she could be.

When their response didn't come after a few minutes, she closed the laptop and stood, cracking her back. She hadn't made the mistake of wearing heels to work again but sitting in the hard plastic chairs they provided for the students and professors alike was murder on her spine. Maybe it would be wise to start bringing a cushion stuffed into her bag. She grinned. That was a little quirkier than she was willing to be.

A yawn let her know her night was coming to a close. She checked the clock and decided she had time for a real bath, not just a shower, and stepped into the bathroom to run the water. For fun, she even poured in some of the bubble bath she kept under the sink. It was a reward for doing so well during her class today—it might have been her imagination, but it seemed like the students had noticed her lack of stress and were responding more freely because of it. If she could be open and engaging, not all uptight and terrified, maybe they could, too?

Marissa undressed and slipped into the steaming water with a sigh. If she could get her career and her love life squared away, everything would be perfect. She knew that the couple—Paul and Adrian, she reminded herself—weren't looking for anything permanent, and this time neither was she. But afterwards, when she'd really figured out what she wanted and what she didn't, she could go looking for a match.

Not Mister Nice and Boring this time, either. Now that she'd felt the spark, she was sure that was what was missing from her past relationships. She had been attracted to Jeff, and Miles before him, but never enthralled by them, never driven to screaming, shivering orgasms by them. They hadn't ever made her feel like

Paul and Adrian had managed to just with a few dirty pictures.

Lita had been right all along—she needed some adventure in her life.

It was Thursday, which was composition class day, full of freshmen and the kids who would probably drop out in the next semester. She tried not to be cynical about it, but really, they wouldn't do the readings, write the papers, or even pay attention during class. It wasn't hard to see they were on their way out from the first day—some people didn't care enough to bother.

To be honest, it drove her up a wall. She'd gone to college with plenty of people who worked every day to get through, and known people who couldn't afford to go at all, and these kids wasted their parents' money to goof off and fail when there were people who wanted it and couldn't go? It was infuriating.

The only thing keeping her from actually yelling at the morons was the e-mail she'd woken up to. "Sounds wonderful. Do you like Italian? I know a good place. If you don't, Adrian thinks seafood is a good choice, too."

She'd replied, "Italian is divine. Where?"

Her auditor rarely came to the composition class, probably because she'd already taught it when she was working on her doctoral degree. It wasn't new to her. She just couldn't wait to get out of doing it ever again. Maybe that was ungrateful, and she didn't want to feel ungrateful, but this was the only part of her job she hated. She looked for him anyway as the class drew to a close, but he wasn't there.

What would he think of her plans for the weekend?

Well, he had no wedding ring, but he probably wasn't the type to encourage young women to have threesomes with strangers. Heat prickled down her spine at the thought—repeating it to herself did that, consistently. *I am going to fuck two men*, she would think, and her belly would go tight. Just the thought was enough, and imagining it seemed to light a wildfire under her skin.

Really doing it might give her a heart attack, but what a way to go.

Saturday came too quickly, yet not quickly enough. At five, Marissa found herself smoothing a dress down around her thighs in front of her mirror. She slipped on her high heels, checking herself out from the back: dark blue slinky dress with a scoop back, but a high front so not too suggestive. The hem was at her knees and no higher. It was sexy without being a party dress, high-class enough for a nice Italian restaurant but not too upscale. She sighed, tugging at the hem again and checking out her legs. Her hair was pulled up in kinky, gelled curls on top of her head in a clip.

It was the best she was going to get, she thought, but she didn't feel terribly comfortable. Marissa would rather wear jeans and a T-shirt than a dress, though academia had taught her to dress up well for official functions.

This was an even bigger sign that she needed a date. Discomfort in pretty clothes, being unsettled by the thought of meeting someone—she wasn't sure she would be up to their standards. Of course, there was nothing she could do about that, so she finally managed to drag herself away from the mirror and grab her clutch bag and her car keys. She had an hour to make it to the restaurant, which was at most a half hour away. She grabbed a book from her bag at the last minute, in case she had to wait.

Her heels clattered on the wooden steps down to the parking lot. One of her neighbors, outside smoking, raised a hand in a wave. She smiled back at the woman and returned the wave, then climbed into her car. The dress slid silkily up on her thighs. She straightened it again, wondering if she should have gone for a longer hem for a dinner date. Was this dress too party-girl? She didn't think so, but she wasn't quite sure.

"It's too late now," she grumbled to herself, frowning, and turned the key in the ignition. "I'm sure it's fine."

Talking to herself often centered her, or made her feel goofy enough that it eased her tension. Throughout the drive, she took each turn with more care than usual, drove defensively, and kept her fingers crossed that she'd make it to the restaurant without any problems. Of all the days to have an accident or get a ticket, today was not the one.

The parking lot was full when she arrived and wedged her small car in between two trucks. She checked the time. It was five forty-five, which meant she was only a bit early. The e-mail they'd sent her said the reservations would be under

Adrian Beck if she arrived early. She took a deep breath to calm her pounding heart, though it didn't do much, and got out of her car. Her legs felt watery. She leaned against her still-open door for a moment, eyes closed.

This was a date, nothing more or less, not yet. It could be more if she wanted it to be, if they wanted it to be. She'd never been so nervous meeting Jeff for dinner, not even the first time, but probably because she'd already known him from college. He hadn't been new, or a stranger, and there hadn't been two of him. Part of the sudden disorientation was a shiver-inducing level of arousal at what she was doing, and what it stood for. The rest seemed to be her upbringing and its expectations having a fistfight in her head with what she really wanted.

After the momentary breather, she lifted her chin and walked to the door of the restaurant, feeling the sway the high heels put in her walk. Her clutch purse dangled on her arm. She hadn't called Lita first to tell her what she was doing. What if they were secretly axe-murderers trying to lure out young women? A sudden rush of too-much-crime-drama fear prompted her to take out her phone standing in the foyer and text Lita that she was on a date and she'd check in later.

Then she stuck the phone back in her bag and went up to the hostess.

"We have a reservation. Adrian Beck?" she asked.

The hostess checked her list, smiled, and said, "Right this way."

Marissa's heart was in her throat as she followed the

woman. Would they already be at the table? In person, would they be as handsome as their photos?

Better yet, could she sit across a table from two men who she'd seen naked, fucking, coming together? Her cheeks burned as she remembered vividly the pictures they'd sent her so willingly. They had seen her intimately, too. How did people do this, meet like they'd never known these sexual details about each other already? To make small talk knowing what someone's cock looked like, thinking about having him inside her? She was almost dizzy.

Luckily or not, the booth the woman led her to was empty. She slid in on one side, ordered a glass of wine, and toyed with the silverware. Adrian, the blond man, always seemed playfully wicked in the pictures. He would be the flirt, she assumed. Paul, on the other hand, was the one who'd e-mailed her. She was fairly sure of that. He was the more serious of the two. She could count on those few small things, but other than that, they were an enigma.

Her glass of wine arrived first, along with a basket of bread lightly coated in garlic butter. She plucked a small piece of it and nibbled. Her stomach was growling; she'd been too on edge to eat the rest of the day. Meanwhile, her eyes scanned the room. She wished the foyer was visible from the table so she could be prepared when they walked in.

The tension couldn't last forever. She checked her phone, saw it was five minutes until six, and tucked her bag next to her in the booth again. Any moment they would arrive in the flesh, these men who wanted to meet her. It was their anniversary, supposedly, but she wondered which. One year? Five? Ten? That would make a difference, she suspected, in how serious this whole affair might be. She didn't want to somehow come between a couple who'd been together for a long time.

Caught up in her imaginings, she almost missed them when they came around the corner into the main area of the restaurant. Her breath stuck in her chest for a moment. They were chatting with each other, eyes skimming the room as they followed the hostess. Paul saw her first, raised one dark eyebrow, and lifted his hand in greeting. She waved back. Adrian responded with a grin and a flip of his own fingers, barely a wave and more of a "wait one minute, I'll be there."

Marissa sipped her wine, wiped her buttery fingers on her napkin, and considered whether or not it was proper to stand and say hello. Men did when a woman came up, but was she supposed to?

Apparently not, as Adrian stepped ahead of Paul, leaned over her, and gave her a peck on the cheek. Up close, his eyes were very blue, almost a lavender color. She felt herself blushing and managed a quiet, "Hello."

"Hi there," he said, finally leaning back from his close scrutiny.

Paul put out his hand and she moved to shake it, but he caught her fingers and lifted them to kiss her knuckles like a courtier. Now she was sure her face was bright red.

"Good evening," he said.

"It's nice to meet you," she said. She was glad it didn't come out as a squeak.

The two of them took the booth seat opposite her, Adrian on the inside and Paul on the outside.

"I'm left-handed," Paul explained. "Have to be careful of who sits where or it's an elbow fiasco."

"Ah," Marissa said, smiling. "My mother is a lefty, so I understand."

A beat of silence settled as they looked each other over. Marissa welcomed the moment to breathe. Paul had on a silky dark green shirt with the top two buttons undone and Adrian was wearing a cute jacket that fit tightly over a plain white shirt with a scoop neck. He looked almost yuppie, but the floppy blond hair in disarray and the grin said he was anything but.

"So," Paul said.

"You said you were shy?" Adrian finished.

She cleared her throat and took a sip of wine to wet her suddenly dry mouth. "Well, I'm not—I don't usually— oh, hell."

Paul laughed, but it wasn't at her so much as with her. His partner smiled.

"I've been very busy," she said. "I just received my doctoral degree and got a teaching position at the university. Let's just say that when you're trying to get your Ph.D. you don't spend a lot of time dating, or exploring, or anything. Just reading and writing."

"Ooh, a professor," Adrian said.

"Down, boy," Paul muttered, prompting a laugh from Marissa.

She was relieved at how her heartbeat had slowed and she didn't feel like she was going to pass out, now that they were really here. They seemed normal, cute, friendly. That was a relief. She'd been afraid they would be overbearing, or it would be too immediately sexual, or something else would go wrong.

"Well, we've been together for three years now," Adrian said. "And both of us like women, too, and have been with girls in the past, so we decided it might be nice to—as you said, explore a little."

"Because we're comfortable enough to," Paul said, his fingers clasping Adrian's briefly on the tabletop.

Marissa glanced down at her drink. It was very intimate, personal, and reminded her this was a happy couple, and she wasn't part of them, no matter what they were going to do together.

"My best friend insisted on me finally coming out of my shell," Marissa confessed. "I've only dated boring guys, and I don't have much real, um, experience."

"Ah," Paul said, and the word held a world of meaning. "Boring like vanilla and bland?"

"Yes," she said, lifting her bread for another bite to distract herself from the embarrassment of talking about her old sex life with two strange men—and being honest about how lackluster it was.

"Which means you're exploring more than a little bit," Adrian said, leaning forward a bit. "I don't mind—"

The waitress arrived and interrupted whatever else he'd been about to say. He sat back again with a smile and ordered an appetizer, some kind of fried cheese, along with drinks for himself and Paul. Marissa asked for water in addition to her wine.

"I guess we should look at the menu and decide what we want so we have time to chat over dinner," Paul said.

Marissa picked hers up and glanced over it. The choices were almost overwhelming; there was so much food that all sounded so good. She eventually settled on a chicken dish with wine sauce and pasta. The prices almost made her wince, but she reminded herself she had a nice new salary twice the size of anything she'd made before getting her real job with her real degree. She could afford it, if just for tonight.

"You know I'm a professor. What do you guys do?" she asked when they seemed finished with their perusal of the menu.

"I'm in accounting," Adrian said.

"I paint," Paul said. He ducked his chin, a boyish and adorable gesture. "And I sell art. I work in a gallery most of the week, selling other people's stuff, but I've also done a show or two of my own."

"Wow," she said. "An artist! That's great."

"Yeah, accounting is boring, isn't it?" Adrian said, pulling a moue of discontent.

She grinned at him. "I'm sorry. Art's more interesting than teaching, too."

A moment later Marissa nearly jumped out of her seat when a cool, bare foot brushed against her calf—her breath seemed to speed a fraction and heat flushed down her body. Footsie, really? Both men were grinning, so she couldn't quite tell who it was. Whoever it was, he brushed his foot down the front of her leg in a teasing carress. It was dim enough in the restaurant that she doubted anyone could see under the booth.

"All right," she said with a hint of breathlessness. "Who's that?"

To her surprise, Paul raised his hand and Adrian cast him a playful look. "It's a date, isn't it?" Paul said.

"We've been here for fifteen minutes, Paul," Adrian replied. "And you're already making her uncomfortable."

"Oh, I'm not uncomfortable," she managed, almost whispering.

Adrian reached over the table and took her hand in his, fingers playing down her wrist until they locked around it. Paul's foot traced up the opposite side of her leg, ticklish soft.

"I just want to be on the same page," Adrian murmured, his stare so intense it made her tremble a bit inside. "I'm thinking about what you look like with that dress off, and so is Paul. It's a little different than a regular date, isn't it, shy girl?"

She let out a shaky sigh, her eyelids fluttering. The heat in her body seemed to be coalescing between her legs. Public—this was so *public*. And she liked it. She liked his fingers cuffing her wrist and the fact that anyone could look over and wonder what they were doing, what they were talking about.

"Yes," she whispered.

"Not so shy," he murmured, leaning further over the table.

She met him halfway in a quick kiss, just a brush of mouths that left her aching for more. He sat back and so did she, her eyes drifting over to Paul, who had watched with a mysterious smile. His foot disappeared when the waitress returned with the appetizer and they placed their orders.

"You look flushed," he said finally. Adrian sipped his drink and smiled.

"Should I tally everything that I like? Keep a running list?" she said. "Because that—was good. I liked that."

"A little dominance, a little exhibition, huh?" Adrian said. He shivered visibly, perhaps on purpose. "I think this might be a perfect match."

"It's odd," Paul said before she had to find a way to reply. "This is something in between a date and a— negotiation, isn't it?"

"That's a good word, negotiation," she said.

"Not only do we figure out if we like each other, which I think we do so far," Adrian clarified. "We get to figure out if the sex we're discussing is going to work out well for all involved."

"It's weird," she said. "I've never talked about sex on a first date before. Or made a date with the, well, intent to talk about it."

"It's a little weird for me, too," Paul admitted.

"See, you're both vanilla compared to me. I used to be in the BDSM scene. Negotiating boundaries, desires, rules and all that is pretty normal," Adrian said.

Marissa blinked at him, surprised. "What was that like?"

"Well," he said coyly. "Maybe I can show you, if we decide to go further."

"*Oh*," she said, almost a rush of breath instead of a word.

"I'm curious," Paul said. "You don't have to answer if you don't want to, but how did you never manage to figure out what you liked? You're almost Adrian's age, and he spent his early twenties on his back, I think."

Adrian smirked. "Not always on my back, dear, I'll remind you. You think you're such a top."

Paul rolled his eyes, and Marissa paused to think. "I'm not exaggerating when I say I was too busy. I worked full time to put myself through school, then there was school itself, and I just had no time. I didn't even hang out with friends. Really the only one I still have from my student days is Lita, and she was in Europe for the past two years."

"Again, if you don't want to answer, don't, but how many men have you been with?"

Marissa had to look at her hands and lock her fingers together. Now she was embarrassed. A year ago she would have been horrified to be in this situation, but this time, she was only humiliated by how little experience she had compared to them. They were going to think of her like a kid, she was sure.

"Two," she said finally.

"Two, ever?" Adrian asked, sounding incredulous.

"Hush," Paul cut him off. "She said she was new to this, and shy, so don't rub it in."

"Thanks," she said, a bit shaky.

"Didn't you ever get lonely?" Adrian pushed.

She looked up then, and he had the most honest look

on his face. He wasn't making fun, he was serious. "Well, of course, but I had to get my life in order before I could make room for anyone else in it."

"Makes sense," he said.

"If it makes you feel any better, he's both younger than me and about three times as experienced," Paul said, gesturing at his partner.

"It does, actually," she said with a smile.

The food arrived, interrupting their conversation, and silence reigned for the first few minutes as they began to eat. Marissa's head was swimming with thoughts and all of this knowledge. They seemed genuinely interested, and the still insistent desire kindled in her wasn't going away, either.

"Is it too early in the date to say that I think I'd like to—to do that weekend with you?" she asked, quiet.

"Not too early," Paul said, meeting her eye. "I was afraid whoever answered the ad would be brash, or demanding, or just not my type. Adrian will put up with more for a pretty face than I will, even for a weekend. But you're perfect."

"I like you, too," Adrian said. "I was a shy guy once. So I can help a shy girl out. From what I can tell, you've got a lot of need bundled up in you, and I think we can help you figure out what you want."

"And he finds being someone's first—at anything—exciting. Doesn't matter if it's sex or, or . . ." Paul trailed off.

"Rock climbing," Adrian finished. "I made you go rock climbing, and you liked it."

"He has a bit of an ego," Paul said.

"How about, when dinner's done, we do one more thing?" Adrian suggested.

The look Paul gave him made Marissa burst into surprised giggles. It was suspicion, love, and wary acceptance all rolled into one. Yes, these were the perfect men to spend a sexual awakening with; they were considerate, not crude, and didn't seem to be like panting fraternity-boy dogs. A worry she hadn't even noticed consciously—that the men she met would look down on her for meeting them at all, for wanting them—flitted away.

"What?" Paul finally asked.

"A movie," he said.

"A movie?" Marissa repeated, confused.

"Well . . ."

Paul rolled his eyes. "I can finish this one. It's dark, it's enclosed, it's sexy, but it's public enough to feel safe. So we can fool around and make a final vote on whether you want us."

"Oh, *that* kind of movie," she said with something like a laugh.

"I'm good at being discreet in the dark," Adrian replied with a wag of his eyebrows that was patently ridiculous.

She dissolved into another fit of snickers. "All right," she said. "I'd like that."

"Movies it is," Paul said. "For fooling around like teenagers."

He was trying to fake disdain, but he sounded too amused and intrigued to manage it. Marissa grinned at them both, because to be honest, she felt the same. Something about these two just clicked with her, which was probably for the best for sex, but maybe not for her heart, since she knew once their weekend together was over, she wouldn't be a part of their lives.

A preemptive twinge settled in her chest as she chased away the worry.

Chapter Four

Their red sporty sedan was easy to follow to the local theater. Marissa had a small box of leftovers tucked away in the backseat that she hoped would keep through the film, and whatever happened during it. A jittery, aroused tension flowed through her body. She'd done the movies-and-making-out thing in high school, with her early boyfriends, and remembered it as being both naughty and cute. It was exciting, definitely. Where would she sit? In between them, or on one side?

She thought she'd best let them guide her, since they were the couple and she the guest. They might prefer to sit together. Honestly, she was happy with either arrangement, but it was a little odd to be so aware of their connection to each other and how it did and didn't include her. Sexually, it seemed, she was a welcome part. But they also had moments of tenderness and obvious knowledge of each other that excluded her, and she knew that if this date went well and they set up their weekend of fun, it was just that: a weekend. Temporary.

"Damn it," she muttered at herself as they parked

in the theater. "I am not going to psyche myself out of this."

So what if it was temporary? That wasn't something she'd ever tried, after all; sex with someone who wasn't her significant other and never would be. Lita seemed to like it with no strings attached, and it was something worth trying anyway, especially if it meant getting to have a roll in the hay with Adrian and Paul, who were so handsome it hurt to look at them together.

Marissa climbed out of her car and adjusted her dress as they came over to escort her. One took each arm, Paul's hand a gentle brush on her wrist as he hooked his elbow with hers, Adrian's a firmer grip. She almost swooned as the sudden press of them on either side of her. That answered the question of where she would be.

"You're so responsive," Adrian murmured into her ear. He was closer to her height than Paul, she noticed. "I like it."

"You like a lot of things," she replied.

"That he does," Paul said, grinning at them.

His arm lined up with hers was a pretty contrast as she glanced down to make sure she didn't trip in her heels in the rough parking lot. Her paleness against his dark skin reminded her of the pictures of Paul and Adrian together, bodies pressed tight. She had a brief image of the three of them with Paul in the center, like an art photo, all beautiful contrasts.

They did make it inside without incident, and they let her go at the ticket line when it became impossible to escort her one on each side. She stood at the front, chilly in the theater in her dress. The air conditioning was up entirely too high for her tastes, like a refrigerator.

"Would you like my jacket?" Adrian asked, already unbuttoning it.

"Thanks," she said with relief as the line moved forward, towing them along with it. She slipped the dark jacket on, inhaling a whiff of his musky cologne, and gave up buttoning it when she realized it would be impossible over even her modestly sized breasts.

"It doesn't match but it still looks nice," he said after a moment's glance.

"And I'm warm now," she said.

"Yeah," Paul muttered to her under his breath. "We'll make sure you stay that way, won't we, Adrian?"

"Oh, we certainly will."

Marissa held in a pleasant shiver and kept following the line's movement to the counter. Paul snagged the tickets with his credit card before she could offer to pay for hers, and she didn't protest. After all, they'd invited her to the movies, and she'd paid her own dinner, mostly because she'd insisted. It didn't seem fair to make them treat her, not yet, not with the possible trajectory of their simple relationship to each other.

The theater room was dim with previews playing when they wandered into their movie—a dark drama, if she recalled the commercials for it correctly. Adrian, in front, led them to the back row and gestured Paul and Marissa ahead of him. She bit her lip to try to control a sudden surge of lust at the realization that they had, as she wanted and suspected, put her in the middle. She took her seat and shifted, thighs pressing together for a split second of delicious friction as she got comfortable. She hugged the jacket tighter to inhale Adrian's cologne again.

The movie began almost as soon as they settled in. Marissa settled with her hands crossed over her stomach, a sudden rush of nervous, shy tension coiling in her to combat the arousal. What was going to happen here? Did she want it to happen? She thought so.

Paul whispered in her ear first, "Relax. I think Adrian wants to play a bit, take it easy, figure out if you're likely to be into the same things as he is."

"Yup," Adrian muttered.

"What things are those?" she whispered, head filled with images of the bondage porn movie Lita had shown her. She could probably handle that. But what else would he show her, introduce her to? She didn't mind him being the first in as many things as he wanted to explore with her.

"You seem like a natural bottom," he whispered into her ear, so close his mouth touched her skin. "You're a little timid, but you were turned on when I grabbed you in the restaurant and when we put you between us outside, right?"

"Right," she agreed.

"So," he whispered, "I want to see if you like being topped. Right here, right now. Say stop if you're uncomfortable."

She gasped in a quick breath as he took her wrist in his hand and laid it firmly on the armrest between them, palm up. His fingertips pressed against her pulse. He did the same with her other hand, leaving her feeling exposed and open in an odd way, without her arms crossed over her midsection.

"Stay like that," he said, low and in control.

Marissa closed her eyes, tipped her head back on the seat, and tried to hold her breath. A strange, hot tension was building in her, like a sweet slow burn. She wanted to be still. Wanted to let them show her things, teach her things, *have* her.

"Don't make a sound," he whispered.

She wasn't sure what she expected, his hand up her skirt or something, but it wasn't. He didn't touch her for a moment. She sat paralyzed, her breath a struggle, arousal running in warm waves up and down her body. He was so right. She wanted it like this, to be told what to do and how.

Dizzily, she recalled she'd always had a thing for commanding older men in the form of professors. How—interesting.

To her surprise, it was Paul who touched her first, his fingers tracing the bare curve of her neck from her collarbone up to her ear. It felt like a line of fire, such a simple caress. His hand slid around to brace the back of her neck, massaging the tightness from her muscles with flexes of his fingers. She melted into the grip and barely held in a sigh, then nearly flinched away when a warm breath touched her ear on Adrian's side.

"Ssh," he murmured to her. "Relax. Enjoy."

He took her earlobe into his mouth with a small nibble, sending a shiver down her spine, and moved to kiss her throat. She locked her mouth shut against a groan as Paul rubbed her neck and Adrian's palm found her knee while he sucked at the tender pulse point on her throat. His thumb traced circles on her bare skin, teasing, while his fingers gripped the very, very edge of her thigh above her knee.

It felt like he was a puppet master pulling her strings, every touch sending jolts of sensation through her. Her breath had begun to stutter as he licked her collarbone and bit her gently there. She hadn't even thought of that spot as erotic, but his mouth burned her skin in the best way. Her nipples were tight against the silk of the bra she'd worn under the dress, aching to be touched.

The movie progressed without her attention while Adrian made love to her neck with his mouth, moving back up to bite at the muscle near the base. As his teeth dug in slightly harder she let out a tiny, helpless whimper. It hurt, but it didn't, and she had no idea it would feel like that. The slow heat had turned into something else entirely, a dull, throbbing echo of pleasure down her whole body.

"Quiet," Paul reminded her.

Marissa opened her eyes a slit to look at him, rolling her head to his side, and giving Adrian more room. He let out a snuffle of a laugh against her neck and ever so slowly released his grip. As the pressure lessened from his teeth, sensation rushed back in. Her eyelids fluttered as he did, and she saw Paul's lips part, his tongue darting out to wet his lips.

He was turned on watching Adrian do this to her, make her come apart. In so many of the pictures, he was physically dominating the smaller man, but she wondered now who was the "top" or if there really wasn't one in their relationship, and Adrian just took better pictures while being fucked.

The hand on her knee shifted and she moved to glance at Adrian, but Paul reached up and caught her chin with his other hand. He kept her turned toward him, stretched on the seat between their hands, her muscles corded with tension. She was nearly panting. His lips hovered over hers, his eyes open and glinting in the half-lit darkness as he watched. She couldn't lean forward any further to finish the kiss; she had to wait. She found that she wanted to wait.

"I want to watch your face," he murmured.

Adrian didn't go under the skirt, as she expected. Instead he skipped over the hem and laid his hand along the curve of her hips, his fingers tucked into the crook of her thigh and the heat of her body. She rolled her hips, wishing for his fingers to move further, but he lifted his hand away.

"Bad shy-girl," he whispered. "Don't move, don't make a noise. You need to listen better, don't you, honey?"

She was watching Paul's smirk as Adrian whispered to her. Her back bowed with a hard shudder at the hiss in his voice and a lance of pleasure seemed to pierce her belly. She almost moaned.

"God," Paul whispered, bending to catch her mouth. His tongue slid against hers, wet and so slick. His lips were soft and damp. She let a tiny groan out into his kiss, and realized her arms were still where they were supposed to be, palm up on the armrests. She'd never thought of moving them, and wouldn't now. Where was this going to go?

Adrian's fingers returned to the crook of her thigh, and he squeezed her gently, encouraging her to spread her legs. She did, letting Paul eat her small noises while Adrian rubbed his palm down the length of her thigh through silk.

"Do you want me to make you come?" he whispered into her ear, his hot breath tickling her. "Or stop?"

Marissa broke from the kiss and Paul let her go, easing her back into the seat.

Adrian pressed his thumb to her throat and she gulped, feeling the ache of a bruise under his touch. That was where he'd bitten her.

"What do you want?" she murmured back.

"Good answer," he said.

She had a moment to be glad the theater was almost empty, because that sounded like sex. Paul's hand shifted to run down her chest, briefly brushing the pebbled hardness of one of her nipples. She gasped. He settled his fingers at the curve of her waist, pressing against her lower stomach.

"I think I want to make you wait," Adrian murmured to her, rhythmically stroking her inner thigh, so close to where she needed him. "I'll think about you going home and running your fingers over your cunt, tweaking your clit, making yourself moan."

He took her hand in his and moved it to himself, molding her fingers around the thickness of him, fully hard in his pants. She flexed her grip and he groaned, resting his forehead against her shoulder.

"And you'll do the same? You'll touch each other, while you think about this?" she said, panting.

"I think I'll fuck him tonight," Adrian said. "I want to keep this mojo going."

Paul purred into her ear, "I'll let him. He's so into this."

"And I want you to think about it while you're coming," Adrian finished.

He drew her hand away and she turned to Paul, taking his cheeks in her hands and drawing him into another kiss. Adrian stroked the line of her back where it was turned to him. Paul hummed a moan of pleasure into her mouth.

"I don't want to leave you out," she murmured.

"I like to watch him work," Paul murmured. "You didn't leave me out."

"We'll have to figure out how to make sure everyone's getting enough attention," Adrian said.

He reached around her, sandwiching her between their bodies as he stole Paul away. She watched from a millimeter away while they kissed each other hard, lips sliding together in passion. She whimpered again, watching so close, and they both looked at her at once. They were both smiling wicked smiles.

"So," Adrian said. "Next weekend? Friday through Sunday, maybe?"

"I can come over Friday night after my last class," she whispered.

"Bring any toys you're going to want us to use on you, if you like," Paul murmured. "We'll work it out from there."

The film credits began to roll.

"We'll walk you to your car," Paul said.

Marissa's legs shook when she stood, but Adrian looked shaky too, and Paul drew in a heavy breath. She wondered how loose their slacks were, and if Paul had been as aroused by the—game. That had been a dominance game. She'd just played submissive under their hands and *loved* it. That made her woozy all over again.

Would she like to be the dominant partner? She'd think about that later, but it was intriguing.

The lights of the lobby were harsh and bright; she thought they all looked like they'd been up to something. Or maybe that was just her. She found their hands and held one each as they walked out into the night. The sun had set while they were inside. It was hard to imagine that whole encounter had taken two hours—in her memory it was already a blur of erotic thrills.

They were silent as they walked to the cars, but it was comfortable, not awkward. At her car, Adrian's hand found her hip and he swept her into an embrace, the lengths of their bodies pressing together. He was still hard, she noticed as they kissed for real for the first time. She swooned against him, hands grasping his shoulders as his mouth possessed hers. She moaned at the slide of his tongue.

"My turn," Paul murmured, pulling her away and spinning her into his arms.

The switch left her breathless and she went willing into the kiss, returning it with fervor. Her legs were truly weak and her skin tight with desire when they finally tucked her into her driver's seat. She rested her forehead on the wheel, knowing they were watching her recover and glad she could show them how they affected her.

One more week until she went further. All the way.

She glanced up to see them, and they waved goodbye. She returned the gesture.

Now she just had to manage to drive home.

The apartment was dark and still when she let herself in. Her body still throbbed with unsatisfied need, lace underwear damp and sticking to her pussy with every step. How had simple making out turned her on so much? No—easy. It had been anything but simple. They'd kept her between them, teased her, stretched her limits, tested her pleasures. She walked into the bathroom and stripped the dress over her head in one movement. The love-bite on her neck, at the curve of her shoulder, was a vivid purple. She touched it and the resultant ache made her quiver.

Did it mean something about her that she wanted to be taken that way, maneuvered and ordered around? Or was it something she could enjoy, could take pleasure from? She thought it was all right to like it. So many other women did, after all, and men too if Paul's admission that he was going to have Adrian top him was any indication.

That image in her mind had her gripping the edge of her sink, pressing herself against the cool marble. She pictured Adrian pushing him down, holding onto the curly dark locks of his hair and guiding his mouth onto his cock, which she'd felt and wanted desperately to stroke.

Marissa stripped off the rest of her clothes and took the clip out of her hair. She could wait a little longer for her satisfaction, wait until she was rinsed clean and in her warm solitary bed, imagining them in theirs together. It would be quick, she already knew that. Maybe just the touch of her fingers to set her off, the lightest tap or tease.

The water was cool still when she stepped under it, but it warmed as she ran her fingers through her hair to work out the curls. A pleased sigh escaped her as she stretched under the spray and let it roll down her back. Her muscles were tight, almost too much so, though it was a well-earned tension. She hadn't realized how taut she was holding herself—and they were holding her—in the theater, until her lower back had begun to twinge on the drive home.

She did halfway wish they'd just gone to the park or somewhere secluded, because they certainly hadn't been watching the movie they paid for, but they probably thought she would have been uncomfortable going anywhere more private. The darkness of the theater seemed solitary, but if things had gone badly, there were other people around and a well-lit hall right outside. It was considerate of them, and she did appreciate that. Next time, though—

That brought her up short. There wouldn't really be a next date. Spending a weekend exploring mutual sexual gratification was not a date, and after that, she'd be back to her normal life again. Her horizons would be expanded, she'd have pleasant memories, and she could start settling down to look for a real date, someone she could be with. It was hard to reconcile that with how she'd felt around Adrian and Paul, though. They made her feel comfortable and eager for more with them, not just sex but other things.

And that, she knew, was dangerous, because they weren't in this for anything but a fun weekend to spice up their relationship. It was coincidence that they were the type to be considerate and interested in helping her discover some things, too.

As if the acknowledgement had drained energy from her, she realized how tired she was. Good stress was still stress, and she was ready to lie down. She turned off the shower and stepped out, rubbing a towel through her hair to dry it some before she went to bed. She'd have to take a real shower in the morning and wash it, but for now the crisp rinse left her feeling refreshed but ready to sleep. The edge of her desire had softened as well without constant stimulation, mental or otherwise.

She padded into the living room to check her e-mail one last time and found a small message from Paul: "Good night, and I hope you sleep well. We'll talk about next weekend later. Call us this week?"

She'd already programmed their home number into her phone. For the time being, though, she closed the laptop with a smile and made her way to her bedroom in the dark, cozy space of her apartment.

Paul was a sweetheart, despite his sultry stares and inherent wickedness, and Adrian's heat and brazen attitude about his sexual allure saved him from being cute and transformed him instead into a shockingly handsome man. Paul was a sweetheart, despite his sultry stares and inherent wickedness, and his handsome features and stature left nothing to the imagination—he must have made girls swoon in school. He looked strong and capable, with an edge of dangerous desire.

The sheets were cool and silky, welcoming Marissa as she snuggled into them. Her hands found her breasts and she cupped them tenderly, thumbs rolling her soft nipples until they hardened. Her own fingers were daintier than either of theirs, but she closed her eyes and imagined them together as she'd seen them that night and in the photos. Adrian would roll the small buds of Paul's nipples between his fingers the same way, perhaps, or pinch—she did the same to herself and let out a pleased sigh as sharp sensation followed the pressure of her fingernails.

She was too tired to draw it out very long, and one hand slipped down to press against the soft heat of herself. She stroked two fingers between her folds and teased her clit with gentle pressure, back-and-forth movements of her fingertips. Another voluptuous sigh escaped as she arched her back and squeezed her breast again, the faintest ache rolling from the love-bite on her neck as she moved her shoulders. The climax was a slow and easy one, a roll of warm and delicious sensation that chased up her spine and down to her toes, relaxing her completely. She collapsed back onto to bed, sated, and shifted onto her side to cuddle one of the pillows.

It wasn't quite as good as her two soon-to-be lovers, but it would have to do for now. Pleasuring herself wasn't the same sharp immediacy of their touch, either. It was just the knowledge that they were thinking about her doing it that made it sweeter, more interesting. She suspected she'd spent more time getting acquainted with herself in the past week than she had since she was a teenager, between the porn and this.

But really, it was worthwhile. She didn't feel bad about it like she had when she was younger, less secure. It was her body and she was allowed to make herself feel good. That thought bolstered her for the fact that she was going to spend the next weekend with two men, fucking in every way they could show her. She smiled, shivered a little, and huddled closer to her pillow.

She was a little nervous, but she still couldn't wait.

Chapter Five

Sunday had been an uneventful day around the apartment, spent cleaning and doing laundry, but Monday presented Marissa with an interesting dilemma. She stood in front of her mirror, tilting her head this way and that. Adrian's bruise, which had been sexy and thrilling to her in private, was decidedly an issue for work. It was too hot out still for a turtleneck sweater or anything like that. She only owned a few scarves and they were all winter weight, not flowy or cute enough to wear with her usual business-casual.

If it were only students, she might not have worried. Let them laugh, and all that. It was the fact that the handsome older auditor would probably be there, and he would probably considering coming to teach her class with a giant hickey unprofessional. The idea of him seeing it, wondering whom she'd gotten it from, made her turn bright red. She wasn't necessarily interested in him, not with Adrian and Paul on her plate and his position in her career, but he was still a nice-looking man and it embarrassed her to have him think about her like that.

Two steps forward and one step back, she supposed. There were still some things she was going to be too shy for, whether or not she made out with couples in movie theaters in public. Showing off Adrian's mark was one of those things—plus it seemed somehow too personal to share. He had left it there to give her something, and it was for her, not for everyone else.

She didn't care if that was a weird way of thinking about it, either. She just needed to find a scarf.

A quick call had Lita on the line. "Hey," she said. "Do you have any gauzy scarves I could wear to work today?"

"Oh, really, now?" Lita said, sounding intrigued.

"I need to cover something." Marissa said.

"What something?" she pressed.

She knew her friend was grinning, had to be. "A mark, all right? A really big one that I can't go flashing at my students and my auditor."

"Yes, dear, I do have one," Lita said. "I can meet you at the campus garage in fifteen. Sound reasonable?"

"I'm wearing a blue shirt," Marissa said. "Will it match?"

"It's gray and shiny, so yes. See you soon," she said.

Marissa hung up feeling relieved and touched the mark again, leaning into the mirror. There were the faintest imprints of teeth in a darker color among the purplish rest of the mark. She laid her forehead against the cool mirror to combat the wave of heat that rushed through her at the thought. It was kinky; so what? She really liked it. Next time he just had to bite somewhere else, where no one would see it—of course, somewhere she still could.

She pressed it again, shivering at the throb of pleasure-pain, and dragged herself away from the bathroom to leave. Lita would be waiting.

The drive was short and uneventful. Lita's car was in the teacher lot, but she wasn't really parked so much as sitting in it. She got out when Marissa pulled in next to her. Her eyebrows went up at the sight of the mark, which Marissa covered self-consciously.

"Wow," Lita said. "Didn't that hurt?"

"Well," she said, ducking her head as her face warmed. Damned blushing. "Yes, but that doesn't mean I didn't like it, okay?"

Lita whistled and handed over the silver scarf. Marissa knotted it jauntily at her throat like a necklace that was also a spill of cloth. It hid the bruise.

"So, spill. How and where? I got your message that you were on a date."

"Those guys from the Internet," Marissa said. She leaned against her car. "They're—fantastic. We met for a dinner date to see if we liked each other, which we really did. I'm going to spend the weekend with them."

She thought her friend's jaw would drop.

"What?" Marissa said.

"You skipped from discovering gay porn to a double-date with two dudes?"

"So?"

"Nothing. I'm just proud of you," Lita said with a laugh and shook her head. "I don't mean to sound so surprised, but I've been wanting you to come out of your shell and be happy for years. If these two hunks of love can do that for you, go on and fuck them 'til you can't walk."

"Lita!" she hissed, looking around them. There was no one else to hear.

"Just be careful," she said seriously. "I know they were nice on the date, but if you need help this weekend, don't hesitate to call me. Or 911."

"Jesus," Marissa said, blinking. "They're not like that!"

"I'm just telling you to be careful. Internet dating has its wonders, but it can be dangerous," Lita said. "That's my soapbox and I'm sticking to it."

"Well, I know that."

"But I want you to do it and have a good time." Lita hugged her, smiling. "I think you'll be way happier if you really figure out who you are, you know, sexually. Everybody needs to know that about themselves."

"Thank you," Marissa said with a roll of her eyes. "You're trying to play therapist with me, aren't you?"

"Maybe a little," she admitted. "Now go to work, and call me sometime this week. We'll catch dinner together."

"Sure," Marissa said. "Thanks for the rescue."

Lita patted the scarf, winked, and climbed back in her car. Marissa set off for the classroom, bag over her shoulder and hickey hidden safely away. She was still so very aware of it on her skin, the mark and its implication. Her friend was right. She needed to know these things about herself, embrace them, and learn from them. It was all part of getting a real life in order: first came the job, now came the self and all the maintenance that implied. Lita really was an excellent therapist.

In the classroom, only cute Evan with his bagel and the auditor were there. She put her things down, back straight, and was surprised at how empowered she felt by her awareness of the bruise on her throat and what she had spent the weekend doing. She had expected to feel nervous, as if everyone could see written all over her what she was up to, or that it should shame her.

Instead, she felt like she had a wonderful, delicious secret.

She smiled at the auditor, and he smiled back, seemingly surprised.

"I forgot a drink," she said. "Would you mind watching my things for a moment?"

"Not a problem," he said with a nod to the door. "Better hurry. I'll mark you tardy if you're late."

She had to grin, because he'd said it with a twist of his lips into a smirk and a bit of a flirtatious tone. Perhaps she wasn't the only one with a healthy appreciation for her coworkers.

The scarf had begun to itch by the end of the day, but Marissa stuck it through until the end. It was a relief to yank it off in the car and toss it in the passenger seat with her messenger bag full of papers, though. They still needed to be graded; she didn't want to take more than a week to give them back to her students but she'd lost her weekend time to the lusty haze of her date with Adrian and Paul. Juggling a career and a romantic life was probably going to be as difficult or worse than managing both while struggling for her degree.

So, instead of going home, she drove to the local coffee shop. At home, she knew she would give in to the urge to get on her laptop and respond to the e-mail from Saturday night that she'd kept reopening and looking at. Getting drawn into another erotic discussion with her paramours wouldn't be conducive to getting any work done.

The café served coffee, tea, and all sorts of pastries and small sandwiches. She walked in with her bag over her shoulder and the scarf looped lazily around her neck. She was glad to see there were empty tables and she wouldn't have to ask to share someone else's. It happened sometimes, and she always felt like an intruder or a distraction, whether or not it was true. The boy behind the counter took her order for a ham sandwich, a pastry, and a mug of chai. The drink was a little sweet for the dinner, but she hadn't had chai for a while, and it sounded delicious.

She picked a table by the wide glass windows that overlooked the street. The tiny lot behind the café had a free space for her car, so she hadn't had to parallel park for once, but it was still nice to have a view outside. That was the great thing about living in the radius of the university—coffee shops, cheap apartments, and a short commute anywhere. Home was never far away. She took the sheaf of papers out of her bag and shuffled through them, sifting them into an arcane order mostly determined by size. The students who'd written over the minimum would come first; they usually had something interesting to say, since they'd done extra work. The short ones, where the students just hadn't bothered to do the whole assignment, would go to the bottom, mostly because they irritated her.

Marissa has just finished sorting the papers how she wanted them when the barista who'd taken her order appeared at her table with her drink and sandwich. He had a winsome smile and she thought she might have seen him around campus. His hair was almost peach-orange, a light and probably dyed color. His eyes were hazel.

"You're a prof, right?" he asked.

"As of this year," she replied, smiling.

"I thought I'd seen you," he said.

He stuck his hands in the pockets of his apron and cast her a shy grin, lashes lowered a bit. It was cute. The moment warmed between them as she returned the gaze and waited for him to continue, distracted from her meal already.

"I'm a grad student," he said. "Mathematics, to be general. Could I ask you to a cup of coffee one day?"

"Oh," she said, her smile widening. Well, wasn't that nice? He wasn't much younger than her, so it was all right. "Yes, sure. Come by my office, I'll get a drink with you. My name's Marissa Ford."

He grinned. "Arthur Miles. Pleasure to actually say hi to you instead of just noticing you across the way."

His candor startled a laugh from her and he chuckled as well. It made her wonder: had her growing confidence begun to show somehow? It wasn't like people had never approached her before, when she was a student entrenched in her work—Jeff, for one, had asked her out. Between this young man's flirting and the auditor's subtle interest, not to mention Paul and Adrian, she felt strangely visible and desirable.

"Thanks," she said. "I'll see you?"

"You definitely will," he said. "And I'll bring that pastry out in a second. You missed the last one, so we have more in the oven. Is that all right?"

"Of course," Marissa said.

They matched another pair of goofy, pleased smiles and Arthur returned to his place behind the counter as a new gaggle of people came in, all in their late thirties by looks, surely from a business nearby. Marissa turned her eyes to her papers and began to read and mark with red pen as she nibbled her sandwich.

The meet-for-drinks, maybe-not-a-date with the young and approachable Arthur made her feel lovely, but it was small consolation for the fact that after the weekend passed, she would have to give up the two-men thing, probably for good. After all, there weren't many bisexual guys who wanted to be part of a permanent threesome. She'd never heard of one, at least, and that was a bit of a damper on her mood.

Still, plenty of people had kinks and fantasies that they didn't act out but once in their lifetimes, she was sure. This could be her one wild, let-loose time. It would have to be enough. She cast a glance at the peach-haired Arthur, who was making a drink for one of the business crowd, and tried to feel a spark of lust or something other than friendly flattery. In her mind's eye, she just saw Paul and Adrian, their lips locked in a passionate kiss.

That was what gave her a thrill.

She sighed, fighting a wave of morose disappointment, and returned to her papers. The motto was supposed to be enjoy it while it lasted, not mourn it before it even happened, let alone ended. Lita would tell her to live for the moment. Hell, she would tell herself to, so why was it so hard to do?

After trading steamy e-mails and watching the bruise fade in the mirror every morning—she'd bought extra scarves at a cheap local market to make it less obvious she was hiding something—Marissa found herself with nothing to do on Thursday night. Adrian had sent her a few e-mails over the week and so had Paul, just to chat and make sure things were still on. But there wasn't one waiting this evening, and she wasn't due to call them until the next morning to figure out where they would meet up on Friday night to spend their weekend. She was comfortable with their home if they wanted, but they didn't want to pressure her and had offered a hotel suite.

Honestly, she didn't know. It was already hard to separate the emotions she kept finding herself having toward them from the desire to be with them for a brief snip of her life, just a few days. Being in their home, among their things, and fucking in their bed did seem a little problematic. And it might make things harder for them to be alone when all was said and done.

She'd been reading up on threesomes, and they seemed perilous for the couples involved if things weren't just right. She found herself adoring Adrian and Paul. Messing up their relationship was the last thing she wanted. So perhaps the hotel was the best choice. Less pressure all around, more anonymous. The decision weighed on her.

Finally, after spending fifteen minutes drumming her fingers on her coffee table filled with indecision and waiting on an e-mail that hadn't come, she took out her phone and dialed her friend. She'd promised Lita a girls' night to hang out, after all.

The phone rang and rang, but there was no answer. She left a message, frowning. It wasn't that Lita was inconsiderate, but sometimes she seemed to be very busy with her own life and only able to make room for Marissa when it was convenient—yet seemed to expect Marissa to move her own schedule to match Lita's. Maybe she was feeling uncharitable because she was lonely and bored. Either way, there wasn't much to do.

She hesitated over the address book in her phone. "Nana" blinked under the cursor. She hadn't called for a few weeks. Her grandmother had been kind enough to raise her when her parents split and decided they didn't want to be in the same state any more, and she hadn't wanted to leave her elementary school and all her friends. She hadn't spoken to her father since, and her mother was a call-twice-a-year situation. They were young parents, sure, but Marissa had never found it in herself to forgive them.

Another moment passed and she closed the phone. She owed her grandmother a call, but what would she tell her? *I'm going to go on a sex-romp with a male couple this weekend, wish me luck?* She snorted a laugh and put her phone back in her pocket. No, definitely not. It was hard enough including Nana in her everyday life when she was at school with steady, normal boyfriends. Having to explain semi-casual dating was a nightmare. This would be a fight of epic proportions complete with a lecture about female humility and responsibility and chastity, she was sure.

Without Lita, and without family to call, Marissa was bereft. It would be weird to call Paul and Adrian. They weren't her boyfriends or even really her friends, though she hoped they might not cease all contact with her after the weekend. She was afraid they might, if it made things easier for themselves—but she liked them as people, and hoped they kept in touch.

"Goddamn," she whispered.

She thought back to the peach-haired grad student who'd asked her to coffee and that was a minor comfort. She'd make more friends, she knew. It would take a little time, though. A drink here, a movie there, a discussion about a book slipped in, and you had a friend to hang out with. Maybe a few co-workers would want to do things sometimes. She kept reminding herself she wasn't so overworked and always busy now that her debts were paid and her degree was in hand, her old job quit.

For the night, she was just lonely. She turned on the television, found the news, and settled in to watch it. Her mind was still circling the issue of hotel-or-home for the weekend, and the rest of her was focused on wallowing in her lack of companionship. It wasn't a particularly enjoyable evening.

She went to bed early, still stressed, and never did decide what her answer would be to Paul or Adrian's call in the morning. Either way, she would be with them, and it would be good. That was enough.

Chapter Six

"It's really your decision," she said into the phone, balancing it on her shoulder as she walked through the hall of her building to the classroom she was due in. "Your house, your choice."

"Shy-girl," Adrian groaned. It had become his nickname for her at some point, and hearing it made her flush with pleasure and amusement. That on its own was worrisome.

"I'm serious!" she protested. "I don't mind either way. I don't think you're going to lure me out and murder me or something crazy like that. It's just that it's your house, so it shouldn't be up to me."

"All right, all right," Adrian said. "Hang on."

She heard him calling for Paul and a brief, off-line chatter of conversation. She waited, walking into her room and dropping her bag on the desk. No one was there yet; she was early. The chair squeaked on the tile floor as she pulled it out and sat, legs crossed. Her light tan slacks were a bit hot and her blouse was sticking to her skin with a faint dew of sweat. The weather had spiked a good ten degrees. Fall was crisp in some years and sweltering in others. This time around, the sun seemed low and heavy in the sky, determined to overheat everything.

"Okay," Adrian said. Marissa leaned forward, elbows braced on the desk and her heart in her throat. This was the moment of decision. "Paul's up for a hotel room for comfort's sake, and I'm fine with either, and so are you. So I guess a hotel it is."

"And I'm meeting you tonight, right?" she asked.

"Yeah," he said. "Dinner to relax first, then back to the hotel. Paul's on his cell making reservations now. I was thinking a light supper, maybe Asian food somewhere?"

"That's fine," she said. "There's a good Japanese place by the campus. Do you know which one I'm talking about?"

"Tiny hole-in-the-wall with a sake bar?" he asked. "Next door to a bookshop?"

"You got it," she said with a smile that he couldn't see.

"We'll see you there tonight around five?" he asked.

"It's a date," she said, and this time the warmth of her smile snuck into her words. "I've got a little suitcase and I'm ready."

"Good," Adrian said. His voice dropped into a purr. "I've been thinking all week about getting you between us, making you come undone."

"Oh," she gasped weakly, eyes darting around the empty room.

"You're at work, aren't you?" he asked with a hint of a laugh.

"Yes," she answered.

"Well, just be glad I didn't get more descriptive. I bet you'd turn bright red if I started telling you how much I've thought about burying my face between your legs and licking you until you want to scream."

"Oh my God," she said, squeaking.

He really did laugh, then. "I'm sorry. I'm too awful, I know, I know. Paul's telling me to stop being an ass."

"Tell him thank you," she said.

"Tell him yourself."

A moment later Paul's voice came over the line. "Is he teasing you too much?"

"It's fine," she said. "Just—different. He's so free with what he says."

"It's because he knows you like it," Paul said. "He's merciless at pushing buttons once he knows which ones are right."

She shook her head. The auditor walked in and she straightened up, tongue suddenly feeling tangled. He cast her a smile and settled into his usual desk.

"How do you feel about all this?" she asked Paul, trying not to give too much away on her end of the conversation with a listener in the room.

"I'm having a ball watching him flirt and you, I'm sure, blush," he said. "I can't wait, to be honest. He's not the only one who wants to touch you."

"You'll give me an ego," she said, almost whispering.

"You deserve it," Paul said, low and sultry. "But I'll let you get to work. We'll see you tonight, Marissa."

The sound of her name rolling off of his tongue made

her want to shiver, but she held it in valiantly and smirked instead. "All right. I'll see you."

Hanging up was difficult, but she would see them once her day's work was over. See them, taste them, touch them—the images swirling around her mind were enough to make her feel lightheaded. Waiting to have a date and sex with Jeff had never made her feel like she was about to combust. It hadn't been bad, but it hadn't been like this, either. Obviously, she was on the right track and moving fast.

"A date?" the auditor asked, and she was sure her face was flaming, because she realized all at once that he'd been watching her out of the corner of his eye while she chatted with Paul about a sex-weekend. Not that he knew that, but *she* did.

"Yup," she said shortly, with a grin that was only a little strained by embarrassment. "It should be fun."

"I'm sure," he said.

She shuffled her papers to give herself a moment to put her brain in order. "Wish me luck."

"Just don't get so damned nervous," he said with a grin.

She rolled her eyes at the teasing. When they were really co-workers on equal footing, she was sure he would be one of those insufferable types, always ready with a quip. For now, she knew he couldn't afford to say more or tease her further even if he wanted to. It would be unprofessional. All the same, she wondered what he was really thinking, and imagined him saying something corny like, "A lady like yourself will always have a good time on a date."

The ridiculousness of it made her chuckle a little, and he raised an eyebrow, but she shook her head. No need to share. The students began to filter in and she stood to start her lesson. The thought, *only a few hours to go,* lingered with her in the form of a shiver.

Sitting in her car with the mirror down to check her makeup, Marissa was on edge. It was a pleasant edge, to be sure, one heated with arousal and uncertainty, but she was nervous all the same. The tiny suitcase with her necessities was in the back, she'd made one hundred percent sure she had extra condoms and was up to date on her birth control shot just in case— not that she'd ever missed an appointment for one; boyfriend or no, it still worried her—and she'd let Lita know the hotel they were going to after Adrian had texted her the location.

"Show time," she muttered to herself and climbed out of the driver's seat.

The Japanese restaurant was busy during the dinner hour. She asked for a table for three and ended up seated in a window booth looking out onto the small lot. It meant that when they arrived, stepping out of their car in the same suave business-casual dress from the last date, she saw them before they saw her. Their handsome beauty stole her breath as Paul reached over with a small smile to straighten Adrian's tie. Adrian smiled back and batted at his hand playfully. They were so *sweet.*

Dangerous, dangerous—that was what sweet was.

She was still smiling wider than she should have been, and she was sure she had a bit of a twinkle in her eye, when the waitress led them to the table. Before she could scoot out of the booth to greet them both men leaned over and planted a kiss on either of her cheeks. The smell of aftershave and cologne mingled and Adrian's longer hair brushed her face.

"Hello to you, too," she said.

They sat opposite her, goofy grins all around. There was a sort of giddy naughtiness in the air, at least for Marissa. She knew what they would be doing, all three of them, as soon as they left this restaurant. It almost made her want to rush the meal, but as she'd always heard, good things come to those who wait.

"Excited?" Paul asked, innocently enough.

Adrian's smirk was anything but.

"Very much so," she admitted.

Her fingers played with the straw in her drink, twirling it between them. It was a nervous gesture but also a flirtatious one, she realized, as both men seemed to zero in on her hand at once, glancing at the way her fingertips teased at the plastic. She dropped her hand to the table after another moment and met their gazes with a grin of her own. These men weren't going to judge her for wanting what she wanted. They were just going to help, and get something for themselves, too.

"What about you?" she asked. "Any second thoughts? I'll understand if you don't feel comfortable after all."

"Absolutely none," Paul said, reaching across the table to clasp her hand in his. He wove their fingers together and gave a comforting squeeze. "You're smart, stable, and out for a good time. So are we. There's nothing to second guess."

"I know Paul, and I know myself," Adrian added with a smile.

"What's that mean?" Marissa asked.

"I trust him, and I trust me, not to fuck this up," he said. He laid his hand on theirs in a Three Musketeers sort of thing. She almost laughed but his voice was serious. "I just want to make sure we're giving you equally as much as we're asking for. I'm not a selfish guy. I want everyone to be happy."

"Thank you," she said, genuinely touched.

"We're comfortable enough to do this and to do it with you, so don't worry too much about getting between us or something," Adrian concluded.

"All right, I won't," she said.

"What about you?" Paul asked. "Are you seeing anyone right now?"

She raised an eyebrow at him. "I've never cheated."

"I didn't mean that. I was wondering if you had any other connections or if you were single," he said.

"Oh," she answered. "No, I told you guys before, school and working to pay it off kept me very, very busy. I just now started making time to date. But I had to . . . I had to know if this was what I wanted."

Adrian nodded, as if something in her answer had satisfied a question he hadn't asked. The waitress returned and their hands slipped apart, away. Marissa ordered a salmon sushi appetizer and Paul tacked on a round of shots. She tilted her head curiously when the waitress left.

"Dutch courage," he said. "Or Japanese, either way."

"Only the one," she said. "I have to drive, and so do you."

"Of course," he said with an answering grin to hers.

It amazed her as they made small talk that she never felt as if she was leaning to one man over the other. They were equally fascinating to her, so different yet so similar. Their senses of humor were almost identical and they shared a few speech quirks that must have come from living together. By the time the main course arrived, she was laughing full-throated at a story Adrian was telling while Paul chuckled, mirth clear in his eyes. It was so good to let loose. *They* were so good. Her laugh caught and she masked the moment with a sip of her drink.

"So, how does this work?" she asked. "Afterwards, I mean."

Paul and Adrian shared a glance.

"I don't know," Paul said.

"We'll work it out," Adrian said with a shrug. "I've known people who could be friends after being, ah, intimate, and people who it was too weird for. I'd like to keep hanging out. You're a great woman. We'll see if you still want to when all's said and done."

"I'm not sure how I'll react," she said truthfully. "I'm not feeling weird right now, so I would think I'd still want to talk."

"You never know," he said, brushing his blond hair out of his eyes. "I hope you do, but it's your feelings at stake, and don't let us pressure you into anything you don't like. At all."

Again with the seriousness, she thought.

"You've noticed Adrian was into BDSM, and still is," Paul murmured, lower, so she had to lean in. "He takes negotiating and fairness to heart. Safe words and mutual consent all around, all the time. Things can get intense. He wants it to stay good-intense."

Adrian nodded.

"I understand," she said, feeling breathless and warmer than she had before at the mention of negotiations, of power shifting between them. "I will absolutely say so if I feel insecure, I promise."

"Good, shy-girl," Adrian chimed in. "I remember what it was like to be new. You want to please so badly, sometimes you let a top get by with things he shouldn't. I won't judge you if you say no, and neither will he. I'm making sure you know that."

"I do," she said.

They seemed content and all leaned back as one, relaxing again from the serious moment. She wondered how it was so easy to go from laughing to mature, responsible sex-talk in a few minutes with them, but it just took its natural course. Now that the heavy things were out of the way Adrian seemed to let himself even further relax, a constant small smile on his mouth, his hands always brushing Paul's or Marissa's when he could manage. The brushes of warm skin on her wrist, her fingers, were like dull electric shocks. They stole her breath.

When the waitress asked if they were interested in dessert, Marissa blurted out a quick, "Oh, no, we couldn't."

The tension had begun to build already, winding between them like a web. Adrian's eyes had tracked down to the mark, mostly healed, that still lingered as a shadow on her throat. The weight of his gaze was like a touch.

"I got tired of scarves this week," she murmured. "Somewhere else, this time?"

He swallowed visibly, and Paul stroked a knuckle down his cheek. Adrian turned his head and caught the offending finger in his mouth for a quick nibble. Paul's eyes narrowed in a sensual, fierce expression. For a moment they were frozen in place, but Marissa managed to move first, edging out of the booth. The sound of them shifting and standing behind her made her back go tight, almost arching, in anticipation.

A hand landed at the small of her spine, as she'd suspected, and she shivered. A quick glance revealed it was Paul, who escorted her gently out the door while Adrian paid the bill. The balmy evening air was cooler than it had been for days, but still warm. She took a deep breath. Paul's fingers found the hem of her dress pants and his thumb stroked a long line across the waistband. She turned to him, appreciating the line of his jaw and the curly, close cut of his hair as she looked up at his face. He was devastatingly handsome, almost textbook gorgeous.

And she was going to be naked, underneath him, before the night was through. She leaned into his open arms and lifted her chin for a kiss, mouths sliding together with the softest of catches, skin on skin. His lips were faintly dry, but the kiss deepened quickly into a damp and slick affair. She gasped into his mouth as he gathered her close, his hands tight around her.

Another body pressed up against her from behind, from hip to the lips that teased her ear. She broke away with another soft breath and Adrian hummed his amusement.

"Starting so soon," he murmured. "Come now, we still have to make it to the hotel."

"I'll meet you?" she said breathlessly.

"Fifteen minutes, my dear," Adrian said and stepped away, drawing Paul with him. "That's not too much longer."

He was right, but it still made her ache to lose the hot pressure of them against her, pinning her. She wove her way through the lot to her car, casting glances back at them the whole way, and caught Paul's eye at least once, Adrian's more than that. Maybe a quickie in the backseat would have taken the edge off, but for now she was starving for their touch.

She wanted so much more than a quickie from this. Her anticipation had grown and grown through the entire week as she researched things on the Web, looked at photos, read stories, expanded her imagination. She wanted to have a little idea of what they might suggest to her before she tried it. She'd found a wealth of kinky, hungry desire in herself that she wanted desperately to have indulged.

Fifteen minutes was only if she did the speed limit, she thought as she got behind the wheel of her car and started the engine. Alternately, she very much did not want a ticket at this juncture of the evening, so despite a lead foot, she kept to the green lights, obeyed the traffic laws, and found herself at the nice hotel in more like twenty minutes. She snagged her suitcase and walked into the atrium with her head held high, reveling in the knowledge of what she was here for.

She found she didn't care if anyone knew. It wasn't their business. That was terribly, wonderfully freeing.

The boys, as she'd started to think of them, were waiting on plush couches for her. Paul stood, took her bag, and handed her a key. They'd already checked in. She could find no words, and neither could they, it seemed. They rode the elevator up in silence, breathing tight and controlled, but with invisible sparks seeming to shatter the air between them in a triangular web.

Her hands shook as she slid the key through the lock and opened the door.

This was it.

She wanted them so badly, so fiercely, that it frightened her just a bit, the way watching a caged lion was frightening. A hint of danger. Safe, but not quite. She flipped the light on. The suite was broad and nice. The outer room was small and held a couch, coffee table, and television. Through a dimly shadowed door she saw the bedroom, and it was expansive. She walked through to it and flicked another light switch.

The huge, multi-jet tub set into the floor in the corner

of the room drew her eye. It was big enough for five, let alone three, to share it at once. The bed was colossal as well. She wondered how much Paul and Adrian had agreed to spend on this weekend, since they had refused to let her pay for a bit of it. It made sense, since it was their offer in the first place, but a part of her did thrill at being so pampered.

"I find myself very interested in that bathtub," Paul remarked.

"Me too," she said.

The moment of silence that followed was tinged with awkwardness as she moved to put her suitcase down and so did they, all three shifting restlessly, eyes catching and skating off of each other. Dinner with them and the easy laughter had made her eager, but now she felt out of her depth, in a hotel room and unsure of what came next.

It was Paul who broke the uncertain moment first. He sat on the edge of the bed, eyebrows raised at both Adrian and Marissa, and quirked a finger at her. She stepped forward with her breath stuck in her chest, nearly trembling—this was happening, it was truly happening—and came to stand between his legs, his thighs warm against hers. He smoothed his broad palms up her arms to her shoulder and kneaded the tightness in them. The light caught auburn highlights in his dark hair. Marissa leaned into the massaging hands, bracing her own on his shoulders.

Adrian crawled up onto the bed behind Paul and pressed against his back, rising up on his knees. He unbuttoned the first few buttons of his vivid blue dress shirt and Marissa found her eyes locked on the peek at his pale chest. Paul leaned his head back and nosed against the fabric, pink tongue drawing a wet line on the bare skin. She stroked her thumbs over Paul's throat, tracing her fingers up and down the warm column of skin. The passion she'd felt before had muted, grown into something encompassing and slow. This first time, they were finding their way—all of them, not just her.

Paul's fingers crept down her arms again and slipped to her waist, dipping under her shirt. The brush of them on her sides nearly tickled and it made her shift in his grip, biting the inside of her cheek as her eyelids fluttered. The quiet of their huffing breaths as Adrian opened Paul's shirt button by button was a heavy caress of its own. Marissa looked down, watching those long, slim fingers tease each button out of its hole and spread the shirt wide, baring a muscled chest. She placed her fingertips on the toned shape of Paul's pectorals and ran her thumbs over his small pink nipples.

He sighed, a quiet noise of pleasure, and Adrian hummed against his neck as he undid the last button and stripped the shirt down his arms. Marissa ran her hands down his stomach, feeling the tautness of his toned muscles under soft skin. He'd been working out since those original photos, she thought, though not too much—he was sculpted, not overly bulky. It made her heart thud faster in her chest. Adrian's questing hands moved to her and tugged at her shirt. There was a confusing moment of too many arms, too many hands, before he pulled it over her head and left her standing in her purple lace bra. It was see-through, and both of their eyes seemed to rivet on the sight of her breasts peeking through the cloth, nipples already firm buds.

They both reached at the same time, fingers bumping to cup and squeeze her breasts. She made a sound that was half laughter, half a moan as four hands petted and teased her through the bra.

"It's been a while, hasn't it?" she murmured as softly as she could.

"I want you," Adrian replied, husky. "I think we should take turns fucking you tonight. It really has been a while."

She reached back of her own accord and undid the snap, easing the bra down her arms. Their hungry attention made her skin prickle. No one had ever looked at her with that much need before, just from the sight of her bare upper body. Paul's thighs tightened around her minutely and she leaned in, hands sliding back to grasp Adrian instead. Paul took the hint, eyes drifting closed, and began to lap at her nipples. Each wet, hot rasp of his tongue brought a shiver over her. The sensation raced in waves through her body.

Adrian's eyes were bright, and he caught her bottom lip between his teeth. He nipped hard enough to make her jump in Paul's arms, then let the bite meld into a kiss, tongue sliding against her sore lip. The ache was sweet. Paul's broad hands clutched at her sides and he pulled her in closer, tighter.

"Too many clothes," she whispered to Adrian, feeling brave as she plucked at his shirt.

"All right, shy-girl," he whispered playfully and eased back.

Paul turned his head from her to watch. Adrian braced himself on his heels, thighs spread on the mattress, and began to undo his cuffs. His cheeks were flushed red and his smirk was absolutely filthy. He took his time, knowing he had their attention, and each button took an eternity. He slid the shirt off just as slowly, coy but heated glances finding each of their eyes as he bared himself. He toyed with his belt a moment next, stroking the black leather in a hint before he unbuckled it.

He stepped off the bed to unzip his slacks and took them down to his ankles with his underwear in one swift movement. He straightened, kicking off his socks and shoes, and grasped his cock in one hand. Marissa's mouth was open in delicious shock and arousal as he ran his fingers up his shaft, teasing the red-blushing skin and the darker head with his eyes on theirs. She couldn't look away. He was average in thickness but long, with a curve that tempted and thrilled her. He climbed back on the bed and crawled toward them.

"Better?" he stage-whispered.

"Yes," she said.

It was like being caught on a roller-coaster, she thought as Paul helped her up onto the bed, his hands on the waist of her pants as she went, stripping her to her panties. They were matching purple lace she'd bought just for this moment, hugging the curves of her hips and ass. He eased off her low heels and stood behind her as she and Adrian eyed one another, her chest tight with desire and sudden nerves.

"You want us to tell you what to do, sweetheart?" he asked. "Too shy to choose?"

"Oh," she gasped, and Adrian smiled.

"Paul," he said.

"Yes?" the other man answered.

She glanced back, settling against the pillows. He was taking his shoes off by actually untying them, unlike Adrian. She wanted desperately to get his pants off, too.

"I'd like to taste Marissa, if you would indulge me and give her something to suck," Adrian said, sounding courtly despite his intent.

It wasn't quite an order, but it was enough of a hint. She stayed still, eyes darting between them, her skin tingling with need to be touched. Adrian's hand slid up her calf and squeezed comfortingly at her knee before creeping further. Paul's pants fell to the floor with a thump and, to her surprise, he moved to lie next to her first. Her mouth was nearly watering with the thought of having him, but he cuddled up next to her side, his erection pressing against her hip. She reached down to palm him, finding that he was a bit thicker than Adrian. The velvety skin under her fingers was hot, smooth. She stroked him gently, running the palm of her hand over the head of his cock.

"Slowly, slowly," Adrian murmured, easing her panties down her legs. She let him, pulse pounding as he stripped away her last shred of clothing, her ability to hide from them. "You're beautiful."

The sight of him curled between her legs, one hand on his own cock and the other on her thigh, was enough to set her to shivering again. He was one to talk—the picture he made was unbearably pretty, suggestive. She wanted his mouth on her.

A part of her mind was still yammering away, "this is it, this is it," as he laid his head against her thigh and just looked for a moment, his breath tickling her most intimate areas. This was where she couldn't take it back any longer. After this, they were having sex, they were fucking, these two men she barely knew but wanted so *badly*.

"Please," she whispered.

Paul's body shifted against hers, cock pulsing once with interest in her loose hand. Her anxiety was equal with her desire for now, but she needed them to take her through this, help her through it, make her forget what she was afraid to try and enjoy what she discovered.

"What do you want?" Paul asked, and Adrian smirked at her from between her legs. "Do you want him to go down on you, or would you rather—" Paul pushed his hips forward, angling his hard-on toward the other man, and Adrian's eyes lit up mischievously. "Watch?"

"Oh, God," she moaned. "Both."

"We can do that," Adrian said.

His hand wrapped around hers on Paul, showing her how to tighten her fingers, where to twist her stroke. Heat washed over her. That was so, so, so fucking hot it was dizzying. Then his head dipped and, without releasing her hand or Paul's cock, his mouth opened over the head. His lips slid down to bump their hands, plump and still dry. His tongue flicked out to taste her fingers mixed with his. She couldn't take her eyes away from the sight of him going down on Paul while they both held him.

"Damn," Paul moaned, long and low.

Adrian drew back with a slurp, guiding their hands to stroke the slickness of spit he'd left behind. Marissa watched their equally pale fingers moving over flushed, dark skin. She couldn't press her thighs together for relief with Adrian between her legs, but he leaned down an inch further and instead his chest moved faintly against her. Tilting her hips to rub herself against him, a little awkward but enough to send pleasure rippling outward through her.

"I love oral sex," Adrian murmured, shimmying down the bed.

The first burning, wet touch of his tongue-tip to her clit jolted Marissa with ecstasy, sudden and undeniable. She cried out softly, gripping the sheets with her free hand. That tongue swirled once, a slippery path of sparks and pleasures, before teasing at her again, just the tip on her. Her pulse seemed to be entirely in her cunt, throbbing, and her head tossed against the pillows as Adrian's ridiculously talented tongue made another circling swirl around the length of her clit. He laved his tongue over her next, almost lapping, broad soft strokes instead of pointed teases.

"Oh, God," she moaned, realizing her hand had stilled on Paul, and resumed stroking, though slower and with more stops. "That feels so good."

Adrian paused. "Vanilla boys ever make you come with their tongue in you?"

"Not really," she panted. Jeff hadn't minded warming her up that way, but they'd usually moved on to sex. "Are—are you—"

"Oh, yes, sweetheart," he purred.

His lips kissed her there, like he would kiss her mouth, sucking and licking and sliding the silken insides of his lips over her. She briefly considered that it must be more like what a blowjob felt like, the furnace inside of his mouth surrounding her. Moans slipped from her and her back bowed as he kept it up, a constant onslaught. Finally he returned to tight, swirling licks centered on her clit that built and built the waves of lust in her. She gasped, letting go of Paul to writhe and grasp at the headboard above her as the pleasure coiled harder, like the circles of Adrian's tongue on the most tender part of her body. He made hungry, moaning noises as he did it and she understood why people called it *eating out*.

He was devouring her, tasting her, consuming her.

She threw her head back as the pleasure crested sharply and opened her mouth to yell but nothing came out. Her muscles went taut and spasmed, shuddering. Adrian licked her through it, softer, easing her down. Paul made a rumbling noise of desire next to her and reached down to ruffle Adrian's hair.

Adrian lifted his face, mouth glistening with her juices, and grinned with satisfaction.

"That took maybe five minutes," he said. "I'm so good, aren't I, pet?"

"God," she laughed, shakily, letting her grip ease and her arms lower again. "Yes, yes, you are."

"Do you feel more relaxed now?" Paul asked quietly.

She ducked her head. "So I was that nervous?"

"You were a little," he confirmed. "Better now?"

"Yes," she said.

Her body wasn't ready to be finished yet, and neither was she. The aftershocks of the quick, sharp orgasm were still tingling in her core but she looked down their bodies, taking in the sight of the erections. They weren't anywhere near done.

"What do you want me to do?" she asked curiously. "This is your fantasy, even though it's mine, too. What do you really want?"

Adrian rubbed his damp face on her thighs. "I do want to take turns tonight. I want to fuck you, make you come, then watch him do it. I want to have every inch of you."

His fingers tightened almost convulsively on her thigh as he looked up, eyes heated. She swallowed hard, imagining that, feeling the contours in her mind—one after the other, having her, pleasuring her. Enjoying being with a woman. A part of her worried that was all it might be about, just her warm female body, but the tenderness in their touch and the fact that they'd thought to relax her first made that seem unlikely.

Yes, they wanted a woman. But she wanted men, men who would touch each other and fuck and love in front of her. So that was very fair. And, if she admitted it to herself, *filthy* hot.

"Condoms," she reminded them.

In her head, she wished for a split second they didn't need them, and she could feel their come inside her while they shared her. The thought ripped a shudder through her that they felt, noticed, and grinned over.

"What were you thinking?" Paul asked.

"Tell us, shy-girl," Adrian prodded.

She had to clear her throat to talk. "Thinking about— your come, in me, when you traded. One of you fucking me wet with the other's come."

Paul groaned into her hair and rutted briefly against her hip. Adrian's gaze seemed to grow even more intense. But they couldn't, that she was sure of. It just wasn't safe, wasn't a good idea—but God, to think about it, that was enough. One orgasm wasn't enough to take the edge off of *that*.

"I want to mess you up," Adrian said.

"You like to talk, don't you?" she said.

"He really does," Paul answered for him. "I think he's got a whole collection of sex metaphors stored in his head. He doesn't repeat himself much."

"If you didn't react," Adrian murmured with a flirtatious grin at his partner. "I would have left off doing it long ago and found something else to please you."

Paul leaned down as Adrian stretched up and their mouths met. The blond man's lips were still damp from her and they both let loose quiet noises as they shared her flavor, lips pressed tight together and eyes shut. Things low on Marissa's body tightened at the erotic sight of them licking at each other's mouths, kissing so hard and deep they might bruise each other. Adrian crawled further into the embrace, rising up on his knees to hover over their reclining bodies.

If she thought watching them kiss was beautiful, watching him finally slip over her and come to rest lying on top of his partner was otherworldly. His smaller frame fit so well tucked around Paul's, legs spread across his thighs and groins pressed flush. Adrian ran fingers through Paul's hair and rocked against him, offering her brief glimpses of their cocks sliding against one another, and the man on the bottom moaned with abandon. Her whole body throbbed in time with that wanton noise. The idea of them with her had slipped out of her mind to be replaced with an unquenchable desire to see them together, as a voyeur, watch them make love to each other as they would in private.

So she said nothing as they bucked and moved together, never breaking their ferocious kiss even to gasp or groan. Sweat dewed their skin. Paul opened his eyes a fraction and glanced toward her. Whatever expression she was making seemed to please him as he closed his eyes again and reached down to grab Adrian by the firm, round globes of his ass and pull him in tighter. Then he rolled to the side, and she moved as well, letting him put Adrian between them.

She spooned herself against his back, wrapping her arms around both of them at once, pushing her hips against his butt. Paul's fingers and knuckles rubbed her hard, almost hard enough to hurt, as she thrust against him. She might not have the same equipment, but it was a delicious teasing pleasure to give herself indirect contact, rutting against his ass. Adrian himself was moaning almost continuously, low in his throat, and one of his hands fumbled back to grasp at her thigh. He pulled her leg up over the tangle of theirs, spreading her suddenly so the slick heat of her pussy ground directly against him.

Marissa gasped into his ear, a sound of pure pleasure. He shuddered. Paul's hands slipped out from between them and he fisted one in her hair, not too tight, but enough to sting sweetly. She yanked against it in a moment of curiosity and the resulting bolt of sensation that slammed down her spine to her cunt made her cry out. The pain was sweet, heady, but not too intense. He seemed to understand and wrapped his fingers tighter, drawing her to lean over Adrian and kiss him, her neck straining and her scalp aching as their wet lips slid together without purchase. They were more touching mouths than kissing, both distracted by the writhing heat of Adrian between them.

"God, switch sides," he begged breathlessly.

"I thought," Paul panted, "you wanted us both to fuck her?"

"Changing my order," he whispered, eyes flashing a glimpse of blue as he rolled them up to look at her. "Want to get fucked. Sweetheart, if you had a strap-on, I'd let you—"

Whatever fantastic filth he'd been about to let loose, which she was sure she would have enjoyed, the wild rush of lust that spun through her at the very suggestion was enough to drive her to capture his mouth with hers. He murmured against her kiss, twisting in their embrace until he was facing her, the pre-come-slick head of his dick nudging at her stomach.

"We'll buy one tomorrow," Paul promised them from behind him, and his hand shifted Adrian's leg over hers, pressing them more intimately together. She wanted to move up an inch or three and let him slide inside her, but not yet, no protection on hand.

With the position, however, she could look down the length of their bodies and see Paul shimmy his toned, muscular body down the bed. His hand on the paleness of Adrian's ass as he spread him struck her again, almost as much as the sight of him pressing his mouth to his partner. Her jaw might have dropped.

Adrian yelped, a cute and still somehow sexy noise, and she assumed there must have been tongue contact. Then his whole body trembled, leg twitching over hers and cock pulsing against her belly. He closed his eyes, mouth open to pant, and she wondered—how good was it? What did it feel like to be licked there? She reached between their bodies and wrapped her fingers around his dick, prompting another gasp.

Paul rolled away, reaching off of the bed, and came back with a condom and a bottle of lubricant. The size of the bottle made her raise her eyebrows, but then again, it was for a whole weekend. She took the foil packet and tore it open, then smoothed the rubber over Adrian's hard-on.

Another twist, another shift, and she was beneath him. His eyes were fever-bright and his lips swollen from kissing, a flush spreading down his pale chest. On anyone else, it might have been ridiculous, but it took her breath away to see him so flustered, the in-control dominant of the movie theater all but forgotten. Her ankles found their way over his shoulders and he bent her backwards, rising up on his knees to lean over her on all fours. The slide of his covered cock against her cunt was a wonderful feeling, so close, so ready. He was ridiculously hard. She was the one to guide him, so he could keep his hands braced while Paul dripped lubricant over his fingers behind them, making a show of it for her benefit.

Marissa held his stare as long as she could, but when the head of Adrian's cock pushed against her, her eyelids fluttered. She kept her fingers wrapped around the base of him, holding him just right so that when he thrust forward, he penetrated her with one smooth jerk of his hips. She gasped, the initial burn of stretch making her clamp her thighs around his waist. He gritted his teeth, eyes closed.

"Tight," he managed to whisper. "God, fuck."

It didn't hurt, or if it technically did, she enjoyed the sensation as he shoved harder against her and slid further in until the soft, trimmed blond curls on his lower belly brushed her. The rolled edge of the condom rubbed against her body. He was all the way inside her, filling her, and she tossed her head against the pillows at the way it felt. She'd forgotten, or never known, what it was like to want to be fucked so badly, to cling to every fraction of sensation as he moved above and inside her.

He was still, though, and she knew why. Paul's arm was moving, his hand hidden by the curve of Adrian's back, but he was obviously preparing his partner. She noticed he hadn't bothered with a condom, and knew he wouldn't, not with his lover. The pang that hit her then was unexpected and sobering, a bit of a distraction from the pleasure eating her up—she was a visitor here, between them. She was caught in their spell, wanting them, adoring them, but they weren't hers.

After the moment passed, neither man the wiser, she moved her hips experimentally, a small rolling shift that made Adrian's cock move perhaps an inch in and out, the smallest glide, but enough to set her nerves aflame. Everything in her lower body seemed to be clenched tight, holding him inside. She wanted more. A moan slipped from her throat. This was about the *body*, the need between them. It was spice that they loved each other, but she promised herself in that moment she wouldn't let their tenderness hurt her. That wasn't what they intended and it wasn't going to happen.

Adrian thrust once, short and sharp, and she clamped her lips shut around a gasp. His eyes were on hers, half-lidded with pleasure and need. He smirked. Paul was moving behind him, rising up on his knees and putting his hands on Adrian's hips.

"Sorry to keep you waiting, sweetheart," he whispered.

When Paul eased inside him, Adrian shuddered over her and thrust again, a short motion, as if he couldn't decide whether to fuck himself backward onto the cock sliding into him or forward into her. He bent his head to her neck and licked a wet, tingling stripe from collarbone to ear. His teeth found her again as they had that night in the theater, and she had no way of holding back the cry that tore free when he bit down. Again, the flash of burning pleasure and the ache of strained muscle as he tightened his jaw and sank his teeth into the meat of her, marking her.

Paul began to move, one of his hands straying up to hold her ankle above Adrian's shoulder while he rocked forward in small thrusts, almost teasing. The breath rushed out of her, their weight folding her nearly double, and Adrian still hadn't let go, their rolling movement and sweet, slow fucking dragging her flesh against his teeth. She nearly screamed, her nails finding Adrian's back and scraping down his spine. He arched convulsively away and into her grip at the same time, crying out, his bite finally loosening.

Marissa tangled her fingers in his hair and pulled, straining, wanting more than the short delicate thrusts they were making, as if Paul was afraid to jar them too hard. The dull, bruised pain from the fresh mark lanced through her, sharper than it had any right to be, as she bucked and writhed under them.

The slap of flesh on flesh increased as the other man bent low over Adrian's back and began truly fucking him, each impact of his hips driving Adrian's dick harder into her. They found a rhythm, a hard and slamming waltz of bodies. Marissa's eyes wouldn't stay open, her spine wouldn't straighten, and there was hair in her mouth. She didn't care.

The intensity was like nothing she'd ever experienced —Adrian's hands pawing and clutching at her while he moaned against her chest, his mouth moving over her breasts. His teeth found her nipple and closed, softly at first but then harder, until she let loose a small scream for him, afraid to arch or shift because she didn't think she could take any more of the sweet starburst of pain. He switched to suckling as soon as she thought she couldn't stand it any longer, easing the ache and sending rushes of ecstasy down her body.

All of that heat and pleasure coalesced in her belly; the edges of his teeth always finding her flesh, the way he jolted and moaned when Paul slammed into him again, fucking him hard, his dick inside her, moving in long thrusts that seemed to stroke every inch of her insides. Paul was watching them, his mouth a tight line of effort as he guided the dance of their movements, sweat glistening on his brow. His muscled chest and abs flexed with each thrust. He was better, so much better, than any of the movies she'd watched. He was *real*.

"Oh, *please*," she begged, her voice tight and breathless from the constriction of the position they had her in.

Her climax teased close and heavy but her hands were locked around Adrian's shoulders and the tight press of her knees near her ears, there was no way for her to give herself that last push over the edge. Just a little more was all she needed, and she wanted it so badly. Her fingers scrabbled at his back, more red marks raised on the pale skin.

Paul, his eyes narrowed and a smirk taking over his lips, found the solution. He wrapped a hand in Adrian's loose hair and *yanked* as he rose up on his knees, drawing Adrian with him so they were both kneeling, Adrian practically howling. The sudden release of pressure on her chest as her legs unfolded with them made her gasp, and the change in angle—Adrian's cock suddenly moving *up* instead of just *in*—made her scream. She came with another cry, weaker and breathless, grabbing at the pillows as her pussy clenched tight and she shuddered, breaking with the pleasure and the consuming waves of it.

As soon as she was finished Adrian slipped out of her and Paul bent him backwards in a sharp arch, driving deeper and harder inside him, where they were joined visible through their spread legs as he reached down and cupped his hand over Adrian's balls, lifting them. All so she could watch. It was too much, the sight of their bodies locked together, and she pressed a hand between her legs. She was wet, burning hot, and she pushed her fingers inside herself up to the knuckle with a gasp.

Adrian was too far gone to watch, shivering and groaning as he fucked himself up and down on Paul's cock, but Paul wasn't, and his eyes were a heady weight on her as she filled herself with her fingers. Paul stripped the condom off of Adrian, shoved him forward, and pushed him down with an arm across his shoulders.

Marissa was awe-stricken and painfully aroused as she

watched him come just from that, the rough handling. He reached down and stroked himself through it, gasping and panting, but she'd seen him start to climax without a touch. He'd been so hot at being thrown around, manhandled. It made her hot, too. She wanted to test Paul's strength that way herself, let him toss her around the bed and drag her where he wanted her. Adrian was handsome and lovely, but Paul was *masculine*.

The sight of his face as he came inside his partner was enough to drive her into a third, smaller orgasm. He bit his bottom lip, eyelids fluttering closed, and drove himself in hard in a few small, tight thrusts. Adrian groaned, weak and fucked-out, his face pressed to the covers. She slipped her fingers free, slick with her own juices, and trembled as she watched Paul draw slowly out of Adrian.

They collapsed next to her in a sweaty, sticky tumble. She heaved a breath, back aching and thighs feeling the strain of the position they'd been in. The tub looked very inviting.

"Bath?" she whispered.

Her voice was wrecked and rough, but Adrian's, "Oh, give me a minute, darlings," was even more raw.

Marissa relaxed between them, her toes touching Adrian's calf and Paul's hand finding her hip. In the circle of caresses, bracketed by their bodies, she felt like she never had before—truly, unabashedly free.

God, I love it, she thought.

How was she ever going to go back to normal sex after this?

Chapter Seven

The tub filled quickly from the two spouts, hot water steaming up the mirrors all around its inset tile area in the bedroom. The door to the bathroom was closed, Adrian was cleaning up inside, and Paul crouched on his heels near the tub to test the water. He flicked droplets of it off his fingertips and stood, unabashedly nude and sculpted like the statue of a god. Marissa slid off of the bed, her inner thighs sore and her stomach muscles tight. A soak would loosen up the aches that had started to set in her body from the active—she might even call it athletic—sex.

"It's pretty hot," Paul said as she came over.

He put one hand on the small of her back, bare skin on bare skin still like an electric shock despite her loose-limbed satiation. She leaned into the touch, resting the side of her body against the length of his as his arm gathered her into a half-hug. His fingers played up and down her side, halting just under her breasts, then switching direction to sweep down to her hip. Her skin tingled.

"I don't mind," she said. "I'm a little sore."

The bathroom door opened and Adrian came out, flicking the light off. He had a lazy grin on his face, his pale body still flushed pink in patches where hands had gripped him and mouths had bitten. He turned mid-stride to show the scratches down the length of his back, raised welts of red that hadn't quite broken the skin. Marissa frowned.

"Did I hurt you?" she asked.

"Oh, sweetheart," he laughed, pressing up against them in a hug of his own, trapping her in the middle of their naked, warm bodies. "In the best way. Are you all right, too?"

His fingers found marks on her that she could catalogue by the way they ached: the bruise of a bite he'd re-inflicted on her throat, a palm-shaped red mark that lingered on her hip where he'd gripped her.

"Yes," she said, nearly groaning. Despite and perhaps because of the little hurts, she felt like she'd had the best sex of her life. And there would be more.

"Tub," Paul suggested.

Marissa sat on the edge of the tile and dipped her feet in, hissing at the scalding heat. After a moment, it was bearable, and she wiggled the rest of the way in. The small shelf seats let her rest with her chin above water and her legs floating, hot water working out all the aches and pains in her joints. She sighed. Next to her, Paul stepped in, sloshing hot water over her neck. Adrian dipped his toes first, made a pleased noise, and took a seat across from her at the far side of the tub.

"You're so pale," she commented, watching his body turn pink in the heat of the water. Everything seemed to turn his skin colors, the slightest pressure or desire bringing up a blush.

"I know," he said, smiling. "I can't tan at all. I think I don't have enough melanin or something."

She hummed understanding and closed her eyes, resting her head on the rim of the tub. For a moment it was a content, happy silence as they all settled and relaxed, enjoying the huge tub. Paul's foot brushed hers and she cracked one eye, tilting her head to look at him. He smiled broadly. She was surprised she didn't feel more self conscious, sitting naked in the bath with them, but then again, they'd just had fantastic sex. Her own comfort in her body was perhaps the biggest shock. She felt good. Just good, not weird or awkward. Paul's gentle, firm guidance of the wilder Adrian and her inexperience made her feel safe and taken care of.

Which made her think of the way Adrian had moaned and cried out as Paul took him from behind, his pace, his body, his hips setting the pace for both of the people underneath him. What was it like, she wondered, to be in the middle like that? Fucking somebody else while being taken, at once dominant and submissive, receiving and giving?

The heat of the water hid the blush she was sure would have taken over her face at the intensity of the thought, and her imagining of it. She'd never wanted to be a boy, but for the moment, it seemed intriguing. Maybe it was the comment about strap-ons Adrian had made, or maybe it was watching them in real life, feeling them intimately above her while they had sex.

"What's it feel like?" she asked Adrian, hearing the husky tint of her own voice and unable to hide it. "You know—to—"

"You've never had anal sex?" he asked, sitting up a little straighter.

"No."

Paul made a curious, aroused-sounding noise. She raised an eyebrow at him, but Adrian was scooting closer to her in the bath until they were side by side. The tub seemed smaller with them so close to her. Paul brushed a hair out of her face and looked back at Adrian. His grin was definitely what she would call wicked.

"Have you ever even fooled around that way?" Paul asked.

"Not really," she said. Now she did feel a little pulse of embarrassment, but it wasn't bad; the interest she had in the direction of the conversation eased it. "But I'm not a guy. You have a reason to do it. Every girl's magazine I've ever read is always touting the prostate and being a good girlfriend by introducing your boyfriend to his."

Paul chuckled, his thumb rubbing the back of her neck. "It can still be good for a woman. You read women's magazines?"

"In waiting rooms, when I'm bored," she said. "They always seem kind of ridiculous."

"That sounds more like you," he replied.

"What do you mean?" she asked.

"I get the impression that you don't have a lot of patience for things that are below your level," he said.

She frowned a little. "I'm not stuck up, if that's what you mean."

"No, I mean you're smart, and it shows," he said. "You don't act like you're twelve, and most of the women I've met who use fashion magazines like a bible do."

"Thanks, I think," she said.

"He likes intelligence," Adrian commented, drawing their attention to him. "I think he has a fetish for competence."

Paul shrugged, and that knowing smile flickered between them again, catching her in the middle. The hesitation she felt—should she speak, interrupt them?— passed as Paul reached out for the soap and the folded washcloths at the edge of the bath. Adrian's hand found hers under the water and she jumped a little as he squeezed. His smile had become inscrutable as their eyes met, and she wound their fingers together. The moment of tenderness had her heart in her throat, almost painful as he planted a small, chaste kiss on her cheek.

"Stand up," he murmured.

She did, planting her feet in the middle of the tub and standing between them. The water still reached mid-thigh, less hot than before but her skin still prickled with cold where it was exposed to the air. Her nipples peaked into tight buds almost immediately. She stood with her hands to her sides, not covering anything, and Paul gathered her in closer. He kissed the curve of her hip.

"May I wash you?" he asked.

"Okay," she said, softly.

No one had done this for her, either, but she didn't feel quite like sharing that, not when the mood had changed from ferociously sexual to sweet and sensual. It would be almost too emotional a confession to say that no one she'd slept with had ever wanted to take baths with her, cared enough to wash her clean after they'd made love. A pain clenched in her chest.

The look that passed between the men again made her wonder if they somehow guessed, and that it was what made her arms rise to cover herself. Adrian caught her wrists mid-motion and pulled them down with a shushing noise, holding her still while Paul lathered the soap in the soft-looking rag. The first touch of it on her damp stomach had her closing her eyes, tilting her head back.

This, Marissa wanted to simply enjoy while she could have it.

Adrian let her go a moment later and she shifted to stand closer to Paul, between his knees. The rag made silky, slippery circles up her torso, gentle over her sensitive nipples and swirling in a delicate pattern between and below her breasts. Paul didn't miss anything, kneeling up to wash her shoulders and neck, the brief tickle of the cloth under her arms and down her sides. She shifted with the touch of his hands, her breath heavy with something more like emotion than desire, and let him give her back the same treatment. His touch was firmer over muscle and he kneaded her through the cloth while he washed her, massaging and cleaning all at once.

Her breath came in a sudden gasp as he ran the cloth between her legs, so delicate there, then over her buttocks. The washcloth hit the water with a wet slap as his bare hands grasped her ass and rubbed in wide circles, alternating pressure as he spread the soap between hard squeezes and soft petting. She swayed on her feet.

It was Adrian who eased her into the water to rinse, onto her knees in the middle of the tub, his smaller, longer fingers swiping over her body under the water. She let her eyes flutter open, convinced the dampness on her lashes was water from the bath, and drank in the sight of them with her, droplets of moisture on their arms as they held her and helped her back onto the seat between them.

"I missed your legs," Paul said quietly. "But there's a shower in the bathroom. Later?"

"Okay," she said. Her voice came out weak and thready.

Paul gathered her into his arms, and tipped her chin up so she would meet his eyes. The intensity there was almost too much but she couldn't look away. Her chest felt tight, restricted. It was just the water pressure, surely. Adrian's hands smoothed up and down her back, soothing.

"Thank you," Paul said.

"It's nothing," she whispered back, shifting to free her chin and bury her face against his shoulder.

She was sure they were looking at each other over her back, but for now, it was okay. They could have their couple-looks, because they were wonderfully sweet and open. She would try not to be the least bit jealous, and it helped that she couldn't untangle whom she liked the most. Whom to be jealous of, when both halves of the couple made your heart pound?

"If this is too much," Paul murmured into her hair, above her ear. "Say so. I won't judge you."

"Me neither," Adrian said. He was hushed, soft-spoken, so unlike his usual self that it almost made her raise her head. "I've told you, I was big into the scene before Paul and I settled down. Sometimes the feelings run too high with certain people, you know? It's not your fault if it happens."

"No," she said. She was proud that she didn't sniffle. "I'm not sad. I promise."

"It's just a lot, isn't it?" Adrian said, still stroking.

"Yes," she said.

"Was he the first one to ever bathe you like that?" he asked.

It took her a moment to respond. "Yes."

"All right," Adrian said. "Why don't we finish washing off and get out of the bath? We can watch a movie on the TV and cuddle. Sound good?"

"I thought—" she started, then didn't know what to say.

"It's a weekend, sweetheart," Paul said, stealing Adrian's little pet name. "Not all of it can possibly be used for sex."

She laughed, then, and felt a bit freer, enough to lift her head and meet his eyes again. It was true, she wasn't—upset. Or sad. It was a lot to take in, though, their doubled attention and the obvious love flowing between them. She'd never—

"I've never loved anyone like you two love each other," she whispered into the quiet, almost immediately wishing she could take it back, but it was too late.

Paul's expression went soft and warm. She looked down again, found herself glancing over her shoulder to see Adrian matching the emotion in the other man's face.

"Yeah," Adrian said. "He's a great guy."

"Let's get in bed," Paul said, and it didn't sound hot. Just comforting.

She climbed out of the tub first, a bit more self conscious now as she bent to pick up a dry towel and began patting herself off. She'd brought pajamas, but she wasn't sure if she was intended to wear clothes or not. Would they think she didn't want them seeing her naked if she got dressed? It wasn't that. She did want clothes, for the time being, until they came off again as they inevitably would.

While Adrian and Paul scrubbed themselves quickly in the bath, Marissa wrapped the towel around her body and padded over the plush carpet to her suitcase. She laid it out and unzipped it, snagging the small pair of cotton shorts and tank top she planned on sleeping in. The towel dropped to the floor and, with her back still to them, she stepped into the shorts. The cotton was smooth and cool on her bare skin. The tank top, too, felt divine and warmed her a bit. The room was slightly too cold to be without clothes.

Turning back to the men, though, she was aware of how the pajamas might look, because Adrian's smile held a shadow of hunger. She looked at herself in the mirrors behind them and saw her breasts, full and round under the cotton, with nipples pressing against the thin fabric. The shorts clung obscenely to her curves. Her own breath caught, seeing herself reflected there and imagining how they must see it. She'd never considered her body particularly bombshell before, but for the moment, the slight softness at her middle only rounded into her hips, and the thickness of her thighs was another addition to her curvy frame.

Looking at herself that way—sexual, sensual, wanted—was startling. She ducked her head, mulling over the picture frozen behind her eyes, and crawled onto the huge bed as Paul stood in the tub and helped Adrian up. They dried each other perfunctorily, more concerned with petting than drying. Again, the sight of them together stole Marissa's breath. They didn't just match in beautiful counterpoints; they seemed perfect for each other in every way.

Adrian found his way over to her while Paul went into the bathroom and closed the door. He paused long enough to grab a pair of soft, fuzzy sleep pants out of his suitcase. They were well worn, silky-soft against her legs, when he lay next to her and cuddled her in close. His eyes were half closed as he met her gaze, a pleased, tired smile spreading over his still kiss-swollen lips. She pressed a quick peck to them, unable to resist the allure. His smile widened.

"Paul's not good at verbalizing," he said quietly. "So let me add while he's in there: I, for one, know that you may feel some intense emotions when we're working through having mind-blowing sex. Sex is a huge part of everyone's psyche, more than most people want to admit. You've already smashed so many of your barriers to get here. You're vulnerable. Don't be afraid of it."

She nodded, thinking. "I was never the kind of woman who would do this, but I like it. I can't deny I've never felt like this before. Watching you together burns me up, and when you touch me, or Paul does, I just can't even speak."

His arm around her shoulder tightened, rolling her in against his body in a closer hug. She laid her head in the crook of his shoulder, fingers creeping across his bare stomach to embrace him in return. The warmth and comfort of him there lulled her, eyes slipping closed and breathing smoothing out. She felt so good, so right.

"That's the barrier I'm talking about," he murmured into her hair. "You keep telling yourself that you're not this kind of woman. What does that even mean? That women who do this are bad?"

"No," she whispered.

"That wasn't convincing," he said. His fingers combed through her hair, massaged her scalp. "You obviously know I'm bisexual, but I lean toward men. Coming out was hard. You're raised with all this paranoia and hate, and it gets inside you, so even when you want to be true to yourself it eats at you."

"It's not that bad," she said.

"Sweetheart, I think it is right now. You're afraid and you don't know what you want, but you want it so badly you can let go of your fear to try. And you're loving it. You're so responsive, you don't even know. It's like a sub who hasn't been ridden hard for a long time. They start to yearn for it."

Adrian took a deep breath, and put his finger to her lips when she started to deny again that she was afraid.

"Hush," he said. "Think of this like your personal sex therapy, not only a weekend retreat. The sooner you accept that you still have some ugly feelings about yourself, about this, the sooner you can let them go. Let them go and *live it* like you want to."

The bathroom door opened and Marissa closed her mouth on the tip of Adrian's finger, flicking her tongue over it and tasting fresh water, the hint of soap. He grinned and pressed another kiss to her head, this time near her ear as she shifted. Paul's body bracketed her a moment later, his pajama pants cotton like her shorts. His hands were so warm they were nearly hot as he snuggled close to the pair.

"Under the sheets?" he asked.

"We have to move, don't we?" Adrian pouted.

Marissa moved with them until all three were huddled under the covers and comforter, with the large LCD television on and a movie playing at a low volume. They were warm, and close, and perfect. She cuddled tighter between them, curling her fingers around Paul's arm where it lay over both her and Adrian and squeezed Adrian briefly with her free arm. They both moved, and she heard the sound of kissing. She looked up to watch them, lit by the television screen, and saw only tenderness and love in the way their lips pressed. Adrian fumbled for the remote on the nightstand and thumbed two buttons: he first turned off the TV, then second the overhead light.

The sudden dark made her flinch, but the moment passed, and she relaxed. Adrian rolled onto his side, and Paul nudged her, guiding her to spoon against his back. Paul did the same, hugging their bodies to his. Hair tickled her nose and she tucked her head in against Adrian's shoulder. Breathing and the shifting noises of the trio settling into comfortable positions, eased her asleep, held secure and safe between their strong, capable bodies.

Chapter Eight

Marissa woke to the subtle, easy movements of the man in front of her trying to sneak out of bed without waking anyone. She grumbled, pawing for him, and he laughed quietly. She blinked, squinting in the morning gloom. The curtains blocked plenty of light, but not all of it.

"Ssh," he said. "I'll be right back."

She let Adrian go, mind slowly clawing back to awareness, and wriggled back tighter into Paul's sleep-loosened embrace. His knees bumped against the backs of hers and she pulled the covers over their heads, but she didn't think she'd be going back to sleep any time soon. What Adrian had said to her lingered in her mind and, after a night of rest, she wasn't too exhausted to think about it.

Was he right? Did she still have what he'd called *ugly feelings* about what they were doing here? A part of her protested. If she did, why was she comfortable sleeping between them, being nude with them, fucking them at all? Another, quieter part seemed to nod its agreement: she was still embarrassed of what she was doing, even if her body ached for it and it made her feel so free. How would it feel to go down to breakfast arm in arm, kisses all around, and have the wait staff know she'd spent the night with not one but two men, who were also together? She shuddered at the thought, but that firmed her resolution to work through these issues. Maybe with Adrian's insightful, incisive commentary along with the mind-blowing sex, she'd be able to. She hoped so, at least. She wanted to be proud of what she had going on. She wanted her reaction to the knowing looks they might get in public to be *pride*, not shame.

So that was a goal, beyond discovering what she really, truly liked.

Her squirming woke Paul after another moment and he made a snuffling, curious noise, his hands patting the bed in front of her to find Adrian gone. She heard the bathroom door open and lifted her head, blearily looking at Adrian as he emerged, his blond hair sticking up in every direction.

He climbed back in with them, this time face to face with Marissa, and his legs tangled in with Paul's over hers. It was close, and almost too hot, but she relaxed into the pressure of them holding her. A shift, and the pressure was an entirely different kind—Paul rubbed the noticeable length of his morning erection against her butt, humming his enjoyment into her ear. She stiffened, then found herself melting into their hands as Adrian ran his fingertips down the length of her torso, between her breasts, ending at the waistband of her shorts.

"Food first, or this?" he asked.

Paul made a noise of sleepy complaint and rolled away. "Be right back," he said.

"Probably food," she said. "I want to freshen up, too, and my mouth tastes awful, I can tell."

"Spoilsports," Adrian murmured but his smile said otherwise. He kissed the tip of her nose and hugged her tight against his body, letting her feel the beginning swell of his growing erection through his soft pajama pants.

"We'll come up again after breakfast," she replied, sitting up slowly.

It was almost impossibly difficult to extract herself from the teasing of his little touches, but she managed, and finally stood on the other side of the bed rummaging through her suitcase for clothes. She chose a soft blue cotton T-shirt and a pair of dark jeans, then made a point of dangling a bright green lace thong from her fingertips as she turned. Adrian sprawled on the bed, his pants riding low on his hips to reveal the suggestive lines of his lower stomach, and smirked at the sight.

Paul emerged from the bathroom a moment later, his hair combed into a more manageable tangle of curls and his pajama pants balled in his fist. Marissa's breath caught at the sight of his nude body, his soft cock drawing her eye. She wanted abruptly to drop to her knees and take him in her mouth when it was so small and seemingly delicate, not like the steely hardness of his erection the night before. The need ached in her in a surprising, sudden wave. She licked her lips. She'd never taken a man soft into her mouth before, never felt him grow between her lips and on her tongue.

So, with a giddy sensation of relief, she put a hand on his hip, dropped her clothes on the floor and sank into a crouch on her heels to put her head at level with him. His breath hitched audibly and his hand found the top of her head, gently tilting it back so he could look into her eyes.

"Let me," she asked.

"Go ahead," he said, low and interested.

He was starting to swell already and she leaned forward, heart pounding, to take him in her mouth. It was a unique feel on her tongue, her palate—loose and soft enough that she could flick her tongue around and over him, pressing and tasting. She could intimately feel the thickening of his cock as he hardened, until she could no longer breathe with her lips against the coarse, trimmed triangle of hair at his groin. He rolled his hips, pushing against her throat, and she shuddered, holding her breath. Could she take him further? She knew he was bigger than this fully erect, and he was still growing in her mouth.

Paul's hand found the back of her neck and she let her hands slide down his legs to rest in her lap, letting him guide her. He tilted her head back a bit, whispered something in a comforting tone that she didn't hear over the pounding of her pulse in her ears, and pushed again. She swallowed convulsively as the head of his cock stretched her throat, scarily new but not painful. It felt like he was fucking her mouth as he would her pussy, working his hips slow and easy to open her up more, make her take him deeper.

She tapped his knee after another moment, lightheaded and now feeling a scrape and soreness in her throat, and he let go. She pulled off with a gasp, mouth full of saliva and throat aching slightly. Paul's dick bobbed in front of her face, fully erect and slick with her spit. She had to gasp for a few breaths. Her lungs protested how long she'd kept them without air.

"You're a natural," he whispered hotly, combing her hair back from her face with his fingers. His thumb swiped over her lower lip. "I don't think I want breakfast any more."

"I want to try," Adrian murmured.

She looked at him over her shoulder. He was lying on his stomach on the bed, chin propped up on his hands and eyes focused singularly on them. His face had the telltale pink blush of arousal that she'd begun to think of as unbearably cute. Her body felt limp but somehow electrified with desire, kneeling there, both of their gazes searching and hungry on her.

"You're feeling it today, aren't you?" Adrian purred as he rose from the bed.

"I don't—" she said, then coughed.

He knelt behind her, gathered her hands in his, and yanked them behind her back with a little more force than was necessary, enough to sting her skin. She cried out, sharp and surprised, back arching and fingers clenching as the lightning shock of it slammed through her like a bite but a thousand times stronger. Adrian let out a husky laugh at the intensity of her reaction.

"You are such a sub," he murmured into her ear.

"I—"

"Hush," he said. He kissed her neck sweetly. "Let us do this to you. Say stop if you don't like it."

She felt him nod, his cheek moving against her hair. Paul took the cue and stepped forward, thumb guiding his dick so it pointed straight at her mouth again. She met his eyes and saw not just lust but also a sort of tenderness there, though heated. She wasn't afraid to be restrained at their mercy, not when he had that look.

"You like to be talked to, praised," Adrian murmured as she opened her mouth again and let Paul slide himself in. "Don't you, sweetheart?"

She moaned. The hot glide of Paul's cock over her tongue and the roof of her mouth made her shiver. Adrian's fingers tightened around her wrists. He held her hard while Paul shallowly thrust, drawing himself in and out in short strokes, rubbing himself over her tongue more than anything. She licked him as well as she could, being immobile, and let them do the work.

"Does it make you hot for Paul to fuck your mouth like this?" he whispered. "Using you to make himself come, while your pussy aches to be touched and we ignore it?"

Paul was the one who groaned, and Marissa dizzily remembered Adrian saying how much he liked dirty talk, too. Her jaw was stretched and her lips tingling, the velvet steel of the man's dick going a little further now with each smooth roll of his hips. She tilted her head the fraction he'd shown her before, relaxing her throat as much as she could, and didn't choke when he slid further in once more. The slickness of her saliva made it easier, smoother, so the stretch didn't hurt.

Paul's voice next came as a shudder-inducing growl. "I like using you like this. Like a wet, hot little fuck-toy."

She did groan around him then, swallowing hard as he slid deep, deeper, cutting off her noise until it was a vibration instead. He gasped, gripping her hair in his fists, and she writhed in Adrian's hold. They were right, so right—her skin was on fire, too small for her, every inch itching with need to be stroked and licked. Paul began to pant above her, his hips moving jerkily, shoving in harder as his control broke. She was along for the ride, trying not to lose the rhythm or choke, her chin wet and hair sticking to her face where it had escaped his hands. It was messy, hard, *hot*.

"Is it okay for him to come in your mouth?" Adrian whispered.

She had no answer but to moan again, hips shifting against nothing, craving touch and receiving nothing. That was enough for Paul. He gasped out a quick, "Oh, yes—" and pulled out far enough that he came in hot pulses on her tongue, letting her taste the rich salty musk of him. She was shaking as he pulled out. Her eyelashes were damp. Her throat hurt in the best way, and a man had just *fucked her throat until he came*. It sounded like something Adrian would say.

"Good job," Adrian said. "You made him feel good, darling. Do you deserve a reward for making him come with your sweet mouth?"

Paul smirked, dropping to the floor with them and lifting her by the thighs so she could uncurl her legs and spread them across his lap. His softening cock was damp against her inner thigh. He pulled her shorts down, his attentive eyes tracking the wetness darkening them.

"You're soaking," he said.

"Please," she whispered, raw and scratchy.

"God, that's hot," Adrian moaned into her ear, moving close with his thighs spread around her waist. The hot press of his cock against her lower back bowed her spine. She needed to be touched, couldn't wait any longer. "Your fucked-out voice. Say some more."

She opened her mouth but found no words, eyes locked with Paul's. She felt limp still, loose in their hands, content to be molded and maneuvered despite her burning arousal.

"It's an order," he corrected. He smirked. "Tell me what to do and I'll do it. But you have to ask for exactly what you want. Otherwise I won't do a thing and Adrian will hold your hands so you can't touch yourself."

Marissa panted, resting her head on Adrian's shoulder. He kissed her cheek, searching for her mouth, and she turned her head to find him. He licked into her open mouth, groaning low in his throat, and she wondered if he was tasting Paul's come. The thought made her gasp again.

"I want to come," she begged into his kiss.

"More specific," he whispered, blue eyes sparkling with desire and pleasure. "Tell Paul."

He helped her shift to look down the length of her body at him, legs propped open over his lap and shorts dangling from one ankle. His hands never left her wrists. Paul waited, patient and darkly amused by her struggle, her debilitating arousal. His mischievous look made things low in her body tighten.

"I want—" She wavered. "Put your fingers in me. Lick my cunt."

Her face flamed, her body seared with heat and lust at the way Paul's eyes narrowed and his smirk widened, obviously enjoying her embarrassment. She was, too, if she were deliriously honest with herself—it was good, it was sweet and pure in a way that shame never was. She just liked to be made to feel *dirty*.

"As you wish," he murmured.

She wanted to cry with relief as his hand moved between her legs, fingers stroking down her pussy and spreading her. He crooked two, pushing them inside with a powerful movement of his wrist. She gasped instead, hips rolling and moving eagerly as he pushed his fingertips up and stroked her insides until he found just the right spot, and her vision went gray at the burst of pleasure.

"Yes!" she cried out, Adrian's grip tighter on her and his breath panting in her ear. Their reactions encouraged hers, she knew—she could be louder, freer, needier with them because they wanted to see it. They wanted her to give up control.

"I think the lady asked to be licked," Adrian growled.

"Yes, sir," Paul said with a grin and bent his head; his tongue flickered over her clit.

She writhed in their grip, Paul's free hand grasping her thigh hard and his other stroking two fingers constantly over that spot inside her that sent bolts of hard, sharp pleasure up her spine. It was almost too intense. The added, sweeter ecstasy of his tongue lapping broad, wet-hot strokes over her clit softened it some, and the crescendo built so fast between the alternating sensations that she was yelling, gasping her pleas for completion without a second thought.

"Yeah, that's it," Adrian encouraged her. He was grinding steadily against her back.

As her legs began to shake and her eyes slammed shut, Paul abruptly pulled back. She bit down on a howl, body quivering and taut at the edge of orgasm but unable to crest. She fought to press her thighs together and end it but his body kept her legs spread, Adrian's hands pinning her wrists so she couldn't touch.

"Oh, God, God, please—" she panted.

"You're leaving out our Adrian," Paul said. "And you didn't order me to make you finish, did you?"

"Your cock," she begged Adrian, rolling her head back onto his shoulder.

He shoved her, and she toppled into Paul's embrace, shimmying up into his lap to press his half-hard dick against herself. She ground down with a moan, feeling him twitch against her with renewed interest. He wrapped his arms hard around her middle and lifted her, squeezing so hard her breath rushed out. His embrace pinned her arms; he held her above his lap so she couldn't rub against him.

"Adrian!" she cried out.

Slippery fingers pressed between her ass cheeks and she froze, stiffening at the wet touch where she'd never been touched before. He waited, Paul waited, she waited. She let her breath shudder out and said nothing. The fingers stroked over her there, teasing skin until she understood what he got from being fucked, if it was anything like being rubbed—ticklish but not, raw sensation, intimate in a way that even touching her pussy wasn't. It required more trust, more willingness to broaden her horizons.

His fingertip penetrated her, slow and gentle.

"You let me know if I'm going too fast," Adrian whispered hotly. "This turns me on so much I'm afraid I'll come before I even get my cock in you."

"Aah," she managed as his lube-slicked finger slid deeper, inexorably deeper, until the press of his hand against her was a comforting weight.

She also felt Paul rising to the challenge of another round beneath her, his cock pressing against her cunt as he grew erect.

"Condom," Paul said.

Adrian passed one over her shoulder and the way his finger shifted inside her made her gasp and clench hard. He groaned at the feeling. Paul leaned back, slipped the rubber over himself and guided her down again, so the head of him pressed against her pussy and then slid inside. He filled her in one long glide and held her still on his lap, stretched around his dick while Adrian probed inside her with a second finger. She felt the press of them together, and it had her shaking, the previously abandoned orgasm rushing up again. She rocked, whimpering, her clit grinding against the base of Paul's cock and his thickness inside her stroking everything he'd primed with his fingers.

Adrian fit a third finger in a moment later, and that burned, though he used more lubricant. Her muscles protested, tightening again around them both, and this time Paul cursed and bucked his hips up, grinding hard into her though he was as far in as he could get. She shuddered.

"Paul, pull out," Adrian said, a thready whisper.

She whimpered as he did, lifting her again. She writhed to keep him inside, but he slipped out, leaving her feeling open and hungry to be fucked. Adrian slid his fingers out. She heard the tearing of a wrapper and then his latex-covered cock nudged at her. She bent forward into Paul's embrace and let out a long sigh as Adrian pushed into her from behind. It burned but not in a way that truly hurt, and even that ache dissolved quickly as he worked in with tiny pushes.

He was being so careful not to hurt her, she knew, especially with his breath racing and his body shaking above her.

"You like—" she gasped, trying to give as good as she got. "Putting your cock in my ass?"

"Fu—ck," he groaned, hips meeting hers as he bottomed out. "Your *virgin* ass, sweetheart, can't forget."

He began to move, and he was right—it did feel good. He kept her back arched, his cock going into her at an angle that sent small rushes of pleasure all through her body. He hugged her to him, mouthing at her neck, constant gasps coming from his mouth. Paul's stare was hot on her face and she met it, knowing and sharing the knowledge that Adrian was losing his control, that she'd made him so aroused that his normally iron will was shattering.

"Coming," he whimpered.

She clenched down hard, the way she had on his fingers, and he actually yelped and slammed his hips against her. She screamed in return, because that was a jumble of pain and pleasure that made her very aware of how careful he'd been. She felt his dick pulsing hard against the muscled ring of her hole as he orgasmed.

"Oh," she moaned, drawing the sound out.

He pulled her back against him, staying inside, and Paul moved up in front. His fingers stroked his own cock, squeezing a little at the head, and he bent to lick her once more. It took three strong swipes of his tongue over her pussy, long wet licks that encompassed her from clit to nearly where Adrian's softening cock was still buried in her, and she was shaking through an explosive peak, voice broken on cries of pleasure. The fullness of Adrian still stretching her insides, owning her virgin ass as he'd so fondly murmured, while she tightened and shivered only drove her higher.

Paul's orgasm was no less spectacular for receiving it from his own hand. He rested his head against her thigh and grunted as he came, filling the condom, his hand moving fast over himself. Adrian shifted and pulled gently free of her a moment later.

"Oh," she groaned, laying herself out on the soft carpet.

Her lower back and her ass had begun to ache, but she was so sated and pleased it was hard to care. Paul carded a hand through her hair and smirked. She rolled her eyes and smiled back at Adrian, who looked both smug and wrecked, more debauched than them both. He really did like being the first, which was such an odd kink, she thought.

But he'd been gentle and made her come, so it was okay. They both got something good out of it.

"Breakfast," he said a moment later, tossing blonde hair out of his eyes. "Though nothing is going to top that, am I right?"

"Oh, darling," she drawled, adopting his brief pet name. "You're both absolutely fantastic."

"Good to hear," Paul replied.

At the hotel table, cleaned up and damp-haired from a quick shower, Marissa found herself at a table with two handsome, sweet and thoroughly debauched men who both had looks on their faces that seemed to announce what they just did upstairs in their room. She wondered if her own expression was as lecherous, suggestive, and open—she doubted it, but wondered. Her body certainly felt sensual and lovely in a way she'd never known it to feel, projecting an air of uncaring satisfaction.

The waiter's eyes lingered on the three of them, eyebrows drawn together in confusion, as they scooted chairs to be close around the small square table. They formed a triangle, Paul in the middle and Adrian and Marissa sitting across from each other.

And, to her joy, she didn't feel the burn of shame she'd imagined when the waiter walked away, still pondering their arrangement. He wouldn't ask; it would be unprofessional, but he was thinking it. They were all covered in love bites and visible bruising shaped like hands, teeth. She instead felt—full, somehow, of life and happiness. She was a part of this for the weekend, this sweet relationship full of trust and open-minded desire.

Jeff would have judged her for wanting these things, for having enjoyed anal sex, for having given her body over to be used by two caring and well-practiced, well-trained tops. This was what she liked, she was sure now. She was more centered, content, and happy than she'd been for years and it was thanks to this sexual awakening, thanks to giving her control up for a little while.

"You look happy," Paul said.

"I am," she said, smiling. "This is perfect. I'm so glad."

"You're a perfect match for us, too," Adrian said. "Don't think you're not, because you blow my mind, sweetheart."

"Me, too," Paul said.

His fingers crept across the table to grasp hers, holding her hand. He smiled in return. Her breath caught, her heart throbbed, and she felt something else: a rush of emotion, sweeter than honey, the first brush of something stronger than desire. Her jaw clenched and she swallowed suddenly, dropping her eyes. Oh, that was not all right. She fought down the feeling and was glad that their food arrived a moment later, distracting the men from her awkward moment.

It was bound to happen, she thought.

After all, she was expecting two horny guys who wanted to bang her brains out and move on. She had been prepared for that. She hadn't been ready for Paul and Adrian, who were so real, human, and down to earth that they had begun to creep into her heart. That, and she'd never done a friends-with-benefits thing: maybe she wasn't cut out for it. Maybe sex made her feel strongly, too, not like Lita and her string of boyfriends.

She thought she could deal with the heartache of leaving when the weekend was through—because the experience so far had been so fantastic, it was worth wringing every minute of pleasure and happiness out of it, and not giving up early.

Marissa had the very clear epiphany that she was already falling for them. Pulling away now wouldn't stop it. So why not enjoy?

In the meantime, she'd been picking over her strawberry pancakes, and Paul's fork crept over to steal a bite. She swatted at him halfheartedly and he grinned, popping the bite of her breakfast into his mouth.

"Eat up," he said. "You need strength for later."

Her face heated and his smile softened along with the blush. He obviously thought it was cute, and if he did, she could, too.

"What are we doing today?" she asked. "I assume

we can't spend the whole time upstairs. I'm kind of sore right now."

"I thought maybe we could go mall-trawling and just hang out for a bit," Adrian said, his voice uncharacteristically soft.

Paul raised his eyebrows and something unspoken passed between them, but she ignored it to say, "Okay, sounds nice."

The pancakes disappeared slowly, aided by the bites Paul kept sneaking off of her plate. She didn't mind. The companionable quiet around the table soothed the building strangeness of the previous conversation—which made her wonder, why was Paul giving Adrian such an odd look about going to a mall to pass the time? Did Paul expect they'd spend the weekend with sex and not do anything else, but Adrian wanted to bond? She wished she knew. Their unspoken communication put her off balance.

A small part of her was afraid she wasn't the only one who was starting to feel something more than lust. What if their relationship wasn't stable enough for this after all? What if she was the one to come between them, entirely by accident?

"Are you both—I don't know, are you all right?" she asked as she nudged her empty plate away from her. Her hands fiddled with the orange juice glass. "Something seems odd."

"It's fine," Paul said.

"Okay, I believe you," she said. "But before we go, I'm going to run to the girls' room. Be right back."

Marissa stood and tucked her chair under, retreating to the restrooms in the back of the hotel restaurant. A glance over her shoulder as she opened the door revealed Paul and Adrian sitting with their heads bent together, blond hair nearly touching dark, an obviously intense conversation under way. She swallowed hard and walked through the doorway, glad for the empty bathroom. She leaned against the sink and looked at herself in the mirror, relieved for the moment alone.

They were talking about her, she was sure. What could they not say when she was there? Were they worrying about how she was feeling, or were they fighting amongst themselves? The thought of unbalancing their sweet, functional relationship made her feel sick. They'd been so certain they'd be able to do this and have it mean nothing, and now she was contending with the ache of growing feelings in her chest, and they were heatedly talking about something related to her. Adrian seemed especially attached already, though Paul was more aloof with them both.

She stared into her reflection, cataloguing the marks on her neck in the scoop T-shirt. If they both felt strongly about her, if they were *both* getting attached—

Marissa shook herself to kill the traitorous thought. She had no place with them after this weekend and she'd never heard of an actual relationship with three people. They had history, years of companionship, and she was a weekend fling. There was no way it would work, and thinking it was just wishful. She splashed water on her face, dried it with a paper towel, and went back out to the restaurant.

They had finished talking and were sitting comfortably again, chatting without a hint of the intensity of before. Marissa took her seat and looked at them both. She wished she could read minds. Paul was smiling with the faintest quirk of his lips, Adrian had his usual smirk. It was as if they thought she wouldn't notice their stiffness, the way they held themselves a bit differently. All the same, she didn't want to ask and turn the morning awkward.

"Shall we?" she asked.

"I got the check already," Paul said.

"Would you like to drive?" Adrian offered. "Or I can. Either way."

"My car's kind of small," she said.

"Ours it is," he said and pushed his chair back to stand.

Marissa looked up at him, the sunlight from the windows lighting up the nearly white highlights in his gold-blond hair. He had the silhouette of an angel, but the expression on his face as he met her gaze and offered her a hand up was anything but angelic. His eyes seemed to be full of mischief, knowledge of contours and spaces of her body that even she had barely thought about.

She took his hand and stood, fingers interlacing, and Paul put an arm around her waist. Managing to walk out of the restaurant pressed together was harder than she'd imagined it would be, the tables not quite far enough apart for three people abreast, and the weight of other people's attention burned on her back. Still, she held her head high and enjoyed the warmth of a hand in hers and an arm crossing the small of her back, Paul and Adrian both bracketing her. She'd wondered since the seating arrangement at breakfast had differed if they'd keep putting her in the middle, but it seemed they hadn't tired of touching her yet and were eager to do as much of it as they could before the weekend was over.

"Time's already passing too quickly," Paul said, almost under his breath. "It's almost eleven. By the time we go out, shop, and have lunch it'll be nearly five. Checkout tomorrow is at noon."

Marissa swallowed a protestation and said instead, "Well, we've got time. Let's make the most of it."

"You don't have a boyfriend, or anybody in mind, right?" Adrian asked.

"I already told you guys," she said with a sigh. "Nobody, no-how."

"Just us," he muttered, and that time the look Paul shot him was somewhere between curious and wounded.

"Come on," she said, her attempt at light-heartedness falling a bit flat. "I thought I was the only angst-riddled, self-conscious mess. If we're all moping we won't have a good time."

"True," Paul said.

He attempted a manful smile and Adrian squeezed her hand. Letting go of them to slip into the back seat of the car was almost physically painful, reminded as she was of their limited time together. She sat in the middle seat and reached up to play her fingers through the blond waves of Adrian's hair where he sat in the passenger seat—best not to distract the driver.

"Mmm," he hummed as she scratched his scalp with the tips of her nails. He shifted in his seat like a satisfied cat. "That's *nice*."

"So, how's your job been going?" Paul asked as he drove, distracting her briefly from wringing more of those contented purrs from Adrian.

"I think it's been going well. I've had—I don't know, it makes me feel weird to say this, but I've had more confidence since I started talking to you two," she murmured.

"You're embracing who you are, and who you want to be," Adrian said with a husky edge to his voice. "We're just helping. You think it's us making you more confident, but it's just you, growing into your skin."

"So, when you found out you were into—BDSM, and all that, you started to feel more secure?" she asked.

"Very much so," Adrian said.

"Accepting that I liked men and women both unlocked so much for me," Paul added. "My art was better, my life was better, and then I met Adrian. You know, he's the first guy I ever dated, and I was his first monogamous relationship for years. It was all pretty new."

"I didn't know," she said.

Adrian turned his head so her fingers ran across his cheek and he cast a glance back at her. It made her feel childish, that these men were barely older than her and so much more aware of themselves. Everyone had to start somewhere, though, and she knew she'd found her inner truth here, with them. This was the kind of woman she was: free, sensual, and still the same Marissa but with a huge weight lifted. Sex with strangers, a weekend of debauchery, hadn't changed who she was. It had just helped her acknowledge it.

And they hardly seemed like strangers now.

"The auditor for my class made me so nervous I could never talk in front of him," she admitted. Her face heated under Adrian's knowing stare. "But when I thought about your mark on me, and what I was going to do, and who I was going to be, I felt better. I felt stronger."

"That's what it's all about," Adrian said.

"Once you're done with us, do you think you'll keep looking?" Paul asked.

That question had an edge she couldn't interpret. The thought of running out for another date on Monday made her feel sick with heartbreak, and she shook her head emphatically, then realized he probably couldn't see, though Adrian could and was cataloguing her reactions.

"Just because I know what I want doesn't mean I can have it," she said.

Adrian made another humming noise, this one displeased, but he didn't elaborate. Paul's shoulders were a bit tighter than before, she thought. Her mouth flattened into a line once Adrian turned away. That—that was a bit too honest, a bit too much emotion leaking into her answer. There was no way they didn't catch on to her tone.

She knew what she wanted: them. It was a shame they weren't really an option.

Adrian twisted in his seat and rubbed her knee soothingly, though he didn't look back, and she relaxed into her seat. The silence wasn't as perfectly comfortable as it had been the night before, but her head was filled with wonderings and worries and she couldn't see the men's faces, couldn't guess what they were thinking.

"I could—" Adrian said quietly, then stopped.

"You could?" she prompted.

"Never mind," he said. "I need to think about it before I say something, okay?"

"Okay," she said, curious now. She caught Paul glancing at him, too.

The mall appeared on the horizon and she leaned up between their seats, the belt pressing hard into her lower stomach. Adrian stretched and sat up straighter. She heard his back pop. Paul found them a space and parked.

"I haven't gone on a mall date since I was in high school," she said.

"We like to go," Paul said. He smiled at her, though his expression seemed preoccupied. "It's nice to walk around and people-watch, if you're comfortable with being watched right back."

She nodded. "I'm ready. I'm okay with that—with people seeing us. Are you, though? What if someone you know sees us? What will they think?"

Paul ruffled her hair and grinned. "They won't question it, trust me. They're all used to Adrian. Nothing shocks them any more."

"What can I say? I like to play games," Adrian said with a shrug.

"You certainly do," Marissa replied, and the teasing in her tone made him smirk.

"Let's go," Paul said.

She climbed out of the backseat and offered a hand to Paul, who wrapped his fingers firmly around hers. Her heart skipped a beat, one dizzying off-thud in her chest as emotion rushed through her. Adrian came up beside them, kissed Paul on the cheek, and took her free hand. The warmth of their grip on her hands hid her sudden chills. This was different than the hotel; there were people from teenagers to elderly couples drifting into the mall and returning to their cars.

Marissa regretted for a moment saying she was ready, because she was suddenly terrified and embarrassed. Her shoulders fought to rise up with tension and her grip spasmed tighter on their hands. Adrian crowded close, pressing the length of his body against hers.

"What's wrong?" he murmured.

"Leave her be," Paul said. His gaze was sympathetic. "Remember the first time you went out holding hands with another guy?"

"Ah," Adrian said. "Sweetheart, everyone's going to be jealous. Even the ones who give you the eye are just jealous."

"Okay," Marissa breathed, calming herself.

She knew it was stupid to be afraid, stupid to suddenly want to crawl back into the car and go back to the hotel and *hide*. Where had the confidence she'd felt facing down their waiter gone?

"It's—" she muttered as they walked slowly, still hand

in hand. "Different. The hotel is farther away. It's like a little universe, no one will know. This . . ."

"We can pretend we're just friends hanging out," Paul offered.

"No," she said, shaking her head for emphasis. "Why am I like this? It's not fair. I like you guys. I liked what we did together. I want to go on a mall date with you."

"You can't kick all the baggage in a day," he answered.

Though Adrian played therapist best, when she looked up at Paul and his handsome face and curly dark hair, stared into his warm brown eyes, she knew he was the one who had experienced more of what she was feeling right then, even if it was a different context. He knew. It soothed her racing pulse just a bit. He wasn't going to judge her for her fear.

"You going to let some grannies and high-schoolers tell you who you're allowed to be?" Adrian asked, his voice gentle though the words were not.

"No, dammit," she said. "Kiss me?"

He smiled, tossed his hair out of his face, and planted a slow, sweet kiss on her mouth. His lips caught against hers, soft and silky. She sighed with pleasure and nipped his lip. He pulled away with a smile and she stood on her toes to give Paul the same, the lush velvet of his lips slipping against her now-damp mouth. She smiled when she dropped back onto her heels. Her heartbeat had calmed back to normal.

"Inside," she said and set off walking.

They followed her with chuckles that had a harmony,

despite the difference in their voices. Adrian had a spring in his step and Paul was a steady, comforting presence beside her. Their hands were anchors in hers, grounding her to the moment. They flowed inside with the crowd, through the food court with its bustling customers and yelling children, and Marissa's eye caught on a sweets shop.

"Oh, I'd kill for a cookie," she said.

"Consider it done," Adrian said.

They gravitated toward the line, hands still locked, and Marissa swore she felt the weight of people staring. She was probably imagining it. Adrian nuzzled close and planted a teasing nip on the top of her ear. She jumped with a tiny yelp, prompting Paul to give her fingers a comforting squeeze. Her pulse sped again, though this time for better reasons than before. The line moved forward and they pressed in close, sandwiching her between their larger bodies, sharing warmth and space.

The clerk, when they reached the front, gave them a snotty look. Marissa guessed he was maybe sixteen, still pimpled and sporting an awkward haircut probably chosen by a parent. Adrian was smirking at him salaciously, which probably didn't help. She cleared her throat and tugged one of her hands free from Adrian and pointed to the peanut-butter cookies.

"One of those, please?" she asked.

"I'd like a marbled brownie," Adrian added.

"One of those chocolate icing cookie-cups," Paul finished.

Adrian made it to his wallet first and forked over a twenty. The clerk raised an eyebrow at the three of them, waited a beat to take the proffered money, and rolled his eyes as he got their desserts.

Marissa bristled. How dare he? Who was he judging, anyway—Paul and Adrian, or her? He was probably a virgin.

"Shy-girl's getting pissed," Adrian singsonged into her ear, under his breath.

It shocked a snort out of her, then a laugh. She reached out for their cookies when the teen put them on the counter and, when she turned back, saw Adrian with his arm around Paul's waist. Now the kid's face was turning red.

"Brat," she said, loud enough to be heard, and wedged herself in between them again with her hands full of cookie bags. Adrian hugged her around the waist and Paul looped an arm over her shoulders. She offered them their desserts. "Eat up, boys. And why do you keep taking the checks? I can treat, too."

"Marissa," Paul said, and hearing her name shocked her into pausing for a moment. "It's our treat because it can be, and we want to. You can have the lunch bill, if you want."

"Okay," she said.

The fact that they'd gotten so comfortable she didn't need to have her name said to know they were talking to her made her feel something not unlike discomfort, but also happiness. It took a long time to get so close to someone you didn't need to use their real name, until you found your own for them. This had only been a few days, really, and a lot of e-mails.

She settled into their arms again, letting them propel her through the loose crowds while she nibbled her cookie and peered at shops. The lingerie store caught her eye, but she wasn't sure if she wanted to go in—buying something for them might be nice; dressing up for the night, maybe.

"You want to pick out something slinky?" Adrian asked. "I think you'd look divine in a corset."

He pinched her butt and her breath caught at the pleasant sting.

"Marissa?" someone said behind her, incredulous and not pleased.

She froze. Her heart seemed to stop. Paul and Adrian flinched with her reaction but didn't let go, and she nearly panicked, but held her breath until the urge to run passed. Too late, now—she'd been caught. She turned, and they turned with her, a move like a dance.

"Eric," she said.

Her cousin's brows were furrowed, his mouth pinched. His wavy brown hair was cut shorter than it had been when she'd left her grandmother's house, when they were both living there. Eric still was. She felt for a brief moment like she might pass out on the floor. Of all the people—

"Who's this?" Paul asked nicely.

"My cousin," she managed.

"We both grew up with Gramma Ford," he said,

and he was glaring now, hard, at Paul and Adrian both. "Who are *you*?"

She took a breath before they could answer. "My dates, Eric. They're my dates."

"Dates?" he repeated.

"Yes. And I'd appreciate it if you didn't pass it along." Her hands were shaking, but their support hid it. Her knees were weak. "Grandma doesn't need to know."

"I think she does, Marissa," he said, shaking his head. He jerked his chin toward them. "Look at you, parading around like you're proud to be a—"

"Say it, and I'll beat your ass," Adrian said cheerily. "You go ahead and say it."

Eric's lip curled. Marissa was reminded abruptly why she didn't like her cousin, why she'd never liked him. He swallowed all the hate and the ideology whole, and believed every inch. She'd never had that kind of blindness in her.

"I'm a grown woman," she said. "And who I date is not your business."

"Whatever," he said. "I'd keep your phone open tonight. She's not going to be happy with you, and after all she did for you, too."

He walked away before she had a chance to think up a retort. Her eyes burned. She fought her hands free and pressed the heels of them against her eyes, breathing deeply. Her face felt like an oven. She must have been blushing bright red. Of all the people to come on her in public, to discover her secret, it had to be Eric, the smarmy little tattletale.

"Do you want to go?" Paul asked, rubbing circles on her back.

"We should talk, I think," Adrian murmured. His hand found her hip. "Have a few drinks, relax in bed. I don't want your day to be ruined because of that asshole."

"He's right," she said into her hands. "I am acting like a whore. But I *like* you, I like this!"

The crowd was parting around them in curious waves, and she was too humiliated to look up. Adrian shushed her, Paul guided her, and by the time they were outside the blur in her eyes was just tears.

"You're not a whore, darling," Adrian said, hugging her tight against him as soon as they made it out into the sunlit day. "You're a proud, liberated woman who knows what she wants and loves getting it. He probably hates queers, too, doesn't he?"

She choked on a laugh. "Oh, God, do they ever."

"They, huh?" Paul asked.

"My grandmother raised me," she said by way of explanation. "She had . . . ideas. Some strong ones."

"Aha," Adrian said.

"There's your baggage," Paul said.

She gladly climbed into the backseat, strained and suddenly tired, waiting to hear the accusing ring of her cell phone. Preemptively, she took it out and turned it off. Adrian crawled in with her and cuddled her against his body while Paul started the car. He murmured pleasant, nonsensical things in her hair, lips pressed to her scalp and hands smoothing up and down her arms. She wouldn't admit she was crying, because it seemed so trivial, just Eric acting like Eric and Grandma being disappointed—but it was a devastating blow, somehow.

She wished she hadn't ruined their date, more than anything.

Chapter Nine

"Because I am your self-appointed sex therapist," Adrian murmured to her as they waited for the elevator in the hotel, "I have devised a novel and intriguingly sexy way to make your afternoon better than your morning, and also serve a psychological purpose."

She laughed at the tone—goofy, overly self-important, designed to amuse her—and reached out to touch Paul's arm. He was giving them a little space while Adrian cheered her up, but she didn't want him to. He belonged even more than she did. It seemed to her that her own issues were waking a few of his, and maybe they could all deal with it together.

"But I will need to consult with my lovely assistant," he continued, nodding to the other man as he stepped in close again with tiny, quirky smile. "So when we get to the room, I want you to sit your pretty self on the couch in the foyer and let me put my plan into action. Can you do that?"

"Is that an order?" she asked, genuinely interested.

"Do you want it to be?" he asked in return as they

crossed the threshold into the elevator, the three of them alone as the door closed. It seemed smaller, hotter, with their bodies next to hers.

What was the game they were about to play? The thought of diving more into those submissive urges and Adrian's skill at manipulating her desires as a top made her shiver. She definitely wanted more of that, more of the skin-tingling, loose-limbed sensation of *giving it up* that she couldn't get enough of.

That, she had less trouble embracing. It bothered her on one level to be a proud, independent woman and still enjoy being ordered around and manhandled, but on another level she could accept that what she liked sexually wasn't what she wanted out of every moment of her day. She knew she wasn't inferior, or anything stupid like that—she just wanted to give away her rigid control. That wasn't wrong.

"What if I say yes?" she countered.

"Then I don't have to ask you if you want to sit in the living room while we get something ready for you," he murmured, voice lower. "I'll tell you to take your clothes off, fold them next to you, and wait on the couch until I come to get you."

"Oh," she managed. Heat raced from her belly all over her body. "Okay."

"Then consider it an order," he whispered, kissing the side of her jaw briefly.

She looked up at Paul to see what he thought, and found his gaze hot on hers, obviously interested. Adrian was the more practiced top, obviously, but

Paul had it in him, too. They were so flexible.

"Will I ever want to—do the part that you do? Be the dominant?" she asked.

"Maybe," Paul said before Adrian answered. "I'm a switch. Adrian is, with an emphasis on topping verbally if not literally, physically."

"I like the sensation of being fucked," Adrian said with a shrug. "Trust me, that doesn't make me a bottom in the D/s sense of the word. I can very much be topping gorgeous there even when I've got his dick in me."

She swallowed hard. The image of that in her mind's eye was breathtaking, and she could so see it, Adrian with his cocky smirk riding Paul's lap while the bigger man was tied down.

"There's still so much I don't know," she said.

"Research and practical exploration," Paul said with a sage tone.

"Maybe I'll try it," she said.

The elevator dinged on their floor and they walked out. The press of their hands on the small of her back now seemed weighted, somehow; they were guiding her, stripping away the vestiges of her control with the simplest of touches. After the disaster at the mall and the tenuous ball of hurt in her chest, lingering and expanding at intervals to make her eyes water again, it was a heady relief. They would take care of her, for now.

I could take care of someone, she thought, *but could I do what they do? Could I be that masterful?*

"Strip and wait patiently," Adrian said when they entered the suite. "I expect you to keep your hands on your thighs, and no wandering."

"Yes, sir," she said.

The words flowed off of her tongue, taking with them another of the burdens weighting her down. It was like flying. She loved the freedom.

They went through the door without her and closed it. Her fingers were shaking, clumsy at first as she stripped out of her shirt and she had to fold it twice to get it neat. She assumed they would want it neat, or Adrian wouldn't have told her to fold them. Next came her pants, and then she unclipped her bra and laid it on the pile. She slipped off her socks, glancing at the door in curiosity, then underwear.

The couch was soft under her bare butt, and she hoped no one else had been sitting on it in the nude, but honestly, it was a hotel room—everything they touched had probably been touched by parts of other people she didn't want to think about. She laid her hands on her thighs, itching with anticipation and the growing warmth between her legs, and waited. Goosebumps prickled her arms at the chill of the room but the core of her body was hot.

What were they planning? Did they want to tie her up? Were they going to roleplay something? Her mind filled in what it could be as she imagined a hundred more and more fantastical scenarios from discipline to bondage to another one of those baths they'd given her where Paul washed her and Adrian fondled her soap-slick skin. She could see where that sort of thing played into the kinky half of the relationship.

The door opened and Adrian leaned out. "Are you ready, sweetheart?"

"Yes, sir," she repeated.

"Then get up and come in here."

He leaned in the doorway as she stood, legs weak at the pressure of his eyes skating down her nude body, past breasts that suddenly felt heavy and in need of touch, to the curve of her hips and further. He made his appreciation blatant with a pleased noise, a low rumble in the back of his throat like a growl, and she let out a quiet breath when she came to stand in front of him, as bare as he was clothed. His hands circled her wrists and he guided her into the room.

Paul had his arms crossed on top of the chair that had previously been at the desk in the corner. It was wood and leather, sturdy, and they'd laid one of the fluffy hotel towels down on it. His smirk was wicked, chin tilted up a bit so he inspected her down the length of his nose, like something he might decide to buy. Her throat was tight and dry, but between her legs was a growing slickness. Adrian guided her to the chair and she sat, one of Paul's hands playing in her hair and twirling locks of it through his fingers.

Adrian said nothing for a long minute, staring down at her with an unreadable but sexy expression. Paul's hands drifted down until they found her arms and he lifted them onto the chair's armrests. The polished wood was cool under her skin. From the bed, Adrian picked up a length of silk that looked to be a green tie and her breath sped.

"I'm going to tie your hands to the chair," he said to her, conversationally. "Because today's about a lesson you should learn all the way to heart, do you understand?"

"What?" she asked.

"I want to make you understand how much you love this," he said, smiling. It was wicked but tender. "You're going to watch. We're going to get naked and do whatever we want to do while you sit and enjoy."

"But I know I like—" she protested.

He cut her off. "Hush. No talking back, darling. You know you like to see your men together, but I don't think you know exactly how much. When you're crying for us to come and touch you, you'll know."

"Oh," she said.

Paul's voice came from behind her, rich and husky with arousal. "When we're done with you, you'll be very, very sure of how much you love this, and no one can take that away. It doesn't matter what they think—it matters what you want."

"Plus," Adrian said as he tied the green tie around her wrist and the armrest. "We'll get to watch you squirm and beg and plead for us. That's definitely a bonus point."

She nodded, testing the knot with a yank of her arm. It was soft enough to not hurt, but the tight knot didn't give a centimeter. If anything, it tightened further. A second tie bound her other wrist and then Paul stepped around the front of the chair. She had a moment to appreciate them, standing next to each other with their eyes on her—the way their bodies differed, the lithe slimness of Adrian next to the sculpted, toned musculature of Paul. Then they shifted, eyes drifting to each other, and the desire there was everything she'd glimpsed between them while they shared her.

Paul moved first, lifting his hands not to Adrian but to unbutton his own shirt. Marissa watched as each button slipped open, baring more of his dark, honey-toned skin. She wondered briefly where his family was from—Middle East? Mediterranean? She didn't care. All that mattered was Paul; gorgeous, kind, and earnest Paul. Adrian's attention was fixed on him just as firmly as he stripped, the shirt fluttering down around his elbows before dropping to the floor.

Next came the belt buckle, undone with both hands and a quick jerk that seemed directly tied to things low in her body. She shivered, thighs clenching together, and nearly groaned as he snaked the belt out of the loops of his pants and wound it around his hand. He surely didn't mean to use it on her, tied down as she was, but she saw Adrian's eyebrows raise a fraction, then lower, an easy smile spreading across his kiss-reddened lips.

"So I top her, you top me?" he asked, husky.

"You've gotten to have all the control, babe," Paul said, tossing out the endearment as easy as breathing. Marissa licked her lips at the casual intimacy. It was as if tying her had allowed them to slip back to their normal, solitary pleasures as a couple. She didn't feel left out or extraneous, but at the same time, she couldn't distract them with a well-placed hand. It was all up to them, every move of this dance. "I think it's my turn, don't you? Aren't you stressed from today, a little worried? Don't you want to let go?"

Adrian swallowed hard, his Adam's apple bobbing visibly. He tilted his chin in a tiny nod. Marissa noticed that he didn't give in as easily as she did. Her body just seemed to melt, to go loose and happy into their dominant touch. Adrian needed coaxing to let go. She wondered, did he enjoy it the same way, or was it different for everyone?

"Good," Paul said. He laid the coiled belt on the bed and Adrian's eyes tracked to it, then to her for one brief, smoldering moment before returning. "You want to make it all better for Marissa, and so do I. It's hard to see such a gorgeous woman so hurt and unsure, isn't it?"

"You know it is," Adrian muttered with a nod. He glanced at her.

"Well, this is how you do it," he replied. "You show her how you let go, and how much you like it, so it's okay for her to like it too."

Her breath caught as Paul grabbed Adrian by the belt and yanked him in close. Adrian blinked, mouth open a bit, some of the tension bleeding from his frame. He moaned a moment later, resting his head on Paul's shoulder. The other man stroked his hair for a moment, cradling him in his arms, then pushed him back.

"Clothes off," he said.

Marissa felt like she couldn't breathe. Adrian lowered his eyes, demure for once, and began to undress. He made no show of it, just efficiently stripped himself until he stood nude and obviously aroused in front of his partner. The clothes were in a haphazard pile, but Paul said nothing of it, just gestured him forward with a crook of his finger.

"There's nothing wrong with this," Paul whispered.

It was for her, even if he didn't look at her. She let a small sigh slip out. Adrian stood with hands at his sides, barely an inch separating his body from Paul's, yet he made no move to touch. Her fingers ached to do it for him, run along that wonderful chest, tweak those small nipples.

"Adrian likes to be treated like a doll, don't you?" Paul said. He didn't wait for a response before continuing. "You like manhandling, Marissa. He does, too, but he likes to make no decisions once he gives it up. Everything is up to me."

She thought about that, didn't know if she had the control to do it. She was already dying to get up and wriggle in between their bodies, touch and lick and suck. Adrian was smiling, she could see, the faintest quirk of lips. His hands were open and relaxed and his posture soft.

Paul tilted his chin up with one large hand spanning his jaw and kissed him soundly, drawing a ragged groan from him and a tremble. Their mouths slid together, Adrian leaning up on his toes as Paul pulled him higher, tongue sliding between his lips. Marissa gasped, eyes tracking down to watch the bounce of the blond man's cock as he stood on tiptoe, wobbling a bit to keep his balance and still breathe through the powerful, owning kiss.

He fell back when Paul pushed him gently, collapsing onto the bed in a sprawl of limbs. Marissa yearned forward in her bonds, toes digging into the plush carpet. She wanted so badly to slide her mouth down the red-flushed length of his cock, fill her mouth with him and then climb up to straddle his waist, guide him inside—

The sight of Paul undoing his pants and stepping out of them distracted her from that. He, too, was fully hard. He wrapped his fingers around himself and stroked once, then let go to climb up onto the bed. She still had a fine view as he reclined against the headboard, legs spread slightly. Adrian watched him through half-lidded eyes, still lax and waiting.

"Suck me," he ordered.

Adrian rolled onto all fours with a hungry growl, running his hands up Paul's legs from his ankles to his hips. Then, aware of his audience, he adjusted his position and tilted his head so that nothing obscured the sight of him opening his mouth and guiding his partner's dick inside. His lips slid down, slowly, inch by inch. He paused three quarters of the way, bobbed once to take a deep breath, and kept going. Marissa shifted, thighs pressed together, her own mouth watering as Adrian swallowed down to the root of Paul's cock.

Paul hissed, a hand on the back of his neck, then moaned. Adrian flexed his hand on the other man's thigh and held, lips pressed to his body, eyes squeezed tightly shut.

"Oh, fuck," Paul whispered. "Breathe, darling."

Adrian pulled off with a gasp, lips glistening wetly and chin also damp. He blinked hard. Marissa groaned and they both looked at her, Paul grinning and Adrian licking his lips. Her body throbbed at their attention, need flickering like fire up her spine. She clamped her lips together, though, refusing to beg—not yet, though she knew she would give in soon. It was deliciously bad to play their game, make them work for it the way they were going to do to her.

The men seemed to grasp her challenging posture and also her trembling desire. Adrian stretched out on the bed, lowering his mouth again to lap at Paul's cock without taking him inside, teasing, then inching down to suck each testicle separately, slowly. The other man groaned his appreciation. He tangled his fingers in Adrian's hair and lifted him up.

"You're having too much fun," he said. "Don't think I don't see you humping the bed like a teenager. Up, hold the headboard."

Adrian was uncharacteristically silent—no joking, no flirting. Marissa guessed it was his way of submitting, of being pliable, to not work his verbal magic and to let Paul lead. He knelt up and grasped the headboard, stretched out on his knees with his head hanging and his cock at stiff attention. It was nearly flat against his stomach, even kneeling.

"I'll give you five with my hand, five with the belt," Paul said, stroking his thighs. His wide palms and fingers seemed to span the tight muscle of Adrian's flanks; Marissa ached to see them dig in a little, squeeze—it was what she would want if she were in Adrian's place. "Not because you've been bad, darling. You've been good. But you want it, don't you?"

Adrian nodded his assent and Marissa watched with wide eyes. She knew now she liked to be bitten, stretched out, tossed around, but would she like this? Didn't it hurt? The tiny pulse of something not quite jealousy pinched at her. Paul knew Adrian to his core, and this made it very clear. He knew exactly what to do and when. Would anybody ever know that about her?

The tension in the room as Paul lifted his hand, his fingers cupped ever so slightly, was enough to cut with a knife. Marissa held her breath; Adrian's fingers were white-knuckled on the headboard and his body trembled; Paul's eyes glittered with fierce emotion. The smack of his palm landing on the other man's upturned butt was like a thunderclap, shockingly loud, and Marissa gasped in surprise before she could stop herself. A pink handprint stayed behind when he lifted his hand again, his attention all for his lover, who was shaking more pronouncedly now, especially through his outstretched arms.

The second slap landed just below the first, on the lower curve of his ass, spreading the pink further. Adrian made no sound but heavy breathing, though his elbows buckled and he lowered himself further, leaning his forearms against the headboard as well. Paul was fixed on his task, shifting to deliver an equal smack to the opposite cheek. Marissa imagined the heat it might bring, the sting, and could not quite grasp the sensation for herself. The fourth spank did draw a small grunt from Adrian, who was clinging to the headboard now. His cock was still stiff as a rod, so Marissa knew he was enjoying it.

Paul reached between his legs then, stroking a hand along his balls and giving a firm caress to his hard-on. Adrian let out a groan that was nearly a cry, shivering suddenly, as if the pleasure had shocked him out of whatever headspace he'd sunken into. The other man smirked, eyes narrowing, and Marissa swallowed hard, again, aching in every part of her body to crawl onto that bed with them. She'd be good. She wouldn't even ask to touch, she just wanted to be close enough to feel their heat. She could practically smell their sweat, the chair was so close to their play, but it wasn't close enough to satisfy her craving.

Paul pinched the back of his thigh a moment later, drawing out a squeak and leaving a tiny red mark. Adrian tossed his hair back and glared over his shoulder, pouting, but his shift in position let Marissa see the way his jaw dropped and his eyes closed when Paul slapped his ass again, hard. He bit his own lip, even, so taken by the feeling. She squirmed with more intent, her pussy wet and her pulse pounding in her veins.

"Patience," Paul murmured, and she couldn't be sure who he was talking to, because Adrian returned to his previous submissive posture, head down between his arms. "Say stop if this is too much."

He picked up the supple leather belt, wrapping the dangerous parts—buckle, latches—in his fist so there'd be no chance of hurting Adrian by accident. Marissa noticed now that it wasn't sewn the way most belts were. It was a softer leather without ridged edges, just a single seam along the far sides that blended in. Adrian moved to draw his thighs together, pressing them in one strong line. There were some things he obviously wanted to protect from the errant snap of the belt, she thought with a sympathetic wince.

Paul paused to look at her. "You seem to enjoy roughhousing, but you might not like this. Adrian enjoys a sharper edge on his submission than most people."

"I'll—" she tried to say, her voice rasping. It caught in her throat, need smothering her. "I—"

"Hush," he said easily.

She did. She had wanted to say *I'll try it*, but couldn't quite manage. Paul went at a side angle with the first strike of leather, snapping harsh and bright red across Adrian's pale thighs. He yelped, jerking with what she thought must be pain and not pleasure, but he relaxed again after barely a moment, still presenting himself for more, and said nothing. Paul's free hand stroked along the raised red mark, tender. Adrian groaned low in his throat and arched into the touch.

His noises of appreciation tapered off when Paul edged back again, switched his angle, and laid an equal stripe across the other thigh, overlapping the first slightly. The crack of leather against skin made her jump. She was so slick now even her thighs were damp with her desire. Adrian let out a low wail, pent-up pleasure and pain equal in the sexually charged sound, and Paul flipped the next strike over his handprint-layered ass. His pale skin took to the marks immediately, red and angry.

Marissa caught herself shifting rhythmically against the towel, clit stiff and throbbing, but she couldn't get enough pressure. This was so hot. Watching them switch their roles, watching in-control Adrian give it up, the way they knew how to please each other. Paul's intense concentration to detail, his desire to cause no harm while giving just the right amount of hurt, was as erotic as the sight of the other man coming undone.

The next two lashes came in quick succession, and she twitched with the sounds of Adrian's cries and the leather hitting flesh. How did it *feel*? The way Adrian collapsed onto his side, eyes fluttering and mouth open on a sigh, seemed so—ecstatic. Paul gathered him close, rolling him onto his back, which prompted a gasp and his eyes flew open. The other man pressed him down against the bed, let him writhe and rub his marked skin against the sheets, and then bent to kiss the curve of his hip.

Adrian stilled, panting hard, wetness on his face—maybe tears, maybe not. She wasn't sure. His hands fumbled to grasp at Paul's shoulders as he lowered his mouth to Adrian's still-hard dick. He took him in, sucking, his cheeks hollowing out with the intensity of it. Adrian moaned, his voice wrecked and hoarse. Two swift pumps of his hips and he was trembling, gasping, coming. Paul swallowed everything, palming his thighs and rubbing the tension from them.

Marissa had managed to keep her mouth closed, her pleas safely inside, for the entire scene. Now, her voice shaking, she managed, "Please—"

Adrian turned his head toward her placidly, a small smile on his mouth. His body was loose-limbed and sated. Paul was still resting between his legs, head pillowed on Adrian's stomach.

"Hmm," he purred out. "Darling, I'm exhausted. Fucked-out. But Paul isn't done yet. Beg him."

"Oh, Paul," she gasped, leaning forward. Her breasts felt heavy, her hair swung into her face. "Paul, please, let me up, please."

His smirk was anything but conciliatory. "Spread your legs."

She did, shifting her hips to show them how wet she was, to prove how much she needed them. Adrian might have been physically done, but the edge that lingered in his voice let her know that he was still interested in playing this game with her. He still wanted to string her pleasure out, tease her until she couldn't take it any more. She was feverishly aware that their theory was spot-on: she was so aroused that she gave no thought to baring her cunt to them, so aroused that no part of her was ashamed of what she was doing, no part of her wanted to stop. She *wanted* this.

It was a desire that she thought, with practice, she could fully own for herself.

Paul slid off of the bed in a sinuous movement, his dick standing out from his body at full hardness. She fought to keep from pressing her legs back together, not out of modesty but out of need for even the slightest pressure on her aching clit. He walked over to her with a sway to his gait, laid his hands over hers. That brief, burning-hot touch made her shudder and her eyes close. She had to have more.

"If we were home," he said. "I'd tie you to the bed and test which toys you liked best, until you were screaming for me. I think the suede flogger would be just right to start. It's soft, but it still feels strong when it slaps your skin."

He patted her inner thigh, barely a smack, and she clenched her jaw to hold in a groan. The second tap of his fingers was harder, sharper, more like a spank. On the tender skin of her inner thigh it stung, but hotly, a warmth that spread up to her pussy. She heard herself panting.

"We could move up to something stronger if you liked it," he murmured. His voice was heavenly, low and dark with want. "Maybe you're like Adrian, you like to hurt once you're revved up."

She wasn't prepared for the full-on slap that landed next. It startled a shriek out of her, a jump in her bonds, but the flare of pain was like nothing she'd ever felt before. She's been spanked as a kid—who hadn't?—but it had never been like this, oh, never. This was unbelievably good.

"Hm," Paul said. He stroked the spot on her leg that was aching now, burning.

"Untie her," Adrian said. She blinked her eyes open to see him propped up on his elbows, watching. Her vision seemed blurry, out of focus. She glanced down at the red mark on her thigh and up at Paul's serious, but still very aroused expression. "Bring her over here and I'll hold her while you play."

The silk slid from her wrists and she tried to stand, but her legs wouldn't support her, shaking as they were with adrenaline and arousal. Paul picked her up, one arm under her knees and the other at her back. He wasn't gentle about it; his fingers dug in and she writhed, helplessly, loving the pressure against her body, the feeling of being crushed against him, held there.

He dumped her on the bed and she bounced, gasping, scrambling to find her balance. She didn't. Adrian grabbed her first, flipping her onto her stomach and grabbing her wrists in his hands. She thought of him as slender but that was only next to Paul's musculature—he was strong. He held her as easily as he would a trembling leaf, stretched out on the bed and dizzy with the manhandling that also made her whole body tense with desire.

Fingers plunged inside her a moment later, three, thick and wide. She screamed for Paul as he fucked her with his fingers, swift and unrelenting, her cunt grasping tightly at him as she shuddered and clenched. The sudden fulfillment after waiting was too much, too soon, and she was left shaking and moaning but unable to climax, waves of raw pleasure crashing over her but not enough to come.

"Slow down," Adrian murmured to Paul over her twisting, shivering body. "Don't let this end so quickly."

She cried out at the loss of his fingers when he pulled away, leaving her unsteady and bereft. The waiting, then the burst of sensation, then emptiness in such quick succession left her nearly sobbing. Adrian shifted her wrists to one of his hands and stroked her hair back from her face, thumb brushing her cheek.

"You're crying, sweetheart," he said. He sounded a bit concerned, but she shook her head, and he seemed to understand. "It's all right. It gets intense, doesn't it? You let go. Just let it all go, and we'll take you high as you've ever been."

The bed shifted as Paul leaned over her to kiss Adrian softly. She laid her head on Adrian's thigh, blinking through damp eyelashes as their mouths pressed softly together. Instead of fighting the loss of control, the bodily confusion, the attacking rush of sensation, she tried to relax and let it happen. Marissa noticed Adrian was half-erect, still partially soft but making a definite effort to continue. She wondered if he had the stamina; it surprised her how much sex they'd been having in such little time.

Their hands, and she could tell it was both of them, helped her stretch out and get as comfortable as she could. She caught her breath and dug her toes into the covers, glancing over her shoulder at Paul. He was smiling. The warmth of it seemed to relax some final knot in her muscles. He laid down along her side, his cock damp at the tip and pressing against her hip. She gave him a pleading glance, but in reality, she had given herself over to this. They could make her wait, and she knew it would only be better.

Adrian passed him a condom from the bedside table, Marissa's wrists still loosely held in his free hand, her body between his legs and head pillowed on his thigh. She shifted in his grip and pressed a kiss to the curve of his hip. He shivered. Paul moved over her, thighs spreading hers, his larger body pressed to her back and his hips nestling against her butt. His cock nudged between her legs, sliding in a long glide against the wet length of her slit. She wriggled back, lifting her hips, trying to get him where she wanted him. His hands stroked down her sides and grasped her hips. As he angled their bodies together, the head of his dick slipping against her pussy, she moaned quietly.

The moan descended into a long, voluptuous sigh as he sank inside an inch at a time, deliciously slow. Marissa felt herself tighten around him, shivers running through her and the heat in her belly spreading out in a flash of desire. Paul made a soft noise as his hips met hers, all of his cock buried inside. Adrian massaged her wrists, switching his grip so he had one hand in each again, their fingers laced. It was less restraint now and more connection. Their interlocked hands tied him into the moment and its eroticism.

Paul lifted her hips a bit further, grinding deeper inside, and reached beneath them. His thumb pressed against the swollen, needy length of her clit. She gasped. He stroked the soft pad of his thumb in a circle and pleasure prickled up her spine. It only multiplied and increased as he drew back, his dick sliding out of her to just the tip, and pumped his hips. The slide of him over the most sensitive parts of her, inside and out, made her breath come quicker. He thrust with intent, shallowly, pushing his dick hard against her g-spot and pulling out a bit just to do it again. Waves of sensation rolled from her cunt outwards, pleasure so sharp and intense that she couldn't even make a sound. She could only pant and gasp.

The thumb at her clit kept moving in a determined, never-speeding massage that stoked her ecstasy higher and higher. Paul was panting above her now, his chest damp with sweat against her back. She felt the tension shaking in his thighs as he fought to keep his measured pace, fucking into her at the perfect angle. She could tell he wanted to let go and just slam into her but he didn't. Despite his panting effort, he kept his pace.

"Going to come," she sighed out.

"Good," Paul groaned. "Me, too."

"You're both so fucking beautiful," Adrian murmured to them, fingers squeezing tight around Marissa's.

She shuddered, a small cry escaping her lips as she struggled to move her hips under Paul's weight and grip. Her body struggled through the wash of pleasure as it crested over her, drawing sharp gasps and shudders as she climaxed. Paul let out a rough yell of his own and slammed deep, bruising and powerful, then did it again. The sudden pounding triggered another hard spasm from Marissa and a short cry as her orgasm continued. Paul came in her with a long groan, grinding their hips together, holding her hard against his body.

"Oh," she gasped.

He managed to roll off of her as he collapsed, drawing himself out. He lay a panting mess, and she equally so. Adrian eased her hands down and ran his fingers through her hair, then reached out to tweak Paul's cheek. Paul grunted and rolled his eyes. Marissa smiled.

"Would you guys like a drink of water?" Adrian offered.

"Yes," she whispered, blinking up at him.

He returned a moment later with a bottled water and pressed it to her lips, letting her sip gingerly in her prone position. Her mouth was parched. She moaned out a thank you and he sat it on the end table.

"You know, I want this to help," he said, eyes on hers. "If I—we—didn't like you as much as we do, we wouldn't be able to go this far. You wouldn't if you didn't trust us, but you do, don't you?"

She nodded. Her emotions seemed to be tied to her body, open and giving. He rubbed the back of her neck, easing tension there, and she relaxed into the grip. He glanced over her at the other man.

"Maybe more than we should," Paul murmured. "What happened to a weekend of kinky, no-strings sex?"

"It's still kinky," Adrian replied, his hand joining Paul's. Their fingers laced and rested on her body. "But you're not a no-strings guy, darling. And I have soft spots, too."

Marissa closed her eyes and wondered if they meant what she thought they meant, but it wasn't the time to think through anything complex. She was too exhausted, wrung-out with pleasure, and a little hungry too. She snuggled in between them, wrapping her free arm around Adrian's waist. Dinner could come later, once she'd had a nap.

Later, alone in the shower stall in the bathroom with the door closed, Marissa gingerly washed herself. There were purpling marks, bites, and scratches all over her. She was actually sore, her thighs weak and shaking. She'd never had so much sex in her life. In fact, she was pretty sure she'd fucked Adrian and Paul more than both of her old boyfriends combined in one weekend, and that was compared to two years of relationships. Still, it was a good ache, even more so because she knew it would stay behind once they were gone, for a few days at least. The weekend was almost over. Checkout was at twelve the next day, and that was it. She blinked hard, rinsed herself off, and denied that her face was wet from tears. It was just the water.

The small bathroom was quiet. Outside, she heard the sound of the men moving around and getting ready for sleep. The dinner they'd had at the hotel restaurant had been full of laughter and warm comfort. It was exactly what she'd needed after the intense, sexual, boundary-shaking afternoon. Even thinking about the sight of Adrian's face as he was spanked, as he left go of all of his iron control, made her tremble. It was so erotic, just the memory could spread a weak heat over her body. She wasn't ready for more, though—she was done. There was only so much a body could take.

Dry and wrapped in a towel, she stepped out into the bedroom. The lamp at the bedside was on. It cast a dim glow through the otherwise dark room. Adrian was already cuddled up with the pillows, blinking lazily at her with a smile. Paul was sitting on the edge of the bed, elbows on his thighs and a book in his hand. He looked up.

"Ready for bed?" he asked.

"Maybe," she murmured.

"Come on in," Adrian replied.

He lifted the sheets invitingly. Paul put his book down on the bedside table and swung his legs up onto the bed. Marissa climbed in between them, nude. Their bodies pressed to hers. Paul switched off the light. In the darkness of the bedroom, naked skin against naked skin, Marissa couldn't hold in the quiet sniffling breaths that snuck out with her tears. Hands of two sizes held her close, breath ruffled her hair, lips touched her neck and shoulder. The men said nothing, comforting her instead with their touch.

It was a long night, and none of them slept well.

Chapter Ten

The sun was too bright. Marissa squinted around the hotel room to make sure she'd missed no clothes or possessions. It seemed strangely bare without their clothes in disarray on the floor. Paul and Adrian had lugged their shared suitcase to the anteroom and were murmuring quietly. She heard their voices but not the words. An inane urge to steal the sheet from the bed, or a towel they'd used to dry after their last bath, or *something at all* struck her. She wanted a memento. They'd taken no pictures. Paul and Adrian had paid, so there wouldn't even be a receipt to treasure.

She swallowed, darted a glance at the door to the other room, and moved quietly over to the bed. She chose something smaller than a sheet: a pillowcase, pulled off the pillow, bundled up and stuck in her suitcase. She zipped it up, feeling ridiculous and a little guilty, but at least she would have something to remember them by once the bow-legged soreness in her inner thighs and the bite marks healed.

After heaving out a sigh and blinking hard to clear the

sudden dampness at the corners of her eyes, she hefted the handle of her suitcase. A quick scrub of her hand over her face and she was ready. Five steps carried her into the anteroom, where Adrian was leaning into Paul and muttering at him with a level of intensity that seemed odd. She paused in the doorway and they glanced at her. Adrian's cheeks were hectic red, his lower lip caught in between his teeth.

"Would you like to—" Paul started, his voice a bit unsteady.

"Dinner? At our house?" Adrian blurted.

Paul closed his eyes and leaned his head back, a gesture that seemed to Marissa a bit like praying for patience. Adrian fidgeted. They seemed so off-balance that it threw her off also and silence settled between them.

"Oh, I mean," Adrian continued. "You don't have to, it's all right."

"No, no," she said, startled. "I'd love to."

"This is awkward," Paul said.

He marched over to her and laid his hand over hers on her suitcase handle. His fingers were damp with nervous sweat, the only thing revealing his discomfort. She glanced down at their hands and up into his eyes. There were tiny crow's feet at the corners, puckered with his tense expression. Her mouth was slightly open as she searched for words.

"I don't want this to be over yet," he said. "Neither does Adrian. I don't want to say goodbye in a hotel at noon."

"God," she whispered. Her weight seemed to shift

without her consent and she leaned into his chest. "Me neither. I want to come. If you're sure."

"I'm not sure about anything," he said. His hands moved to pull her into a hug.

"Sorry," Adrian muttered. "I was nervous, okay?"

Marissa looked around Paul's side and smiled at him. "I got to see you nervous. I'm okay with that. I thought you were totally unflappable and in control."

Adrian huffed comically. Her smile widened.

"Would you like to follow us to our house? I can give you directions, so if you lose us you can still find the way," Paul said.

"Okay," she replied.

They stepped apart and she made sure to cross the room and draw the other man into a similarly soft embrace, burying her face against his throat and inhaling his musky but lavender-tinged scent.

"You still smell like that bath soap," she murmured, then glanced up at him.

His blinking was a bit too rapid to be anything but fighting off some emotion. She let him go and grabbed her suitcase. Paul tore off the sheet from the top of the hotel stationary sheet, on which he'd written directions, and handed it to her. She tucked it away in her back pocket.

"Shall we?" Adrian said.

There was gravity to the request that had been missing, though hinted at, all weekend. Marissa had to take a deep breath before she managed to say, "Of course."

This dance was new to her. As they made their

way to the elevators in peaceable quiet she struggled to figure out what steps came next in the waltz of companionship. Something had shifted if they weren't ready to part yet, if they wanted her to come to their home. But it could have been simple sentimentality, wanting to prolong the weekend and get the most out of it. Or maybe, like her, they couldn't bear the thought of letting go.

In the lobby, she kissed them both on their cheeks as they meandered toward the counter to check out. She had to stand on tiptoe for Paul. Walking out the door while they settled up the room, staying behind, was like crawling through taffy. She dragged her feet, glancing over her shoulder every few moments to catch another glimpse. She would have felt worse if they weren't both doing the same thing. Their eyes tracked her as she struggled to leave. Finally, the sliding doors shut behind her and she stood under the sunlight, blinking hard and trying to remember where she'd put her car on Friday evening.

It was a little ridiculous how much her chest ached, as if a fist was squeezing her ribcage. She was going to their house, to spend more time with them, and being apart for the length of a car ride wasn't so important. It was just difficult to convince herself of that. After heaving her suitcase into her trunk, she climbed into the driver's seat and rested her head on the wheel. Halfheartedly she pulled out her cell phone and turned it back on.

There were five messages. She winced.

One was from Lita—the other four, her grandmother. With a fortifying gulp of air, she pressed the "voicemail" button and put the phone to her ear to listen. Lita's message was first, from Friday, and all she did was wish Marissa luck and adventure, then ask for gory details later. It made Marissa smile. She wasn't sure she wanted to tell too much about the weekend. It was too personal, too perfect.

The next message wiped the smile off of her face.

"Your cousin cannot be right about what he saw you doing," came her grandmother's voice, tight with anger. "Call me. I want to talk about this fit of yours."

The next three went downhill in invective and anger, more incensed by her lack of response than anything. As if she owed an explanation, an apology, then a swift promise to dress in a drab gray apron and never see a man in private again. She snapped her phone closed and jammed it back into her pocket.

For once, she was angry, too. She loved her grand-mother, was eternally grateful to her, but honestly, she was an adult, and this made her happy. This was who she was. Like Adrian, like Paul. If they could embrace their own needs and publicly be proud of them, so could she. That was all there was to it. She blew out a breath and started the car. At least the weekend wasn't over. She could put off what she would say to her gran until later and enjoy another few hours of happiness with her—lovers.

The drive to their house was scenic, through a lovely suburb outside of the city proper. It would be at least thirty minutes from the university campus. She tried to cancel out thoughts of how she could visit and when because that hadn't been put on the table. She had no idea what to expect now, and it wasn't up to her. It was their relationship, their partnership she was nudging in on. They had to say it first. They had to ask. She couldn't, and she knew that.

It worried her a little that she knew she would say yes to another date right away.

Their car was already in the drive, the front door open with a glass outer door closed against the outside. It gave her a glimpse of their living room. The open door was inviting. The outside of the house was dark red brick interspersed with dark gray bricks at odd intervals to create a pretty pattern. It was a ranch-style, large in comparison to her apartment though the same size as its neighbors on a small but well-kept lot. She was impressed and a bit daunted. It would take her another ten years of working and saving for her to get a house like that.

Marissa turned her car off and stepped out, tucking her hands nervously in her pockets as she walked across the yard and up the three steps to the porch and the front door. She knocked on the metal edge of the glass outer door. Almost immediately, Paul appeared and opened it, ushering her in. She glanced around the living room. Warm, dark brown leather furniture was arranged in a semi-circle around a TV and entertainment center. Paul must have been perched on the armchair closest to the door.

"Adrian's fixing some lunch," he said. "We were pretty hungry, so we figured you would be too."

"Absolutely," she said.

Paul laid his arm over her shoulders, cuddling her close to his body, and walked her through the wide archway to the kitchen. Adrian was wielding a spatula at a pan with a determined look on his face. The smell of cooking meat was heavy and delicious in the air. He glanced over his shoulder at them and smiled.

"Hamburgers acceptable? It was all I could thaw out on quick notice."

"That's just fine," Marissa said.

She took the chair that Paul pulled out for her and settled at their four-seater table. He sat across from her, lacing his fingers together on the tabletop. It was a homey scene, Adrian cooking and Paul sitting with her at the table. That didn't make it any easier for Marissa to relax. Tomorrow was Monday. Back to work, away from this.

"I don't know what to say," she admitted.

The other man cocked his head and gave her a searching look. "About?"

"Damn," she said with a laugh. "I don't even know. I just—this. Being with you guys. It's so . . . comfortable. I've never been this comfortable. It makes me nervous. I mean, I can't stay. It's temporary. We're probably treading on unsteady ground by doing *this*." She gestured expansively at the house.

"It's harder to let go than I thought it would be," Paul admitted.

Adrian came over and put a plate of hamburgers in between them on the table. His expression was more solemn now, less playful. "Nobody was counting on how intense everything got. I was really expecting the woman who answered our ad to be somebody from the BDSM community who was used to this kind of thing. I'm glad we got you instead."

"Thanks, I think," she said.

He half smiled and swept away to gather up buns and condiments. Paul and Marissa sat, thoughtfully quiet, until he returned and set the table. She was glad to know she wasn't the only one feeling so off balance, but it worried her that she'd obviously affected them. What if their relationship didn't work the right way any more?

"I hope I haven't made problems for you," she murmured.

"No, no," Adrian said. He patted her on the shoulder and took the seat at the head of the table, between them both. "Things just happen this way sometimes. You're— I'm very fond of you, already."

"Me, too," Paul said.

"I like you both a lot," she said.

"Now that we've got that settled," Adrian said. "Let's eat. Then we can cuddle. I want to get another cuddle in, before—well. You know."

She nodded her understanding and began assembling her sandwich. It was all very normal. The steady pulse of an ache that was growing in her chest wasn't, but she'd be damned if she'd let the sorrow set in early and ruin her last few hours. Lunch itself passed quickly, quietly. It was a companionable silence despite the discomfort they were all sharing. A weekend of sex had been wonderful, but the strings that had appeared over the nights together weren't.

"Let's go to bed," Paul suggested, sounding weary, as he pushed aside his empty plate. "There's hours of day still left."

Marissa took Adrian's offered hand and Paul hooked a finger through his partner's belt loop, so they walked connected down the hallway. She glanced in the guest room and a small office before they reached the door at the end of the hall and went inside. Their bedroom was painted a pleasant chocolate color with cream highlights and baseboards. It made the space seem warm and inviting. Their bed was huge and piled high with pillows, some of which had spilled onto the floor. No one had tidied the covers before they'd left for the weekend.

Adrian tugged at the waist of her pants and she jumped a bit, giving him a shy glance. It was a little different, stripping in broad daylight in their bedroom without the pressure of lust guiding her. All the same, she pulled her shirt over her head and unhooked her bra, dropping them into a pile. She saw them both disrobing as she stripped out of her pants and underwear. Nude, she climbed up onto the broad, soft mattress. The sheets were crisp under her knees and hands.

"Mm," Adrian murmured contentedly as he climbed in beside her, pulling the covers up. Paul's taller body pressed against her other side and she rolled onto her back so she could see them both, touch them both. "I need this."

His voice was raw, unexpectedly emotional. Marissa looked away from the revealing emotion on his face and found Paul was staring at him, a soft look like wonder on his own. Adrian guided her onto her side with a push so she faced Paul and huddled against her back, his hands wrapped tightly around her stomach. He buried his face in her neck. She felt the slight dampness of tears. The warmth and smoothness of his body pressed against every inch of her from calves and up was soothing.

Paul tangled his legs with theirs and dropped an arm over them both, facing her. She was eye level with his chin. A brief tilt of her head and she pressed a kiss to the side of his mouth. He shifted to give her his lips and she planted a sweet, close-mouthed kiss to them. He moved to press another to the top of her head and gathered them in against him. It wasn't that her body didn't react to all of their beautiful, naked skin against hers, but that it wasn't about sex. They'd had plenty of that, plenty of ways.

This was what she needed, they needed, to say goodbye. She breathed in the musk of Paul's cologne, her face in the crook of his shoulder, and relaxed into the feeling of being held. Adrian's hands were still gripping her as if he was afraid she'd slip away. She fumbled one of hers back to grasp him in return, clumsily hugging him closer with a hand on his hip.

He sighed against her hair, almost a sob, and Paul clutched them into a tighter hug. She felt her own eyes stinging. The overwhelming heat and presence of these men and their candid emotional intimacy were too much.

She cried quietly, without much movement, but knew Paul must have felt the wetness on his skin. He said nothing to reprimand her. If anything, she thought he might have been crying too. The catharsis of holding each other and letting out the impending sorrow was perfect.

"I don't want to go back to my apartment, or work, or anything else," she confessed weakly. "You've gotten under my skin."

"I know, sweetheart," Adrian whispered. "Damn, I know."

Paul kissed her forehead, then her nose, then her mouth. She sighed into the touch and let him deepen the embrace, their mouths sliding together. She felt his restrained passion and his unspoken need. What were they going to do? There was nothing for it but to go home, and deal with the life ahead of her. It was a good life. It just seemed empty without Paul and Adrian in it.

"But I know you must be a good professor," Paul murmured. "So I know you want to go back to that."

She nodded.

"And you'd get tired of not having any clothes to change into," Adrian joked. "So you'd have to go home sometime."

That forced a small laugh from her. "I'm sorry. I know I'm being a pain."

"No, you're not," Adrian said.

"It's hard for us, too," Paul reminded her.

Marissa snuggled in tighter between them, hugging them as if it meant that time would stand still. But it wouldn't, and she knew that.

"Let's just nap," she said. "I don't have to go yet."

"Amen," Paul said.

It was easier than she thought it would be to fall asleep cradled in their embrace, despite her internal upheaval. She drifted off into a dreamy haze within moments. The soft murmur of their voices woke her halfway at one point when the light was low, but then they quieted and she heard a small snore from Adrian. He'd fallen back asleep. Paul's eyes were half-lidded and he met her curious, sleepy gaze.

"A little longer," he breathed.

"Yes," she replied.

But the spell of sleep was broken, and now she tried instead to memorize the feel of their embrace and the way they touched her, touched each other. Adrian stirred finally after what could have been another hour or only ten minutes, she wasn't sure. The light from their windows said it was evening. Time to be heading home.

"I have to go," she said.

"I know," Adrian muttered.

"We'll see you out," Paul said. "Don't lose touch. Please."

"I have your e-mail address," she said.

Dressing was like a dream in and of itself, hazy and slow with reluctance. Marissa found herself lingering over straightening her hair in their bathroom and staring at herself in their mirror. It was time. She went out to the living room and they put on a brave front of meeting her at the door, arm in arm.

They hugged as one unit, mouths finding mouths and hands questing for a last grab and a last feeling. She was out the door and on the way to her car before she could stop herself. It was almost like running away because if she stopped to speak she wouldn't be able to go. Moisture blurred her vision. She managed to get behind the wheel of her car and saw them standing on the porch, waving.

It was easy to lift her hand in return, easy to smile, but impossible to start the car. She found she could do it even though she thought she couldn't.

She was halfway home before she had to pull over at a gas station and sob, her heart breaking like she'd never felt it break before. She'd never been in love until now, she thought, and wasn't that just a damn shame.

Work the next day was a harsh snap back to reality. The scarves had made a return just because she needed to cover the lingering marks on her neck and long sleeves were necessary because somebody had left a hickey on her inner elbow. She didn't even remember that happening.

So when Marissa collapsed into her chair at the podium before her classroom filled, she was exhausted and hot, already tired before the day even started. She'd barely slept the night before. Too long of a nap during the day and too much hurt balled up in her chest. It wasn't Paul or Adrian's fault. It was just having to give them up so soon. But really, they'd never been hers.

The auditor came in smiling but his expression had a damper once he looked at her.

"Are you ill?" he asked.

"A little," she lied. "I just feel under the weather. I'll be better soon."

He frowned but nodded. "Don't hesitate to take a personal day if you're sick. I won't grade you down for that."

"I know," she said with a smile. It was mostly forced, but not completely. He really was a nice guy. "Like I said, I'm sure it'll pass."

Lita was waiting for her when she got home with a bottle of gin and a bag of limes. Marissa barely had the energy to raise an eyebrow at the fact that her best friend had appeared on her apartment steps with liquor. Her neighbors were going to think she was an alcoholic or some kind of party girl. Lita's smile mellowed when she looked her over.

"Not a good time?"

Marissa sighed. "Great time. Too great."

"Oh, honey," Lita said.

The hug almost undid her. "Stop, I'm going to cry."

"Let's get you inside, lovebird," Lita murmured and ushered her over to her own couch once she opened the door. She found herself divested of scarf and briefcase and with a drink in hand in short order. "Now. Was it good?"

"Oh, God." Marissa half-laughed. "It was better. It was perfect. It was—everything I ever wanted. I loved it. I loved *them*."

Lita shook her head and settled with her own drink. "Then we're going to get all kinds of fucked up tonight and you're going to cry it out and feel better. Once the lonely passes, you'll be able to enjoy the memories."

"Have you ever—" she started and couldn't finish.

"Fallen in love too quickly?" she whispered. "Yeah, honey. I just don't talk about it. If it's meant to be, it's meant to be. If it's not, you have to move on."

"My grandmother found out," Marissa confessed.

Lita winced. "Oh."

"I know. I don't know how to deal with it."

"You know, maybe you shouldn't," Lita said. "It's her problem, not yours. You were happy. She's the one who's upset."

"I know that in my head."

The lime-and-gin drink was too strong and it tasted a little bit like Pinesol. Marissa drank it anyway. Lita had the right plan: get tanked. She hadn't done that in forever, years at least. Now was a good time. Especially since she doubted she had any e-mail from the men she wished were a part of her life.

"I'm going to make an appointment with a therapist. A kink-friendly therapist," she announced to the room or Lita or both.

Lita said, without pause, "Thank God."

They both laughed, surprised, and Lita toasted her. Their glasses clinked. Marissa smiled, and it was watery, but it was there. She had a life to live. She had to learn to accept herself. She had to get out there and do things with the newfound passion locked up inside her.

For the time being, though, it was all about moving past the pain in her gut.

Chapter Eleven

Marissa's pen flowed in smooth black lines over the pages in the small leather-backed notebook. She had her feet tucked under her, sitting in her bed with her laptop open at one elbow. The nights were coming so soon now. It seemed like barely a week since she'd been grasping at the last of summer, starting her first semester teaching. There was only one week left before the winter holidays. The air was crisp and sharp outside. She'd taken to wearing scarves again, though not to hide anything—just because she liked the colors.

The notebooks were the best suggestion Doctor Ringel had given her. As she wrote her dreams and fantasies, so many of them starring those-men-who-will-not-be-named, they came to life for her. They weren't a burden but a joy, something to thrill in. Not to mention, the constant effort at writing beautiful erotic scenes to make her body warm had improved her craft significantly, if she said so herself. Even her essays and scholarly work had more flair.

The sudden jangle of her phone ringing made her jump, pen skidding on the paper. She huffed, tossed the notebook aside in the middle of a scene about having two pairs of hands caressing her body, and picked up the cell phone from her bedside table. The number showing on the screen had her heart in her throat in an instant. She hadn't forgotten it. Three months wasn't such a long time that she would have let the memory of that number slip away.

"Hello?" she answered. It was mostly a steady sound, only a little bit of a quaver.

"Hello there," said Adrian. The sound of his voice, the teasing lilt to it and the rich warmth of his affection was enough to make Marissa close her eyes and just breathe for a moment. Her chest was tight with renewed emotion. "Is this a good time?"

"Yes, sure," she babbled. "What are—what have you been up to lately?"

It was such an awkward sentence that she winced. "Paul and I have been thinking quite a bit, mostly. Is it the end of the semester yet?"

"In a week," she said.

"Damn, misjudged it," he said with a snort of laughter.

"What is it, Adrian?" she asked.

He was quiet for a moment, though she heard his breathing. When a week had passed, she'd just assumed they weren't going to contact her again. A month, and therapy, made her even more certain. It wasn't that the good doctor had advised her against seeking them out—the opposite, really—but she'd decided to wait. It was their relationship she would be intruding on. It would have to be their first move.

"We were wondering, if you . . ." he paused mid-sentence, clearing his throat. "God, this is hard, darling. Are you seeing anyone?"

"No," she answered.

It was a thoroughly uncharitable but still somehow sweet thrill she got, listening to suave Adrian behave like an awkward teenager. She would let him continue this at his own pace.

"Would you like to be?" he asked.

"What are you boys offering?" she asked.

"Us," he said, and it was so desperate that it made her heart skip a beat. She heard longing, and perhaps a bit of pain, in that one word. "Just us. Would you like to talk to Paul?"

"I assume you've spent the past three months debating this amongst yourselves, and you've decided it's the right choice?" she asked. "I want to be sure, you know. I don't think I could take another weekend and then having to leave again."

"I'm sure," Adrian said. There was the sound of shifting bodies, then Paul's voice, "I am, too."

"Hi there," she said.

"Hello," he replied, his voice low.

"So what is this going to be?" she asked. "Are you asking me on a date, so we would be dating, the three of us?"

"I'm not looking for just sex," he said. "Neither is Adrian. We want you to be with us. We want to at least—try. I can't let it go without trying, seeing where things lead."

She closed her eyes and sighed out a breath. Her heart was pounding, her mouth dry, her brain yammering at her to just say yes, say yes, say yes.

"Where would you like to have our first date?" she whispered.

"Thank you," he said fervently.

"Italian?" Adrian suggested, muffled.

"I heard him, and that sounds fine," Marissa answered.

There was a beat of silence. "I missed you," Paul said.

"I missed you, too," she said. "I thought some distance would make it less intense, but—talking to you both, it all comes right back."

"We had to give you space, and us space to figure it out," Paul said. "It would have been a bad idea to jump right in. Even if it hurt to say goodbye."

"I agree," she said. "You know, I've been seeing a therapist. I think you'll find I have a few ideas of my own now, about what I like."

"Really?" he said with interest. "What about your family?"

She sighed. "Things are strained, but I refuse to pretend to be something I'm not or to feel guilty about it. We'll come to terms eventually."

"I can't wait to see you," Paul said.

"Me, neither," Adrian added.

She smiled. "We should really have just done a three-way call, you know."

"Too late now," Adrian said cheerfully. He must have

stolen the phone back. "So, we'll see you tomorrow night? Or would you rather wait 'til Sunday?"

"No, Saturday's fine," she said. "I'll meet you there?"

"I'll e-mail you the address. Around six?"

"Absolutely," she said.

Another long, heavy pause.

"Sweetheart," Adrian said, and this time it was he who sounded choked up. "I can't tell you how this makes me feel. You'll see us again?"

"Of course I will," she said. "I haven't thought about anyone else since I left."

"I—" He stopped. She imagined the words he wanted to say and wouldn't, not yet. "I'll see you tomorrow."

"Goodbye," she said. "And sleep well."

"We will," he said.

She hung up with more effort than it should have taken and flopped back onto her bed. Her eyes were burning, hinting at tears, but they would be of joy and not sadness. Her e-mail program pinged a moment later. Adrian had sent her a short message, just the address, and a small heart typed in at the end. She closed the laptop and moved all of her work onto the floor. She was ready for sleep now, and knew she'd have excellent dreams.

She was going to see them again. They weren't gone from her life. They wanted to date. She had wished for it, dreamed it, but never thought it would be real. She tried to remind herself that there were no guarantees it would work out, but she couldn't convince her own mind to be less happy. It just wasn't going to work.

*

The first thing Marissa noticed when she entered the restaurant—unfortunately fifteen minutes late, as her car had been nearly out of gas and she'd had to take the time to fill it—was that Adrian's hair had grown longer. It was a curtain of pale blond around his face now instead of just a shaggy mane. Paul, who had his back to her from the angle of their booth, still had the same short haircut. She moved through the tables toward the booths at the far side of the restaurant where they were sitting.

Adrian noticed her first, and the way his face lit up with a smile made her chest feel tight. He really was happy to see her. She felt her own lips move in response, grinning. Paul turned in his seat, one arm tossed over the back of the booth, to look at her as she approached. He, too, couldn't hide his pleasure at her arrival.

"Hi," she said, sliding into the booth next to him. Under the table, Adrian's foot found hers immediately, pressing them together. "How are you?"

"Better now that you're here," Adrian said.

Paul hummed his agreement and dropped his arm around her shoulders to hug her against the line of his body. It was still a familiar, pleasant sensation, as if it had only been a day since she'd last hugged him. She inhaled the musk of his cologne and leaned up to press a kiss to his jaw.

"We barely managed to wait," Paul admitted. "I wanted to call you the next day. But—we thought letting you finish your semester and get things settled might be better. Give us steady footing to start this, whatever it'll be."

"I had a lot going on," she admitted. "I think the doctor I've been seeing has really helped. She's very, ah, 'kink-positive' is the term she used, I believe. I'm much more comfortable."

"Good," Paul said. Adrian nodded. "I'm glad you're happy."

"Not as happy as I could be if I had you," she said to them.

"Well," Adrian said. "Here we are. I want to do this. I want to date. I want a *relationship* with you, with Paul, with all of us. Is that what you want?"

"It won't be easy," she said, glancing between them.

"It never is," Paul said.

"Just as long as we're clear," she replied with a smile. "I want to be with you both, too. I want this to be equal."

"Then we're all on the same page." Paul hugged her tighter for a moment, then let her go so she could pick up the menu and look it over. "Nobody here has to work tomorrow, right?"

"I don't," she said. "I'll have finals to grade next weekend, but for now, I'm free."

"Would it be uncouth to suggest we break the not-on-the-first-date rule?" he asked.

She looked between Paul's handsome, boyish grin and Adrian's flirtatiously wicked expression, a warmth kindling in her belly. They'd waited long enough, she thought. To hell with the rules.

"Your place or mine?" she asked.

"Is your bed big enough?" Adrian asked.

"Who says we have to use the bed?" she replied.

His smirk deepened. He winked. "*Touché*."

"God," she said, almost a sigh. "I missed you both so much, you don't even know."

"You won't have to miss us any more," Paul said. He kissed the top of her head. Adrian reached across the table to grasp her hand, squeezing reassuringly. "You're our girlfriend now."

She shivered, blinking hard to keep her eyes from watering. "And you're my boyfriends, aren't you?"

"Of course, darling," he muttered against her hair.

"Good," she said.

The spectacular bruise on Marissa's lower back had not yet faded by the last day of her classes. She sat gingerly in the hard plastic chair behind the desk and watched students scribble their final exams. The pile of their graded essays on the corner of the desk drew a longing glance every now and then from someone half-finished with their exam. It was a fifty-fifty split for the grade: half paper, half test. They were understandably nervous.

Her auditor was there, a cup of coffee in his hand that he toyed with absently. Their eyes met every few minutes over the students' heads. She shifted to try and take pressure off of the aching spot on her back.

It hadn't been either of her boyfriends' faults, really. It was just that the kitchen countertops weren't as sturdy in her apartment as she'd thought they were, and they were definitely more slippery, so when Adrian's foot slipped on the tile and he dropped her a few inches she slammed her lower back against the ridged edge of the counter.

He'd apologized profusely and the yelping had brought Paul from the living room to see them half-clothed and suddenly unable to continue fucking, judging by the expression on Marissa's face. It had hurt more than she'd expected. Adrian felt suitably awful and went out to buy her a heating pad. He'd applied it to her back, and licked every inch of her in apology until she was moaning with something much better than pain. After he'd made her come with his mouth, she'd watched them together. They had traded blow jobs, messy and wet and thoroughly delicious to see.

The thought made her smile. They were due for dinner again after her last class of the semester. She couldn't wait. It was still a fresh, new, exciting relationship, but there were emotions running deeper than any of the three were quite ready to discuss yet. She suspected they would be, soon enough, but for now it was still scarily new and intense.

The timer on her desk dinged and students put down their pencils reluctantly. She handed out papers, collected the exams, and finally found herself in an empty room, except for the auditor.

He stood and approached her desk.

"How did I do?" she asked.

"Very good," he said. "You won't have to worry about keeping your job. It's settled. You're a fine instructor."

"Thank you," she said.

"And now I'm going to do something unprofessional," he said. She blinked up at him, noticing a faint flush on his cheeks, almost hidden by his beard scruff. "Would you like to have dinner with me?"

"Oh," she said. She smiled, gently. "I'm afraid I'm already seeing someone, but thank you."

He nodded, then gave a little shrug. She was glad he didn't seem terribly put out. Benefit of age, she supposed. "Too late, huh?"

She took the hand he offered her up and gathered the exams into her bag.

"Yeah," she said. "I had to get some things sorted first, but I think things are going pretty well now."

"Well, congratulations," he said with a smile. "Lucky man."

"Men, actually," she said with a laugh. He raised an eyebrow and she grinned. "Have a good night."

"You, too," he said.

Marissa walked out of the classroom with her bag over her shoulder, head held high and grinning. She was off to dinner with her boyfriends, then there were three weeks before the start of the next semester. That was plenty of time to get acquainted.

Three in
Love

Chapter One

Heather dropped her carry-on bag just inside the apartment door and collapsed onto the leather couch with a sigh. Every muscle in her body ached. An eight-hour flight with one short layover was just ridiculous. Through the still-open door she heard thumping, a muffled curse, and a masculine grunt.

"Don't drop my suitcase," she called. The leather, warm from the afternoon sun streaming in the windows, soothed her. The boys had been right about wearing hot-weather clothes. Back in Ohio the air was still crisp, but in southern Nevada, barely into April, it was already broiling.

"What did you pack?" Andy gasped, hauling the huge black case through the front door. His brown hair stuck to his face, damp with sweat and framing his strong cheekbones and hazel-green eyes. "Your brick collection?"

"This one's worse," countered Daniel. She rolled her eyes at them while they settled the two suitcases and closed the door. "I know you had to pack a lot of your stuff in here to save shipping the rest, but goddamn."

"That's why I've got two big strong men to carry them for me," she said with a grin, looking over the back of the sofa at them. Daniel was less sweaty than Andy, but his tank top clung to his muscular chest in all the right places. She could see his nipples through the thin white fabric. His short cropped hair was almost midnight black and his eyes were a deep, chocolate brown; the slight tan of distant Asian ancestry gave him a perpetual glow.

Andy's hand slid around to cup Daniel's hip while he grinned back at her and she clamped down firmly on her libido. They were not for her to sample; oh, no. Andy and Daniel had been dating long before they'd moved out to the sunny west and left her behind. A few fumbled kisses in their teenage years weren't enough to count. They were firmly, happily in love. She'd just have to find somebody new.

"I'm so glad you decided to come out here," Andy said, flopping onto the couch next to her. "The graduate programs here really are great. You'll have to meet my advisor."

"I couldn't stand it any more," she said. His hand found her upturned palm and squeezed it. "I missed you both so much. And after I graduated, it wasn't as if there was any reason to stay."

"Yeah," Daniel replied, planting himself onto the arm of the couch on her other side. "We were hoping. That's why we got the two-bedroom place."

She rolled her eyes. "No, you just have bad financial planning."

"Or we knew you couldn't resist our lure."

She laughed. It was true. No matter how much it seemed to hurt her other attempts at dating, she couldn't get her mind off her best friends. Nobody else measured up, and she had a feeling they never would. Being in their apartment and seeing them, their photos of her, and their old leather couch was like stepping into a home she'd temporarily lost.

"It's good to be here," she said warmly.

"Let's get washed up," Daniel said. "Then we can take you out on the town and show you all you need to see. Unless you want to unpack some of that ton of stuff?"

"I only have one more big box in the mail," she reassured them. "Books. I sold the furniture. It was crappy anyway."

"True," Andy said. "And you should have space in your room for a shelf. Want to see it?"

"I'll go hop in the shower while you kids look around," Daniel said.

Heather lost her response as he stripped his thin tank top off and tossed it on the couch. His back looked like a Greek statue, all fine muscle and sleek curves. He glanced over his shoulder at the pair of them frozen, watching, and smiled before sauntering down the hall. She swallowed and stood straighter. That show had been for Andy, and if she was going to live with them—both of them—she needed to stop thinking about those casual touches and hints back home. A year was a long time to forget about someone. They were settled and happy without her messing things up trying to wedge into their relationship.

"This way," Andy said after a moment.

The apartment wasn't anything special by design; to the left of the living room was a kitchen with an open dining room. On one side of the hall was the bathroom, its door shut and water running within. On the other, an empty room beckoned her. Andy and Daniel's room was at the end. She stepped into her new home, taking in the bare walls. The boys had an empty computer desk ready for her, but there was no bed or dresser.

"Obviously, I'll need to pick up a few things," she said. "But I really like it. Thanks for letting me come."

"We weren't joking about getting the second bedroom for you," Andy said, bumping her shoulder. "We missed you."

"You know, some people would think this was odd," she joked.

"Like Devin?" he said, lips curving into a frown.

"Oh, hell," she said, rolling her eyes. "We broke up as soon as you guys moved. If he couldn't handle me having guy best friends, we couldn't date. End of story."

"I recall him accusing me in one sentence of both being a fag and trying to steal his woman," Andy deadpanned.

"Well, like I said. We broke up shortly thereafter."

"Good," Andy murmured. The water cut off across the hall. "Want me to drag the suitcases in here?"

"Sure," she said. "I'll help."

"They're kind of heavy," he said, raising one fine eyebrow.

"I got them to the plane, didn't I?" she said, grinning. "No wuss, me."

"You're just a regular Amazon," he replied with a smile.

She smiled back. It was good to be home, even if that home ended up being across the country. Andy strode out of the bedroom and she followed. Daniel cracked the bathroom door open and peered out at them, his hair still damp and glistening with water.

"Forgot to get a towel," he said. "Pass me one?"

"Oh, yeah," Andy said, brushing past Heather to open the hall closet. "The closet is out here in the hall instead of in there. There's a lot of streaking going on around here, thanks to that."

"Ah," she said, trying not to leer. Her attempt wasn't successful, but Daniel just laughed and grabbed the towel from Andy with a wink.

The other man shrugged and went back to her suitcases. She tipped one onto its rollers and grunted at the sudden weight on her arms. While scrambling backwards down the hall wasn't exactly an attractive maneuver, it kept her from losing her grip or balance. Andy laughed, but he imitated her, lugging the second case. The bathroom door opened again just as they finished dropping them in the middle of the room.

"Damn," Daniel said, striding out in a pair of dark jeans and nothing else. "I missed the show."

"Wasn't that entertaining," Heather said, stretching

to crack her back. The shock of seeing him in the flesh again hadn't worn off yet; a heat burned in her belly as she took in the fine muscles of his abdomen and chest.

"You next," Andy said. "Then you can unpack while I clean up."

"All right," she said. "There won't be any hot water left."

Andy snorted. "With the temperature outside, I'm okay to take a cool one."

"True," she said.

Daniel stepped out of the doorway to let her pass and she was careful not to brush his warm, damp, inviting skin. She snagged a towel out of the hall closet and ducked into the bathroom before she could spontaneously combust. In the privacy of the still-steamy room she let out a sigh and inspected herself in the mirror. The draw to them hadn't been so bad before the separation. Before it was just a tension; now it was like gravity. A year apart had made a world of difference. Could she even live with Andy and Daniel, or would it cause too many problems?

She yanked off her sweaty clothes and tossed them on top of Daniel's in the corner. The water was still warm when she turned it on and stepped in, but not too much so; she hummed with pleasure as it cooled her down. She snagged the soap, still wet, and glanced around for a washcloth. There wasn't one, which meant Daniel had rubbed that same bar of soap all over his body. A little thrill ran up her spine, heat pooling in her belly. It was a weird thing to be aroused by, but as she stroked the soap around the heavy curves of her breasts, she didn't mind. Her nipples tightened and rose into firm, deep pink buds. She squeezed her breasts and sighed, wishing for bigger, rougher hands on her.

They wouldn't notice if it took her an extra few minutes in the shower. She was a woman, after all, and wasn't it expected for her to dawdle? She smiled and soaped the rest of her body with efficient strokes. The water cascaded in a half-cool curtain down her body. She leaned against the back wall of the shower, angling the spray to hit her lower stomach. Behind her closed eyes, the fantasy was as quick and easy as washing had been: Daniel and Andy, tangled together in their bed. The sheets would be on the floor, or somewhere else entirely. Daniel's firm, tan back would ripple with muscle while he pinned Andy and kissed him, their bodies rubbing and slick with sweat.

Heather bit her lip and slid her fingers down her stomach, through the ticklish spray of the shower and to her already-slick pussy. She slipped two fingers inside and pushed the heel of her hand down on her clit. A small gasp tore free. She rubbed one of her breasts with the other hand and undulated her hips. Pleasure built in sparks and snaps. She pictured Daniel wrestling one of Andy's legs over his shoulder, thrusting against his firm belly and sliding their dicks together. They would both be thick and long, she imagined shamelessly, pinching her nipple until it stung faintly.

"Hey," one of them called from outside the bathroom door. She bit her tongue to hold in a squeal and came, suddenly, muscles contracting and fluttering around her fingers as her back arched. "You want to get takeout or explore, have a nice meal somewhere?"

"I," she managed, her voice breathy. Her tongue throbbed. "I'd like to go out."

"Okay," he said. She thought she might have detected a hint of humor, but with the rush of the shower, it was hard to tell. "We'll be waiting."

She groaned under her breath and rinsed her fingers under the water. It took only another minute to wash her hair. She wrapped her towel around her middle—it barely covered her ass if she pulled it up high enough to hide her peaked nipples. To say she wasn't excited by the prospect of them looking at her would have been a lie, but it was wrong to provoke them when they were perfectly happy.

That wasn't the kind of thing best friends did.

Of course, as soon as she shuffled out of the bathroom, both of them came out of her new room. Her breath caught. Two hot pairs of eyes ran from her bare feet up to the curling dampness of her hair, lingering especially hard over her breasts. Heat blazed in her cheeks. Her hands ached to throw off the towel and grab both of them by the hair for a kiss.

"We'll just let you get dressed," Andy said.

They stepped apart from each other but didn't move down the hall. She held her breath as she brushed by them, close enough to feel warmth on either side like the touch of a hand. As she shut the door behind her, she thought she heard one of them sigh. That was probably just her imagination again. She toweled her hair dry and dug through a suitcase, feeling absurdly naked instead of just nude in her empty room. She hadn't locked the door, hadn't wanted to.

This was going to be a problem if she couldn't get it under control. At least she fantasized about them together instead of with her; surely that made it less of a betrayal of their relationship. Surely that would make it easier not to want to fling herself into their arms. Heather ruffled her hair until it settled in what she hoped was an artful mess and straightened her tank top and skirt. The boys had the best taste in restaurants. She couldn't wait to try everything they recommended.

She walked to the living room and paused in the doorway. Daniel was sitting with his head pillowed on Andy's shoulder, one hand resting on his leg. His eyes were closed. Andy smiled at her, and her heart ached. It was like being shut out in the cold, watching a happy couple by a warm fire.

"Are you going to take a shower before we go?" she said.

"Yeah," he replied. "Just a quick rinse. I'm too sweaty otherwise. Come keep Daniel company while I clean up."

He shifted and Daniel moved to let him up. As Andy passed by her, he put one hand on her shoulder and planted a quick, soft kiss to her temple. She gave him a startled look. They were always touching her, but it had been a long time since she'd felt his lips on her skin.

"I'm glad you're here," he said, smiling.

"Come on over," Daniel called from the couch, one of his arms draped over the back. "Don't let him steal all your attention."

Heather rolled her eyes and walked over to him, standing with her hands on her hips. He raised one eyebrow. She sighed and flopped down in a swish of skirts, his fingertips brushing her neck and sending a sweep of heat into her chest. He curved them over her bare shoulder a moment later. It wasn't quite cuddling, but it was close.

"What's up with the skirt?" he said, plucking at the thin fabric.

"I'm way too pale for anything shorter than my ankles, and this is much cooler than a pair of pants," she said. She pulled up the hem to flash her leg. "See? White as chalk."

He smirked. "I happen to like pale-skinned girls. And if you hadn't noticed, Andy's approaching ghostliness too. Suntanning is bad for you, after all."

"Says the man with the natural glow," she replied.

Comfortable silence settled. Heather closed her eyes and enjoyed the warm, callused weight of his fingers on her shoulder. The shower ran in the other room, a distant hiss of noise. The ache in her chest loosened its hold, just slightly, as she enjoyed Daniel's company. She loved them both and had since high school, but it was starting to occur to her that the depth and breadth of that feeling might have changed while they were away. Or, possibly, that she was more aware of it while sharing a small space with them.

"I think we'll have Indian," Daniel said, startling her. She jumped. He pushed her back against the couch with gentle fingers. "There's a great, great place down the street. Huge piles of food, excellent flavors."

"That sounds good," she said. Her heart slowly calmed its racing. "You surprised me."

"You looked deep in thought," he said, grinning. "I figured I'd get at least a flinch if not a whole jump. You're so easy to startle."

"I missed you, too," she said with a huff.

His smile was so bright, the ache flared in her chest again. It wasn't fair to be so close to perfection and stuck right outside the lines. The shower cut off in the other room and she looked at her hands. First thing to do, besides buy a bed, was find a new boyfriend. That might make it easier, just a little, if she was lucky. It hadn't ever worked before, but things could change. Feelings definitely could change.

Andy came in a moment later and put his shoes on by the door. Daniel and Heather stood up in one movement and followed him down the flight of stairs to his car. It was a cream-colored sedan with dark leather seats. Daniel's sports car was prettier, but it was only a two-seater. She climbed in the back before Daniel could offer her shotgun. Andy was his boyfriend, after all, and that meant he had dibs.

The jet lag settled heavy on her shoulders as Andy eased the car out onto the street. She closed her eyes and leaned her head against the window. Soft music played and her boys were quiet. Just as she began to drift, the car stopped. She lifted her head, blinking.

"We're here," Andy said. "Next time I'll go somewhere farther away so you can nap."

"Hm," she groaned, stretching. "I'm just exhausted from the flight. Is the fold-out bed in the couch ready for me?"

"Yeah," he said as they climbed out of the car. "We got the sheets put on it this morning and folded it back up that way. All you have to do is pull it out when you're ready to go to bed."

"I'll probably turn in early," she said. "I'll be more fun tomorrow, promise."

"You're fine," Daniel said.

A waiter seated them and took their drink orders. Heather flipped through the menu. Indian food back in Ohio hadn't always been a treat—it usually wasn't actual Indian, for that matter—but the menu here looked authentic. She picked a curry dish, closed the menu and looked at the men sitting across from her.

"Just like we never left," Andy said.

"Perfect," Daniel agreed.

"Yeah," Heather said, resting her chin on one hand.

They placed their orders when the waiter returned with their drinks. She stirred her soda with the straw in slow, clockwise swishes. Someone's foot bumped hers under the table, then returned and pressed against it. She raised her eyebrows at her dining partners but neither of them did anything but smile the smile of the innocent.

"You decided where you want to go for your grad degree?" Daniel said.

"I've got some applications ready, and the materials. Mostly I need to find a job. There weren't any bookstores

I could transfer to out here," she said. "Neither of you guys know anyone who's hiring, do you?"

"No," Daniel said. "I mean, even if you weren't an arts major, the firm I signed up with is full. I was the last newbie they took in, and that was mostly because I aced all the exams. Most of us junior lawyers are all the same on paper until you check the grades."

"Unless you want to work in a kitchen, no," Andy said. "And trust me, while you're going to finish your degree, you don't want to be full time in a kitchen. I'm moving up the ladder but you'd be like a waitress or a dishwasher."

"Damn," she sighed. "I hate to be a burden. I've got some money saved to help pay my bills the first couple of months, at least."

"Don't even think about it," Daniel said with a little smile. "We can more than afford that apartment, honey. You keep your money until you've got a job."

"Dan," she protested, slipping into his old nickname easily. "I can't do that. That's your money. I can't just let you support me."

"Yeah," Andy said. "I really think you can."

"But—"

"No buts," he replied, smiling. "I've missed having my sweet peach to take care of."

She pointed at Daniel. "There's the peach you're supposed to be taking care of!"

"Hon," Daniel drawled. "Face it, as soon as you moved in with us, you got stuck with us again. We're going to make sure you live a nice comfortable life whether you like it or not."

She sighed, exasperated, and sipped her drink. Every bone in her body seemed to argue the idea of letting her best friends pay her way, but she had a feeling she wasn't going to be able to sneak money into their wallets at night. They just wouldn't have it. She knew them well enough to hear that in their tone of voice. They were making her their responsibility and there was nothing to be done about it. She chafed to think of herself as not being independent, though.

"So, where's good to hang out around here?" she said.

"Bookstore," Andy replied immediately.

"There's a bar down the street from the bookstore, too," Daniel added. "Good drinks."

"You know how I feel about publicly humiliating myself," she said.

"We'll make sure you keep your top on," he said, his dark eyes twinkling with delight. "I can't have the whole world looking at those luscious tits."

"Hey!" she said, her face heating. "Don't talk about my breasts like that."

Andy raised one eyebrow, theatrically slow. Daniel just grinned.

"You aren't going to tell me you haven't noticed that you're, ah," Andy paused. "Stacked. Completely, utterly stacked, and you have been since you were like, fourteen."

Heather buried her face in her hands, heaving with laughter while both men descended into giggles that weren't quite befitting of their stature. She caught a glimpse of her breasts bouncing as she laughed and burst into another fit of snickers. They were big, but it just wasn't nice of Daniel to make such a big deal out of it. Hearing him say "tits" had hit her like a jolt of heat to the belly, anyway, and that was the last thing she needed at a good dinner with her friends.

Their dinner arrived moments later, while Andy rubbed his eyes to brush away any tears of mirth. Daniel beamed a smile at the waiter, who returned it with a touch of confusion before leaving. Heather laughed again. It seemed like she hadn't laughed since her boys had left home, not until that moment, when all the weight of her loneliness lifted.

Then Andy planted a kiss on Daniel's supple lips and the balloon of her excitement began to sink. No, she wasn't alone any more, but it would still be possible to be lonely. Best not to forget that if she wanted to truly enjoy her life in Nevada. Maybe she could meet someone at the bookstore or the bar, or both. Once her bedroom was set up, of course, though the thought of rutting with some handsome stranger on the couch while Daniel and Andy listened in from the other room was, well—

She swallowed a deep gulp of her soda to cool her ardor, and it didn't work.

"So, I guess after we eat you just want to go home and get ready for bed?" Daniel asked, picking a piece of chicken off of Andy's plate. His lover did the same in return.

"Probably," she said.

She didn't tell them that even though she was tired, she was also turned on, and wouldn't it be nice if they would give her a backrub before bed? She almost shuddered to remember the one time they'd tried that. Two pairs of hands rubbing her down from toe to scalp, excited breathing against her neck. But they'd been young, and unsure, and it hadn't ever gone any further. Maybe if she'd rolled onto her back and pulled her top off, asked them each to suckle her nipples . . .

"Your face is flushed," Andy said. "Are you all right?"

"Spicy," she lied, taking another bite of her curry. It *was* a little hot, but not enough to make her turn as red as her imagination. There were many times she wished for Daniel's darker skin. She bet it hid all sorts of reactions.

"If it's too hot, I can trade," he replied.

"No," she said. "I like it."

"I'm with her," Daniel said. "Spicy is good."

He winked. She bit her lip to keep from asking how "spicy" he liked it. Silence settled for a long moment while they ate. The food left her feeling more energized than she had been on the ride to the restaurant, most likely aided by the sugar in her soda.

"Can we go to that bookstore?" she asked, pushing her empty plate aside.

"Sure," Andy said. "I thought you were tired."

"Not too much all of a sudden," she said. "I mailed my books, but some of the ones I knew I could find again I just sold. I need to stock back up."

"All right," he said. "Sounds like fun."

"I guess I should just make a list and not buy anything, though," she said, frowning. "I need that money to last me until I can find work. I can always get books later."

"And I repeat," Daniel said. "We are taking care of you. That means you can buy books. I mean, don't go spend your whole savings or anything, but I trust you won't just slack off because we're paying for the apartment. You're not that kind of girl."

"Damn right I'm not," she said. "I'm never going to be able to talk you out of this, am I?"

"No," they both said at once. She sighed.

"To the bookstore, then," she said.

Andy snagged the bill before she could ask for it to be split and paid it with a satisfied grin on his face. It made her wonder just how much they were making with their new jobs to be so happy about spending all of their money on her. Had they been preparing for the eventuality since they'd moved? Probably. She smiled.

The sun was starting to set as they walked out the door. The heat pushed like an invisible hand, its weight palpable. Heather slid into the stifling back seat and leaned up into the front for some air conditioning once Andy started the car. Sweat prickled the back of her neck.

"It'll get colder once it's nighttime," Daniel said.

"Thank God," she replied. Andy chuckled. "Oh, come on. You two have had time to get used to it. I'm miserable!"

"Hate to tell you, but you don't really get used to it," Andy said. "It's still just as hot for us as it is for you. But I like this area, and it's a damn sight better than being stuck with the same group of people we went to high school with."

"That is true," she said. "I never have to see another one of their faces again. How nice."

"Isn't it, though?" Daniel said.

They parked in front of an old brick building with several doors and concrete patio tables outside. People sat with coffees and sodas, flipping through magazines and books. Heather looked it over. They hadn't said it was an independent store, but the atmosphere was interesting already. She climbed out of the car and followed her boys inside. The door chime rang and a young blond man glanced up at them from a notebook.

"Hey, guys," he said. "And who's your lovely companion?"

"Best friend from back home," Andy said. "She's come to live with us."

"Heather," she said, offering her hand. He shook it. His grip was strong. "Nice to meet you. What's your name?"

"Jamison," he said. "I guess I'll be seeing you around pretty often?"

"Probably," she said. "I'm quite a reader."

"Awesome," he said. "Coffee shop is through that door there."

He pointed to the back of the store. A big wooden doorway with no door led to a café, or what she could see of one. People milled around the stacks. She glanced around, taking in all of the sections and towering shelves. The walls actually had stepladders to reach the top. That must have been interesting to stock. She put her hands on her hips and pondered where to go first.

"Be free," Andy muttered into her ear. "Explore the wilds of your new domain."

She laughed, nudging him with her elbow, and walked up a small flight of stairs to a raised section. She started with the first shelf and picked through the titles, plucking up new books and replacements. The sign on the register had said ten percent off purchases over twenty-five dollars, after all.

She looked down at the back of Jamison's head and thought about him for a moment. Strong handshake, pretty hair, pretty eyes. He had expressed a friendly interest, too. It probably wouldn't be best to involve herself with someone she'd have to see on a regular basis, though, if things went south as they usually did. Across the store, Andy and Daniel had their heads bent over some book, their hair mingling in a strange mesh of brown and black. She looked back to the stack in her arms and shuffled to the counter.

"Can I put these here?" she said.

Jamison's eyes lit up. "Oh hell, yes, you can. Like he said, be free. Go explore."

She rolled her eyes. "You don't need to love money so obviously, you know."

"Hey, I'm just glad the books are getting a new home," he said defensively, one hand over his heart as if wounded. "You're cruel."

Heather giggled. Maybe he wasn't such a bad choice after all. He waved her off into the stacks again and she started afresh. Ten percent off was a good deal, after all.

"Are you buying the whole store?" Andy said just behind her. She jumped. "Got you!"

"Oh, damn," she said, gasping. "Don't scare me like that!"

He grinned. "It's too hard to resist, honey."

"I guess I could be done with this much. It's mostly new so I'll have things to read while I try to find something productive to do." She lifted the new stack of paperbacks in her arms. "I've been meaning to pick up a lot of these new authors, too. Hard to find in the chain stores."

"That's why I love this place. It's huge and they've crammed every inch with books," he said. "I think Daniel's looking at the gay porn again. Let me go assure him we don't need to pay for it."

She sighed as he whisked off to the magazine rack and his lover. She put down her stack on the counter, enjoying Jamison's sunny smile, and approached her boys. Daniel had a magazine in his hand with a tanned, muscular man posing in tight underwear. His fingers framed his considerable package. She plucked it out of his grasp and walked back to the counter. She knew they'd be staring after her with fish-faces, so she didn't have to look. Jamison's laugh told her all she needed to know. She put the magazine on top of the pile.

"All right," she said. "Now I'm done."

"I love a woman who's not shy," he said with a wink.

Heather winked and handed over her card. The total would have been swoon-worthy if the boys hadn't subsidized her rent payments, but she'd saved up a lump sum and now had very little planned for it. Three bags of books on her arms, she walked out to the car.

"Are you having your car shipped here or just getting a new one?" he said as she put her bags next to her in the back seat.

"I sold the old beast," she said. "So I'm going to buy a new one. I figured I'd do some shopping online tomorrow while you guys are at work, then maybe we could take a trip to whatever dealership has the best one for me."

"Going to finally get a sports car?" Andy asked.

"I don't think so," she sighed. "We need more than one car with a back seat."

"I would appreciate that, yes," he said, grinning at her in the rearview mirror.

She closed her eyes again and leaned her head back against the seat. It was still "we." We need a car, we need to do this, we want to have dinner. She was part of that "we." It hadn't narrowed down to Daniel and Andy somehow, in the time apart and their time together. They had kept some Heather-shaped space in their lives, just waiting for her. How could it be the three of them against the world if two were lovers and the other was watching and yearning? She opened her eyes and resettled the bags full of books on the seat. One had started to tip over.

Andy parked them right in front of the stairs to the apartment. The word home still felt strange in her head. It was theirs, not hers. Not yet. Maybe not ever. She couldn't bear the thought of being separated again, though. Moving out on her own would be a separation, even if a small one.

"Home, sweet home," Daniel said.

She followed them up the stairs and dropped her purchases in the middle of her empty room. They'd have to find a good-sized shelf, too. Even without half of her old collection, the books she'd bought and the books still on the way to her would fill a up medium-sized one. She turned and found Daniel waiting in the door frame of her room.

"Are you okay?" he said.

"Why wouldn't I be?" she replied, heart throbbing.

"I don't know," he said. "But you know you can tell us anything."

"Yeah," she said. "I think I'm just sleepy. Want to fold the bed out for me while I get changed?"

He nodded and disappeared down the hall. She nudged the door shut and stripped out of her clothes. Her boxer shorts, worn thin with wear, hung loose around her hips. She pulled on a tank top and padded out into the hallway. Someone had hit the lights and doused the whole apartment in darkness. The only light shone from their bedroom. She looked around the living room but Daniel had already gone. The fold-out bed had dark-green sheets on it and what looked like five pillows; four too many for one woman. She smiled and cuddled down into the sheets, pulling the comforter up around her ears. The warm glow from down the hall lessened suddenly as the door clicked shut.

Even with the blinds pulled and the lights off, the living room still seemed bright. The blackout curtains in her suitcase were designed for the bedroom, though, not the big balcony doors in the living room. She pulled the covers over her head and sighed. Now that she'd lain down, she wasn't quite so tired. There was always the television, or one of her new books.

She sat up and heard a noise. It sounded—she froze. Another low, soft moan came from down the hall. A creaking sound followed it, like a bed shifting. Her heart raced, pulse suddenly pounding. She strained her ears to hear more. A short cry, followed by silence, then the rhythmic creaking of bedsprings; it was impossible to think they were doing anything else. The muffled noises made it hard to tell who was making what sound. Every quiet groan and sharp gasp seemed magnified in her ears. Liquid warmth pooled in her belly and lower. Was it wrong to get off listening to Andy and Daniel make love?

Heather slipped her fingers under the band of the boxer shorts and cupped her hand over her sex. Damp heat slid against her fingers. She pressed the heel of her hand down and shuddered. The creaking from the other room continued. The short gasps were growing louder, turning to whimpered cries. She could imagine Andy on knees and elbows, Daniel thrusting and straining above him. Sweat would glitter like diamonds on their bodies. She had no trouble at all picturing their tryst.

Finally, one hoarse moan rose about the other noises and cut off short. Another man's gasp followed it. She huddled down under her covers again, holding her breath. The creak of a door sounded, then soft footsteps that hesitated in the hallway. She could feel someone's gaze on her back. She hoped the line of the sheets hid that she had her hand in her underwear. The bathroom door clicked shut after a moment. She slipped her fingers back and forth, rubbing, sliding in the slick wetness. She froze again as the door opened with another click.

She wished hard for whichever of her boys was there to come climb under the sheets with her, his cock still soft after sex, and push his hand down her shorts. Instead, the bedroom door closed again. She buried her face in the pillow and rocked her hips against her stroking fingers, imagining a bigger hand touching her. The orgasm was sudden and sharp, prompting a short groan into the pillow. It rippled in waves down her back and from fingertip to toe. She shuddered. The pleasure receded.

Heather blinked away dampness in her eyes and wiped her hand on the sheets. She didn't feel like getting up. They would surely hear her and wonder if she'd been awake the whole time. Of course she had been, but they didn't need to know. It certainly wouldn't make life any easier. After a long quiet moment, she finally managed to close her eyes and drift to sleep. The warm haze of sex followed her into her dream.

Chapter Two

Heather turned her head toward a soft clinking coming from the kitchen. A dull, buttery light pooled in the living room. It seemed to be lighter outside the curtains than when she shut her eyes, but not quite day-bright yet. Daniel came around the corner with a cup of coffee in his hands and froze. She sat up, groggy.

"What time is it?" she said.

"Damn," he said. "I was hoping not to wake you. It's about seven. I was getting ready for work."

She looked him over, lingering with sleepy interest on his bare chest and lightly furred legs. His boxers covered the best parts. He cleared his throat and she swallowed, looking back up at his eyes.

"Sorry," she said. "I'll lie back down, then."

He smiled and started back down the hall. She watched the round, firm shift of his ass while he walked. The boxers didn't leave much to the imagination. Her own were clinging to her, stuck to her trimmed thatch and her thighs. She tugged on them under the covers and settled down. After blinking at the wall for some time, listening to rustling and shuffling in the other room, she sat up again. Maybe it was the jet lag, or the early night, but she was awake and there was no changing it.

She wondered when Andy had to go to work and figured it wouldn't be until later in the day. He was cooking, after all, and most of the good restaurants didn't even open until four. Neither of them were in the hall as she went to her empty bedroom and changed into a light summer outfit; another swishy long skirt and a T-shirt. It wasn't the classiest thing in her suitcase but it was comfortable. She dug her laptop out of her bag and sat it on the computer desk. There was a plug right behind the wooden desk, so she hooked it up to charge.

"Hey," Daniel said, cracking the door to her room and peering in. "There's pancake batter in the fridge you can fry up if you're hungry. And eggs and bacon. Basically anything you might want is in there. Andy keeps us stocked."

"Okay," she said. "Blueberries?"

"You know it, babe," he said with a grin and shut her door.

A moment later, she heard the front door close. The apartment was silent and dark, just edging into morning. Down the hall, their bedroom door was shut. She crept over to it and turned the knob with slow care. It never creaked. She leaned in. Their room smelled faintly of musk and the heavy warmth of sleep. Andy's brown hair stuck up in tufts from under the blankets and his bare feet peeked out the other end. He didn't stir. She closed the door quietly behind her and walked to the kitchen. The carpet was pleasantly thick and soft between her toes.

She flopped down on the unmade fold-out bed and sighed, arms crossed over her knees. No car yet, so she could hardly go exploring, and Andy wouldn't be awake for some time. Daniel was at work. The bookstore, of course, was within walking distance. Jamison might be there. If not, she could get a coffee and read a newspaper. Better than sitting and feeling lost in a new city without company. She ducked into the bedroom and grabbed her bag and a pair of sandals.

The heat wasn't quite oppressive yet. She walked down the steps, flip-flops flapping on the wood. A longer walk might have called for sneakers, skirt or not, but if she was going to make eyes at the cute bookseller, it would be good to look less homeless. She flipped the bag over her shoulder and started walking. The sidewalk was almost empty, even as she emerged onto the main road. A lone jogger on the other side, his head bent with concentration and sweat pouring from his clothes, was her only company. The coffee shop door was just opening as she approached. An older woman with her hair pinned up in a bun glanced up and smiled.

"Early morning beverage, sweetie?" she said.

"Just what I came for," Heather replied. "When does the bookshop open?"

"In another hour at nine," she said. "We have today's paper, though."

"Okay," she said. "Do you know if Jamison will be there?"

The woman gave her a shrewd look. "He'll probably be there eventually, if not at open. He's the assistant manager, you know."

"Oh," she said. "No, I didn't. That's cool."

"Come on in," the woman said.

Heather climbed the three steps to the café and glanced at the big, chalkboard-style menu taking up the whole back wall. One corner was a giant shelf covered with jars of coffee beans, all different flavors and imports. She chewed her lip in thought.

"You might want an Italian iced soda to pep you up," the woman suggested, stepping behind the counter. She pulled a name tag over her head that said Linda. "Sugary, fruity, but not too heavy. And chilled."

"Okay," she said, looking at the list of flavors. "Blackberry sounds perfect."

"Coming right up," Linda said. "Find yourself a seat and settle. I'll bring it to you."

Heather sat at one of the wooden booths and picked up the neat, new paper sitting on the table. The far wall with windows was all tall barstools, but she had a feeling she might step on her skirt and take a fall if she tried to climb one. The booths were safer by far. A fan turned in big, creaking circles overhead, its blades almost as wide as the room. Every pass pushed cool air down on Heather and rustled the paper. The big wooden door frame to the bookstore was closed with a sliding door that disappeared into the wood whenever it was pushed in; she certainly hadn't noticed it before.

Linda walked over a moment later and sat a tall plastic

cup in front of her. The soda inside was a rich purple color, dotted with fizzy bubbles. She took a sip and hummed without intending to as bright, sugary flavor burst on her taste buds. It was like sunshine.

"Wow!" she said.

Linda smiled. "Glad you like it. By the way, Jamison loves fantasy novels, if you want something to talk to him about."

"Me too," she said. "I like it all, but fantasy or sci-fi would be my favorite."

"I would have pegged you for romance," she replied, grinning.

"I like romances fine," she said, returning the smile. "Especially when they're mine."

As she sipped her soda and waited, flipping through the paper, loneliness settled again. Linda went behind the counter to take care of the customers dropping in for their morning drinks. Some found chairs; some left for work. She didn't recognize anybody, and it disheartened her to think she wouldn't. Not like back home, where everybody of a certain age knew each other. It was just the change wearing on her, the first big change of her life, and she knew it. That didn't make the ache any easier.

She glanced up as the door chimed again and a familiar blond man strolled in. Heather sipped her soda and watched him. He moved with muscular grace; his pants hugged a round, firm butt. He leaned against the counter to order his drink and his T-shirt flashed a bit of flat stomach. He was certainly handsome, and her heart may have fluttered a little, but he just wasn't Andy or Daniel. But that wasn't the point. She shook her head to clear it. He was handsome and probably smart, and that was all that mattered to strike up a conversation.

He walked by with an iced coffee, on his way to open the bookstore, she supposed.

"Hi," she said.

He glanced back, then paused and smiled. "My new customer," he said.

"Heather," she reminded. "How're you this morning?"

"Fine," he said. His smile was bright and pleased. "You already doing more shopping?"

"No," she said. "But I'm new in town and the boys both have to work. I don't even have a new car yet, so I'm pretty stranded. This is the only place I know so far."

"So it isn't for my company," he said, his smile turning to a bit of a grin. He looked in her eyes. She smirked back.

"Maybe it is," she said. "I don't know yet."

"Why don't you come look at some magazines and when the other guy gets here I'll take you to lunch?" he said. "If you don't mind waiting."

"I really have nothing else to do," she said, sipping the blackberry soda.

He tipped an imaginary hat and unlocked the sliding door to step into the bookshop. She watched his butt again while he walked inside and put his coffee on the counter to start opening up the register. He winked at her when he noticed her looking, but he seemed pleased, so she kept her chin on her hand and tried not to be creepy about it. He turned the sign to "open" and propped open the front door. If it got any hotter, he'd have to close it or risk running all the air out.

Heather got up and wandered over to the store. "Mind if I take a book and sit there while I wait?"

"Nah," he said. "You get special permission. It's not really against the rules anyway. Linda watches when people bring over merchandise. Nobody really tries to steal from here. They go to the big chains for that."

"Well, good," she said. "I'll look, then."

She plucked a volume of short stories off the fantasy shelf and saw him smile at the choice. He didn't say anything, though. She retook her seat and flipped the book open, soda in one hand. It was delicious. Splurging on them wouldn't be good, but once she got her own job, they would be a regular treat, she was sure.

Her cell phone rang after some time, startling her. She put down her almost empty cup and answered it.

"Heya," Andy said on the other line. "Where'd you disappear to?"

"The bookstore," she said. "This café is wonderful. Jamison offered to take me to lunch when his employee shows up."

"Ah," he said. She frowned at the tone in his voice. "I just thought we might go look for cars today."

"Oh, are you off work?" she said. "Babe, I'm sorry, I didn't know. I can give him a rain check. I don't think he'll mind if I tell him I need to go find some transportation after all."

"Daniel didn't tell you," he sighed. "Sorry! You must

have thought we were both bailing on you on the first day here."

"No way," she said, shocked. "You both have lives that I'm trying not to disrupt too much. It can't be fun having me sleeping on your couch right now, I know that. I can get an air mattress for the bedroom if you want."

"No, no," he said. "It's totally okay. Why don't I come pick you up and we'll go eat and shop? That sound good?"

"Sure," she said.

He hung up and she crossed to the bookstore again. Jamison looked up from the book he was reading, his big smile brightening her heart a little.

"I have to bail on you today," she said. "Turns out Andy took the day off to help me go get a replacement car and Daniel forgot to tell me. I'm so sorry."

"But are you interested?" he said, his eyes serious. "I won't be insulted if you just changed your mind, you know. No hard feelings."

"I'm very interested," she said. He raised his eyebrows. "What? I thought you liked girls who weren't shy."

"I really do," he said, waggling those eyebrows suggestively. She rolled her eyes. "Just come leave me a note here when you want to have dinner. We'll make a date."

"Wonderful," Heather said.

He ran a hand through his thick, gorgeous hair. It seemed to glitter in the sun with gold highlights. She wanted to purr, but instead she sat the book on his counter and winked. She felt him watching her as she walked outside to sit at one of the stone tables and wait for Andy. She'd have other days for a new date; there was no way she could blow her best friend off.

Even if it felt like maybe he hadn't wanted her to see another man. He had seemed disappointed, but that could have just been because he'd been planning a day already and Daniel had forgotten to tell her. She was sure that was the real reason. Andy's car rolled up next to her table and she tossed the empty cup into the trash before climbing in the passenger seat.

"You know, I should probably do some Internet research first," she said. "I wasn't planning on going to get the car today at all. Should we wait till later this afternoon?"

"We've bought both of our cars from the same lot. I figured we'd go look there. The prices are great and neither of ours turned out to be junkers, so I assume it's a good place." He shrugged. "But it's up to you."

"Can't hurt to look," she said. "Where are we eating?"

"I thought we might go to a pub for lunch," he said. "There's a great one we like a lot."

"Okay," she said, turning in her seat toward him slightly. He smiled at her. "Do you not like Jamison? You seem kind of tense."

"Oh, it's not that," he said, his brow furrowing. "I'm just irritated Daniel forgot to tell you about today. I know he's got a terrible memory so it's sort of my fault, but it irks me."

"Don't worry about it," Heather said. "It's not as if it messed up our day."

"True," he said.

She watched him as he drove. His lips were still pressed tight and he had both hands on the steering wheel instead of one; unless he'd woken up with a headache or some other ailment, she wasn't buying that he was just a little annoyed at Daniel. If he didn't want to say what was wrong, though, that was his business. She did hope it wasn't about Jamison, because he seemed like a friendly, attractive man. He was someone she could see herself falling into bed with and enjoying every moment. Considering it had been months, the thought of all his pale skin and muscled curves beneath her fingers sent a shiver down her spine.

It wasn't that she'd never gone without sex before, but she wanted to be with somebody. Filling in the Andy- and Daniel-shaped hole in her heart was the first thing she had to do if she expected to live with them without a problem. Jamison might not be enough for that, but he could distract her, and he could be kind. Still feeling as unbalanced as she did, kindness was a bonus.

"Here we are," Andy said, pulling into a tiny and packed parking lot beside an old converted house. "I think you'll enjoy it. The beer list is huge and the food is to die for. Wait till you try the bread."

"I believe you," she said, fighting a smile. Andy and food went together so well.

Heather twirled her new car keys on her finger while she and Andy walked up the steps to the apartment. Daniel's car was already in the lot. The sleek, lovely black sedan she'd brought home seemed to glimmer in the evening sun. Her stomach rumbled. She sincerely hoped Daniel had dinner ready or at least a plan for where to go.

She opened the door with her key, Andy watching and smiling. Daniel peered around from the kitchen as they came in. She kicked off her flip-flops and collapsed onto the couch.

"Hard day?" Daniel said.

"Car shopping," she said. "Successful car shopping, though."

"That's great," he said. "Did you manage to stay within your budget?"

"Yes, actually," Andy cut in, leaning over to give his boyfriend a quick kiss. Heather looked away. "She found a great one. Just in the price range."

"Awesome," Daniel said.

"I'm planning on having lunch with Jamison sometime soon, too," she said. "He seems nice. I need to make new friends in town. Can't afford to be a hermit."

Neither man laughed, though Daniel managed a short hum of what might have been approval. She frowned over toward the kitchen but neither of them was watching her. Andy leaned in the kitchen doorway, intent upon whatever Daniel was cooking. Maybe they'd been less than enthusiastic about some of her other boyfriends, but it stung her. What right did they have to cast any judgment when they weren't exactly welcoming her with open arms into their bed? She got up and brushed past them to the fridge for a beer. Daniel had some red brew on hand, so she popped the cap off on the countertop and took a swig.

"Missed my beer, huh?" he said, glancing up from his saucepan.

"Yup," she said. "What's for dinner?"

"Chicken marsala," he said. "It's good. Promise. Why don't you two go wait out there? You're crowding up my kitchen."

His grin eased the shooing. She rolled her eyes and shuffled past him to go back to the couch. The kitchen was pretty small. Andy flopped down next to her and snagged her beer. He wrapped his lips around the neck of the bottle in a way that made her pulse flutter. His throat worked as he swallowed.

He handed it back and she took the bottle with limp fingers, eyebrows raised a little. He just smirked. It wasn't fair that cock-tease tricks worked as well on her as they would on Daniel; she couldn't help but picture him on his knees in front of the other man.

"Think I have time for a shower?" she called out.

"Sure," Daniel said. "Twenty minutes left until it's all done. Go ahead and wash up."

She passed her beer to Andy and pushed off the couch. "I'll be back in twenty, then."

Heather made a quick duck into her room to get clothes and, discreetly, the silky-smooth dildo in its fine silk pouch at the bottom of her suitcase. She bundled it all up together and slipped across the hall into the bathroom. Sleeping on the couch hardly gave her the privacy to enjoy a real self-love marathon, but a little time in the shower would have to be enough. She started the water and laid out her clothes. She had just stripped down to her underwear when she realized she didn't have a towel. With a roll of her eyes, she cracked the door to peek out and see if Andy was still on the couch.

Her jaw dropped. He certainly was. One of his bare legs was draped over Daniel's back, his shorts and underwear dangling from that ankle. Daniel's dark head was buried in his lap, bobbing up and down. The expression on Andy's face was one of complete ecstasy; his damp lips were open and his eyes were fluttering but closed. She shut the door again before he opened his eyes and noticed her watching. Her heart pounded, heat racing through her blood.

Twenty minutes, Daniel had said. Obviously he didn't need to be in the kitchen the whole time. He was giving Andy a timed blow job while she showered barely a few yards away. She glanced in the mirror and saw her nipples hard and pink. She plucked at them, eyelids lowered. Her reflection shivered. She palmed the round globes of her breasts and lifted them, squeezing until they stung faintly. The dramatic stretch of Andy's bare leg over Daniel's back flashed in her mind's eye again.

Heather leaned her back against the door and slipped the dildo out of its pouch. The toy wobbled in her hand. She looked in the mirror again, her eyes drawn as if it was some kind of magnet. The clear, realistic cock in her hand was a good seven inches long. She could imagine both of her boys being endowed like that, or maybe bigger. She closed her eyes and pressed the tip of the toy to her lips. It wasn't warm, but it was strangely smooth and hard like the real thing.

She imagined she was Daniel and slid the toy into her mouth, tongue pressing at the veins and ridges. Not the same as being pressed up against the genuine article with all of his shuddering breaths and clutching hands, but she opened her jaw wider and sucked the toy like it was Andy's dick. She slipped it free with a pop after a moment and gazed at herself in the mirror. Fog crept around the edges from the hot water. She spread her pussy with two fingers, sliding in the dampness. The reflection hid nothing from her.

Her breath sped. She pressed the toy up against herself, blocking her view with her arm. The head, slick with her saliva, nudged against her. She pushed. It slid in slowly, haltingly, still wide enough to sting without any other preparation. She gasped and spread her legs farther, leaning harder against the door. Another quick shove buried it fully inside her until it bumped the end of her body with a little spark of something like pleasure, or possibly pain.

Had Andy come yet? Would Daniel drink him down or let him come all over his face, in long spurts that would leave the scent of semen on his skin for hours? She worked the toy, pressing the silky fake balls against her clit. The door stuck to her back as she writhed and wriggled, praying it wasn't thumping on its hinges too noticeably. Finally, she closed her eyes again and devoted all of her attention to the pleasure building in her core. The toy pounded her, sliding past her G-spot on every thrust, and her clit throbbed with the constant soft rubbing. Her body had heated it to the point that it felt real. It felt just like it would if she walked out and seated herself on Andy's spit-wet dick, sliding down until he filled her up. She squeaked, one short, uncontrolled sound, and came. Her body trembled with the wash of pleasure that tickled every nerve and whited out the fantasy in her mind.

"You about ready?" someone called, not quite through the door. Probably down the hall. She laughed under her breath, shivering still.

"Almost," she yelled back. Sliding the toy out made her tremble again with aftershocks. She rinsed it in the water and laid it to dry on the counter before stepping in for a quick rinse.

She peered out the door a moment later, dripping wet.

"I forgot to get a towel," she called.

"We won't peek," Daniel replied, but Andy got up off the couch and plucked one out of the closet. She took it with a smile. He didn't even bat an eyelash at her flushed face. Must have thought it was the shower.

Heather patted herself dry and tousled her hair. She pulled on her jeans and another T-shirt, then bundled her old clothes around the dildo. She darted across the hall and hid the toy in her suitcase again. Her muscles still felt liquid with release, her legs faintly weak. Had Andy come, too? She'd given them long enough. She took a deep breath and let it out before walking back down the hall. There were three plates on the coffee table with three glasses of wine. Daniel and Andy both smiled at her.

"A girl could get used to this," she said.

"That's what we're hoping for," Andy said, nudging Daniel to scoot over so they could all fit on the couch. "If we get you used to being pampered, you'll never want to leave."

"Why would I want to leave?" she said, raising her eyebrows. "You boys are my favorite people in the whole world."

"You could find somebody else," Daniel said, uncharacteristically quiet.

"Oh," she said, blinking. "I haven't managed to get stolen away yet. I don't see it happening any time soon. Nobody ever measures up to you two."

Andy shrugged. She looked at them both. The silence was slightly oppressive. Her brow furrowed with confusion. Daniel cut the first bite of his dinner and the moment dissipated, but Heather mulled it over as she ate. They seemed to want her all to themselves, but they were together and she wasn't included. That was hardly fair. It actually stirred a little ember of anger in her gut. She had needs, too, and if they weren't interested in her, they had no right to want her to stay single and lonely.

Andy turned the TV on after minutes of continued silence. They ate without arguing but Heather made a promise to herself to go see Jamison the next morning. He could take her to lunch before she went hunting for good jobs that would work around her graduate classes. The sun was just starting to set, casting gold and red bars of light through the balcony doors, when Daniel gathered up their plates and whisked them into the kitchen. Andy glanced at her.

"You seem bothered," he said.

"I just left the only city I've ever lived in to come live with you two and you're getting huffy about me making new friends," she murmured back. "I'm a little irked, yeah."

"I'm sorry," he said, deflated. "It shouldn't come across like that. I don't know why we can't keep our mouths shut. We ruin every relationship you try to have."

"That's not true," she said.

"Sure it is," he replied. "Even if it's not intentional, guys take one look at you with us and run for the hills. There's being secure in your masculinity and there's being aware that you're never going to measure up to your girl's best friends."

She frowned at him, but he shrugged again. Daniel came back in and wedged back into his corner seat on the couch. Heather leaned forward and propped her chin on their hands while they watched a comedy movie that had barely started. She wasn't sure whether or not she was actually paying attention to the film, or if the conflicting images of Jamison's golden beauty and the way her boys looked together were the only things in her mind.

Chapter Three

The workers at the café were a boy and a girl she didn't recognize, both college aged. Linda was nowhere to be seen. Heather ordered herself another iced soda and took it over to the bookstore. The boy behind the counter was a brunette, but she caught sight of Jamison's blond ponytail bobbing behind a shelf. She ducked around it and smiled at him. He jumped, rattling the little cart of books he was shelving, but grinned back.

"Hello again," he said. "Ready for our date?"

"You should see my new car," she said. "Not to say that it's better than you or anything, but I'm glad I took that rain check. I don't think the lot would have held onto it another day."

"Great," he said. "Let me finish this pile of books and then I'll tell Chris we're off."

"All right," she said. "I'll be in the magazines."

Jamison must have shelved the cart as fast as was physically possible, because Heather had just started reading an article on "the creative mind" in some science journal when he put a hand on her shoulder. She smiled at him. "Ready?" she said.

"Yeah. Want sandwiches? I know a good deli."

"Sounds fine," she said. "You want to drive since you know where it is?"

"Drive, hell," he said with a laugh. "It's just down the block. All of us at the store practically live there."

"Oh, awesome," she said. "Another place I can walk to from the apartment."

"I would ask if you've known those two devils long, but all they did was talk about you before you moved here," Jamison said. He grinned. "Seems like you three got in plenty of trouble back in O-hi-o."

She rolled her eyes at the fake, nasal northern accent in his pronunciation. "First thing, we don't talk like that and you know it. Second, we were totally a pack of hellions. But we were bored and young. You can't blame us."

"When you live in a state where gambling and prostitution are main thoroughfare business, it's pretty easy not to be bored," Jamison said, waggling his eyebrows. Heather laughed. He pointed to a green car parked in the alley by the café. "That's mine. In case we ever do need to drive anywhere."

"Showing me you can support yourself?" she asked, grinning.

"Of course, my lady," he replied.

She grinned. He offered his elbow and she tucked her arm through his, a warm flush stealing across her cheeks. Jamison smiled down at her. His eyes weren't quite brown; they were actually hazel with flecks of green. His chin came to the top of her head, so he had to have been at least six feet tall. It was interesting how many things she noticed once she was in his personal space. His cologne was musky and rich.

He pushed open the door to a shop. A little bell jingled above their heads as they stepped in and a woman, leaning against the counter and reading a battered paperback, looked up. She smiled.

"Hey, Jamison," she said. "And who are you?"

"Heather," she answered. The woman offered a hand and she shook it briskly. "I just moved in with Andy and Daniel, if you know them?"

"Oh, yeah, they eat here all the time," the woman said. "I'm Lucy."

"Well, hi, Lucy," she said.

Jamison let go of her arm and they ordered. He took a seat at the table by the window and she scooted her chair up across from him. A moment of silence stretched between them until Lucy brought over their drinks and sandwiches in baskets, with fries on the side.

"Oh, cool," she said. "Free fries!"

"Yup," Jamison said. "She takes care of her regulars."

Heather smiled at him, popping a fry into her mouth. He grinned back. His foot bumped hers under the table and, when she didn't move away, stayed there. She was momentarily overcome with the urge to ask him to bring her back to his apartment, but took a bite out of her sandwich to prevent it from coming out. Too forward was creepy or awkward, but Daniel and Andy's constant touching and lovemaking, which she couldn't seem to avoid, had put her nerves on edge. She wanted desperately to soothe them.

Jamison, with his golden hair and nice pale skin, seemed like just the thing.

"So, what do you like?" he said. "Movies or books or music?"

"Books and music, then maybe a good movie," she said. "They just cost a lot, when you add in all the drinks and snacks and stuff."

"Sneak in soda and candy. It saves on the cash."

Heather chuckled. "I suppose that's right."

"So, would you like to catch a movie?" he said, raising one eyebrow. "I'll bring food."

"Okay, when?"

"I'm off tonight," he said. "I actually get out at five. Maybe nine? I can pick you up and take you to the theater, if you want."

"Sure," she said, wiping her fingers on her napkin. "I'll let the boys have the night to themselves. They, uh, need their privacy."

Jamison coughed, his cheeks turning slightly pink. "Yeah, I would imagine."

"And I'm sleeping on the couch, because I haven't got a bed yet." She sighed. "I didn't want to pay to ship the frame. I'm kind of rethinking that at this point."

"Ah, couches," he said with a wince. "I know they're a little touchy-feely in public, so I can sort of imagine what it's like in private."

She grinned. "Especially since we grew up together,

all the awkward years and stuff, we're used to seeing things most people would think are private. It kind of weirds out a lot of my dates, because we're so close. But they're not interested in me, so I don't get why it bothers other guys."

"Probably because they're, ah," he paused. "This is going to sound pretty gay, but they're damned gorgeous. Even I don't measure up to them."

She blinked. "But you're so handsome."

"But they *are* gorgeous, and there are two of them," he said, grinning. "Any guy's going to feel a little competitive with you consuming all that eye candy on a regular basis."

"What about you?"

"Nah," he replied. "I like those guys. I think I can handle you ogling them."

"I certainly do not," she said archly.

"Uh-huh," he said. "Right. Like I don't look at fine women when they walk by."

"Exactly like that." She tried to hide her smile, but her lips quirked anyway.

His smile deepened into a grin. A warm tingle ran down her back. A movie in a dark theater sounded like a wonderful idea, the more she thought about it. Maybe she could do the innocent-arm-over-the-shoulder move first. Jamison seemed like the kind of man who would be amused by it. Andy and Daniel would have an evening to themselves—she pictured them tangled together on the couch, briefly, the pale shocking line of Andy's bare leg over Daniel's shoulder—and she would try to find a new lover. Hopefully, someone who might not leave just because she loved two other men. Jamison fit the bill, or seemed to.

"These sandwiches are great," she said after another pause.

"Told you," he said.

"Do you know if she's hiring?"

He see-sawed one hand in the air. "I think she's always looking, but I've never seen her hire anybody besides herself and the three college kids who've been working here since they were in high school."

"Ah. What about the bookstore or the café?" she said, pondering. "I'm looking for a job I can do while I'm in grad school."

"No and no," he said. "We pick up some people around Christmas, but we usually have to let them go again once it's over. Nobody ever seems to quit, you know?"

"Damn. Worth a shot."

"There's one of those chain stores about twenty minutes from here," he said with a grimace. "I won't hold it against you. I hear they're not bad to work for."

"I'll try for local first," she said. "There's got to be a job somewhere."

Jamison stood up and took their baskets to the trash. She pushed her chair back to get up and he stepped in front of her. She looked up the long line of his body. He offered her a hand and she held her breath as he pulled her up against the warmth of his chest. She tilted her head back. His breath tickled her lips.

"May I?" he murmured.

Heather answered him by leaning up and pressing her lips to his. They were soft and dry, slightly chapped. He cupped his hand under her chin and tilted his head, deepening the kiss. Her nerves lit up like fire. The wet brush of his tongue against her lips made her gasp. He licked into her mouth, warm and slick, wonderfully sensual. She pressed forward, her breasts crushing tight to his chest.

"Hm," he murmured, breaking away. "Movie at nine, then?"

"Yeah," she whispered back, hungry for more. Her lips tingled.

"Time to go back to work," he said. She pecked another quick kiss to his damp lips. He smiled, a little goofy and a lot pleased. "You're a nice lady."

"Glad to hear it," she said, grinning back.

Daniel and Andy sat cuddled on the couch, and Heather stood at the doorway to the living room, hand on her hip, frowning at them. They hadn't said much since they found out she was going to a movie with Jamison. Daniel actually had a faint frown on his lips as he watched the television. It hurt her a little to watch them be so selfish. She'd never tried to keep them apart just to preserve her own happiness. The fact that they were angry she was going on a date only made her want to do it more. If they weren't going to love her, they couldn't own her, either.

"How do I look?" she said.

Both men looked up, weighing her with their eyes in a way that made her feel warm and excited. Andy's attention seemed centered on the tight skirt she'd picked out in royal blue while Daniel was glued to the ripe, round cleavage showing with the small black tank top she'd chosen. Her feet were encased in black spike heels with open toes.

"Damn," Daniel said.

"Yeah," Andy agreed. "Too bad you're taking that out there, not keeping it right in here."

"Oh, like you have a use for me," she said, maybe sharper than she intended. "You boys have a nice private night tonight. I'll probably be home late."

"Sure," Daniel said. "C'mere."

She strode to the couch and stood with her feet slightly spread in front of them, gazing down at them. Daniel's tanned hand rested possessively on Andy's pale neck, fingers curled down over his collarbone. Her breath caught when he laid his other hand on her waist, just at the juncture of skirt and shirt. Warm fingers brushed a band of her skin. She stared down into his dark eyes.

"Be safe," he said, his thumb pressed to the curve of her waist. "Please?"

"I always am," she said.

Her mouth was dry and her pulse raced. Daniel let her go and she glanced into Andy's half-closed eyes. He was watching her, too. She turned on her heels and walked out of the apartment at the sound of a horn honking down below. Her heart wouldn't stop racing. Her skin burned from the touch of Daniel's fingers pressed to her body. She clattered down the stairs and climbed into

Jamison's car. He leaned over and planted a quick peck on her cheek.

"Hiya," he said.

"Hi," she replied, hoping she didn't sound too breathless.

"You look great. I love the skirt."

"I'm glad," she said. "Color in the middle is a daring dress idea."

"I approve." He turned onto a road she hadn't taken yet. The summer sun had just set and the sky was still slightly lit. She could see the shop fronts, at least. "That boutique is run by one of my exes."

She blinked. "Which one?"

"Tara's Designs," he said. "She's nice, though. She likes girls better than boys, turns out."

"Oh," she said, grinning. "Always a shock."

"Did you know Andy and Daniel were gay when you were younger?" he said. "I mean, if you don't want to answer, that's cool."

"Actually, they're not," she said. "They're pretty bisexual."

"Oh," he said. She watched his color rise again in his cheeks. "I see."

"Do you think they're attractive?" she said, a little husky.

"I already said so," he muttered.

"Do you like boys, too, Jamison?"

"Maybe a little," he said, glancing at her. His face was very red. "Mostly just to think about it. Do you like girls?"

"I've slept with a woman," she admitted, shifting in her seat. Silk panties slid between her legs tantalizingly. "I prefer men, but it was interesting. Nice."

"Oh," he said again, more emphatically. "Wow, that's beautiful to think about. Hope that's not weird."

"I would like to have sex with you at this point," she said, solemn. "So no, it's not weird."

"I would like to have sex with you too," Jamison replied, but he couldn't keep the laugh out of his voice. "So that's cool. Movie first though, we can't be too improper."

She looked up at the theater rising on the horizon and realized she had no idea what was playing and frankly didn't care. The admission stage, which was usually so much more awkward, had gone well. Jamison didn't seem to think she was easy, just fun. And there was no damn reason a woman couldn't pick her own dates and decide when to sleep with them. Jamison excited her; his tawny gold looks and easy smile were keys to her libido, if nothing else. He was nice, too.

He found a parking space in the crowded lot and climbed out. She tottered on her heels for a moment, holding the door, but he didn't seem to notice. She didn't wear them enough to be used to getting out of cars. It was sort of difficult. She snickered at herself and closed the door. He offered his arm again and she placed her hand on the crook of his elbow, allowing him to escort her up to the theater.

Jamison had apparently mastered the male trick of paying before the woman even noticed there was a tab. He handed his card to the teller for their tickets before she could even offer to pay. He flashed her a cheeky grin and a wink. She rolled her eyes at him.

"Share a drink?" he said. "Maybe popcorn, too?"

"Sure. I thought you liked to sneak your own in."

"I can't smuggle in a jacket in this heat. It wouldn't look right." He shrugged. "Next time, bring a big purse and we'll load it up in the car."

"That sounds like a plan," she said. "What are we seeing again?"

He laughed, guiding her to the snack counter. "Some horror movie, guaranteed to be less interesting than the person next to me."

"Oh, good," she said, refraining from leering suggestively, even though she wanted to. Heat crackled between them, like static, as she brushed her fingers down his bare arm. "I like those."

Jamison leaned down and brushed his mouth against the shell of her ear, hot breath sending shivers down her spine. "I'm glad."

Two words, that was all it took, and she trembled again. The husky darkness in his voice had an edge, the taste of sex to come. His desire was rich and ripe. The knowledge of it, of his want for her, made warmth spread in her belly and lower. All the banter, the civilized conversation, provided cover for this: need, want, lust. Her own hands just weren't enough to satisfy. She ran her fingers down to his palm as they entered the dark showing room and grasped his hand. His fingers were strong and thick, not too large, and the thought of them inside her forced her pulse to speed and her breath to catch.

They took seats in the very back row without con-
sulting each other, but by some general instinct and
experience. Heather spread her feet slightly, glad for the
dark and the short skirt. He might not take advantage of
it, but it made her feel wanton and deliberately sexual.
Jamison put up the arm rest and pulled her closer with
an arm around her shoulders. She leaned against the
warm, strong line of his body, her fingers resting on his
thigh. The muscle there was taut and perfect; she could
only imagine what he would look like nude. Adonis in
the flesh, probably.

Warm, slightly callused fingers landed on her knee.
Jamison's thumb pressed against the crook of her leg.
The previews flickered by. She half-watched them,
intent on enjoying the sensation of his skin on hers. He
hummed when she laid her head on his shoulder, his
fingers moving in little circles. She shivered.

"What would you like to do after this?" he
murmured.

"Your place?" she said. "If it isn't too soon. I'm not
easy, I just—"

He waited while she searched for the words to encom-
pass how she felt.

"I want to connect. I'm kind of alone here. Daniel and
Andy have each other, but all our other friends are back
home, and so is my family. I want to make new friends,
have new lovers. You're funny and cute, and I like you.
You sell books."

He snorted a little laugh. "Okay. I don't think you're
easy. You just know what you want."

"Agreed," she whispered against the warm skin of his neck. He swallowed hard. She licked a quick, short stripe up to his earlobe and nipped it. "I figure that even if this doesn't quite work out, we can be good friends. But I'd like to try it."

"Yeah," he said, walking his fingers up to the edge of her skirt. "I would too."

"Watch the movie," she whispered.

He pressed a kiss to the top of her head and stilled his hand, fingertips pressing against her inner thigh. The comfort of continued contact warmed her and dissipated the little core of loneliness that had been nagging at her since she arrived. She inhaled his musky cologne. This was what she couldn't have from Andy or Daniel, this closeness. Not any more. Not since they'd become a couple and they'd all grown up. It wasn't proper, and though she'd never thought propriety would dictate how they touched each other, it had.

"Hm," she said halfway through the film, drowsy despite the screaming, dashing, terrified characters playing out their story on the screen. "This is so nice."

"Yeah," Jamison said. "I haven't gotten to just sit with someone and hold them in a while. I forgot how good it can be."

"Do you want to just leave now?" she said, tilting her head up. He smiled down at her.

"If you want to," he said. "I haven't paid attention to this whole damn movie."

"Me neither," she replied with a grin.

"Let's go, then," he said, standing. She shuffled down the aisle behind him, her heels clicking on the steps in the dark. Her ankles ached a little, reminding her how long it had been since she'd worn date shoes.

The light in the hallway was bright. She blinked hard, eyes stinging until she adjusted. Jamison's hand on the small of her back spread tendrils of heat from every point of contact. She raised an eyebrow at him when she noticed he was looking straight down her shirt.

"Sorry," he said, pale skin flushing again. "It's kind of low cut, and I was just glancing down, and—well. Couldn't make myself glance back up."

"I don't mind," she said with a laugh. "We're going back to your place so you can touch them and lick them and play with them."

He growled a little; a tense, masculine sound. His eyes were slightly darker when she looked up again, the pupils dilated. She smirked. The heat in his eyes was almost enough to burn her skin where it touched.

"You like having your breasts touched?" he murmured as they passed through the crowd, just low enough that only she could hear him. "Is that your favorite thing?"

"One of," she whispered back. They stepped out into the warm night air. "You've probably noticed I have a lot to work with in that department. I like to have them rubbed. It feels good."

"You do have beautiful, beautiful tits," he purred. She hummed back at him, climbing into his car. "I like the heels. Would you like to leave them on?"

"I can do that," she said, placing her hand on his thigh, close enough to the zip of his pants to feel the warmth radiating from him. "What else do you like?"

He placed his hand over hers, thumb stroking her wrist. "Nothing too special, I guess. Just you and me together. I think we can figure it out from there. You keep the heels, I massage your breasts. Sounds like a good time."

He waggled his eyebrows suggestively and she giggled, pleased and comfortable. Jamison had a way of making himself just silly enough to amuse but still sexy enough to titillate. He wasn't taking things too fast, or too slowly, or too seriously. Back at the apartment, Andy and Daniel were probably rolling around naked in their bed, as noisy as they wanted to be since she was out for the evening.

Tension—tangible and wonderful—stretched between them as Jamison drove past the bookstore and into a neighborhood right after the apartment complex she'd moved in to. He pulled up to a small, well-kept house with a little garden out front. She raised her opinion of him at once.

"Rent or own?" she said as they got out of the car.

"Own," he said. "It belonged to my older sister until she had kids. She sold it to me for less than she should have, but I couldn't make her take any more money. I keep her garden the way she had it in return."

"How much older is she?" Heather asked, suddenly aware she had no idea how old Jamison was. "Actually, how old are you?"

"I'm twenty-eight, she's thirty-four. There's an older brother in there who's, like, thirty. I think. He may be thirty-one." He shrugged, grinning sheepishly. "It's hard to keep track. I'm the youngest."

"You look younger than you are," she said, pressing up against him as he unlocked his front door. He shuddered at the brush of her breasts on his back.

Heather followed him inside. The living room was colorful and packed to the brim with bookshelves, every one of them layered deep with books of all shapes and sizes. The television, in comparison, was small. She liked that.

"Want a beer?" he said, his lips turning up in a flirtatious smile. "Or should we just go on to the bedroom?"

"Bring one to the bedroom," she said.

Excitement tickled down her spine like questing fingers. Jamison winked at her and pulled off his shirt in one fluid motion, the muscles in his arms rippling beautifully. She admired his toned chest and the luxurious looking pelt of golden fuzz that trailed down to his jeans. He disappeared into the kitchen and she walked down the hall. The guest bedroom had more bookshelves, one of them nearly empty, and a computer with a wooden desk bigger than a small bed. The next door was the bathroom, and she assumed the closed one led to his bedroom.

The sound of his footsteps let her know right before he leaned against her, one arm dangling over her shoulder with an open bottle of Guinness. She took it and sipped the bitter brew delicately. The solid weight of him draped around her made her want to moan, and though his hips weren't pressed to her backside, she could imagine the hard line of his cock and how it would feel against her body.

"Open the door," he murmured against her ear.

She turned the knob and stepped in, his arms slipping away from her. He flipped the lights on. There were no shelves in the smaller bedroom, just a dresser and a bed too large for the house. It must have been bigger than a king. She glanced over her shoulder at him.

"I sprawl out when I sleep," he admitted. "It's the best bed I've ever had. I couldn't get rid of it when I moved in here, even if it totally doesn't fit."

"Well, at least we have a lot of space," she murmured, putting her beer on the dresser. Jamison did the same. She watched him watch her, silent and still, for a moment. The air thickened with unspoken desire.

Jamison moved first, both of his hands on her shoulders to pull her against him. Their lips met in a wet, wonderful kiss that sent sparks raining down Heather's body. She leaned against him hard and felt the hard heat of his dick at the curve of her hip. She pushed up on her tiptoes to rub against him, drawing a gasp. She groaned into the kiss at the sound, tongue sliding against his. Fire ignited between them, in her body, raging sudden and swift.

Heather skimmed her hands down his back and grabbed firm handfuls of his ass. He groaned into the kiss, reaching down to tug her skirt up and palm her thigh. She gasped as he tumbled her back onto the bed. She bounced, giggling, and he crawled up on top of her.

His legs wedged hers apart, forcing the skirt to ride high around her waist like a belt. He looked down at her green silk panties and made a husky, pleased sound.

"Beautiful," he said.

"You, too," Heather purred, her fingers playing on the bumps of his spine, from neck to waistband and back. "Strip?"

"You first," he replied, sliding his hands under her top.

She moaned when his hands cupped the bottoms of her breasts through the bra, thumb finding the hard peaks of her nipples. She wriggled and pulled until her shirt came off and tossed it off the bed. Jamison's hungry, dark eyes settled on her pale breasts, still half-hidden by a black cotton bra. She lifted her chest as he slid his hand back and grinned at the expression of concentration on his face while he tried to unlatch it. After a long moment, the straps came loose and he slipped it down her arms. He sighed with pleasure and bent his head to her chest, licking a line across the small space between her breasts. Faint stubble rubbed her on both sides of his cheeks, drawing a sharp groan. His hands squeezed and rubbed the tender flesh, feeling every inch of her skin. She bit her lip to keep from crying out. His thumbs pressed against her ribs as he cupped each breast and licked one nipple, then the other in quick succession. He returned to the first and suckled until the pleasure crackling across her nerves became a sweet pain and she tugged on his hair.

Jamison smiled up at her then, for just a moment, before switching to the other nipple and nibbling. She wrapped her legs around his torso and dug her heels in, but not too hard. He shuddered and moaned against her. His hands never left her breasts but he lifted his head and kissed her again, lips ripe with sucking and plump against hers. The tight coil of lust in her belly clenched.

"Please," she whispered into his mouth. "More, now."

He reared back and undid the button on his jeans. She shimmied out of the skirt and kicked it off the bed. Jamison stood up, removed his shoes, and paused with his hands on the zipper of his pants. Heather smiled, cupping her hand over the silk barely covering her intimate parts. She rubbed, sliding the wet cloth against herself and gasping. Jamison slowly eased down his zipper, revealing royal blue boxers. He hooked his thumbs in the waistband of both and peeled them down.

Heather watched, teasing herself through her panties, as his dick bobbed free. She swallowed, suddenly aware of her mouth filling with saliva. He raised one eyebrow and smoothed a hand down his stomach, grasping himself. She whimpered as he stroked once, tip to base, highlighting exactly how big he was. And he certainly was. Her toy had nothing on Jamison.

"Come here," she whispered.

He climbed back up onto the bed, moving to bend down to her pussy, but she put her hand on his forehead. He rolled his eyes up to look at her, obviously confused.

"I want to suck you," she said.

"Oh," he replied, nearly gasping. She smiled. "How do you want me?"

"Lie on your back," she said. "It's easier that way."

Jamison rolled onto his back next to her. She stripped off the damp panties and dropped them on the floor. Her heart pounded so loud she thought he might be able to hear it, pulse racing in the throbbing of her clit. She settled between his legs, running her hands up his thighs. He stroked her hair with one of his hands, not tugging yet, just petting. She paused as her fingers framed the sweet round globes of his balls and the closely shaved base of his cock. She stroked his skin all around, searching for stubble, and found only the slightest brush.

"Are you always shaved?" she asked.

"I like it," he said. "I wax. Keeps me from getting itchy stubble."

She hummed, another wave of lust racing down her nerves. Face to face with his cock, she wondered how wide he was. It would be weird to ask if he'd ever measured, though. Instead she sneaked her index finger and thumb around the base of him, finding that her fingers didn't quite touch. He held his breath for the space of heartbeats while she lifted his cock from his belly. Stroking her hand up the silky, hard length made her pussy flutter with anticipation. She licked the smooth skin of his balls first, lapping between them and around. Jamison's breath came in short gasps. His dick pulsed once in her hand. She moaned and licked a long stripe up the length of him.

There was nothing quite like the feeling of a man aroused, subject to her desire. She rubbed her cheek on him, savoring the wonderful sensation, and finally opened her mouth wide to fit him in. Her jaw began to ache as she worked to take more, teeth pressing into her lips, the musky heat and taste filling her mouth.

"God," he sighed. She stroked what she couldn't fit once he bumped the back of her throat. He was too wide to go any further. It had been too long since she'd taken any man so deep. "You're great at this."

She slurped back, her tongue dragging up the thick vein on the underside. He shuddered and rubbed her shoulders with gentle fingers.

"Condom?" she said.

"Not before I taste you, too," he said.

Heather let him push her onto her back and spread her legs as he knelt between them. Instead of lying on his stomach, he stayed on all fours. The view of his round, lovely ass only made her moan louder at the first touch of his hot, slick tongue to her folds. He licked her with surety, long strokes of his tongue that teased her pussy and fluttered over her clit. She grabbed the sheets in handfuls and panted. The pleasure, like his attention, came in waves and crests. It wasn't the kind of concentrated licking that would make her come; instead, his sweet skill built layer after layer of ecstasy.

"Please," she cried out, finally, her body trembling. He looked up at her. "Fuck me!"

"Anything you want," he managed, his mouth shiny with her juices.

She lay gasping for breath, her body on fire, as he dug through his nightstand. She heard foil tear and lifted her head to watch him roll on a condom. Her whole body quivered with need and hunger. He put one hand on the soft plane of her stomach and lifted one of her legs over his shoulder. Sweat glistened on his brow. He smiled down at her and slid his dick against her body. She shuddered. He pressed harder, fitting the head of his cock to her, and she nearly screamed as he pushed inside. He held still, his arms trembling with the effort. She heaved for breath, holding on to his shoulders. The stretch wasn't too much, it wasn't; the burn was good after she waited a moment to adjust.

"Okay," she managed. "Go."

He let out a long, soft moan as he pushed again, deeper, seeming to fill her up forever. Heather's eyes fluttered shut. He kept thrusting, tiny and shallow movements to work himself in further. His hand pressing down on her stomach was strange and intimate, as if he could feel himself inside her that way. She opened her eyes again and looked down the length of their bodies. Desire poured over her like molten liquid as she saw that she'd taken almost all of him.

"Please," she whispered. "More."

He bit his lip and drew out of her while she watched, her breath coming quicker as each inch slipped free. When she could feel just the head teasing the tight rim of her body, he plunged back in, hard and fast. She cried out, tearing her eyes away to meet his gaze. Heat and pleasure threatened to consume her. He bent his head and caught her mouth in another kiss as he thrust, fucking her deep and hard, so that the end of each thrust met a little spark of pain that pushed her further, faster. She found herself whimpering into his kiss, nails clawing at his back and the leg he didn't have over his shoulder tight around his waist. She hardly knew if she was digging the heels in or not, but if she was hurting him, he didn't mind.

The ecstasy built upon itself with each shove of his hips, each glide of his thick cock inside her, touching every nerve and secret space. She closed her eyes and let the pleasure fill her, focused only on it and her breathing. The soft grunts and gasps Jamison made as he fucked her only drove her higher. She let her body go limp so he could move more, harder. He seemed to understand that she was close and lifted a hand to one of her breasts, squeezing and massaging just shy of pain. She cried out again at the flare of desire that arced down her spine.

"Come on," he gasped. "Come, baby. Please. I'm so close."

Hearing the strain in his voice was the final push. She climaxed on the next thrust, struck silent and gasping by the weight of the pleasure as it crushed her beneath it. She raked her nails over his back and he yelped, thrusting suddenly sharper and faster. She opened her eyes in time to see him bite his lip again and come, his eyes closed, his face beautiful in its joy.

"Mm," she moaned, aftershocks rippling through her as he slid out a moment later. She felt boneless, sated. Some rustling and a prod at her leg made her lift her head.

Jamison lifted the cover in invitation, a sleepy smile on his face. She smiled back and crawled under the sheets next to him. His heartbeat was loud and quick when she laid her head against his chest, but his breathing had started to slow, and so had hers. A fine ache started in her lower body.

"You're wonderful," she said, hearing in her own voice how dazed and pleased she was.

"You, too," he said against the top of her head. He kissed her there, softly.

Chapter Four

Heather padded into the apartment, eyes heavy with tiredness and her heels dangling from her fingertips. The light in the kitchen was on, half-illuminating her rumpled fold-out bed where one of the boys must have pulled it out for her. The clock on the cable box said it was three in the morning. A brief nap and a snack at Jamison's house had eaten up the rest of the hours of the night. Her insides still ached and her legs were sore, but the lassitude that blanketed the rest of her was beautiful. She made it into her empty bedroom, grabbed a pair of sleeping boxers and a fresh tank top, then climbed in the shower for a quick rinse.

That was one thing she didn't like to do with new lovers. She sighed with relief as she rinsed the sweat and fluids from her body, tender and sated. She hoped Andy and Daniel had had just as good of an evening, with just as much wonderful sex. The thought of Jamison's thick, long cock in her mouth and hands made her shudder again. The ache, though, was something she might not want to get used to. The well-endowed weren't always such a pleasure, at least not afterwards. Maybe an inch or two shorter would have been better. She smirked at herself for her mental commentary, decided she loved the sex one way or the other, and shut off the water. She heard a door creak as she toweled herself off.

"I'll be out in a minute," she called softly through the bathroom door, pulling her sleepwear on. She opened it and found Andy leaning against the wall and looking rumpled, like he'd just woken up. "Sorry if I woke you."

"No," he said. "I wasn't sleeping well. Didn't want to call and check up on you like some kind of mother hen, though. I figured if it got too late I might make sure he wasn't a secret axe murderer or something."

"I'm sorry," she said, reaching out to enfold him in a hug. He pulled her tight against him, shocking her breathless, the slide of his bare arms and chest against her barely covered skin sending a bolt of desire through her. Her satisfaction melted away under its heat. "I didn't mean to make you worry. He's very nice."

"I'm sure," Andy muttered into her hair, his voice tense and ragged with some emotion. She would have thought it might have been jealousy, but that didn't make sense.

All the same, she laid her head on his shoulder and melted into the hug the way she would have when they were younger. He sighed, his breath tickling her ear. She ached fiercely for him to carry her back to their bed, if not for sex, then for closeness. To be held between their warm, delightful bodies, to be cosseted and comforted. To be loved. She bit her lip and squeezed her eyes shut tighter against the crushing grip of loneliness as it, too, roared back to life.

"Hey," Daniel said. She looked up, dazed, to find him leaning in their doorway. "You okay? Did he hurt you?"

"No," she said. The need to beg to come to their bed pushed against her throat, her lips, like a hand. She held it in with a hard swallow. "I'm just tired. That's all."

"Okay," he murmured. Andy released her, his hands skimming down her arms and back. He stepped into the bathroom and shut the door quietly.

Daniel stood staring at her and she stared back, hands loose at her sides, her hair wet and plastered ridiculously to her head. There was some chasm between them that she couldn't cross, one that had never been there before. And she wanted to be with him terribly; the pain of a lonely bed with no one she knew so well to whisper goodnight was like nails in her heart.

"Sleep well," he whispered, eyes dark and shuttered from her.

Heather backed down the hall as he disappeared back into the shadows of their room. Andy came out of the bathroom and closed their door behind him, leaving her in the dim living room, cold in her pajamas and wishing for someone to hold her again and mean it. She huddled under the sheets and bit her lips until they were raw to keep from crying. After the wonderful night with Jamison, she'd felt good, but nothing could wipe away her feelings for Andy and Daniel. No man ever could. It was more than looks and desire, more than lust; she loved them. She loved them passionately, deeply, painfully.

Sleep was long in coming, despite her exhaustion.

The soft shuffling of Daniel making his coffee woke her, but she groaned and put her pillow over her head. Her eyes were gritty with tiredness. Her lower back ached. She twisted onto her back and stretched. Daniel came around the corner, mug in hand, squinting and exhausted. She raised one arm over her head, the covers riding low on her stomach. The tank top stretched over her chest. He looked down at her.

"Sorry I woke you," he murmured. "You going to go bed shopping today?"

"Probably," she said. "Is Andy off?"

"No, but he will be tomorrow," he said. He reached out and smoothed a stray lock of hair off of her forehead. Her eyes closed involuntarily. Her eyes prickled as his thumb rubbed her temple. "What's wrong?"

"Back hurts," she said, squeezing back the tears. "I can't get comfortable."

"Hold on, I'll get you some ibuprofen," he said, disappearing back into the kitchen.

Heather huffed out a sigh and rubbed her eyes. What did they expect from her? Short of moving away again, she couldn't move past them, and didn't particularly want to. It was just the ache, the pain, of watching them be happy without her when she loved them so much. She sat up when Daniel came back in. He dropped two pills into her hand and passed her his coffee. She swallowed them with a sip and handed it back.

"That fold-out's no good," he said. "Why don't you go sleep in our bed?"

She glanced up at him. "With Andy?"

"It's not like it'll be the first time," he said. "You can stay with us tonight, too, if you can't get a bed delivered. It's just stupid to make you sleep out here; we've got the room."

"Okay," she said through the lump in her throat.

Daniel offered her a hand out of bed. She wrapped her fingers around his, leaning into his arms for a split moment as she stood. He gave her a brief hug and guided her down the hall. She realized she hadn't actually been in their bedroom yet. Daniel put his coffee down on the dresser and flipped on a little desk lamp. Andy lifted his head and blinked at her.

"The fold-out's hurting her back," Daniel explained.

Andy hummed and shifted, pulling the covers back. Heather crawled up onto the bed—it wasn't quite as big as Jamison's, but it was big—and curled up. She watched Daniel dress in the dim light, pulling on his shirt and tie, his armor against the world. Andy's palm was warm and large on her back. She stifled a gasp as he slid it down from her shoulder to the curve of her waist and shifted, spooning them together. Her breath rushed out in a sigh.

"Go to sleep," he whispered into her hair.

His arm around her waist and his mouth at the back of her neck were like anchors to a warmer, better world. The warm length of his thighs pressed against her legs. She wasn't sure if he was wearing anything or not. Her shorts were still on, after all. It didn't matter. Nothing mattered but this. Daniel turned off his lamp and shut the door behind him, enclosing the room in darkness. Andy's breath against her skin tingled and tickled, but as he relaxed back into sleep, she fell with him. It was so much easier.

An alarm beeping and Andy's reaching over her to turn it off woke her. It still felt too early to be up. She grunted her disapproval, prompting a little snort of laughter from her bedmate, and pulled the covers over her head.

"That'll teach you to have a late night out," Andy said. "Come on, it's noon. Time for lunch and living and all that."

"Damn you," she groaned, peeking up from the edge of the blankets. Andy's bare, beautiful chest and stomach drew her eye. "Are you naked?"

"No," he said, grinning naughtily. "I sleep in boxer shorts. Keeps things from sticking to other things."

"Ah," she said and rolled her eyes. "One of the many issues I never have to worry about."

"I assume that you, uh," he cleared his throat. "Had a good time last night?"

"He's very nice," she said, ignoring the real question. "We did have a good time together. I wish there was an opening at the bookstore. That would be a great job."

"They never hire anybody new," he said. "Nobody ever quits."

"That's what Jamison said," she said and sighed. "I still need to go job hunting, then. Nowhere I've been so far has been hiring. It's kind of a tight market."

Andy shrugged and slipped out of bed. His underwear clung to the round curves of his ass. Heather watched with her chin propped on her hand while he got dressed and smoothed out his hair in the mirror on the dresser. Her stomach rumbled and he glanced at her.

"Lunch?" he offered.

"Daniel said there was food in the fridge," she said. "I don't want to keep spending your money by eating out."

"Consider it part of your job search," he said, shrugging. "Check everywhere we go to see if they're hiring. Have you heard back from that grad program yet?"

"No, but I should soon," she said.

"That's good," he replied absently. "I guess I'll go look through the coupons and find somewhere to eat. You get dressed."

She followed his gaze to her chest and noticed the firm buds of her nipples lined quite obviously by her tank top. She huffed again and he just laughed, walking out of the room. She ran one thumb over the bump in the fabric and twitched at the sore shock of pleasure. Maybe Jamison had paid a little too much attention to her breasts the night before if they were still sore in the morning.

She did feel better, though, after spending a few hours sleeping in Andy's arms. Happier, at least. Her back was still stiff and sore, but as she shuffled to her bedroom, she had to admit the ibuprofen had helped some. The softer, bigger mattress probably hadn't hurt, either. She pulled on her jeans and checked her phone for a message, then realized she hadn't actually given Jamison her phone number yet. She laughed at herself under her breath. Desperation was an ugly word, but it was accurate. There were no words for the subtle, constant pain of watching Daniel and Andy in their separate orbit. Jamison's affection hadn't managed to cancel it out either; he'd only helped her put it aside for a few hours.

If she didn't want to risk breaking up her best friends, it would almost be worth telling them how she felt. The chance to ruin their relationship was too large to ignore, though, so she didn't. She kept it to herself and let it hurt.

Heather ducked into the bathroom and straightened her hair with a few quick swipes of the comb. She brushed her teeth and rinsed with the mouthwash already on the counter, despite it being the awful orange flavor Daniel liked. When she came out, Andy had his shoes on and a little leaflet in hand.

"Twenty percent off a purchase of twenty dollars or more at the Italian place down the street," he said. "You in?"

"Sure," she said. "I like Italian. Maybe they need a waitress. I'm not too good for that."

"Good," he said, fake-glaring. "Because I'm a kitchen worker and very proud of it."

She leaned in and gave him a peck on the cheek, a faint brush of lips. He smiled at her, sweet and pleased. "I have to get my shoes, hang on," she said.

Heather rushed back to her room and pulled on her sneakers, then followed Andy down the steps to his car. His T-shirt was tight across the wide muscled expanse of his back. She enjoyed the view, but she was still sore, and each little flutter of arousal almost made her wince. She was starting to rethink her opinions on big men. Jamison would have to be more careful next time, if there was a next time. She wasn't sure. It would be frankly wrong to lead him on when her heart was somewhere else. Being friends was probably the best, most honest route.

"Thinking?" Andy asked her after the long silence, shops and streets drifting past outside the windows of the car.

"Yeah," she said. "I think Jamison and I would probably be better friends. It's never fair when I start a relationship and my heart isn't in it, and my heart's just never in it for—"

She stopped. She couldn't say, *anyone else but you two.* Andy wisely didn't finish her sentence for her, and the silence held until he parked the car in front of a red-brick converted house with a hand-painted sign that read, "Best Lasagna in the State."

"Does it have a name?" she asked.

"Not really," he said. "I just call it Dino's. He's the guy who owns it. His son runs the kitchen. Good guy, friendly. I would work here if it wasn't family run and I had the chance, you know?"

"Yeah," she said. "Good people, good food."

"Absolutely," he said. "Let me order for us. Trust me, they'll give us a feast."

"Okay," she said, intrigued by the close, slightly smoky atmosphere as they stepped inside. The lights were dimmed even in the back; natural light from the front windows gave everything a nice glow. "Where do we sit?"

"Wherever," he said, choosing an empty booth across the restaurant from the little corner bar. "A waiter will find us pretty quick."

Before he'd even finished the last word, a young, handsome man swept up to their table. His long hair was tied back in a casual knot and his white shirt was dusted with what looked like extra oregano from the kitchen.

"Hey, Andy," he said. "What can I get you and the lady? Tell me you aren't running around on Danny. That's just wrong, man."

"No," she said, grinning. "I'm their childhood best friend. He's safe with me."

"Good, good," the waiter said.

"The platter special," Andy said. "And two Cokes. We're starving."

"We'll get you taken care of," he said with a wink to Heather. She smiled at him.

Andy raised an eyebrow when he walked back to the kitchen. "He's married."

"I wasn't interested," she said. "But it's still polite to respond to casual flirting."

"Yeah, I guess," he said. He fiddled with the parmesan shaker. Heather frowned and watched him while he stared resolutely down at the little jar in his hands. "Do you feel like something's not right?"

"Hell," she said. "I don't know, Andy. I moved all the way out here because I care about you two and I can't live without you. I'm just lonely. Daniel's never home, you two are dating, and I'm on a fold-out sleeping by myself."

He looked up at her then, frowning also. "I thought that was why you went out with Jamison. Didn't you have a good time?"

"Yes." She sighed. "He was fantastic, and the whole time I was in his bed I was happy, but then I came home. I always have to come home, and then nobody else is ever enough."

"Well," he said, taken aback by the ferocity in her voice. "I don't know what to say."

"Yeah," she said, burying her face in her hands. Her cheeks burned with shame. "Me either. I didn't mean to unload that on you. I left my family, and our other friends, and here I can't even find a job or furniture and I'm just intruding on this life you've built for yourselves."

"Are you saying you want to go home?" he whispered.

"No!" she said, startled. "No, I want to be happy here. That's all. It's just relocation blues. It'll pass. That's how it works."

Andy stared at her, and she shied away from his gaze. Her heart sped up. This was getting too close to the truth of the matter, and she didn't want to let it slip out that all she wanted was Andy and Daniel, any way she could have them. It would sound pathetic. Andy would feel guilty. It wasn't worth it.

A different waiter brought them their drinks and a small plate of cheese-covered breadsticks with a thick, rich butter sauce in a cup and another cup with marinara. Heather plucked one off the plate and nibbled it, then made a sound of joy and took a bigger bite.

"This is great!" she said.

"Told you," he replied, still subdued. "I have to go to work after this, by the way. Are you going to go bed shopping?"

"I am," she said. "That fold-out sucks, and I can't sleep through Daniel making his coffee in the morning. I always wake up."

"I usually sleep through him getting dressed," he said. "We just didn't get much rest last night. Jamison's a cool guy, but you can never tell, you know?"

"Yeah."

"Like that time we had to take care of Jake for you," he said, biting his breadstick more viciously than was entirely necessary. "The son of a bitch."

"Don't talk about that," Heather said shortly. "You know I don't like it."

"I can't forget about it," he said. "Not when you go out with other strange men. Any one of them could try to hurt you, and I couldn't deal with that."

"You two put him in the damn hospital," she said. "After I already Maced him in the eyes. That was sort of unnecessary."

"No, it wasn't."

The waiter came back and put in front of them two small plates of baked spaghetti topped with meat, olives, and mushrooms. Heather twirled some onto her fork and nibbled. The flavor was rich, yet tart. She didn't have to say again how wonderful it was, because Andy's satisfied smile let her know he agreed.

That was the best part about being close to a cook. They knew the best restaurants.

"Consider the subject dropped," she said after another few bites. "I should go to the bookstore and tell him we should be friends instead. Or maybe I'm just trying to get out of developing a functional relationship."

Andy sighed. "Psychiatrist babble. You're perfectly functional and so are your relationships. If you don't want to be his girlfriend, don't."

"I was thinking lover," she said, almost laughing. "We're a little old for boyfriend–girlfriend, aren't we?"

He gave her meaningful eye contact, though she couldn't quite figure what his point was. "You're never too old to be sweet."

"I suppose," she said, smiling.

Chapter Five

Heather opened the apartment door, brushing her sweat-damp hair back from her face. The TV was on, but no one was in the living room. She nudged the door shut and collapsed onto the couch. Daniel's car was in the lot downstairs, so she knew he was somewhere in the apartment. It had taken hours to find the right furniture for the right price and arrange to have it delivered; she'd settled for a scratch-and-dent set of cherrywood. It was beautiful, and so was the dresser that came with it, but the delivery couldn't come for two more days. Expediting it would have cost a ridiculous fortune instead of a small fee.

A door opened in the back of the apartment and Daniel strode into the living room.

"When does Andy get home?" she said.

"Restaurant closes at ten thirty," he replied, sitting on the couch next to her. "So, about two hours. Sometimes more depending on how much cleanup he does."

"Hm," she said. "I guess I'll have to adjust to the schedule. Dinner's at eleven, then?"

"Yup," Daniel said. He draped an arm casually over the back of the couch. "I did talk to him earlier. He said you might not date Jamison any more."

She sighed. "You boys are damned gossips, you know that?"

"Well?"

"I suppose," she said. "It isn't fair to string along thoroughly nice people when I know I just don't have feelings for them. I mean, not to be too graphic or anything, but the sex was amazing. But I'm not the kind of woman to use somebody like that."

Daniel looked at her, almost staring. She turned her gaze to the television without really seeing what was on. He turned his head, too, after another moment of quiet. Andy seemed bothered by her loneliness, but Daniel looked like he was chewing it over and trying to figure it out. She wasn't going to come out and say she was in love with them, but surely he would put the pieces together and leave her alone?

"Do you remember what happened before we moved?" he said.

She froze. Her cheeks colored. "You had just started dating. We had a going-away party. That's all."

"That's not all, honey," he whispered. His fingers brushed her shoulder. "You're being dense now. You can't have forgotten."

"I don't want to talk about this," she said, hunching over.

Daniel went quiet, but the image burned itself on her brain, fresh as that night. The party over, all of their friends gone, an empty bottle of Jack Daniels in her lap along with Andy's head. He had been drooling on her shorts. She remembered that vividly. She also remembered the moment when Daniel collapsed on the couch next to them and buried his face against her neck, one hand on her breast and the other on Andy's head. Then Andy had awakened with a slurred gasp and pressed his mouth to her belly.

She'd said no and stumbled to bed, leaving them to have messy, loud sex on her couch. She'd made herself come twice, despite the alcohol, while listening to them, her skin burning with the memory of their touch. But it would have been wrong. She knew that. They had all been intoxicated. Ruining their fresh love for each other in one night hadn't been on her agenda then any more than it was now.

The door opened and startled them both. The smell of meat and butter followed Andy's exclamation of, "I'm home!"

"You're early," Daniel said over the back of the couch.

"Elmer gave me leave to go," he said, piling bags of food on the table. "He heard from Lucio that we had a lady friend in town and that I hadn't been keeping her company."

Daniel snorted. "That's an interesting way to phrase it."

"You know Elmer," Andy said with a grin. "Come eat. I know you two must be tired, and tonight you don't have to wait up on me. I brought home steaks with bourbon butter and a little bit of salmon I skimped off an extra plate that got made by accident."

Heather smiled, relieved to have his boisterous happiness filling the apartment instead of her gloom and Daniel's sudden curiosity. Andy handed her a plate with a scoop of mashed potatoes and a small helping of broccoli, plus her steak and a little piece of fish.

"You're trying to fatten me up," she accused, taking her plate to the coffee table.

Daniel sat down with his own and two sodas in the crook of his arm. She plucked one free and opened it for herself. It seemed a little uncultured to have it with a steak, but she didn't really care. The taste was all that mattered. Considering the silence as they feasted, she wasn't the only one thinking along those lines.

True to Andy's words, her eyelids began to droop as she finished her last bite. Shopping was surprisingly hard work.

"Go on to bed," Daniel said, patting her on the back. "We'll come in there in a minute."

Heather remembered in one feverish rush that she was going to be sleeping pressed between her boys, and the thrill of it threatened to wake her right up. Andy patted her leg and she stood, leaving them to clean up the leftovers and the kitchen. She grabbed her pajamas and changed in her empty room before padding down the hall. She heard the soft murmur of voices in the living room and couldn't quite figure what they were saying. Probably talking about her loneliness and her bad dating habits. She snorted. There was nothing they could do about it; they'd realize soon enough and give up.

The empty bed seemed huge as she flopped down on it and buried her face in the pillows. The sweet musk of their scent filled her senses. She wiggled under the covers and hummed contentedly to herself. The mist of sleep had begun to drift over her when the door creaked open and soft footsteps came into the room. She lifted her head briefly, blinking at the silhouettes of Daniel and Andy as they stripped for bed. A warm, purring moan slipped from her when one of them—she thought Andy, by the calluses on the hand that wrapped around her middle—pressed up against her and shuffled her to one edge of the bed.

She laughed; it was definitely Andy. Another hand settled on her upper arm, draped over both of them, belonging to Daniel. She closed her eyes and basked in the warmth and comfort. This was what happiness meant. Her breathing leveled out and her mind drifted.

A rustle of fabric and a bitten-off gasp woke her again. She didn't move or tense, afraid to give herself away. Andy scooted his hips back away from her butt, his fingers tightening on her side. Along the small of her back, she felt the brush of knuckles that she knew must have been Daniel's, which meant he was touching Andy. Heat raced from her fingers to her toes, igniting everything in between with fire. The bed shifted, Andy whimpered, and Heather tried to keep her breathing even and steady.

"Hush," Daniel whispered. "You'll wake her."

Andy answered only with hard breathing. Heather desperately wanted to reach back and feel what they were doing. She imagined Daniel shifting Andy's legs and pushing inside him with slow, careful movements. So careful not to jostle, not to wake her. Her fingers crept down her belly, but she couldn't figure a way to get them lower without brushing Andy's hand with her arm.

"Or do you want to?" Daniel whispered again, the faintest hint of noise. The bed rocked ever so slightly and Andy gasped. "Do you want to push her onto her back and fuck her while I'm on top of you?"

"Yes," Andy hissed.

Heather didn't gasp but she bit her lip so hard so tasted blood in her mouth, copper like pennies. Another slow rocking of the mattress followed with a tiny noise. They shifted, and it took all her focus not to moan as what was unmistakably the naked, hot length of Andy's cock bumped her lower back and rubbed there. He hissed again. A little streak of wetness tickled the bare skin between her shirt and shorts.

"Don't come," Daniel whispered.

She couldn't believe they were doing this right next to her, and not too quietly, either. Unless they wanted her to wake up, wanted her to hear what they were saying. Her breath sped with her pulse, beyond her control. There was no way—they were so happy together, they hadn't included her in the beginning. Why now?

"I want to touch her," Andy whispered back, his voice husky and tight. "Don't you?"

"Sure I do, pretty boy," he murmured. "Always do."

She held still, fighting not to press herself back onto them, fighting not to touch herself. Not until she heard more. Not until she knew what they really wanted from her. Childhood lusts were one thing, but she wanted love. She wanted them to love her, need her, like she needed them.

"Not fair," Daniel moaned, a little louder. "Not fair to want somebody so badly."

"Who won't have you," Andy replied. The bed shifted and creaked with the force of Daniel's next thrust, and Andy keened low in his throat. "I miss her."

"Me too," he answered.

Heather stifled a whimper, but not low enough. They froze. She heard them breathing, her too. She could always pretend to be asleep. But they wanted her. Wasn't that enough? If they didn't love her, they wouldn't have asked her to move in with them.

Someone's hands grasped her breasts, suddenly, through her thin top. She cried out, her hands flying up to grip them. Bigger palms; that meant Daniel. She writhed back into Andy, rubbing the whole length of his erection against her butt and back.

"When did you wake up?" Daniel whispered.

"Never fell asleep," she replied.

"Hm," he murmured, flexing his hands until she whimpered again. The tank top abraded her nipples, his fingers touched bare skin at the edges. She wanted more. "You can say no."

"I don't want to ruin this," she said. "You two. I don't want to break you up."

"Honey," Andy said with a short, not-so-humorous laugh. "We've been waiting for you to join in since day one."

"But I thought—" she started. A wet, hot mouth fastened at the crook of her neck and shoulder, freezing her words with a moan.

"You thought wrong," Daniel said. "We missed you so much. We thought you didn't love us anymore, always going around with those other boys."

"I hated it," Andy said, sounding raw. "We were made for each other. You know that, too, just like we do. Don't pretend."

A whole lifetime's worth of lust came crashing down on her at once. She let go of Daniel's hands to skim down her shorts, and shimmied bare on Andy's still-hard cock. He gasped. She wriggled again until she got him positioned between her legs and squeezed her thighs. He thrust shallowly against her and Daniel grunted at the movement.

"Do it," she moaned. "Please, make love to me. Please."

"Don't have any condoms," Andy managed, his fingers creeping down to grip the curve of her hip. "We'll have to improvise."

"I'm safe," she said, reaching down to fondle the slick head of his dick. He gasped again.

"Believe you, baby," Daniel said. "But you can still get pregnant."

"No," she said shortly. "On birth control, too. I'm a big girl. I take care of myself."

"More foreplay next time," Andy promised, spreading her legs with one hand hooked under her thigh. "Roll onto your stomach."

She did, panting already, the sweltering heat under the covers and the sweet, wonderful knowledge that they had always wanted her and always would burning her up. Hands guided her to lift her hips a fraction, then the velvety, hot touch of Andy's dick pressed at her. She pushed back as he thrust forward and cried out at the perfect, endless sensation of him sliding inside her. He gasped and shoved forward harder after a moment and a second pair of hands found their way to her body.

She let herself reach back this time and trace the curve of Andy's ass until she found where they were joined. She stroked the base of Daniel's cock with her fingertips, making him jerk forward and press her hand between their bodies. Andy gasped again. Heather was so wet she could feel herself dripping, her thighs slick as Andy's cock as he thrust shallowly again.

Pleasure wracked her completely. This was what she'd waited for her whole life, this joining, this moment. The swelling of her heart and the joyful dampness on her eyelashes only added to the physical sensations.

"I love you," she managed, muffled by the pillows.

"Me, too," Daniel said.

"God, yes," Andy gasped, working his hips faster and deeper now. Daniel stroked the line of her sides, then moved his hands, she presumed to Andy.

Heather ground up into each thrust, taking him as deep as she could, despite her soreness from the previous night. Even the twinges of pain couldn't distract her from the rising tidal wave of her orgasm. She balanced herself on one arm and slid the other hand down her belly, between her legs. The faintest brush against her swollen clit made her shudder, but instead she spread her fingers around Andy's dick, feeling in every way how he pumped in and out of her body. He moaned at that.

She didn't want it to end. She'd waited so long, so patiently, for the touch of their skin on hers. With each movement, though, the crest of her pleasure grew closer. She ground her hips against her palm in counterpoint to Andy's thrusts, like a dance. Daniel's panting rose over their noises, and then he cried out, slamming forward hard enough to crush Andy against her. Andy shuddered, gasping and moaning as short shoves pushed him again and again deeper into Heather, who just whimpered with it.

"Come on, honey," he panted against her ear. "Feel me in you. Come."

It was the combination of his husky voice and another full, deep thrust lighting up every nerve in her body that made her climax, nearly screaming, a gush of hot fluid bathing her fingers. Andy cursed, short and sharp, and bit her shoulder. She cried out again, writhing under him while he pumped his hips in hard bursts, coming with his teeth on her skin and his hands on her waist.

Daniel threw the covers back and the sudden cold air made her shudder, which in turn made Andy gasp and push deeper one last time. Daniel sighed, obviously content, and she turned her head to look at him as he sprawled out on the bed in the dark. The shadows hid most of him, but she could see the dampness of sweat glistening all over his body. Andy pulled out and nudged her until she lay down between them on her back.

"Well," Daniel said. "That only took ten damn years."

She laughed, startled into it, and Andy chuckled. Her mind was stuck on the sudden split: life before, life after. She found each of their hands with hers and wound their fingers together. She knew she needed to get up and clean off, or wake up sticky and uncomfortable, but the only thing that seemed to matter was touching them. Making sure they were real, and so was she. The enormity of the situation threatened to overcome her, like a different kind of wave.

"Hey," Andy murmured in the dark, kissing her shoulder. "It'll work. I'm not worried."

"I hope so," she said, squeezing their hands. "I really hope so."

Daniel's alarm went off too early. Heather groaned and rolled away from him to curl up against Andy. Daniel shut off the horrible beeping and rustled around in his drawer, finding clothes. She blinked at Andy's slack, still-unconscious face. Obviously he was either used to the alarm or he slept more deeply than she remembered. She traced her fingers down the curve of his cheek, his neck, his chest. The thrill of just feeling him, and being allowed to do it without consequence, woke her up further.

Daniel stepped over to the bed and stroked a hand over her hair. She rolled onto her back to look at him, his warm smile in the dimmed morning light like a miniature sun just for her. He tugged the covers down to reveal her breasts and her breath caught. He bent and pressed a tender kiss to the top of each, then one more peck to her lips.

"I love you," he said, relishing the words.

"I love you, too," she whispered, pulling him down for another, deeper kiss. His dry lips caught on hers and slid, a tender brush of tongue sending shivers down her spine. She broke away. "Now go to work, lawyer-man."

He smirked. "You two are going to sleep the day away, aren't you?" he said.

"I hope so," she said with another smile.

"Nah," Andy said from his cocoon of sheets. "You've woken me up now. Where's my good morning kiss?"

Daniel rolled his eyes and climbed up on the bed in his good suit, knees pressed to Heather's side as he bent to kiss their lover. She sighed with thorough enjoyment at the sight of their mouths pressed together. Daniel pulled back and stood up again, brushing the wrinkles from his slacks.

"She's right," Andy said. "Time to go to work."

"You make me wish I could take a day off," Daniel sighed, giving them a heated once-over. "I've been waiting a long time for this to work out, and now I don't even get to spend the day with you enjoying it."

"You'll come home," she said. "And then we can cover all the territory we've been missing. Sound good?"

"Hell, yes," he said. "You two have a good day. I'll see you later."

He closed the door behind him. Andy turned his head

on the pillow to smile at her, and she rolled so her back was facing him and scooted. He pulled her in tight, his hands on her wrists, cuddling her as close as he physically could. She sighed again, long and pleased.

"Perfect," he murmured.

"Yeah," she said. "I can't tell you how long I wanted this."

"As long as we did," he said. "We just didn't ask you the first time because you were already dating, uh, Hank, I think."

"Nobody else has ever mattered," she said, her voice breaking slightly. "You could have just asked. I would have said yes. I love you so much."

"I know that now," he whispered. "I'm sorry. We hurt you."

"I hurt you, too," she replied, blinking back sudden and unexpected tears. "If we had talked about this, it would have been so much better."

"We didn't want you to feel pressured," he said.

"And I didn't want to ruin your relationship," she said.

"Guess we're evenly stupid, then," he managed to say with a short chuckle.

"Yeah," she said. "Perfect matches, all the way."

"Want to go ahead and get up?" Andy said, thumbs rubbing her wrists soothingly.

"I don't see why not," she said. "Make me pancakes, my chef."

He chuckled and sat up. Heather rolled onto her back and gazed up the line of his body, mouth watering, suddenly unsure if it was all right to have sex without

Daniel there. She assumed it was, but then again, the rules for this kind of relationship had never been written anywhere she could read them.

Andy smirked and ran his fingers in a hot line from her neck, between her breasts, to the edge of the covers at her lower stomach. She shuddered, raising her arms over her head to grab the pillows. He peeled the covers down, slowly, baring her to his hungry eyes. She spread her legs slightly, stretching to make a long line of her body.

"Beautiful," he murmured.

She looked, equally turned on, as he shifted down the bed. The curve of his hip and butt peeked out from the covers. She tugged them down further, baring his lower body also. He kissed the crook of her knee and licked a long line up her thigh, until she moaned.

"Is this all right?" she said, winding her fingers in his hair.

"I don't see why it wouldn't be," he replied. His eyes sparkled with desire and happiness. "You're our lover. That means you're my lover, too."

"Good," she said, the sound ending on another moan as he licked the trimmed triangle of hair at the apex of her thighs, not quite low enough. "Yes, please, more."

"I haven't done this much," he murmured against her skin. "Tell me what feels good."

He spread her folds with his thumbs and swirled his tongue in a hot spiral up her clit. She gasped and massaged his scalp, pleasure tickling her nerves. He repeated the swirl again, almost like he was making figure-eights with the tip of his tongue. She moaned. He dragged the flat of his tongue up, almost too intense, and she clamped her fingers down. He made an inquisitive noise.

"Too hard," she said. "More swirling, less direct."

Andy lifted his mouth to press a kiss to her belly, the faint swipe of his tongue making her giggle. His thumb pressed gently at the little throbbing bud of her clit, stroking up and down in wonderful small motions. She sighed her enjoyment, smiling at him.

"Think I can make you come like this?" he said.

"Only if I get to do the same," she murmured back.

He grinned and bent his head again. His fingers played gently at the entrance to her body, stroking while his tongue circled her clit. She wriggled, groaning, and he slipped two fingers inside. She cried out as he crooked them and rubbed, sending shocks of pleasure through her. He murmured something, possibly "right there," his lips moving, smooth and delicious on her pussy. He thrust his fingers gently, stroking her inside as his tongue flickered over her throbbing clit.

"Yes," she whispered. "Oh, yes, keep on doing that."

The warm waves of desire lapped at her until she was moaning and gasping, her hips working up in tiny thrusts against his mouth. He thrust his fingers harder, sped the motions of his tongue. She pulled his hair as she came, digging her feet into the mattress. Andy kept licking her.

"Enough," she gasped as the pleasure became too intense. He bestowed a tiny kiss on her aching clit and rolled onto his side, burying his wet mouth against her side. "Damn, you're good."

"I aim to please," he said huskily, and rubbed his jaw. "That works a whole different set of muscles. Weird."

She giggled, reaching down until her hand met the hard length of his cock. He hummed and pushed into the touch. She stroked her fingers slowly up and down him, loving the velvety sensation on her skin.

"Actually," he said after a moment. "Pay me back after breakfast. I'm starving and I kind of have to pee."

Heather laughed harder, letting go of him. "Pancakes sound great."

Andy rolled out of bed and snagged a pair of boxers out of his drawer. Heather watched him as he walked out of the room with them in hand and sighed luxuriously rolling on the warm sheets.

Life couldn't get any better.

She stood up after a moment, wincing at the twinge in her back, and hobbled down the hall. The bathroom door was closed. She pulled on a tank top and a loose skirt without a bra or underwear. She wanted a shower before she got fully dressed; her whole body was sticky with sweat and sex. The slickness between her legs was irritating now that they were finished.

The bathroom door opened and she stepped past Andy.

"I want to get a shower," she said. "Do I have enough time if you're cooking?"

"Just enough," he said, winking. "Since you won't

have to get off while you're in there, should be perfect timing."

She felt herself blushing. "You, ah . . ."

"We figured, yeah," he said.

She rolled her eyes at him and shut the door. The shower heated up quickly and she rinsed herself off, then soaped her hair and stood under the spray. The hot water pounding at her aching muscles was wonderful. She felt a twinge of guilt. She would need to tell Jamison what had happened, and ask if they could still be friends. It wasn't quite regret—she had enjoyed their time together, but now she wished she hadn't done it. He would inevitably be hurt by her sudden turnaround, even if he half-expected it.

Heather turned the shower off and toweled herself dry. Being clean felt so much better, but it still couldn't quite erase the guilt. She hoped that neither of the boys would be irritable when she told them she needed to talk to Jamison alone. Daniel might. He was more possessive than Andy. While it was sometimes flattering, it was also aggravating.

She emerged into the kitchen after dressing again. Andy, in his boxers, glanced over his shoulder at the stove. The smell of bacon and frying butter filled the air. She sat down at the kitchen table and cupped her chin in her hand, watching him cook.

"Blueberries or strawberry chunks?" he asked.

"Huh?" she said.

"Or chocolate chips. In your pancakes." He grinned. "Exciting pancakes."

"Blueberries," she said emphatically.

He reached across the small kitchen space to the freezer and grabbed a bag of blueberries, shaking a few of them into the pan, she presumed onto her pancakes. Her mouth was dry and her stomach rumbled.

"I might go check the mail," she said. "Does it come this early?"

"Actually, yeah," he said. "We're right next to the post office, so we get ours at like, six in the morning. It's always here when I get up."

"Okay," she said. "Be right back, then."

Heather grabbed her keys off the coffee table and toed on her flip-flops. The air outside was warm and slightly humid. There were clouds looming on the horizon, black as night. She raised an eyebrow and walked down the steps. The mailboxes for their building were across the parking lot, so she walked past their cars and unlocked the slot for their apartment.

The first letter on the stack was from the university she'd applied to. She grinned and flipped through the rest; bills and one letter from her mother. She plucked both of hers out and climbed back up to the apartment. Her plate and a tall glass of milk waited on the coffee table, complete with a bottle of real maple syrup. She put the mail on the kitchen table with the other assorted junk taking up its space.

"I'll be in there with the bacon in a sec," Andy said.

She smiled again, giddy with the knowledge that her life had changed for the best. Andy and Daniel were her lovers. They loved her the way she loved them. A warm glow settled in her belly and spread. It seemed so quick.

After years and years of flirting and talking and needing each other, one night had changed it all.

Andy sat down next to her, balancing two plates in one hand and his glass in the other. She took the bacon from him and put the plate between them. Half of it was crispy and half softer. She laughed.

"I like it chewy," he complained, plucking one of the pieces for himself.

"I know," she said, still giggling. "Trust me, I know. Had that argument before."

"So, you get any mail?" he said.

"Yeah, something from the university and from mom," she said. "I hope it's not money. She knows I'm well taken care of."

Andy turned on the television, but neither of them could find anything even mildly interesting at eight in the morning. He muted an infomercial about a fruit-chopper and they dug in. Heather loved the way he made his pancakes: crisp around the edges with gooey fruit chunks and sweet syrup. She made a purring noise and he chuckled.

"Pass me that letter," she said a moment later. "I want to see when I start."

Andy got up. She admired his butt in the thin boxers while he picked up the mail and passed it to her. She opened the letter from her mother first, and found a check for one hundred dollars with a note that said only, "You'd better cash this."

He laughed. "She's still the same."

"Never changes," Heather sighed.

Her heart beat a little faster as she picked up the college envelope. It seemed a little light, and she frowned. She hooked her thumb under the edge of the envelope and tore it open. The folded letter inside was printed on heavy paper, only one sheet. Andy leaned over to look. She opened it and her stomach sank to her feet.

"Oh, honey," Andy said. "Damn."

"They turned me down," she said quietly. "I can't believe it. I have perfect grades, my samples were great. I don't get it!"

To her embarrassment, her eyes began to water. She rubbed them fiercely, letter still clutched in her fist. Andy pulled it gently from her fingers and wrapped an arm around her shoulders. He cuddled her to him, pressing her face to his shoulder while she sniffled and fought the tears still leaking from her eyes. It felt like a giant, awful void had opened in the center of her fresh new life. What was she going to do without school? How could they have turned her down in the first place?

"Hush," Andy murmured. "There are more colleges than that one around here. We'll find you something. And if nothing else, there's always the spring semester, right? Don't give up yet."

"I just don't understand," she managed, hating the reedy sound of her voice. "They're competitive, but I entered with perfect everything."

"Unless the slots filled up before you applied," he said. "Don't forget about that. Doesn't matter how competitive you are if there just aren't any spots."

"Still," she said, rubbing her eyes again. "What now? It's too late for most places."

"Apply for spring semester," he said with a shrug. "It won't be the end of the world to wait another four or five months, will it?"

Heather shook her head, but inside she still felt like someone had kicked her. Andy might say it was because she applied too late, but what if it really *was* because she wasn't good enough? Then what? And she hadn't found a job yet, either. Nothing was working out. Andy's hand on her shoulder reminded her that there was some good in her life—namely, her best friends who had finally become her lovers—but the outlook seemed hopeless.

"I don't work and now I'm not even in school," she said, morose. "I'm a burden."

"No," Andy said sharply, tilting her chin up. She looked him in the eye. "Don't say that. You're a strong, independent woman. You're never a burden on us. It's a hard job climate and this—" He pointed at the letter. "Is bad timing and coincidence."

"Whatever you say," she said and sighed.

Inside, it still felt like she'd fallen into her mother's role: stay at home, read books, take care of the house. That wasn't enough for Heather. She wanted to teach, to make the world a better, or at least different, place.

"I can at least take care of the house and cook," she said finally. The words came out raw. "I want to be good for something, okay?"

"Okay," Andy said, ruffling her hair until she frowned

at him. "Finish your pancakes. Then get together your early application for the spring semester."

"Yeah," she said, picking up her syrup-sticky fork again. The food seemed less appetizing than it had fifteen minutes before. Rejection could do that, she supposed.

Chapter Six

The bookstore clerk who looked up from the desk when Heather came in wasn't Jamison or the boy she'd seen the day before. This woman was in her early thirties with bright, flaming red hair tied back in a loose ponytail. She smiled helpfully.

"What do you need?" she asked.

"I was looking for Jamison," she said. "Do you know where he is? We had a date a few nights ago and I forgot to give him my number at the end."

"Sure, babe," she said, sliding off the stool and scribbling something down. "Here's his number. He's off today. I'm Betty, if you need anything else."

"Thanks," Heather said.

She stuffed the scrap of paper in her pocket and went next door to the café for another iced soda, this time blueberry. Daniel and Andy were both busy, but at least it was Friday. Andy might not have the weekend off, but Daniel would, and she really hadn't been able to spend much time with him since she'd moved. His day job made it a little harder than Andy's flexible, mostly unpredictable kitchen hours. She missed him and his darker charm. Andy provided the perfect sweetness to the mix, but as unstable as Heather felt after her rejection—a night spent in their arms had lessened the blow slightly, and Daniel had been thoroughly sympathetic when he got home—a little dominance wouldn't be unwelcome.

Daniel had been gone when she woke up, and Andy had to go to work early to take care of some mysterious dinner party or catering, something she hadn't quite grasped. It was the best time to see Jamison, when neither of them could fuss about it or be worried.

She pulled out her cell phone and dialed the number. He picked up on the second ring.

"Hello?" Jamison said, sounding confused.

"It's Heather," she said. "I got your number from Betty. You're going to be mad at me when I tell you why, but would you like to meet for lunch somewhere?"

"Sure," he said. "Sandwich shop?"

"Okay," she said. "I'm at the bookstore now, so I'll walk. Meet you there."

She hung up and heaved a sigh. The sun beat down unrelentingly on her dark T-shirt and jeans. A skirt and tank top would have been much cooler, but she wouldn't have needed those every day back in Ohio. She wasn't used to the new weather yet, and wasn't quite sure she ever would be. At least the soda kept her cool while she walked to the deli where Jamison had taken her for lunch, before Daniel and Andy made their confession.

Heather sincerely wished they had gotten around to it, oh, before they'd ever moved out to Nevada. That would have been nice. Saved her some heartache, at least, and other men, too. When she walked into the shop, Jamison wasn't there yet, so she took a table, placed her order and got a drink. Lucy seemed pleased that she'd bothered to buy one even though she already had another soda.

Jamison walked in, startling in his golden handsomeness, as soon as she sat down. She smiled at him and he returned a grin, putting his own order in. He sat down across from her and leaned in.

"What am I going to be mad about?" he said.

"Well," she said. "I've been thinking about our date. Do you think we could just be friends? You're an awesome guy, and I don't want you to stop talking to me."

"Ah," he said, then sighed, looking a bit crestfallen. "It was the sex, wasn't it?"

"What?" she said. "No, that was great."

"Oh," he said. "Sometimes the size is, uh, prohibitive. What's wrong, then?"

She sipped her soda and tried to look him in the eye. Her face began to heat. He raised an eyebrow, watching her blush.

"Daniel and Andy," she said after a moment. "It turns out they've been waiting for me this whole time and thought I wasn't interested in them. But I, er . . ."

"You were," he said, leaning back in his chair. His smile was a little wan, but it was still a smile, and that was better than she expected. "You moved out here to live with them. They're men. The only reason a woman willingly shares space with a man is if they're in love. It fuzzes over all the horrible habits we have."

"I'm sorry," she said.

Lucy brought over their sandwiches and Heather poked at hers. The bread was still crisp and hot. Jamison sat silently, chewing his sandwich. She sighed and picked up her own. At least they could have a nice lunch, if nothing else. He didn't seem angry, but that didn't mean anything. He could have been holding it all inside. She hated the thought that she'd destroyed a friendship before it had even started.

"Seriously," he said once they were halfway through their meals. "I'm not mad. I kind of expected it, to be honest. I think we could be friends. I'm glad you and I spent that night together, but it doesn't mean I expect you to date me."

"Okay," she said. "I'd like that. You're a nice person."

"I like to think so," he said with a smile. "If your boys are okay with it, maybe we could get lunch sometimes. I like you."

"I like you too," she said. "Thanks for understanding."

"Hey," he said, grinning. "I'm not going to stand between you and your two hunks of man meat. You're the perfect sandwich filling, if you get my drift."

"Jamison!" she exclaimed, half-laughing. "Stop that!"

His grin mellowed into another smile. Heather returned it.

"Did you park at the bookstore?" he said.

"I walked. I'll walk back, too. I got turned down by the university and I still don't know where I can work. I don't want to get all tubby sitting around the apartment."

He rolled his eyes. "You finally said something I'd

expect from a woman. Why not walk for heart health? That sounds much better."

"Sure," she said. "I'm doing it for heart health. And my belly."

He laughed. "I guess I'll see you soon, then?"

Heather picked up her empty sandwich basket and took it over to the trash cans. Jamison put a hand on her shoulder, then gave her a quick, friendly hug. She returned the squeeze and watched him leave. A quick check of her phone showed it was four o'clock, which meant Daniel wouldn't be home for another two or three hours. She started the walk back to the apartment, sipping her blueberry soda.

By the time she made it up the steps, sweat drenched her hair and clothes. She gasped with relief as she stepped into the air conditioning. The blinds were closed so she stripped down to her underwear in the living room and started down the hall.

"Whoa!" Andy said, leaning against the bedroom doorway. "Take off the panties, too, honey."

Heather squealed, reflexively covering her breasts. He laughed and came down the hall to pat her on the back. She glared at him. He just grinned, unrepentant, taking as much enjoyment as they always did in startling her.

"What are you doing here?" she said.

"I finished catering the wedding and got the night off," he said. "We trade around that crap so it's fair. Where were you?"

"I went to tell Jamison we couldn't date because I had

fallen into bed with you two," she said. "He took it well. He still likes you."

Andy winced. "I didn't think about how much that would suck for him. He's been looking for a smart, pretty girlfriend forever. He finally finds one and the gay guys take her."

"You're hardly gay," she said, copping a feel of his half-hard cock through his jeans. He jumped. "The sight of my breasts wouldn't do that if you were."

"Tits," he said. "Call them tits. Please."

"No," she said. "I need a shower. What should we make Daniel for dinner?"

"I'll think of something," he said. "Want to go to the porn store and buy something sexy to surprise him after dinner?"

She leaned up and planted a little kiss on the corner of his mouth. He grinned and palmed her ass through the thin silk of her underwear. She wriggled into his hand and pressed herself to him, back to chest.

"I take that as a yes," he purred.

"Yes," she said, then stepped into the bathroom. He winked at her as she shut the door.

Heather slipped off her panties and hopped into the shower for a quick rinse. If they were going to have vigorous, kinky sex later, which she sincerely hoped they were, she'd just have to wash again. Once she dried off and walked out, Andy was waiting with his shoes on. He grinned at her as she did a little dance in the nude before stepping into her room. Joy and silliness in equal parts filled her heart.

"You really like porn stores, huh?" he called from the living room.

She dressed before coming back out. He stood and ushered her out the door, smiling with obviously wicked intent. It would have to be a quick trip if they wanted to cook Daniel dinner before he got home, but she had a feeling Andy knew exactly what he was looking for. She wondered with equal parts arousal and amusement what it would be.

As soon as they got in the car, Andy reached over and put his hand on her thigh, midway up, just high enough to cause a tiny stir of excitement in her. He kept it there through the drive, flexing his fingers at random intervals and glancing at her to watch her shiver each time. Her arousal built like a slow fire, ember lighting ember in turn with each squeeze. By the time they parked at the boxy, plain brown-sided building, her panties were damp and her clit ached with need.

"Let's go," he murmured, patting her leg once before stepping out.

She followed him in, sighing to alleviate some of the pounding desire. The first thing she saw upon entering was a poster of a nude woman with sticky notes over the appropriate places. When read in order, they spelled out: "ID please! Thanks!" She laughed and dug hers out of the pocket of her jeans. As they rounded the corner to the inside, an older, bored-looking man checked their birth dates perfunctorily and waved them in.

Heather put her hands on her hips and looked around. The racks of porn were to the right, and all of the fun toys were to the left. She went to the left. Andy followed behind, practically bouncing on his feet.

"What were you thinking?" she said.

"Well," he replied, dragging the word out. "Something for me, and you, and Daniel."

"And what's that?" she said.

He waggled his eyebrows and led her down an aisle that consisted primarily of dildos in various sizes, colors, materials, and shapes. She admired the selection with a little smile, aware of her arousal like a twisty, shivery thing in her belly. Andy held up something in his hands.

It took her a moment to put together what it was. Heat rushed down her nerves in a scalding wave. He grinned at her gasp. The harness was obviously designed for wide female hips, with a silky, cushioned triangle for the crotch and a not-too-large realistic cock bouncing from it.

"This is the display," he said. "But do you want one? It's got a built-in vibrator."

"Wow," she said, breathless and turned on. "Oh, yeah. Who am I using it on?"

"Me first," he said with a dirty grin. "Then I can get Daniel to beg when I tell him how amazing it feels. Nothing like seeing him on his knees, gasping and whimpering for it."

"Damn," she said, feeling almost woozy. "I can imagine."

And she could: the picture of Daniel sweaty and naked, his back flexing under her fingers while she fucked him—almost too much, very nearly, for public consumption. It wasn't as though she didn't get turned on by the thought of them together, or by feeling and seeing it, but she'd never imagined "being the man" instead. The thrill was thick and sweet, like honey.

"We're getting it," she said, reaching out to fondle the fake dick. It was silky-smooth, and so was the cushioning for her end of things. "This is nice."

"It's the best," he said. "We'll split the cost, how about that?"

"Do I even want to know how much?" she said.

"Honestly, no," he replied with a laugh. "But it's the best, and you want it. Let's get it."

She stroked the cock slowly, staring into his eyes, and watched as he swallowed suddenly. The heat in his eyes burned in the best way. She smirked at him and gave her new "appendage" a little squeeze.

"Get me the packaged one. I want a little porn, too. Can we look?" she said.

"We have time," he replied, grinning back.

"You know what would be better than waiting till after dinner?" Heather said.

"I'm all ears," he replied, strolling over to the porn racks with the discreet package in his hand. "What have you got?"

Heather lay sprawled on the couch, absently running her hand up and down the smooth dildo while Andy, nude, stood at the edge of the window, waiting. She palmed one of her breasts, teasing the nipple back to hardness.

It was odd and sexy to have the strap-on staring up at her from her lap where there had certainly never been anything before. She stroked it again, weighing the dick and palming its silky balls.

"You just can't stop touching it, can you?" Andy murmured, shifting from foot to foor. "Oh, damn, here comes his car!"

"Staging!" she cried out, and giggled.

Andy bounded over to her and buried his face against her stomach to muffle his laugh. The dildo bumped his chin; she felt the push against her lower belly. Strange, and perhaps not completely arousing, but interesting at least. Andy winked up at her and dragged his tongue showily up the length of the flesh-colored dildo, flickering at the tip. She turned on the little bullet vibrator and tucked it into the pouch. The instant stimulation made her gasp.

Andy hummed and mouthed at her toy again, his fingers wrapped in a loose circle around the base to guide it. Her breath sped. She might not have even needed the thorough vibrations with the sight of him getting ready to suck her "cock." It was painfully arousing, like being doused in lust.

He grinned as the door opened and plunged his mouth halfway down.

"I'm home—" Daniel started. Heather moaned, flinging one hand back to grip the couch cushions. "Oh."

He walked around the couch and she opened her eyes. His mouth was slightly open, his eyes hot as he took in the sight of Andy fellating her toy with enthusiasm, slurping up and down the shaft with little moans. How did the vibration feel on his tongue? Daniel ran a hand through his hair, still speechless. Heather watched the bulge in his pants grow at eye level and leaned over to mouth at his slacks in just the right place. He groaned and palmed the back of her head.

Andy looked up at them and pulled back to say, "Bedroom?"

"Yes," Daniel replied, his eyes glued on the bobbing, spit-slick cock between her legs. She put her fingers around it again and he swallowed, hard. "That's a mind-fuck, right there."

"Good, isn't it?" Andy murmured. "You want to watch our girl fuck me, don't you?"

"Hell, yes," he said. Heather grinned at his half awe-struck, half turned-on expression.

"You're so kinky," she said, standing up. The toy was a strange weight between her legs, the vibrations making her weak-kneed. "This is our second time together and we're already playing gender games."

"Oh, I don't want you to be a boy," Daniel purred, his hand slipping between her legs from behind. She squealed and fell against him as he pushed two fingers inside her, enough sudden stretch to make her ache a little. He pumped his wrist, still rumbling a little laugh. "I like this sweet cunt."

She spasmed, crying out. The words flicked across her nerves like a whip, sharp and perverse and wonderfully arousing. Andy crawled over to mouth at the fake cock again. She panted, writhing onto Daniel's thick fingers. He bit the curve of her neck, one arm supporting her around her chest and the other hand buried between her legs.

Andy's hands worked between them and she heard and felt the zip of Daniel's pants coming down. A moment later, their lover had worked his hard-on out of his slacks and underwear. It pressed against her ass, a solid, thick weight. She thought he might have been bigger than Andy, though it was hard to judge when she was so turned on. He slipped his fingers out and shifted his grip around her shoulders, his arm pressing ever so slightly against her throat. She knew a second before his cock head pressed to her what he was going to do. Andy smiled up at her, wicked and pleased.

He thrust, holding her with an arm across her chest and the other spreading her legs. She gasped as he sank halfway in, stretching her wide and filling her up. Her slickness eased the way, but he was definitely bigger than Andy, at least in width. The other man wiggled the fake cock above his lips, teasing, and she pushed forward to entice him. He swallowed it down again and Daniel groaned, fucking into her with more force. She wobbled on her unsteady legs. He couldn't get much traction or depth, but the drag of his dick on all of her most sensitive parts was enough. The vibrations on her clit and the sight of Andy sucking her fake cock like it was the real thing helped, too. Daniel pushed against her in tiny thrusts, moving barely an inch each time, just enough to rub her G-spot with each grind.

"Gonna make you come," he murmured into her ear. "I want to feel you fluttering around me. I want to feel you pour your juices all down my cock, honey."

She moaned again, the pressure of his arm across her throat adding another layer of knife-sharp sensation. Andy massaged her thighs while Daniel thrust and whispered delicious filth into her ear. The vibrations from the little bullet never wavered. She gasped and gasped, higher in frequency as the sensations built. They lanced through her as she climaxed, a piercing blade of pleasure. She screamed. Daniel moaned and shoved deeper, making her tip forward and grab Andy's shoulders for balance.

He pulled out a moment later as she was still panting, leaving her feeling empty and drenched with come and sweat. Andy let the toy fall from his mouth. They took her by the arms and led her on shaky legs back to the bedroom. Daniel gave her a gentle push and she went tumbling to the bed, still shivering with aftershocks. Andy climbed up on top of her and pressed their lips together, stealing a sloppy, hot kiss. His cock nudged her belly. She looked down to see him rubbing against the toy and groaned. The endless vibrations were almost too much for her sensitized clit.

"That was just an appetizer," he whispered, husky and a little hoarse. "You know, after we do this, I expect I'll get to fuck your ass, too."

"Yeah," she managed, grabbing a handful of his hair. "Okay."

He went with it when she pulled his face down for

another kiss. Daniel climbed on the bed with them and tumbled Andy to his side with a push of his fingers. He immediately got up onto all fours and wiggled his butt at Daniel, who gave him a firm slap. Heather swallowed a mouthful of saliva as he squeaked and the skin turned pink.

"I'll get him ready," Daniel said. "Give you a minute to catch your breath. And you like to watch, don't you?"

"Oh, yes," she said. "I want to see."

Daniel's lascivious grin tightened her lower belly all over again with desire. Andy made a questioning, hungry noise. The darker-skinned man poured lube over his fingers. Andy watched over his shoulder with quickening breath. She turned off the vibrator for the time being and sprawled onto her side to get a better angle. Daniel ran his slick fingers down the crease of their lover's ass and he shuddered in turn, spreading his legs wider. Heather watched, rapt, as Daniel pressed at the tiny, pink pucker of skin with his thumb until it opened for him and Andy gasped. There was an element of trust with such delicate maneuvering. It was more than simple sex.

His thumb, slick and shiny with lube, slid in and out slowly until Andy began to move back against it in tiny increments, as if he couldn't keep himself still. Daniel hummed, pulling it out and pushing two fingers in, so smooth and practiced that Heather knew it was their regular routine to do it this way. Her belly tightened with imagined sensation and desire as he twisted his fingers, pushing as deep as he could. Andy pulled at the sheets and moaned. The muscles in Daniel's arm flexed and strained as he stretched the other man.

Heather thought she might die of anticipation. One quick orgasm wasn't enough to keep her sated through watching the pair of men while they touched each other. She almost wanted to just throw out the idea of the strap-on and watch them make love. There would be other times for that, though, and the strange, unexpected thrill of being the physically dominant partner wasn't something she wanted to give up quite yet.

"Do you ever bottom?" she murmured to Daniel. He glanced at her.

"Of course," he said. "But Andy likes it more, and I like to top more. That doesn't mean we don't switch around sometimes."

"Yeah," she said. "I want to see that."

"You'll see everything eventually," he said, winking. "Welcome back home, honey."

"Less talking," Andy groaned. "More fucking."

They both looked at him. His sweat-dappled face, his plump, bite-swollen lips, and the curved line of his back were all enticing. Daniel pulled his fingers free and, still grinning, slicked lube over her toy. She let him guide her into position, a hand on Andy's lower back to ease him a little lower. Her breath caught. Daniel steadied the dildo and tugged their lover backwards. Heather flicked the switch for the vibrator again at the moment the head of the toy slid inside him.

Andy cried out, working his hips back without Daniel's encouragement. Heather put her hands on his hips, entranced by the sight of the toy opening him up and sliding in, inch by inch. This was what men got to see, this angle and intimacy, the stretch and give of her body as they fucked her. Lust and pleasure rushed down her nerves. She let Andy dictate the pace by his gasps. Finally, his butt bumped her hips, only the faintest bit of the toy still visible between them. Andy trembled in his awkward position, moaning.

She temporarily forgot Daniel—not an intentional slight, but she wanted so badly to do a good job at this, to pleasure her lover. She put her hands on his back and eased him forward again, making a slow and, she imagined, pleasurable slide of it. Judging by Andy's groan, she was right. Once he was settled more easily on his knees and only the head of the cock remained inside him, she pushed her hips forward.

"Good girl," Daniel murmured. She twitched at the shock of his breath on her ear. "Now lean over his back. Spread your legs for me."

Without thought, only desire, she did as he asked. The change in position made her go deeper into Andy, who leaned on one arm so he could stroke himself with the other. Daniel bit the back of her neck, then shoved into her, drawing a tiny scream from her throat. This time he bumped the end of her body and ground deep, his hands on her hips, guiding her to move back against him. She did, and he thrust forward, driving her into Andy. She saw the plan behind the motions.

Andy moaned continuously, rocking on his knees to give himself exactly what he wanted. She gasped into his shoulder while Daniel fucked her, the length of him stroking her insides like a knowing hand. Down his back, she could watch herself fucking him. It was odd, not knowing the angle she needed or how it felt to really be inside the other man. That was something she'd simply have to imagine. Hot, and tight, and silky. She'd fingered herself before and she knew what that was like. Daniel stroked his thumb over her ass, teasing at the little pucker there. She groaned, unsure whether she wanted to try it or not. While the loop of their pleasure was amazing, she couldn't quite reach the crest of her orgasm. It tingled out of reach, even though every time Daniel pounded into her she felt a shockwave of pleasure.

The thumb returned, slippery, and she gasped as he pushed it slowly into her. There was the stretch, and a slight burn, but also pleasure. She could feel his cock and thumb both inside her, stimulating the thin skin between them. The extra ache and fullness added to the sensation. Andy cried out suddenly beneath them, his back bowing. He plunged himself back hard enough to jolt Heather against Daniel, held himself there for a moment, and then let out a shuddering sigh.

"No fair," Daniel murmured. "We're not done yet."

"I'll watch," Andy gasped out, wriggling free of the strap-on and collapsing beneath them, half on his back.

Come streaked his chest. Heather bent to lick it up, hearing him sigh his pleasure above her head. She traced her tongue up his belly, searching out every last bittersweet taste. Daniel panted behind her, his thumb sinking deeper as he slammed his dick in again. She cried out, scrabbling at the edge of climax.

Andy wrapped his fingers in her hair and jerked her

head up. Her gasp cut short at the tingling, sweet pain in her scalp. He held her there, smirking, caught between himself and their lover, straining to her breaking point.

"If I could get hard again so fast, I'd make him stop so I could fuck your ass," he said, low and husky. "Then after I'd come inside you, he'd have you, too. You'd be dripping wet and covered in our spunk. You like that?"

"Oh God," she gasped, shuddering.

"Yeah, you like that," Daniel growled from behind her.

She recognized the quick switch of thumb to fingers as he did it to her, stretching her wider, going deeper. His knuckles burned a little, but it wasn't quite pain, just another sensation of letting him have her however he wanted.

"Should I keep going?" Andy murmured. She couldn't nod, because of his hand tight in her hair, but he smiled. "I like to think about you wet with come. We could tie you to the bed and use you all day and night for our personal fuck-slave. Every time one of us could get it up again we'd have you. Maybe leave you with a plug to keep your ass ready in case we wanted you that way. What do you think of that?"

Heather heaved frantically for breath, eyes closed, picturing everything he described for her. The stretch of a plug in her, the slick stickiness of their come on her breasts, her pussy, her lips and face. Waiting for one to return and make her come again, because they would. That was how her boys worked. They would never leave her unsatisfied.

She heard a drawer creak but when she opened her eyes, Andy was already relaxing back to his reclining position. Whatever he'd gotten for Daniel, she couldn't see it. She had some guess, though, and it thrilled her.

"Imagine," Andy whispered, pausing. Daniel's fingers slipped out of her and there was a nudge of something wider, cooler. She wailed as it breached her and slid inside, its silky material like heaven on her body. "That's me. Just imagine us both inside you, wanting you, loving you so much we can't even take turns. We have to have you at once."

It didn't precisely hurt, but she was unprepared for the strength of the sensation as the dildo pushed deeper and deeper inside her while Daniel kept up the steady grind of his hips. The counterpoint stroking was alien and absolutely mind-blowing. She gasped, clawing at the sheets, and when Andy pressed their lips together, she came undone. The orgasm was sudden and sharp, making her clamp down, trembling and shuddering. Daniel shouted his relief and release, pulling out at the last minute to paint streaks of his spunk across her back.

Heather collapsed onto Andy, who walked his fingers down her spine until he found the base of the toy. He pulled it out so slowly she thought she might come again just from the stimulation of her already-exhausted body.

"Wow," Daniel moaned, flopping next to them. "You made us work for that one, honey."

"Yeah, yeah," she muttered, eyes drooping shut. "It was good and you know it."

"Andy's got such a filthy mouth," he said proudly. "I'm glad you like it, too."

"I don't want to cook now," Andy murmured. "I'm tired. Want to go out?"

"God, I need to rinse first," she muttered, wiping her hand through the mess of come on her back. "Throw the sheets in the wash, too."

"Go hop in the shower, babes," Daniel said, heaving himself up and off the bed. "I'll get the sheets. I need less washing."

Andy rolled off the bed and offered Heather a hand, which she took gratefully. Her legs wobbled under her as they walked to the bathroom and her body was achy, but still tingling with pleasure. They were going to kill her with sex, she knew it. But when Andy smiled over his shoulder, a pink handprint still glowing on his butt, she just smiled back.

Heather frowned across the table at Daniel and the angry tilt to his dark eyebrows. Andy sighed and poked at the remains of his steak as though the meat would transport him somewhere else entirely.

"I don't get why you think I shouldn't have gone to see Jamison," she said. "It's fair to tell him we aren't dating. He's a nice guy. He deserves that."

"But you're hanging out with a man who—" Daniel stopped and breathed through his nose for a long moment. "You and he were intimate, okay? I don't like it that you're still talking to him."

"That's ridiculous," she said, pushing her plate back.

"I like him. He's a cool guy. I need to have friends, Daniel."

"But do they have to be male friends?" he said, a pained look on his face. "Male friends you've slept with?"

A sharp wave of anger flickered through her. "Is this about me sleeping around?"

"No," he said, rubbing his face. "I just don't like it. I don't trust him."

"You like him," she accused. "You said you liked him when you introduced me. You don't trust me!"

"Shut up," Andy said suddenly. "Both of you. Daniel, you're being irrationally possessive. Heather, consider the fact that we've had to watch you date other men for at least two years and it fucking hurt."

She shut her mouth and seethed. Daniel frowned thunderously. The air was thick and tense with their irritation. Andy stabbed at a bite of steak. The waiter dropped off their check and disappeared into the ether, as if he could sense the anger rising.

It had only been a couple of days and they were already fighting. Heather sighed and tucked her arms against her chest. It was her right to have whatever friends she wanted, but on the other hand, was it fair to rub her sexual exploits in Daniel's face? Even if that wasn't her intention, it was obvious he saw it that way. But that was before she'd known they even had an interest in her. How unfair.

Andy paid the tab and they went out to the car in silence. Daniel sighed again once they settled, trying to find something to say.

"I'm sorry," he said. "I just hate it. I do."

"I know," she said. "I don't approve. I love you, and you love me, but you don't own me."

"It's not about ownership!" he burst out.

"Guys!" Andy said. "Seriously. Wait till tomorrow. Think this through. For now, be quiet. We can sleep on it."

Heather settled back in her seat, biting her lip to hold back the burn of tears in her eyes. Daniel, in his own huff, huddled in the passenger seat. Andy ground out an aggravated sigh and started the car to drive them home. She leaned her head back on the back seat to keep the tears from falling. They didn't ever fight enough for her to be used to it, but she wasn't about to let Daniel walk all over her. He had an alpha personality, but she couldn't let him get away with pulling the strings of her life. Love was one thing, but she'd had experiences with ownership before, and she didn't like it.

Plus, Jamison was truly well meaning and under-standing. She wasn't about to throw that sort of friendship away.

Chapter Seven

Heather woke up to an empty bed and the clock reading eleven in the morning. She sighed and curled up with her pillow. It was Saturday, and she'd expected to have a great weekend, but Daniel was angry with her. To be perfectly fair, she was upset with him, too. She'd seen Andy have this fight with him too many times to count, in little and big ways.

On the other hand, it wasn't as if she would be willing to leave them for anything short of the end of the world, so really he could say whatever he wanted. That depressed her. Being stuck between loving someone so much she couldn't live without him and disagreeing with him about the direction of the relationship—it sucked. She cuddled the pillow tighter and wondered what they were doing, since they were obviously up. She felt almost ridiculous to have expected a perfect, glossy, fight-free relationship. Daniel was an alpha male, she had a volatile temper, and Andy was a grudge-holder extraordinaire. There was nothing they could do about any of that.

She rolled onto her back and watched the ceiling fan turn in slow circles.

She'd have to go out there eventually. Going to sleep with them all tense and grumpy had been hard enough; she wasn't sure how she felt about trying to have a civil lunch. Not to mention the fact that she was still unsettled. The university's rejection threw all her plans into the wind. She couldn't find a job, couldn't go to school, couldn't get along with her boyfriends.

It wasn't fair.

As soon as she thought that, she pried herself out of bed, because life wasn't fair. It was what you made it. If Daniel had a problem with her talking to Jamison, they could try to work that out somehow. She wouldn't give up a new friend, but maybe they could reach some kind of compromise. She could only imagine the faintest half of the pain they'd felt watching her flirt around with half of the men in their hometown. Of course she'd done it because she thought they wouldn't have her. That had hurt, too. Maybe apologies were due all around.

She opened the bedroom door and padded down the hall to her empty room to grab something to wear for the day. She settled on jeans and a T-shirt again. By the time she went to the bathroom and straightened her hair, she assumed they would have noticed she was up, but when she went into the living room she found a note instead.

"Be right back, if you wake up," it said in scribbled handwriting.

Heather sighed and rifled through the refrigerator until she found a chocolate pie that was only half eaten.

She sniffed it, determined it was still good, and cut herself a slice. Chocolate would help with the gloomy mood. She still couldn't quite believe that their relationship was already on the rocks after such a short time. That might have been normal adjustment, though. She didn't know.

She took her pie to the couch and tried to get comfortable. Her lower back ached and so did her breasts. In fact, almost every tender spot on her body seemed to be sore. There was such a thing as too much sex, she supposed, especially when it was so vigorous.

The door opened as the finished the last bite of her impromptu breakfast. She looked over the back of the couch to find Andy and Daniel, their arms laden with shopping bags, squeezing inside. They laid their loads on the kitchen floor and then Andy disappeared down the stairs again.

"Grocery shopping," Daniel said, his hands shoved in his pockets. "He's shutting the trunk and bringing up the last of the stuff."

"Ah," she said. "What are the plans for today?"

Daniel took a deep breath and sighed. "I thought we might see if Jamison wanted to come hang out with us at a movie or something."

"I see," she said slowly. "So you're not mad at him anymore?"

"I never was," Daniel replied, frowning. "You blew it all way out of proportion."

"Don't start," she said.

"I'm not starting anything. I'm just saying that I wasn't as angry as you make me out to be," he snapped.

"Andy's always bitching at me that I'm too possessive, and I try to keep it under control, but you guys have got to try to understand me. I don't want to lose you. It has nothing to do with trust."

"Right," she sighed. "Movie it is. You want to call him or shall I?"

The silence grated between them until Andy came back in.

"Oh, you're kidding me," he said. "Quit fucking fighting, already. I'm going to go out by myself and have a drink somewhere if you can't act like grownups."

Heather frowned at him, too. Daniel just scowled at the world. She appreciated what he was saying, but it didn't change the fact that he didn't seem to grasp he'd been rude and demanding. She wondered if he ever would. That wasn't exactly his strong suit. Could she learn to live with that, if it meant getting to be with the men she loved?

"Sorry," she said. "I get angry too easily. I appreciate what you're doing. I'll call him, if you want. It's up to you."

"Me, too," he said, flopping down on the couch next to her. "I just want you to understand it's not about trusting you. Or even Jamison. He's an all-right guy. But I can't think about losing you now that you're finally with us."

"Daniel," she said. He looked at her, sharp and serious. "Every relationship I've tried to have has failed because I'm in love with you both. Do you honestly think I would manage to leave you? It's not as though I'd have any success at it."

He laughed a little, though it didn't hold much humor. "I guess. That's why I'm trying to reach out. What do you think, Andy?"

They both looked over to their lover. He shrugged, unpacking groceries into the cabinet. His shoulders were tight and his frown was tense. He wasn't pleased with them, and he wasn't the fighting type, either. He would just seethe.

"We're sorry," she said. "Don't be mad at us."

"I forgot how much your personalities clashed sometimes," Andy said finally. "I suppose it's best to just let you argue it out until you reach a conclusion."

"Usually works," Daniel said.

"Let's just go to the movies," she said. "We'll talk to Jamison some other time. I want us to be okay first."

"Can't believe I thought this would be a smooth transition," Andy griped from the kitchen.

Heather rolled her eyes. "Lunch first?"

"Sure," Daniel said. "I'm starving. Want to cook or go out?"

"Go out," she said.

"Agreed," Andy said as he came back into the living room. He pointed mock-threateningly at Heather. "By the way, you're putting the groceries away next time since we went and did the shopping."

"Deal," she said, a weight lifting from her shoulders.

Andy's smile was still strained, but Daniel had relaxed a little, and she wasn't quite as angry. Lunch and light conversation would help bridge the tense gap between them, she hoped. It was hard to brush off

Daniel's yelling at her, but he genuinely felt bad about it, and that helped. There were other things that soothed anger, too, she thought as she ran her eyes down the length of Daniel's body from his dark, beautiful face to his muscular arms and toned stomach. She reached out and touched his bare forearm, wrapping her fingers around it. The heat and strength sent a thrill up her arm to her belly.

"I'm not leaving," she said.

Daniel's eyes were suddenly hot with desire. Andy shifted closer. She ran her fingers up his arm and grabbed a handful of his hair. His lips parted. She leaned in and pressed their mouths together. The hot catch and slide of their lips made her sigh with pleasure.

"Okay," he whispered into her kiss.

Another hand petted her hair and she tilted her head back. Andy kissed her from behind the couch, his lips pressing harder and more intently to hers. He was still angry, it seemed, but that only fueled his passion. Heat rose in her body.

"Lunch," Daniel said.

"Sure," she replied, breathless. "But later we're picking this up where we left off."

"Of course," Andy murmured. "I always want you both."

Daniel smiled at him and tugged him down by his shirt collar for a kiss. The sight of it stole Heather's breath. Their lips, flushed with kissing her, pressed together. Daniel's hand cupped the back of Andy's head and held him still. The brown-haired man groaned.

"I'll never get tired of this," she said honestly, emotion thick in her voice. "I love you. I really, really do."

"Yeah," Daniel said. "I love you too."

"Me too," Andy said.

He put his arms around both their shoulders and hugged them all close, bent awkwardly over the back of the couch. His breath tickled Heather's cheek. She smiled against his throat and planted a little kiss there. It was true: she couldn't get enough of them. She never had been able to. Andy and Daniel were her boys, and they were the most important thing in her world. Being able to touch them, kiss them—it was almost too much for her. She laughed against his throat and squeezed them both tight. Daniel hummed his pleasure.

"Where do you want to eat?" Andy said, gently breaking the moment. He pulled back and popped his back. "I'm thinking Chinese food. You?"

"Okay," Heather said.

"I don't mind," Daniel said with a shrug.

"I swear, all we do is eat and make love," Heather said.

"We have to keep our calorie intake up if we want to survive all the sex," Andy replied, grinning. It was like watching the sun come out from behind a cloud. He had forgiven them, at least for the time being.

She stood up first, smoothing out her jeans and walking over to the door to toe on her flip-flops. The boys followed her down the stairs and Andy ducked ahead to unlock his car. She took shotgun seat and Daniel gracefully accepted the backseat as his due. After all, she'd ridden in the back last time. She put her hand on Andy's knee and studied the lines of his face while he drove. He cast little amused glances at her every few moments. She memorized the plump pinkness of his lips, the high curves of his cheekbones and the little smattering of freckles across the bridge of his nose. He was lovely. It hit her again, harder than usual, that he was hers now in every way. All of his subtle handsome beauty was for her and Daniel, nobody else. She smiled and laid her head on his shoulder, though it required a little stretch over the armrest.

Clouds gathered overhead as Heather walked to the car, Andy and Daniel each holding one of her hands. The sky had gone dark while they were in the movie theater, and the rolling underbellies of the clouds were nearly black. She stared up at them, tasting rain on the air.

"That looks bad," she said.

"Yeah," Daniel said. "When it storms here, it means it. We need to get home."

"Okay," she said, a little alarmed. "So you don't think I have time to fill out this application and hand it back in before we leave?"

She held up the little packet of paper for the movie theater. She wasn't too proud to do a teenager's job if it meant bringing in some income while she waited for the spring semester to open up its application process.

"Uh," Andy said, pointing to the clouds again. Lightning lashed like white fire inside them. "No. We can do that later. I don't want to be on the road when that lets loose."

"I see your point," she said, climbing into the back seat and giving Daniel the front again. Fair trades were a good way of keeping each other happy until someone invented a car with three front seats. "Drive fast, I guess."

Heather watched the sky while Andy drove, pushing the speed limit but never going too far over. Everyone on the road was speeding a little. Being stuck in the storm wasn't safe. She doubted the police would pull anyone over. The first fat drops of rain began to splatter the windshield as they pulled into the apartment building's parking lot. Daniel made sure all the windows were up, then bolted up the stairs. A boom of thunder rattled the windowpanes and the first sheet of real rain poured from the sky. It was as dark as evening outside. Heather looked out the glass balcony doors at the torrents of water pouring almost sideways from the clouds. The wind whipped at the small trees scattered around the apartment complex.

"Wow," she said.

"Yeah," Andy replied, coming over to stand behind her. "It's intense."

"I would say we should go play in the rain, but I think it's coming down hard enough to hurt," she said. Another arc of lightning flashed from the sky to the ground. "That, too."

"Probably not safe," he agreed.

Daniel started putting out long taper candles in little holders all over the coffee table and the kitchen. He walked down the hall to get the bedrooms and Heather raised an eyebrow at Andy. He shrugged.

"We usually end up losing power," he said. "We don't have underground lines, so they have a tendency to get torn down when it storms. Transformers blow, lines get pulled out, you name it."

"Wonderful," she said, rubbing her arms. They prickled with nervousness. "No tornadoes though, right?"

"Not usually," he said, patting her back. "Come on. I know what'll take your mind off of the big, bad storm."

She let him guide her down the hall. They came in the bedroom as Daniel was setting up more candles on the dresser and bedside table. Andy helped her up onto the bed and rolled her onto her stomach. He climbed up on top of her, his thighs bracketing her hips and his weight warm and comfortable on her legs. He tugged on her shirt and she wiggled until they managed to peel it off without her getting up. The bra came next. She stretched her arms out, topless, and waited.

"Pass me the massage oil," Andy said.

She heard a cap pop, then slick, cool oil drizzled down her spine. She shivered. The bed shifted and creaked. She turned her head to see Daniel sitting next to her, still holding an unlit candle in his hand. Her eyes fluttered closed as Andy's slightly callused hands spread over her back and rubbed. He dug his fingers in with just the right amount of pressure. She sighed while he worked out all of the tension she'd barely been aware of, each swirl of his hands stoking another fire. She arched and trembled with desire by the time he made it down to the hem of her jeans. The bed creaked again and she managed to open her eyes. Daniel walked out of the room.

"Where's he going?" she said.

"Ssh," Andy murmured. "Let us take care of you."

She subsided. His fingers worked under her belly and she lifted her hips so he could unbutton her jeans and pull them off with her panties in tow. She lay naked under his clothed body, the friction of fabric abrading her thighs in a way she could only find arousing. She waited to feel the hot length of his dick against her, but instead he kept rubbing her back. Daniel came back and a wet cloth landed on her shoulder. She jumped, even though it was warm.

"Thanks," Andy said to him.

He wiped her down slowly, cleaning every trace of the thick oil from her skin. She sighed, almost disappointed. It would have been nice to have him rubbing their nude, slick bodies together. His fingers dipped between her legs a moment later and tested the wetness there, sliding against her pussy, but nothing more. She pushed against them and the fingers disappeared. A little groan of displeasure worked its way out of her.

"Patience," Daniel said. The click of a lighter drew her eye as he put it to the single white candle in his hand. Her breath quickened as the flame took. "Have you ever tried this before?"

"Yes," she said, eyeing the wax as it began to bead around the heat.

"Did you like it?" Andy murmured in her ear, following it with a quick swipe of tongue.

"Yes," she hissed, trying to rub against him. His clothes and the angle of their bodies prevented that.

Daniel smoothed his hand down the length of her spine, making her shudder again. He held the candle over her back, and no matter how she strained she couldn't turn enough to see it. Andy held her down gently, his fingers circling her wrists and his weight on her thighs. The first drop of wax pattered onto her skin from afar, lukewarm and strange. He was being careful.

"Closer?" Daniel asked.

"Mm-hm," she murmured.

The next droplet, landing just below the base of her neck, was hot enough that she moaned. It wasn't too much, yet. Her skin tingled under the little flake of wax as it dried. Another landed below that, equally hot and equally sensual. She writhed as her nerves lit up, the tiny edge of pain adding to the sensation. Andy's weight bracketing her, holding her down, made her breath come faster. Excitement rained with the little drops of wax all down her spine in a long, burning trail.

She gasped as Daniel flicked away the first dried flake with his nail, scraping the tender flesh. The sensation flashed through her like the lightning in the sky outside, bright and blinding. The nails continued, scraping away each dried bit of wax until it reached the base of her spine. She struggled because she couldn't stay still; pulling and jerking and panting.

A sharp slap on her ass made her cry out, but she subsided, still gasping for breath. Daniel pulled gently on her hair until she lifted her head. He smiled wickedly and pressed their mouths together, his tongue sweeping against hers, wet and perfect. She moaned into the kiss.

Andy massaged her wrists, playing his fingers up and down her forearms.

A crash of thunder made all three of them jump. The lights flickered once, then died, taking the alarm clock with them. Heather groaned and it wasn't a sound of pleasure. The wavering light of the candle was their only illumination. Daniel stood up and walked to the other candles in their holders. She watched as he lit each one in turn until the room glowed with dull bronze light. It was more romantic than she'd expected. He stripped his shirt off while she watched, shadows gliding over his muscled chest, and then undid his jeans. She made a quiet sound of desire as he pulled them off, and stood nude in the candlelight. Andy, too, growled his interest.

Daniel grinned at them, climbing back onto the bed. Andy let go of her and moved so Heather could roll over onto her deliciously sore back. Daniel ran his hand down her body from shoulder to hip to knee, skipping all of the parts that ached to be touched. She would have turned to face him, but Andy began to strip, and her attention stayed firmly on him. He made less of a show of it, casually tossing his clothes into the hamper and lying down next to them.

Heather sighed as they cuddled her between them, skin sliding on skin. She turned onto her side to face Daniel and Andy rubbed against her back, his arm draped around both his lovers. She palmed Daniel's butt, squeezing the firm globes and pulling him against her. His cock pushed against the crease of her hip. She reached down to take him in her hand, testing the weight and thickness of his arousal with her fingers. His eyelashes fluttered. She purred while she stroked him. Learning the shapes and contours of his body was wonderful; she didn't think it would ever get old. He gasped when she twisted her wrist a little on the upstroke.

Andy moved one of his legs between hers, spreading her thighs, and pressed his dick to her pussy. She leaned harder against Daniel, her leg shifting over his hips to open herself up wider for Andy. Daniel watched her face while she moaned, writhing with need as Andy simply rubbed himself against her without pushing inside. The smooth, hot skin against her, teasing at the bud of her clit on every glide, made her gasp and whimper.

"Do you want it?" Andy murmured.

"Yes!" she said, frustrated, then moderated her tone. "Please."

He laughed, his knuckles brushing her thighs as he gripped his cock and guided himself into her. She ground backwards as he thrust; a moan tore from her at the angle. He thrust shallowly, pushing himself almost directly against her G-spot. Daniel kissed her and swallowed her sounds, tongue playing on her lips while she gasped and groaned. Andy worked his hips in circular thrusts, not much depth but so much pleasure, sharp enough that it was almost too much. Daniel put his fingers up to their mouths and licked them. She clutched at him. He leaned back to watch her while he pressed those two fingers to either side of her swollen clit and began to rub.

She cried out softly, stuck between the two pleasures: one sharp like a knife and the other soft and sweet.

Daniel kept rubbing, Andy kept thrusting. His breath was hot on her throat. He moaned, struggling to keep his rhythm. Heather squeezed her eyes shut and clung to Daniel while the ecstasy rose and rose.

"God," Andy gasped a moment later, slamming his hips against hers, suddenly going so much deeper. She screamed, a short and surprised sound of pleasure. "Fuck, yes."

Daniel bent his head to lick her breasts, messy and wet, dragging his tongue from the nipple to the plump underside and back up. She dug her nails into his shoulders and cried out again when Andy pulled out almost all the way and shoved back inside with all his strength. A nova of pleasure burst behind her eyes.

"Again," she begged. "Don't stop."

"Gonna come soon," he panted, hands gripping her hips harder.

He did as she asked, though. While Daniel stroked her clit and licked her breasts, his cock pressed to her thigh, Andy pounded into her, each thrust as forceful as the last. She found herself gasping, frantic and high pitched, as her climax approached, spurred on by each deep shove. Andy bit her neck hard, and muffled his cry against it. She felt him pulse inside her, but he kept thrusting, whimpering against her skin. It was that sound that pushed her over the edge, groaning, her body spasming and fluttering around his cock. He moaned again, weakly, into her shoulder.

"My turn," Daniel growled, hiking her leg up further. Heather went with the movement as he rolled her on top of him. Andy's come dripped from her onto his belly, and he swiped his fingers through it. She thought he'd offer them to her, but he sucked them clean, looking between the other man and her. Her knees were still weak with aftershocks when he guided her to sink down on his dick. She cried out at the sudden fullness, stimulation on already overworked nerves.

"Hold still," she gasped. "Too much."

"Too much?" Daniel said. "Or just enough?"

She opened her mouth to answer. He bounced her on his lap, just a bare inch or two, but it stole her breath. Andy huffed a laugh from next to them. His eyes were filled with joy and pleasure. Daniel smoothed his hands over her back and ass. She leaned down over him to rest her head on the crook of his shoulder, still shivering. He bucked his hips, driving deeper inside, and she cried out at the burst of intense pleasure.

"Just enough, I think," he murmured into her hair.

One of his hands came up to hold her face to his shoulder, keeping her body arched over him, and the other landed on her thigh. He held her still while he rocked his hips in hard, small thrusts. Heather panted and gasped against his skin, pinned and overwhelmed with pleasure.

"Do you want to come again?" he murmured.

"You," she gasped. "You first. I'm done."

He hummed his understanding and rolled them over suddenly, his weight a hard pressure on top of her before he lifted himself to his knees. She wrapped her legs around his waist and let out a yell as he slammed his hips forward. She pried her eyes open to watch his face while he fucked her, harder and faster than before, so much that it all blended into one loop of pleasure, every thrust melting into the next. His face was dappled with sweat, his eyes closed, lips parted. She moaned. His eyes fluttered open and he managed a grin before orgasm forced them closed again. He cried out, stilling above her, his only movement an uncontrolled shivering.

Heather groaned when he pulled out a moment later, a devilish glide of his still-hard cock that sent one last tremble of ecstasy up her spine. She lay panting between them again and hoped this would be the way most of their nights ended: sated, loved, comforted.

"Need a shower," she said.

"Wait till the power comes back on," Daniel said, stroking his hand down her thigh. "Otherwise you won't be able to see. Bathrooms get pretty dark even with candles."

"I suppose," she said. "What now?"

"I'm not sure," Andy said. He pressed a kiss to the curve of her shoulder. "I suppose we could all grab books and huddle under the covers for a read-in."

"We have a gas stove, so we can still cook," Daniel said. "If you two are hungry yet, I can put something together. What do you think?"

"Sure," she said. "Make us a pizza, my fine lover."

He laughed and climbed off of the bed. "Get dressed and come in the living room. I'll light all the candles so you two can read. Don't forget to blow these out when you leave the room, though."

"Yes, sir," Andy said, rolling his eyes.

Heather bundled her clothes up and went to the bathroom to clean up. Daniel was right: even though she'd lit one of the candles, it was still almost pitch black. There was no way to keep candles in a shower, either. She shook her head and got dressed again. By the time she came out of the bathroom, Andy was sprawled on the couch. The book she'd been reading was sitting on the coffee table. She smiled and picked it up, settling under the weight of his legs. He grinned at her.

"By the way," Daniel said, leaning around the door frame to the kitchen. "No pizza. I'm making lasagna. Sound good?"

"Of course," she said. "I can wait a little longer. Andy?"

"Yeah," he said, glancing up from his book again. "I'm only a little hungry. Give me another hour and I'll be starving."

Daniel nodded and disappeared back into the kitchen. Heather wiggled her bare toes in the soft carpet and opened her book. The flicker of the candlelight didn't make it easy to read, but she managed. The comfortable weight of Andy's legs over hers and the sated soreness of her body didn't hurt, either. She didn't need electricity to be happy as long as she had her boys; that was certain.

The time passed quickly. When the oven timer buzzed, she jumped, and so did Andy. Daniel just smiled at them from the recliner across the room then stood and made his way to the kitchen. Andy swung his feet down to the floor and nudged all the candles on the table into a semi-circle around where their plates would go. Daniel came back with two steaming helpings of lasagna, which he placed squarely in front of them, then returned with his own plate a moment later. They scooted to make room for him on the couch.

"Not such a bad day," he said. "At least we got to finish the movie before the storm came through. Hopefully, we'll have power back by the morning."

"It's Sunday anyway," Heather replied. "We can just spend the day sleeping and making love if we want to. You don't need lights for that."

"So true," Andy said.

Heather smiled and they settled into dinner. The candles provided wavering light, and outside it was notably silent. No air conditioner, no television. She hoped the power would come on before the freezer started to defrost, but it was nice to enjoy real quiet for once.

"Hey," Daniel said. She looked up. He was silent for a moment and she waited while he struggled to find his words. "I want to talk about this. Us."

"Oh," she said. "Okay?"

He laid his fork down and took a sip of his drink. Andy made a quiet, interested noise, but didn't say anything. Heather leaned forward in her seat to look at him, frowning faintly at the serious expression on his face.

"Damn," he said. "This is way harder than it should be."

"Just get on with it," Andy sighed. "You're going to say something stupid either way."

Daniel gave him a dark look but he shrugged and waved his hands between them in an encouraging gesture. Heather bit the inside of her lip, her stomach twisting. Was he about to dump her? Was the week together only to satisfy some old lust?

"I love you," he said finally. "You know that. But I have to be sure what you want from this relationship."

She frowned. "What I want?"

"Yeah," he said, tapping his fingers nervously on his knee. "What do you expect from us? Where do you want it to go?"

"I want to be together, that's about it," she said.

Daniel sighed, agitated. "Not what I mean. Do you want kids? A house? What are you looking for in five years?"

Her jaw dropped just a bit. She stopped herself from answering right away, because the enormity of what he seemed to be asking was overwhelming. She looked between them. If she wanted kids, who would be the father? How could she possibly decide on one over the other? How could they do it without jealousy? Buying a house was a less shocking prospect, but still huge. She couldn't wrap her brain around it.

"We've basically been together for ten years," he said. "Tell me it's too soon and I'll leave you alone about this. But it doesn't feel too soon to me."

"I don't know," she managed. "I just don't know. That's a lot to dump on me at once, Daniel. Do you want kids?"

He shrugged and so did Andy. She flopped back against the couch in a huff and closed her eyes. It was dizzying. None of the relationships she'd had had progressed to the point where they could talk about a life together. Was it right to try to decide those things after a week as lovers?

"How do you even know this is going to work?" she said, her voice more raw than she'd have liked. "We don't know that this is a functioning relationship yet. How can you ask me to decide if want to have children or a house or God knows what else?"

Daniel flinched. "I don't mean it like that. You don't think this will work?"

"I don't know!" she said. "You can't ever know, not for sure."

"Exactly," Andy said quietly. They both looked at him. "You can't know. You can only hope. Make plans and trust and hope, that's it. I believe you're going to be with us, loving us, fifty years down the road. Do you?"

She opened her mouth and he put his fingers over her lips before she could speak.

"Think about it," he said. "Think about all of this, both of you. You're not ready to have this conversation yet. Just try to decide if you can see us still loving each other as much as we have for the past ten years."

Heather blinked hard, her eyes burning, and Andy planted a soft kiss on her mouth when he moved his fingers. He leaned over to Daniel and gave him a peck, too. Then he stood up and left the room, his dinner only half finished.

They stared at each other.

"You know," Daniel said. "Sometimes I feel like we swallow him up between us, and all it does is hurt him."

"Yeah," she said, her chest hurting. "I feel like that, too."

Chapter Eight

The plethora of job applications spread out on her table at the café made Heather's eyes ache. Jamison sat across from her, sipping an iced coffee. He cast a glance back into the store every now and then to make sure his employee didn't need any help, but otherwise he was trying to help her sort them into piles, or least likely and most likely.

"I'm going to kill myself," she groaned, dropping her head into her hands. "All these jobs suck. It's not like I'm under qualified for something good! Why wouldn't the stupid chain bookstore take me? I worked at one for years."

"Life sucks," he said and passed her the iced coffee. She took a sip and handed it back. "Where are your boyfriends?"

She sighed. "At home. At least the power's back so I could go out. I told them I needed to go hunt down applications and have some time away from the apartment."

"Problems already?" he said. She frowned at him. "Sorry, you just seem down."

"Not a problem," she admitted. "But still uncomfortable. Daniel asked me last night about kids and a house, and where I see us in five years. I don't know. I want to hope we'll stay together forever and all of that, but what if we really aren't compatible as lovers, only as friends?"

He put his chin on his hand. "Not sure what to tell you."

"It's not that I don't have faith. I don't think they'd cheat or anything, and I know I won't. Things happen, though. We could be better friends than anything, and then where would we be if we had this whole life set up together?" She pulled on her hair. "I can't answer him! And he thinks it's because I don't want to think about a future together, like I'm going to up and leave them."

"Pretend it's not happening for now," he said gently, fanning out the applications. "Drink your soda, and my coffee, and figure out where you're going to try to work. You'll feel better if you're producing some income, I guarantee it. Plus, more books."

"Yeah," she said, sighing. "I'm running low on reading material already. I need something bigger next time. Maybe a collection. Those take me a while."

"I'll start looking for some good, hefty reads for you, then," he said, winking.

Heather smiled and put her pen to the first application, a waitress job. A half hour later, Jamison rapped his knuckles on the table and she looked up. A small pile of completed papers sat next to her elbow. He gestured back to the store.

"He needs to get home," he said. "So I guess I have to bail on you. Sorry. You going to take the rest of those home with you?"

"I'll drop off the ones I've filled out," she said, shuffling through them.

"All right," he said. He put his hand on her shoulder and gave a quick squeeze, friendly and a little awkward. "See you later."

"The boys might invite you to dinner with us sometime," she said. "Daniel will probably call you. I might see you before then, though. We'll figure something out."

He nodded and went back through to the bookstore. She watched him give a high five to the clerk, who yanked off his name badge and stuck it beneath the counter. He waved to her as he left, and she smiled, waving back. She wasn't quite sure what his name was, but she'd make sure to read the tag next time she saw him.

She gathered her piles of paper and drank the last sip of her soda, tossing it in the trash on her way out the door. She was surprised neither of the boys had called her yet. She checked her phone. It was almost dinner time. As she climbed in the car and started of toward the location of one of her potential jobs, she dialed Daniel's number. He answered on the second ring.

"Hi," she said. "I'm dropping off half the applications now. Want to meet me somewhere for dinner? It's a little early, but I'm starved."

"Okay," he said, sounding subdued. "How many apps did you find?"

"Hm," she said, thinking. "About twenty, I guess. Hopefully at least one of them will pan out. I don't really like any, though. It's all stuff I hated doing when I was a teenager, let alone an adult."

"I'm sorry," he said. "Why don't you just get an office position somewhere and quit when spring semester comes around?"

"Because I don't want to have a six-month employment on my record," she said. "I like to try to appear reliable, you know?"

He sighed. "You're a college student. It's to be expected."

"Still," she said. "How about that Italian place Andy's friends own?"

"Sure," he said, perking up some. "I love their breadsticks. When should we meet?"

"Forty-five minutes," she said, calculating the distance to the places she still needed to drop off applications at. "That should be plenty of time."

"Okay," he said. Then, quieter, "I love you."

"Oh, honey," she said. "I love you too. Please don't forget that."

He made a noncommittal noise and said, "Bye. See you soon."

"Fine," she said, hanging up.

Her heart ached. He sounded so sad. She never wanted to make either of her boys hurt, but here she was again, dragging them through nails. But it wasn't fair to expect her to just decide, split-second, what she wanted to do with their lives together. Weren't those things supposed to take time, anyway?

She dwelled uncomfortably on it while she made her rounds and smiled at managers and employees alike at the stores she applied to. As she'd told Daniel: none of them was what she wanted, but she would take what she could get.

And it hit her, all at once, that she'd been living her whole life on that principle since Andy and Daniel hooked up and moved away. She sat in a parking lot, car rumbling but going nowhere, and stared at her hands. Was that the kind of person she was? Someone who settled for what they could have instead of working for more? There was no way, but the more she thought about it, the more she considered it might be right.

Daniel didn't want her to settle. He wanted her to be happy.

Her eyes burned and she rubbed them, feeling like a complete and total ass. Her phone alarm buzzed to let her know she needed to head to the restaurant if she wanted to be on time, and she clicked it off. They could talk about life over dinner. Daniel's approach might not have been perfect, but she wanted him to know she understood his intentions.

Heather sped to the restaurant and parked in the little lot behind it. Daniel's sleek car was already there. She went inside and relief welled up in her at the simple sight of him and Andy chatting at a table, one on each side of the booth, easy expressions on their faces. They were happy. She wanted, more than sex or even comfort, to be a part of that. To be another piece in the puzzle, locked together with them for anyone to see.

Andy looked up first and spotted her. A grin broke out over his lips and he waved. She smiled back and started toward the table, heart fluttering in her chest. She slid into the booth next to Daniel and planted a kiss on his cheek. He turned toward her.

"I'm sorry," she said.

His eyebrows drew together, furrowing. "What for?"

"I don't care if we have kids or a house or anything," she said, almost whispering, staring into his dark eyes. "I want us to be happy. I only want to be together. Everything else can wait."

He pulled her into a hug. Andy reached across the table to squeeze her shoulder, the best he could do without standing up to hug them both. She smiled at them. Daniel stroked her hair.

"I still want to know about the kids thing," Daniel murmured.

"Well, you tell me first," she said archly. "I still have to graduate from my master's program. I can't be pregnant for that. We'll figure it out when the time comes."

"Wise words," Andy said, eyes sparkling with familiar warmth. "I wouldn't mind a little one running around."

The idea was mammoth to Heather. She shook her head. "Not yet. I'm not ready."

"I know," he said. "But maybe one day. I'm casting my vote, so you both know."

Daniel nodded. Their waiter brought out a huge plate of cheese-covered breadsticks and the wonderful garlic butter. Heather plucked one for herself. She couldn't stop smiling. Some of the weight had lifted, at least. She still had no idea what to do about school or work, but Daniel was happy with her again, and so was Andy.

It was enough for her, so long as they were together.

Heather had just stepped into the shower when she heard the bathroom door creak slowly open. She smiled to herself and kept lathering the shampoo in her hair, wondering if she was casting a curvy silhouette on the curtain. It worked like that in the movies. There was the sound of fabric shifting and something clinked on the floor, possibly a button. She ducked her head under the spray, still grinning.

A moment later the curtain eased back and a warm male body pressed up against her back. Strong hands circled her waist and massaged her hips; a smooth, wonderfully hard cock bumped the small of her back. She purred and leaned into the embrace.

"Came to tell you to hurry up," Andy murmured. "Daniel's waiting in bed for us with all manner of wicked plans."

"Oh?" she said, tilting her head back onto his shoulder. He smiled at her. "Like what?"

"You really do like it when I talk dirty," he said, pressing a kiss to her forehead. "That's cute. Appropriately filthy, but cute."

She laughed and wriggled in his arms, rubbing their water-slick bodies together. His breath caught and he dipped his hands lower, cupping them over her pussy. She moaned quietly and rocked her hips, forward into his hand and back against his dick.

"I think he wants you to suck him while I fuck you," he whispered into her ear. She shivered. "Do you like that, having a cock in your mouth and one in your pussy, caught between us?"

"Yes," she hissed, looping her hands backward around his neck to give herself more balance as she spread her legs. His fingers delved between her folds, rubbing up and down her tender flesh in long strokes.

"Maybe then, before he comes, he'll pull out and move behind me. You want to watch us, don't you? I'd pull out too, and you could lie on your back and touch yourself while he sucked my cock. He'd do it so he could taste you on me." Andy ground himself harder against the curve of her butt, panting slightly.

She whimpered, toes curling, thrusting her hips against his fingers in little rocking motions as she climbed closer and closer to the height of her pleasure. His ragged breath on the back of her neck sent pulses of fire down her spine. She cried out, tensing—and he pulled his fingers away, leaving her bereft. She gasped, shuddering, her climax stolen suddenly. Her body pulsed with need, ached with desire.

"Not yet," he growled. "Come to bed?"

"God," she gasped, turning the shower handle to "off" a little harder than was necessary.

They climbed out and he toweled her dry before she could quite comprehend what he was doing. Down the hall they went—Heather in a haze of sexual euphoria, hungry for more. She wanted to come. The sight of

Daniel spread out on the bed, his hand stroking his big cock, made her mouth water.

Andy didn't have to guide her. She climbed up on the bed and between Daniel's spread legs. He gave her a dirty grin and held his dick up for her with a thumb at the base. She moaned and wrapped her fingers around him, slipping the head into her mouth. He rubbed against her palate, silky and hot. She worked her mouth down further, loving the way he groaned for her.

A moment later, Andy's hands guided her hips up into the air. He curled his fingers in her hair and pulled her off Daniel's cock. Saliva stretched between her bottom lip and his body, pornographic and lovely. She shuddered and started to protest. Andy's hand smacked down on her ass, a sudden sharp pain that made her squeal. Daniel ran his fingers over her cheek and down her throat, resting his thumb on her pulse. She watched his face, his excitement. The other man spanked her again, on the other cheek, a little softer. The angle was different.

"Now, that was no good," Daniel murmured, rising up onto his knees. "Do you want me to show you how it's done? That was a wussy slap."

Andy growled. Heather strained against the hand in her hair for another taste of the cock that bobbed, still spit-slick, in front of her face. She whimpered when he crawled away, behind her, and tried to twist her head to see. A smack of flesh on flesh made Andy gasp, his grip loosening. She rolled onto her back.

Daniel winked at her from behind Andy and hooked his forearm across the other man's neck. He stilled immediately, panting, held up on his knees by the careful but unforgiving cage of Daniel's arm under his chin. Heather appreciated the view: a long lovely stretch of Andy's muscled body, his cock practically begging for touch.

"See?" Daniel murmured. "I told you we were going to play some discipline games. But I didn't actually say who was going to be the bottom."

Andy groaned, reaching back to find a hold on Daniel's hips. A shiver of lust ran down Heather's spine. They writhed together in a sexual dance, Daniel grinding himself against their lover's ass and Andy panting for breath past the gentle restriction on his throat.

"Heather," Daniel said. "Open the second drawer and get out the cuffs. They should be on top."

She leaned over and opened the drawer, momentarily awestruck by the sheer selection. Daniel said nothing as she inspected the blindfolds, bindings, floggers, and so many other toys. She picked up the black leather cuffs and pushed the drawer shut with a twinge of regret that they wouldn't be trying out any of the other implements. She could imagine the soft suede of the red flogger slapping across her butt and back, leaving warm patches of sensitive skin in its wake. She shivered.

"Loop the chain around the slats in the headboard," Daniel instructed. His hand crept around to cup Andy's balls, rolling them tenderly just to hear him moan. She did as he asked. He put his mouth to Andy's ear and whispered, "Put your hands in the cuffs, boy. Face down, ass in the air."

Andy gasped when Daniel released him. Heather scooted over to give him room to do as Daniel asked. She stroked his wide wrists and wrapped the leather of the cuff nearest her around one, black on nearly white skin. The latches held firm, but not so tight as to cut off circulation. Daniel fastened the other buckle. Andy's body made a fine, tempting arch. Heather ran her fingers down his spine to see him shiver. His eyes were bright with desire when he turned his head on the pillows to look at her.

"Get over here," Daniel said. She smirked at Andy and crawled around behind him with the other man. "Do you know how to give a good spanking, honey?"

"Of course I do," she said. "I learned how to do it when I dated Anna."

She watched as his eyes darkened. He licked his lips. "I jerked off thinking about you and her at least ten times. Maybe more."

"So you like to think about me with other women?" she asked, half curious and half turned on. "Do you like the thought of me licking their pussies, pressing our breasts together?"

He shuddered and pulled her into a kiss. She moaned into it as his fingers found her nipples, twisting just hard enough to sting a little. His tongue played against her lower lip until it tingled with sensation, then Andy made a curious noise. Daniel pulled back, but before he could lift his hand, Heather swatted their lover on his upturned butt. Andy gasped, mostly from surprise.

Daniel grinned. She raised one eyebrow. He edged

back to give her room and she positioned herself behind Andy, studying the firm globes off his ass, slightly pink with their attentions. A hot flash of desire spread through her as she thought about the same sight while she fucked him, listening to his breathy moans. But that wasn't what today was about, and as interesting as being the "man" had been, it wasn't going to be her preference. Daniel and Andy were bigger and stronger, and most of the time she just wanted them to hold her down and make her come as hard as she could.

Not this evening. She rubbed both hands over his warm ass, kneading her fingers at the crease of his thighs. She dipped her fingers lower and caressed the delicate skin of his balls. He sighed his pleasure, spreading his legs, but she drew her hand back.

He tensed a moment before she landed the first slap on his right cheek. A little gasp tore from him. She rubbed the handprint, then ran her nails over it. He shuddered, pushing back into her touch. She smiled and bent to press a tiny kiss to the mark. He groaned at the flicker of her tongue on his sensitive skin.

"Nice," Daniel murmured. She glanced at him, lazily stroking his cock while she spanked their lover. "You have technique."

"I'd like to see yours later," she said huskily.

He nodded and she returned to Andy before he started to feel neglected. She cupped her hand before she brought it down on his other cheek, and this time he actually cried out, shifting forward slightly, then back again as she dragged her fingernails over the red patch.

She patted his thigh so he would spread his legs farther, reaching between to fondle his hard-on. He was stiff as she'd ever felt him, little sticky drops of pre-come rolling down the shaft.

"You like this a lot, don't you?" she murmured.

"Fuck, yes," he gasped, pumping his hips shallowly into her hand. She stroked him twice and let go, licking the bitter musky fluid off her fingers. Daniel growled at the sight.

"You want more?" she asked.

"Please," Andy begged.

Daniel sat up from his reclining position and winked at her. She shifted to give him room and he smacked Andy's ass hard on the crease, making him yell. He strained in his bonds, shuddering. Heather's breath caught at the restrained power of Daniel's slaps as he delivered one to the top of each thigh, raising bright pink spots. Andy's breath hitched and rushed out, hitched again. His shuddering continued nonstop, a faint trembling in every limb.

"He can come this way," Daniel said, stroking his fingers down the hot skin. "Get me a plug out of the drawer. Medium sized, I think."

Andy groaned weakly, watching her while she dug through their toy drawer again. She found a shimmery blue one that seemed about the same width as Daniel's cock at first glance. He nodded his approval as she passed it to him. She brought the bottle of lube over as she crawled back to his side.

"This one vibrates," he said, flicking the switch on the bottom she hadn't seen.

It buzzed to life in his hand. She shivered, imagining how it would feel. Andy just whimpered, hips swaying. Daniel drizzled lube over his fingers and spread Andy with his other hand, working that slickness all over the crease of his butt. Heather reached beneath him again to squeeze his rock-hard dick. It pulsed in her hand when Daniel twisted two of his fingers inside, followed by another groan. Andy's eyes were closed, his face tight with pleasure and anticipation. Her body throbbed with its own desire, clit aching, wetness on her pussy and thighs. She wanted to finish it, though, wanted to watch him come just from their spanking and one toy, no one even touching his cock. She half-believed he couldn't do it. She hadn't seen anything like that in her explorations with other men, not once.

Daniel stroked the toy, spreading the lubricant on it, and put one of his hands on Andy's hip. Her breath caught as they shifted together—Andy back onto the plug, Daniel pushing it slowly and carefully into him. Andy groaned long and loud, thrusting against her hand with little jerks of his hips. She gave him one last squeeze and slipped her fingers away, despite his pleading noise. Daniel grinned at her and ran his hands down the other man's thighs.

"Close your eyes," he murmured to Andy, petting his skin where it was still pink.

Heather gasped as she ran her fingers over her sex, slipping in the wetness there. Daniel scratched his nails down Andy's back, making him arch and shudder. The faint buzzing of the toy was a constant undercurrent to his little whimpers of pleasure. She waited, almost as tense as Andy, while Daniel raised his hand. He smacked it down on the supple curve of Andy's ass and he writhed, crying out, his cuffs rattling on the headboard. She gasped, playing her fingers over her clit. Sparks of pleasure crackled up her spine. She didn't want to come yet, so she kept the touches light.

She kept count while Daniel rained slow, hard slaps and spanks all over Andy's ass and thighs. He gasped into the pillow with each strike, his body trembling harder and harder. His legs shook, his fingers clenched on the chain of the cuffs. Heather pushed two fingers inside herself with a little gasp, startled by the intensity of pleasure that rocketed through her at the simple stretch and glide. She was so aroused that anything would have felt like heaven.

"Come on, baby," Daniel murmured. "Do you want to give up? Is it too much?"

Andy just moaned, his hips swaying, eyebrows drawn tight together. Heather watched his face while Daniel struck him again, an open-palmed slap that rang out like a shot. He gasped once again. With the next spank he cried out, and her eyes were glued to his cock. A bead of come dripped from the tip; on the last slap, he came all over the sheets. Heather ground her hips against her hand, thrusting her fingers, and the fire of lust flared high in her. She bit her lip.

"Not yet," Daniel growled at her.

He pulled her hand away and toppled her onto her back. He looked feral in his desire, poised over her.

When Andy whimpered, he reached out and turned off the plug's vibrations. She tilted her head to see Andy watching them as she'd watched him. She didn't have a chance to comment on what a voyeuristic lot they were before Daniel hooked his arms under her legs and lifted her.

She screamed as he plunged inside, thrusting hard and fast. Her nails raked across his shoulders without purchase to let off some of the sudden shock and pleasure. The switch from nothing to fucking so quickly threw her, she reeled with the pleasure underneath him. Her own orgasm, already close and strung tight in her belly, caught her unaware. She bit down on his arm, the nearest thing, and screamed again as her muscles fluttered and spasmed with pleasure. He groaned, slamming harder and deeper. The loop of ecstasy continued. Heather wailed, throwing her head back and writhing under him. Each thrust seemed to propel her climax further, higher. When Daniel shoved deep and stilled, she shuddered. The waves of pleasure receded as he came, too, quicker than she'd ever seen him before. He bent his head and planted a kiss on her lips, tender and certain. She sighed into it, her hands dropping away from his body.

Andy muttered something, and Daniel laughed. She turned her head to look at them. Daniel undid his cuffs and massaged his wrists one by one. Andy rolled onto his back and pulled the toy free with a flutter of his eyelids.

"I wonder if we'll ever just have boring, normal sex," he said, breathless.

"I hope not," Daniel purred, his long muscular body stretched out between them. She plucked at his hard nipple with her nails and he jumped. "Not again, not yet!"

"Oh, I know," she said. "Me, neither. I just like to play with you."

He grinned as she did, too. Andy rolled his eyes, throwing one arm over both of them. She laced their fingers together, her thumb tracing the contours of his hand, each bump and divot. There was a little scar on his thumb that curved around the base.

"That's new," she murmured.

"Kitchen," he said. "I caught myself with my knife. We were rushing and I was careless."

"Hard to see you being careless," she said.

"It happens to the best of us," he replied, sounding sleepy and sated.

Heather closed her eyes and listened to them breathing, Andy's hand on hers, until she drifted off. There was nothing better than sharing a bed with her boys.

Chapter Nine

Heather nibbled the end of her pen, staring down at her notes for the application to the spring graduate program. Andy milled around the kitchen, preparing their supper. Daniel was sitting on the couch reading with the television on mute, pictures flashing in distracting waves of color. She sighed and dropped the pen.

"I just don't know what to say that I didn't say last time," she said and groaned.

"You'll get it," Andy said, gesturing with his spatula. "You still have two weeks before the application window even opens, right? Keep reworking it. You'll get there eventually."

"Are you sure one of you can't write it for me?" she said.

He raised an eyebrow. "I work in a kitchen. Seriously, you want me to write your application? I may read a lot, but I'm not that good with the creating half."

"I could," Daniel called from the living room. "But I write dry, witty legalese."

"No, thanks," she said.

"Just keep trying," Andy said.

She pushed her chair back and walked up behind him, wrapping her arms around his waist. He made a pleased sound, stroking his fingertips over her arm. She smiled against his back. He prodded at the chicken in the saucepan.

"Dinner's almost done," he said. "Want to get the plates?"

"Sure," she said.

The warm domesticity as she set up three plates and forks made Heather smile. He served out a piece of chicken with red, creamy sauce and mushrooms onto each plate. She inhaled deeply, mouth watering. Her stomach rumbled. She hadn't eaten since breakfast, and lunchtime had passed by while she read and worked on her application. The paper she had turned in for her sample wasn't perfect yet, either. She had only flipped through it. The real revision work would take much longer. She could almost see why she hadn't made it in.

"I smell dinner," Daniel said. "Kitchen table or in here?"

"Un-mute the damn TV," Andy said. "We'll eat in there."

Daniel laughed and the sound of the television came on a moment later. Andy took two of the plates and Heather grabbed her own, following him into the living room. Daniel scooted down to the end of the sofa to give them room.

"So," he said after a moment. "There's something I want to show you."

"Daniel," Andy said.

"Hush," he replied.

Heather raised her eyebrows. Daniel reached under the couch and pulled out a little sheaf of papers. He laid it down on the coffee table and twisted his fingers together. Heather bent to look. It was a bank account statement. Highlighted were the words "savings" and a total that made her breath catch. He'd also written "goal" at the bottom. She flipped to the next page. It was a print-out from a real estate site of a lovely two-story brick home on a decent lot with a privacy fence and a pool.

She raised her eyes to him. His cheeks were flushed.

"Sorry," he said. "I know it's sudden, and we can wait until you find a steady job, but I don't think we're going to leave each other. So Andy and I have been saving up for a place. Obviously we were hoping you'd be there too, but now we know, so—"

"Honey," she said, cutting him off. "Calm down. Can we go walk through the house first? I want to see it."

"Yes," he said, hugging her. She smiled against his neck while he squeezed her. "Please, let's get a home together."

"Told you she'd like it," Andy said under his breath. "By the way, Heather, how much did you bring with you, if you don't mind me asking?"

She told him, and he scribbled it on the paper with their accounts.

"Can we eat now?" she said, smirking.

Daniel rolled his eyes. "I guess I could have waited. But I wanted to get it over with."

"I know," she said. "You're adorable when you're flustered."

Andy laughed. Daniel frowned at them both. She smiled back and he pushed the papers across the table. Her heart beat fast in her chest as she pictured it: a home for the three of them, with a library room, a big kitchen, and maybe even an office or an exercise room. A real place they owned, not just a rental. She hadn't thought much about owning her own home because on her own it was nearly impossible, but the living with her boys was wonderful.

"Thank you," she said. "I know you're going to insist I only contribute enough to bump us up to the goal, but I promise I'll buy the furniture if I can. You boys shouldn't be paying for everything."

"Actually," Daniel said. "Yeah, we should. You're still in college, and that's like a job on its own. I've got, like, a real career already. You can make it up to me once you become a teacher, yeah?"

"Fine," she said. "You always win these discussions."

"Because I'm right," he said with a winsome smile. She smacked his arm.

"Eat," Andy interrupted them. "I'll be offended if you let the dinner I made get cold."

She smiled at him, and he returned it. Heather dug into the fragrant chicken dish. She wanted to purr; Andy was the best cook. She had no doubt he'd go far in the restaurant world. As it was, she was thrilled to have him in her life.

"That was delicious," she said. "Dessert?"

"I'll bake a pie later," Andy said.

His hand crept around Daniel's back and flicked her bra strap. She grinned. He ran his fingers down to the hem of her jeans and tweaked them, too. Daniel's fingers found her upper thigh. She leaned back against the couch and he ran his palm delicately over the zipper of her pants.

"I see," she said. "What's on the menu this evening?"

"I don't know," Andy said. "What do you want to do?"

"Something different," she said, leaning against Daniel's warm body. "I want to see Daniel on the bottom."

Daniel gave her one of his terribly amused looks and kissed her on the cheek. She smiled back. He wrapped his free arm around Andy's waist and propelled them up, until they were all shuffling down the hall together.

"You're such a voyeur," he said.

"I know," she replied. "I can't help it. You're just so gorgeous together."

"Once we get that new house, we have to christen every available surface in it," Andy said over his shoulder.

"Of course," Daniel replied.

Heather, last in the line, closed the bedroom door behind her. She leaned against it, hands behind her back, while her boys stripped off their tops. They glanced at each other hungrily. Pants dropped; so did underwear. Heat raced through her as they came together in a grappling, power-struggling kiss. Andy's hands gripped Daniel's ass, pulling their hips together. Daniel yanked his hair to get the best angle, plundering the other man's mouth with his tongue. They moaned and breathed heavily, clutching at every bit of skin they could reach.

"Wow," she said breathlessly.

Andy looked over at her from their embrace and grinned.

"Get naked and lie down," he said.

He didn't have to say it twice. Heather skimmed out of her clothes and jumped onto the bed, bouncing on the mattress. Daniel made a pleased sound at the sight of her breasts jiggling. She cupped them in her hands and lay back on the bed. They were watching her now. She bent her knees and spread her legs, massaging her breasts. Eyes closed, she ran one hand down her belly and spread herself with two fingers so both men could see. She moaned.

Daniel growled and the bed shifted.

She opened her eyes and stared up into his, dark with lust.

"I thought you were going to let him fuck you," she said.

"Nobody said we couldn't have you first," he said, grabbing one of her ankles.

She squeaked as he hauled her leg up over his shoulder, pressing the length of his cock against her pussy. She rubbed against him, moaning, that delicate skin providing the perfect friction on her clit. He pushed down on his cock with his thumb, giving her more pressure. She glanced at his wicked expression and kept writhing, using his dick to pleasure herself in the literal sense. Andy walked to the side of the bed and guided her to turn her head. His cock tapped her lips.

She took him in with a hungry sound, filling her mouth and stroking her tongue along his hard-on. He sighed his pleasure, petting her hair, his hips pumping shallowly. The tension in her body coiled tighter while she moved her hips, her own wetness allowing Daniel to slide against her easily. The pressure was almost too much, the faintest hint of over-stimulation, but she kept gasping and undulating.

Her toes began to curl. The tension wound tighter and tighter. She whimpered around Andy's dick, shuddering with the beginnings of climax. Daniel shifted his hips, pulling himself away at the last second. She nearly cried out her loss but he thrust inside immediately, one hard lunge that lit up every nerve in her body. She clawed Andy's hip, her throat opening to take him in deep as she came. The orgasm seemed to go on and on while Daniel jerked his hips and fucked her in hard, small thrusts, intentionally dragging himself back and forth over her swollen G-spot.

As soon as she pulled off of Andy with a gasp, he slowed and stopped his motions. She looked up at him. His brow was dappled with sweat and his mouth was open, lips bitten red. She imagined she looked much the same: mouth plump from sucking and body glistening with exertion.

"Now," he said. He pulled out, making her shiver all over again. "Do you want a toy to use while you watch?"

She ran her fingers down her slick, hot pussy, slipping her fingers inside. She sighed. Her body was furnace-hot and so slick. She wondered what that felt like for them. Both men seemed entranced by the sight of her fingers disappearing inside her body. She twisted on the bed, wrist pumping, a long moan spilling from her throat.

"Damn," Andy groaned. "I'll get you one."

She watched Daniel watch her while Andy dug around in their drawer. She could have gotten her own from her suitcase, but it was smaller than Daniel, and she doubted anything else would satisfy for the moment. She was still feverish with desire, every nerve tingling. One orgasm wasn't enough. But she also wanted to see them together, trading power dynamics. She wanted desperately to see Daniel's handsome, tanned face slack with the ecstasy of being taken, being filled and fucked. She shuddered, her pussy clamping tight on her fingers. She moaned again.

Andy dropped the toy of his choice on her belly. It jiggled. She recognized the material: it was the same ultra-real kind she loved. She lifted it to her mouth and raised an eyebrow at both men's enraptured gazes. She licked it, warming up the soft, silky material and getting it slick. Her body tingled with anticipation. It was as big as Jamison, wider around than her fingers could fully clasp at the base.

"That one's new," Daniel purred, his eyes locked on her mouth. "We bought it for you after I saw the one you were sneaking around to the bathroom. Do you think you can fit it, or should we have gone smaller?"

She rolled her eyes, too turned on to care that he was peering at her sex toys. He'd seen more of her than that, now.

"If it was first thing, no, I couldn't," she murmured, stroking the toy. "But you've got me warmed up. I think I can manage."

"Let's see," Andy said.

"This was all some great plan to watch me masturbate, wasn't it?" she said.

"No," Andy replied. "I really am looking forward to having him panting under me, trust me. This is a bonus. Come on, I want to watch you."

"You first," she said, grinning.

Daniel opened his arms to Andy and let the other man tip him onto his back. She sighed as they pressed their bodies together: long muscular planes and soft curves all matching so perfectly. Daniel's legs wrapped loosely around Andy's lower back. They kissed, slower and deeper. Heather rubbed the silky toy over her pussy, shivering with anticipation. Andy fumbled for the bottle of lubricant on the nightstand and she handed it to him. The angle made it so she couldn't quite see once his hand dipped between their bodies, but after a moment Daniel groaned, his legs clamping around the other man's back. Andy growled, his arm moving in shallow thrusts.

"Slower," Daniel gasped.

Andy bit the side of his throat. The motion of his arm slowed, eased. Daniel let out a long sigh, his eyes fluttering closed. Heather shifted and spread her legs farther apart. Lust and heat like fire raced down her body.

The look of subtle concentration on Andy's face and the ecstatic pleasure on Daniel's were enough to make her shudder. It was obvious they didn't switch much.

"Think I'm ready," Daniel managed, opening his eyes. He looked up at Andy with a mixed expression: love, desire, trust. She swallowed hard.

"Sure?" Andy murmured, rubbing against him. "You're ready for all this?"

"Yeah," he moaned, nails raking across his back. Andy gasped. "Give it to me."

Andy sputtered a laugh at the pornographic dialogue. Daniel grinned. Their easy humor and comfort made Heather smile, too, but a moment later Andy shifted back. He picked up the lubricant again and stroked a handful of it up and down his dick until it glistened. He eased one of Daniel's legs over his shoulder, then the other. It left most of his weight on the small of his back. Daniel reached over his head and fisted the sheets, his lip caught between his teeth. Andy bent to kiss his mouth open again, tongue lapping at him until he was moaning.

This time she could see. She had nearly forgotten about the toy while watching them. Andy guided his cock with one hand, the other petting Daniel's. He wasn't quite stroking, just gentle rubbing to provide a distraction. Daniel hissed a little as he slid inside, despite his careful slowness. He didn't stop. Daniel clutched at the sheets, his hips moving ineffectually. She imagined the slow slide of taking Andy into her that way, if she did. How each inch would stretch and burn just a little, just enough that he had to ease her pain. Daniel groaned when he bottomed out, hips pressed to ass.

"Okay?" Andy whispered.

Daniel growled, yanking him down for a kiss. Andy's hips flexed, drawing a whine from him. The next movement was almost a thrust: a withdrawal and push back in, though barely an inch. Daniel dropped his head back and groaned, long and loud. Andy huffed a small moan of agreement, taking each of Daniel's wrists in hand and pinning them over his head. His fingers twisted in the sheets. Heather saw his cock twitch against his belly at the restraint and smiled a little to herself. One more thing to remember.

"Hey," Andy said, glancing at her. "Isn't your pussy feeling lonely?"

"Yeah," Daniel rasped, eyes fluttering at another slow, deep thrust. "Go on. Want to watch you come."

She shivered, sliding the toy back and forth over her slick pussy to make sure it was properly slippery. It was so wide she thought it might give her an appreciation for the pleasure Daniel was feeling: strange, different, intense. How long had they pictured seeing her with it, she wondered. She shifted her hips for a better angle and relaxed. As she pushed, slow and sure, she kept her eyes on the sight of Andy and Daniel moving together, their eyes locked on her. She groaned as the head slipped in. It didn't hurt, but she would be sore later, she was sure. Daniel groaned. Andy kept pumping his hips at the same pace. A slow slide out, hard push in. It was as if he was dancing a waltz with two beats, dictated by some internal rhythm.

Heather bit her lips and tried to keep watching while she tapped the base of the toy with her fingers, shaking it a little. The sensation made her gasp. She picked up the discarded bottle of lube and poured a generous amount over herself. It made a shiny, slick mess, but the next time she pushed on the base, the toy slid in further. It stroked every nerve, every inch of her. She moaned.

"Yeah," Daniel growled.

Andy bent him forward at a tighter angle until his knees nearly touched his chest, still pinning his hands. Daniel's breath came short and sharp. His eyes shut again. The next time Andy repeated his slow withdrawal and shove back in, he cried out. Pearly fluid gathered at the head of his cock and dripped onto his chest. Heather gasped, the sight sending a shock of lust through her.

"That's it," Andy murmured. "Slow and easy, want to watch you come all over yourself."

Daniel groaned. Heather constrained herself to moving when Andy did, imagining herself on the other end of his attention. Each thrust in prompted more cries and groans, more frantic shivers. Her climax built, but seemed out of reach. It was a sweet mountain of sensation. Every time she pushed the toy back in, every time Andy thrust, another layer of pleasure settled over the three lovers.

"Please," Daniel gasped.

"Like this," Andy replied, his voice husky and thick. "You can. I know you can."

Daniel thrashed beneath him, no leverage to work his hips faster. Andy growled, never speeding his pace even as Daniel gasped and moaned, his cries like sobs of pleasure. Heather moved her wrist faster. She couldn't take it any more. She put her free fingers to her clit and began to stroke gently, adding sparkling ecstasy to the thick stretch and glide of the toy.

"Love watching you come apart," Andy managed.

Daniel was beyond words. Andy kept him pinned, helpless, and didn't speed his pace. She watched, her breath coming so fast it ached in her chest. Daniel's cock throbbed at each slam of Andy's hips. A mess of slick pre-come shone on his chest. His thighs and arms strained in the tight position. He moaned continuously. Andy panted, his hair sticking to his face.

Heather cried out as she came, entranced by their picture, the controlled abandon and ecstasy flowing between them. Andy flashed her a smirk and picked up his pace just a fraction. Daniel practically howled, almost screaming. There was no pause between thrusts now. Andy still eased out slowly but he didn't make Daniel wait before lunging forward over him and driving back inside. Daniel gasped for each breath.

"Please, baby," Andy moaned. "Let go. Do it."

Daniel whimpered, fingers flexing and toes curling. His body strung itself tighter and tighter, muscles shaking. Andy suddenly stepped up his pace to harsh speed, fucking him hard and fast without mercy. Daniel did scream then, coming, his dick pulsing untouched. Heather writhed, a third, smaller orgasm crashing over her as she thrust the toy in and out in imitation.

Andy froze, his mouth open in a silent yell, eyes closed.

He shivered as he climaxed. Daniel panted fiercely, as if he'd run a marathon. Come dripped from his chest in little runnels onto the sheets. Heather eased the toy out, feeling boneless and sated.

"Mmmm," Daniel said.

"Ditto," Andy groaned, easing off of him and rubbing his legs to soothe the stiff muscles.

Heather heard a faint ringing and leaned off the bed, fishing through her pants pockets for her cell phone. She answered it, still half off of the mattress.

"Hi," Jamison said. "Got a minute?"

"Sure," she said, rolling onto her back. Daniel crawled off the bed and wobbled on unsteady legs down the hall, probably to clean up. Considering how sticky she felt, he had the right idea. "What's up?"

"Well," he said. "You still looking for a job, or did one of those apps already pan out?"

"Still looking," she said cautiously. "Why?"

"Jackie just got accepted to some big California college," he said.

"Who's Jackie?" she said.

"One of my employees," he said. She swore she could hear him grinning. "So if you still want to work in a bookstore, nab an awesome discount and hang out with me . . ."

"Really?" she exclaimed. "You're joking!"

"Nope," he said.

Andy stirred, curious. He raised his eyebrows at her. She waved him off.

"When?"

"Well, he won't be leaving for another month," Jamison said, a little more subdued. "But I can start you on training hours in two weeks. It won't be much till Jackie actually goes, but if you can wait a month, I'll give you plenty of hours."

"Of course," she said. "Oh, damn. This is great!"

"Yeah, I know," he said. "You actually read, you're smart, and you're not a horribly evil sociopath. That's pretty much our criteria."

"Hired any sociopaths?" she said.

"Actually, yeah, once," he said with a laugh. "Story for another day. I'll call you tomorrow and let you know when I can work you in for training, okay?"

"Yes," she said. "Thank you so much!"

"My pleasure," he said. "Bye."

She hung up and grinned at Andy. "I have a job in a month. At the bookstore."

"Great," he said, smiling. "I figured by your end of the conversation, what with all the squealing."

She rolled her eyes and flopped back against the pillows. The room smelled of sweat and musk. Andy hugged her close, his warm skin sticking to hers. She giggled, burying her face against his chest. Daniel climbed up on the bed a minute later, sandwiching her between them.

"She got a job," Andy said. "Bookstore. Perfect timing."

"So," Daniel said, ruffling her hair. "Want to go house-hunting tomorrow? If we combine our savings, we can get anything we want. Well, not anything, but you know what I mean."

"Yes," she said, closing her eyes and savoring the words. "I do."

She might never be able to say them in a chapel, or sign a marriage certificate. Daniel kissed the top of her head. She felt him smiling. This was enough. Even if she never got into the school she wanted and had to settle for something less next year. That was something to deal with later. It was another hurdle to jump, that was all. She could be happy without it.

Being held in between her best friends, warm with love, would always be enough.